NATIONAL ACCLAIM FOR JAN BURKE'S IRENE KELLY NOVELS

GOODNIGHT, IRENE

"Readers who want nonstop action, spare dialogue, and a heroine who's a combination of Nancy Drew, Katharine Hepburn, Lois Lane, and Lauren Bacall, should snap up *Goodnight, Irene* at the first opportunity."

—*Booklist* (starred review)

"Jan Burke writes with a verve that makes this an eminently satisfactory debut, one that bodes well for the future."

—*The San Diego Union-Tribune*

"Jan Burke has created a sharp, witty, and utterly endearing detective."

—Susan Dunlap, author of *Death and Taxes*

"Extraordinary, crackling first novel. May there be more!"

—*Murder ad lib*

SWEET DREAMS, IRENE

"A compelling mystery . . . virtually nonstop drama. It's hard to see how Burke can top this one."

—*The Drood Review of Mystery*

"A highly readable mystery with a rapid heartbeat and a thoroughly modern point of view. [Burke's] detective is a welcome addition to the world of the contemporary mystery."

—*The Dallas Morning News*

"A joy. . . . A beautifully crafted book, played against an intriguing backdrop."

—*Orange County Register*

BOOKS BY JAN BURKE

Nine
Flight
Bones
Liar
Hocus
Remember Me, Irene
Dear Irene,
Sweet Dreams, Irene
Goodnight, Irene

JAN BURKE

HOCUS

AN IRENE KELLY NOVEL

POCKET BOOKS

NEW YORK LONDON TORONTO SYDNEY SINGAPORE

POCKET BOOKS, a division of Simon & Schuster, Inc.
1230 Avenue of the Americas, New York, NY 10020

Copyright © 1997 by Jan Burke

Originally published in hardcover in 1997 by Simon & Schuster, Inc.

ISBN: 0-7434-4453-1

First Pocket Books printing September 2003

10 9 8 7 6 5 4 3 2 1

POCKET and colophon are registered trademarks of Simon & Schuster, Inc.

Front cover illustration by Ray Lundgren;
photo credit: Zefa Visual Media/Index Stock Imagery

Manufactured in the United States of America

For information regarding special discounts for bulk purchases, please contact Simon & Schuster Special Sales at 1-800-456-6798 or business@simonandschuster.com

To Siblings Without Rival

Tonya, Sandra, and John
and
Tommy, Susie, and Michael

ACKNOWLEDGMENTS

Laurie Bernstein deserves thanks first and foremost for this one, for believing in it from the start. Simon & Schuster has offered unfailing support.

In addition to friends and family who cheered me on, I am indebted to Lisa Baldridge and Sandra Molen, research librarians, and other members of the staff of the *Bakersfield Californian,* who were so generous with their time and help when I visited there. Fictional Brandon North wouldn't last a day if he had to compete with Ms. Molen, who is much more competent and organized. Patrice Black of the Bakersfield Chamber of Commerce helped me to locate Bea Harriman's house and provided other information about the area. I appreciate the help given by the staffs of the Kern County Museum, the University Library at CSU, Long Beach, the Long Beach Public Library (especially James Washington and Eleanor Newhard), and the Beale Memorial Library in Bakersfield. As with the staff of the *Californian*, the librarians in this book resemble those of the Beale only when they are brilliant and helpful.

My thanks to Joel Hendricks, engineer, California Department of Forestry, for fire-fighting information; to Skip Langley for his expertise on medical and industrial gas systems; Ranger Patty Bates of the U.S. Forest Service, Greenhorn Ranger District, Sequoia National Forest, for information on the Kern River and wildlife in the canyon; to Mike Brewer of the San Diego Zoo for additional help with wildlife behavior; to Dan Coburn for information on aircraft; Andy Voelkel for computer help; California offices of the Southern Pacific and the Atchison, Topeka & Santa Fe Railroads for information on freight trains.

Medical questions were answered by Dr. James Gruber, emergency department physician, Dr. Ed Dohring, orthopedic surgeon, and Kelly Dorhing, R.N. Tonya Pearsley helped with information on the psychological aspects of elective mutism and in other ways too numerous to mention.

Law enforcement and investigation expertise was generously given by several members of the Long Beach Police Department, most especially Detectives Bill Valles, John Gill, and Corporal Henry Erickson. Additional help came from Vic Pietrantoni, Los Angeles Police Department Robbery-Homicide Division; Vernon Pitsker, private investigator; the Long Beach office of the Federal Bureau of Investigation; the Bakersfield office of the California Highway Patrol; GTE Security. I am also grateful to my nephew, John Pearsley, Jr., who was recently sworn in as an officer with the El Cajon Police Department and of whom I am exceedingly proud.

Regina and Greg Szal are more remarkable than their fictional namesakes, and I appreciate the help they gave with astronomy and speech therapy.

Several individuals at the Richard and Karen Carpenter Performing Arts Center at CSULB kindly offered information on theaters new and old when I visited there; I am very grateful to my good friend, Sharon Weissman, director, who helped me to explore the catwalk and other areas, and to Kathyrn Havey, production manager, who read the rough draft and provided insights on stagecraft and design.

Debbie Arrington again provided invaluable assistance with information on reporting.

Joyce Matsumoto and Chef Mavro (George Mavrothalassitis) are two reasons the Halekulani is indeed worthy of paradise. Mahalo.

Cappy, thanks for warming my feet. And if home is where the heart is, Tim Burke is my permanent address.

Hocus (Hō′kəs) vt.

1. To play a trick upon; dupe, hoax.
2. To drug (a person), especially for a criminal purpose.

ORIGINS

*E*VEN BEFORE HE STARTED KINDERGARTEN, *he had figured out that his favorite superhero flew with strings. Now, just over four years later, he wished he had been wrong. They could use a hero with a cape. Escaping into his imagination, he pictured someone with true superhuman powers coming to save them. A soft moan brought him back to the dark room. He hated the way the room smelled: musty and metallic. Whatever form their hero took, he needed to get there quickly. His friend was hurt—a broken arm, maybe. His father would have known.*

Best not to think about his father.

Their mothers wouldn't miss them yet. It was hard to know what day it was, but he didn't think a week had gone by. And maybe the bad guy knew where their mothers were. Maybe their mothers would never come for them. He almost started crying again.

Don't be a wussy, he told himself. Don't.

He thought instead about his friend. If anything happened to his friend, he didn't want to live. No one else would ever understand him, no one else would know what this had been like.

Intermittently, over the last few hours, his friend had been moaning softly, but now he stopped and held himself silent—they could hear the door opening. Someone was coming down the stairs. The boy trembled, afraid their tormentor had returned. His friend reached out and held his hand.

The voice was not the voice of their captor. This man was calling out something about the police, but that didn't fool the boys. Not this time.

They stayed silent. The man's clothes were as dark as the room, and he was carrying a flashlight. He said something about Jesus when he saw the bodies of their fathers, the pools of blood. He kept moving the flashlight, and finally it lit the boys' faces. The man drew in a sharp breath, then said very gently, "Hi. It's okay. Don't be afraid. You're safe now. I'm a policeman."

"A real one?" the boy asked.

"Yes," the man answered, slowly drawing nearer, holding the light up high so they could see him.

"So was the other one," his friend whispered, but later, neither boy would tell anyone what he meant by that.

1

I TOLD THEM I WAS GOING to try to get some sleep, but I don't think I fooled anyone. None of us would sleep that night. I hadn't even tried. I was still wide awake, sitting in a chair across the room from the too wide bed, staring at it as if it were a stranger in my house; thinking too much; repeatedly, relentlessly recalling that the last thing my husband and I had done together was to part in anger. I do not know of any potion as bitter as the realization that one may have lost all opportunity to ask forgiveness.

Hours earlier I had been more complacent about making apologies. Frank didn't show up for dinner, but I figured work had held him up. After all, a homicide detective's schedule is not one you can set your watch by. As a reporter, my own hours are fairly irregular. This was not the first night one of us had eaten across from an empty place setting.

I didn't have much of an appetite. I sat there, wondering how a week that had begun so gloriously had so quickly gone to hell. On Monday Frank had been instrumental in breaking a major case: his work had led to the identification of two members of Hocus, a group that had been on a destructive rampage in Las Piernas for several weeks. On Tuesday he had discovered the whereabouts of the suspected ringleader of the group, one of two men who were then taken into custody.

Wednesday, life made an about-face. A story about the arrests appeared in the *Las Piernas News Express,* an article that painted homicide detective Frank Harriman as a hero. That might have been cause for celebration, except the article didn't give much credit to the other cops who had worked on the case, and worse, it included details apparently leaked straight out of classified police reports. It didn't take long for a department that had been patting Frank on the back to start pointing a finger at him, the only cop married to an *Express* reporter.

The Hocus story had been written by our crime reporter, Mark Baker, an ace who does his own work and has no need to consult with me. It never would have been my story anyway—because I'm married to a cop, crime stories are off-limits. But most members of the police department and the district attorney's office are cynical about the press to begin with, and few would buy any of Frank's explanations about our ground rules. Frank's pressures at work quickly became pressures at home.

Perhaps peace would have been restored in our household if that were the only difficulty we faced, but problems rove in packs, it seems. Trouble arrived in a trio this time and left us silent and distant throughout Thursday, shouting at breakfast on Friday.

Friday afternoon, tired of worrying over the magnitude of our current rift, I had called his office. Big of me, I thought.

My noble intentions were wasted. He wasn't in. I called his pager. No return call.

I tried a second and a third time, to no avail.

At home, while cooking too much dinner, I considered the possible explanations for his lack of response. One was that he didn't have the pager with him. Unlikely, but possible. Another was that he hadn't found time to call back. Maybe. Most likely, I decided, he was ignoring me.

By eight o'clock the leftover chicken was in the refrigerator. The dogs, Deke and Dunk, had been walked and fed. They lay at my feet but watched the door. Cody, my big tomcat, more attuned to my mood, was restless, prowling from room to room, tail snaking and snapping in displeasure. He went into the guest room, where the lights were out, and yowled. When I went in to see what his problem was, he sped out of the room, waited for me to settle into a chair, and then repeated the performance in the kitchen. We toured the house in this fashion. I had just about decided that I could make a nice pair of booties from his pelt when the phone rang.

I ran to catch it before the answering machine picked up.

"Irene?" a man's voice said.

"Yes. Hi, Pete." Not a good sign, I thought, to have his partner make the call.

"Is Frank there?"

"I thought he might be with you," I said. My worries started to shift direction.

"No. Christ, I thought he'd be back by now."

"Back from where?"

"Riverside."

"Riverside?"

"He drove out there this morning. He had to talk to a guy out there. A witness."

"Oh."

"Yeah, I stayed here," he said, and I could hear the edge of uneasiness creeping into his voice. "I had a lot of other stuff to follow up on. You know."

Might as well face it, I thought. "He's being kept out of the office because of the leak on the arrests, right?"

"Yeah, probably because of the leak. You know, if you'd just get that other reporter to name his source—"

"If that didn't work for Frank, why the hell would it work for you?"

"I guess you guys fought about that this morning, huh?"

I sighed. "Did he tell you what we had for breakfast, too?"

"He said he left without breakfast."

"Shit."

"Don't get all hot and bothered about it, Irene. Frank and I have been partners longer than you've been married."

This is one of Pete's favorite things to say to me whenever I object to his sticking his nose into our business. Before I could reply, his wife picked up the extension.

"Pete Baird, you are ten pounds in a nine-pound bag," Rachel said. "What's this, Irene? Frank isn't home from Riverside?"

"No," I said, suddenly feeling as if I were admitting that he might not want to come home. But Rachel was on a different track entirely.

"Something's not right, Pete. Use the other line to call the department. Ask when he last checked in."

As Pete hung up I asked, "What do you mean, something's not right?"

"You sure he hasn't been trying to call you? You been on the phone?"

"No. The only time I've used the phone was to page him earlier today. Who was this witness?"

"The witness? It was—"

Before she could name him, I heard Pete shouting to her in Italian. I couldn't make out what he said, but he was obviously telling her not to talk to me about the case. The clean part of her response, also in Italian, was, "I'll tell her if I want to," and something to the effect of, "Here's a nickel; with that you can buy twice as many brains as you're using right now."

To me, quite calmly, she said, "It's nothing to worry over. The man he went to see, he's an informant. Frank and Pete have talked to him before. He's not a prince, mind you. Just a junkie. Never been involved in anything big. Never hurt anybody."

I finally used a nickel's worth of brains and saw exactly what she was trying to avoid saying to me.

"Oh, Jesus."

"Irene, don't do that to yourself."

"You think something went wrong out in Riverside. That something has happened to Frank—"

"Wait," she said. "Pete's trying to tell me something." She covered the mouthpiece with her hand, so that I heard only the muted sounds of their brief discussion. There was a stretch of silence, then she said, "Look, I'm going to come over, okay?"

"He didn't check in, did he?"

"Listen to me, Irene. For all we know, Frank is sitting in some bar, drinking with the local cops and thanking them for their cooperation, right? So I'm just coming over to keep you company, so that you don't drive yourself crazy thinking about what might or might not be making him late. Pete's going to go down to the office and get the informant's address and phone number. Pete can find out who Frank talked to in the Riverside PD."

"Tell Pete I want to go with him."

"What are you, nuts? That department is not exactly singing praises to the *Express* right now. They aren't going to let you walk in past the front desk. I'll be honest with you. They think of you as some kind of Mata Hari right now. They're sure you seduced a story out of your husband the cop. Pete told me that Frank was actually happy to get out of the building today. I guess their lieutenant has really been leaning on him. He's got almost everyone convinced that the only way the *Express* could have learned the details of the arrests is through Frank."

Rachel was at my front door not much later. She took one look at me, divined what I had been imagining, and said, "Look, I'm not going to bullshit you. Even though I think it's the least likely possibility, Frank might be in trouble. *Might be.* You can't do anything about it one way or the other, so making a nervous wreck out of yourself does nobody any good at all."

Rachel retired about a year ago—while in her early forties—from working homicide in Phoenix; she's now a PI. I figured she knew this kind of worry from both sides: former cop, cop's wife.

"If it were Pete—" I began.

"I'd be concerned," she said. "But not as upset as you are. Not until I had more reason to be." She paused. "It's harder if you've had a fight, maybe."

"I'd say I owe it to Frank to keep my mouth shut for now," I said. "But you probably know more about it than I do. Sounds like he's told Pete quite a bit. Come on in and tell me what you already know."

Once we were seated and the pets had settled in around us, she said, "Okay, I know Frank was upset about the article. That's understandable, but I'm with you. Frank and Pete don't have any right to try to ask you to do something that's going to get you in trouble at work."

"Frank has risked that much for me now and then. It's more than just getting in trouble; it's much worse than that."

"What do you mean?"

"Look, I understand why Frank's upset. To him, finding out who talked to Mark looks like an easy thing for me to do."

"This Mark guy is a friend of yours, right?"

"Yes, he's a friend."

"So just ask him to tell you who the source is—"

"But I can't do that," I protested. "In part, because Mark is a friend. If he's promised anonymity to a source, I can't use our friendship to get him to break his promise."

"So you're saying it's an ethical issue?"

"Yes."

"I don't suppose your editor would be too pleased with you, either."

I nodded. "He'd have a right to be angry. To fire me."

"I think Frank understands that. He's just frustrated."

"I know, I know. But he made this into a question of loyalty: where's my loyalty—with him or the *Express?*"

"Ah, I begin to see."

"It made me furious. I was a reporter when we first got together. We've talked about this, talked it over before we got married. We had a whole system worked out, a way to avoid this problem. I've never taken anything he's told me about a case into the newsroom—not unless he's told me it was okay."

"And he doesn't talk about your work at the paper with the cops—not even with Pete, no matter what that little troublemaker says."

I quieted down. "I know. I know he doesn't."

After a long silence she said, "Just like you know he doesn't have any interest in his old girlfriend."

"Oh, hell. Does Pete know about that, too?" I sighed. That meant Pete was up on two out of three of our recent problems. Frank was usually more discreet, even with Pete. "What did he tell you, then?"

"I've got a better idea. Why don't you tell me your version of it?"

Before I could reply, the phone rang. I hurried to answer it. It was Pete.

"Have you heard from him yet?" I asked, all irritation forgotten.

"No, not yet. He hasn't answered any of our pages. Riverside PD hasn't heard from him since he called to let them know he was going out to talk to the junkie. Junkie hasn't been paying his phone bill, so there's no way to call his place. Riverside is on its way out to talk to the guy, find out when Frank left. Is Rachel there?"

I handed the phone to her.

So Frank wasn't out drinking with the Riverside cops. Pete must not have told them that his partner had a fight with his wife. If he had, he might not have convinced Riverside to send a unit out to the junkie's house. Then again, Pete could make such a pain out of himself, they might issue an APB for Frank just to get Pete off their backs.

I looked at a clock. Quarter after nine.

Rachel's half of the conversation didn't take long and was in Italian. I couldn't understand more than a few pronouns and endearments, but her tone of voice would have been understood in any language: she was trying to calm him down, to ease his worries. Mine escalated in direct proportion. I started to pace.

"So," she said when she hung up, "you were going to tell me about this old girlfriend."

"Former fiancée," I said. "Frank moved from Bakersfield to Las Piernas to be with her. She's with the highway patrol."

She waited.

"You know all this, and I don't want to talk about it anyway. I want to know what's going on with Frank."

"Of course," she said. "But we don't have any way of knowing what's going on with him, do we? So we can sit here and stew and let you wear out the rug pacing, or we can distract ourselves."

I sat down. "Her name is Cecilia Parker. Frank's mother wishes he would have married her instead of me."

"Even now?"

"Well, no, maybe not. I don't know."

"Cecilia lives in Bakersfield?"

"Yes. She moved back there, and Frank stayed here. They both came from Bakersfield, originally. He was a detective in Bakersfield, met her, and they got engaged. She wanted to take a job here. So he followed her, even though it meant that he had to go back to uniform here."

"Then she changed her mind about living here?"

"Right. She didn't give it much of a chance, I guess. At least, that's how he tells it."

"From detective to uniform—that's not easy on anybody," she said. "Pete told me that Frank made detective in Las Piernas in record time, but still—he gave up a lot to move here. He must have been steamed when she wanted to go back."

"I don't know all the details. I know he liked it here, wasn't in a hurry to go back."

"But his family is in Bakersfield? His mom and his sister, right?"

The question came close to another area of trouble, and I wondered briefly if Rachel knew that when she asked. That would make Pete three for three. But just in case Frank hadn't mentioned that problem, I decided she'd have to be more direct.

"Yes," I said, "Frank's mom wants him to move back to Bakersfield. And she's close to Cecilia's mom."

"Hmm. I begin to understand. So why did this Cecilia call?"

How much should I tell her? "Just to talk to him about his family, people they knew in Bakersfield. And to tell him that she had some of his things."

"What kind of things?"

"I don't know. Records, books, a few papers, I guess. Apparently, she's splitting up with a live-in boyfriend. Told Frank she ran across some of his stuff when she was packing up to move out. Invited him to come up to dinner some night so she could give it back to him."

"Invited him to dinner?"

I smiled at her look of surprise. "I see Pete didn't relate the entire story."

"Maybe she doesn't know that Frank's married now. It hasn't been so long. . . ."

"Rachel, you weren't listening. Bea Harriman and Cecilia's mom are friends. I've met her mom. Trust me, Frank's mom has told her that their hopes have been dashed."

"Oh."

"I figured Cecilia could mail his stuff to him, or leave it with his mom. Frank said she wouldn't do that, and besides, he got the feeling that she needed him. That sent me over the edge. So he tells me I'm treating him as if he isn't trustworthy. I told him that I trusted him, but I didn't trust her. He didn't buy it. I thought it over today, and I guess I decided he was right. Two to tango and all that."

"What?"

"Worst case, she wants him to come back to her, right?"

"Maybe. Or maybe just *un chiavata al momento*. You know, a quickie."

"Whatever. He'd have to want it, too, right?"

Her look of skepticism made me laugh.

"Men!" She said it like a swear word.

"We're back to what you said a while ago, Rachel. I do trust him. The rest—that's her problem."

Rachel shrugged.

"Besides," I added, "she touches him, I'll punch her perkies inside out."

She laughed. "That's more like it!"

We passed some time posing theories on Cecilia's motives. I kept glancing at the clock. Rachel tried hard to keep me distracted.

At 10:25 the dogs suddenly clambered to their feet, tails wagging, and scrambled toward the front door.

"He's home!" I shouted, exactly like a little kid, feeling just that excited and twice as relieved. I hurried down the hall and threw open the door.

The man who stood there was a fearsome sight. Tall, clad in black leather, scar faced. His head was shaved and he wore an earring. His tattooed arm was raised in a fist, but only because I had pulled the door open before he could knock, and the look on his face was astonishment, not aggression.

"Oh, it's you, Jack," I said to my next-door neighbor.

The dogs, who consider Jack Fremont their alternate owner, were rubbing up against him, rolling on the ground, panting in delight.

"Well, at least the dogs are happy to see me," he said, reaching to pet them. "As far as you're concerned, though, I'm clearly a big disappointment."

"Sorry, Jack. No, of course not. I—come on in."

He was puzzled but followed me back to where Rachel waited.

"Hi," he greeted her. "Pete and Frank out on a case tonight?"

I briefly explained the situation.

"Maybe he's still steamed after that fight you two had this morning," he offered.

"Damn it to hell, does everyone in the city know about that?"

"Possibly," he replied. "After all, you were shouting at each other in the driveway."

I turned red. "Sorry if we awakened you," I muttered.

It was the last thing I said for a while. They discussed a variety of subjects. Jack spent a lot of years as a rover, Rachel as a cop; between the two of them there was no shortage of stories. I think Rachel was relieved to share the burden of distracting me, but that part of it was pretty much a sham all the way around. I could think only in sets of a few words at a time, and I didn't say them aloud: Please be safe. Please come home. Please call. Please don't be hurt.

This rapidly turned into praying. Sort of. I worried that maybe that was a sham, too. Every time I pray, I end up telling myself that I have no business praying, especially not if I am going to swear and doubt and misbehave in as many ways as I do. This has become a routine between me and the Almighty, like letters that say, "I think of you more often than I write." I'm sure I will hear about it later.

Rachel and Jack kept exchanging glances and trying to get me to do more than mumble and look between the clock and the front door. At one point Jack came over and sat beside me. Although we hadn't known each other very long, he had helped me deal with more than one crisis, and he was also one of Frank's closest friends. I thought about this, and the fact that I wasn't the only person in that room who was worried, and found myself joining their conversation again.

At eleven-thirty the phone rang. Rachel was still sitting next to it and answered it on the first ring.

"Yeah, Pete. It's me," she said, watching me stand up.

She turned away from me. That's when I knew the news would be bad.

2

"JUST TELL ME," I said when I saw she was searching for some way to carefully phrase news that had obviously shaken her.

I hadn't interrupted while she'd sat hunched over the phone, resting her forehead in her hand, talking to Pete. Not even when she'd quickly switched to Italian. I'd stood there, arms folded to prevent myself from grabbing the phone, hands clenching my elbows so hard that it hurt, even as she'd scribbled notes on a scratch pad, asking Pete to slow down, repeat things.

Now I wanted to know what was going on, no matter how difficult it was for her to tell me.

Jack stood up beside me. "Is he okay, Rachel?"

"Nobody really knows."

"What the hell does that mean?" I snapped.

Jack took my hand.

"Sit down, Irene," Rachel said in a strained voice. "I'll tell you everything Pete told me."

I sat, and Jack sat down beside me, still not letting go of my hand.

"Riverside sent a patrol car out to the junkie's place," she began. "Two officers—a rookie and his TO—his training officer. Frank's car was nowhere in sight, but they knew this was where he was headed. So they went up to the house. Some shack of a place the junkie was renting—kind of isolated, I guess. Only one light on in the whole house. They knock on the front door, and it just swings open. The junkie is in there, shot to death."

"No. . . ."

"Frank wasn't in there," she went on quickly. "Just the junkie. They saw signs of a struggle. The rookie got on the radio, the TO looked around. No sign of Frank."

"Frank is missing?" I asked, knowing that was exactly what I had just heard but hoping that some-one would tell me I had heard wrong.

"Yes," Rachel said.

"Someone has taken him?"

She hesitated. "There are other possibilities."

"Such as?"

"Maybe he's gone missing for reasons of his own."

"No. Not Frank."

"Irene is right," Jack said. "You know that as well as I do, Rachel. He wouldn't leave the scene of a crime."

"Which makes me wonder if he made it there," Rachel said. "Look, all I'm saying is, we can't jump to conclusions."

I barely heard what she was saying. Like Jack, I would never believe that Frank would voluntarily leave the scene of a homicide. The death of that informant meant Frank was in danger. Whether he failed to arrive before that informant was killed or was forced to leave afterward, he was in trouble.

A mixture of fear and blind rage jolted and twisted right through me, and I felt like screaming or hitting something just to get it out of my system. The thought of anyone harming Frank—

The thought of anyone harming him made me come to my senses. I didn't scream or cry or use my fists. I took a deep—if shaky—breath and promised myself that I could go into hysterics at some future date. Even revenge would have to wait.

Think.

"What's this junkie's name?"

"I don't know," Rachel said. "Pete never told me. Just calls him 'the junkie.' They try to protect informants, so they don't usually refer to them by name." She paused, then added, "Not that I would have wished the guy dead, but the fact that they found the body there gives me hope for Frank."

"Because if someone—" It was so hard to make myself say it. I took a breath and tried again. "Because if someone was going to kill Frank, he would have done it right away. Left two bodies behind, not one. He might have a reason to keep him alive."

"He or she or they. We don't know. And again, maybe Frank left the scene because that's what he had to do to be safe. We don't know."

The dogs came to their feet again, barking this time. The doorbell rang. Jack got the dogs to be quiet, and I looked through the peephole, wondering who the hell wouldn't just knock after midnight.

The Las Piernas Police Department, as it turned out. Or its representatives, anyway. As I opened the door for Reed Collins and Vince Adams, I figured I was lucky. Although I hadn't always been on good terms with either of them, they liked Frank. I could think of others who might have drawn this duty and made life more unpleasant.

"Hello, Irene," Vince said. "Mind if we come in?"

"Not at all."

They were walking ahead of me, blocking my view of the end of the hallway, but I knew exactly when they saw Jack. Their steps slowed, and they seemed suddenly wary. Reed was the first to ease a little. "You Frank's neighbor?" he asked.

"Yes. Jack Fremont."

Rachel called out a greeting to them as they shook Jack's hand.

"Can I get you a cup of coffee, anything to drink?" I asked.

"No. No, thanks," Vince said.

Reed watched me for a second, then said, "Yeah, I could use a cup. Thanks."

"Anybody else?"

Rachel and Jack shook their heads.

As I moved to the kitchen, out of the corner of my eye I saw Vince make a questioning gesture to Rachel, who gave a quick nod.

Yes, I know my husband is missing, I wanted to shout, but busied myself with grinding beans and measuring out water instead.

Cody came in, snaked around my legs, then went over to Reed. He sniffed Reed's shoes, then rubbed against him, too. Reed reached down and lifted the big lug into his arms. "You're not going to scratch me, are you?" he asked, apparently aware of Cody's reputation.

"Don't trust all that purring," I said. "How do you take your coffee?"

"Black, thanks."

I stared at the coffeemaker as if it were really important for me to keep an eye on it, as if an automatic coffeemaker were some delicate instrument that might require my attention in order to operate properly. In fact, what was so wonderful about it at that moment was that it did exactly what it was supposed to do. I needed *something* to be normal.

I reached for a couple of mugs, not wanting to test the steadiness of my hands with a cup and saucer. Reed put the cat down. As I handed him his mug he said, "You know why we're here."

A statement. I nodded.

"Is there a room where we can talk?"

"Just a minute—" Rachel began, but I shook my head.

"They're here because they want to find Frank," I said. I turned to Reed. "We can go into the guest room, or sit outside."

"It's a little chilly out, down here near the water," he said. "The guest room would be fine."

"Do you want us to leave?" Jack asked me, earning a dark look from Rachel.

"No. Please stay. I mean—if you're tired, don't let me keep you. Same with you, Rachel. If you need to go home to Pete—"

"Pete's on his way to Riverside," she said. "I'd be up anyway. I can never go to sleep until I hear his car—" She clasped a hand over her mouth. Tears started welling up in her eyes.

"Hear his car pull into the driveway?" I asked. "Yes, I'm the same way. It's good to have you here with me, Rachel. But I've never seen you cry, and this would be a stinking time to start."

"I'm not crying," she said. "I thought I was going to sneeze for a minute. That's all."

I nodded and walked off toward the guest room, Reed in tow. I could hear Vince ask Rachel something in a low voice and heard her reply loudly, "Did you see her face? Did you? Of course she didn't call the newspaper, you clueless pinhead!"

If Vince said something back, I didn't hear it. He followed us into the guest room.

I motioned Reed and Vince to the two chairs in the room and then sat on the edge of the bed. With three of us in there, it was pretty crowded. The door creaked open, and we turned toward it in expectation. Cody came sauntering in, then jumped on my lap. I was going to have a friend in the room after all.

Vince stood up, closed the door, and leaned against it, arms crossed. He ignored a look from Reed. Reed sighed and took out his notebook. The warm-up speech—how sorry they were to be in this situation, were doing everything they could but needed help from me—was quick and painless. It gave me a little time to pet Cody, to try to go numb. Reed did the talking. Once he had my (previously undreamed-of) permission to allow my phone line to be tapped, he worked his way to the questions.

"When was the last time you saw Frank?"

"This morning, when he left for work."

"About what time was that?"

"About seven-thirty."

"What was he wearing?"

"A suit. Gray suit. White long-sleeved shirt. A dark red tie." One I bought for him. He looked good in it. He looked good no matter what he wore. "I'm sorry, what were you asking?"

"Shoes?"

"Yes, he had shoes on." I felt my face turn red. "Sorry. That's not what you meant. Black leather shoes."

"Was he armed?"

"Yes, he had his shoulder holster on, his gun in it."

"Are you sure?"

"Yes. I watched him dress." I looked down at Cody. "I—I saw him put the shoulder holster on. The gun was in it."

"Did you talk at all this morning?"

"Yes."

There was a brief silence.

"What did you talk about?"

"Personal matters."

They waited. So did I.

"Could you be more specific?"

"No. Contrary to your lieutenant's opinion, we don't tell other people what we talk about privately."

Vince snorted.

"Vince, get me a refill, would you?" Reed asked, lifting his mug.

Vince gave him a stubborn look, got one back, and relented. When Vince had gone, Reed said, "Look, Pete told us you two had a hellacious fight this morning."

"As Frank has said so often, Detective Baird has a big goddamned mouth."

Reed sighed. "Yeah, he does, and he sticks his nose into everybody's business. And right now, we are all just as worried as Pete is about Frank. Pete may be his partner, but the rest of us are sick about this, too. I figure there's only one person on the earth who's more worried than we are right now, and that's you. Help us. Don't let Vince and his attitude get in the way."

So I told him, in a nutshell, about the argument—not all of it, I admit. But I told him about two out of three bones of contention. If he already knew about the third, a Harriman family secret, he would have to give me some hint of that knowledge before I talked about it. My own connection to that family might be only by marriage, my opinion about such secrets contrary to the Harrimans' own—none of that mattered. I owed it to Frank to keep my mouth shut.

Reed kept his face completely impassive. If he agreed with Frank about asking Mark Baker for his sources, Reed never let any judgment show. If he thought Frank was crazy to let his wife know the former fiancée was beckoning, he kept it to himself. If he knew the family secret, he wasn't letting on.

Vince came back in with the coffee. Cody put his ears back and hissed at him.

Reed tried, but for all his former composure, now he couldn't hide a smile. Vince told him to shut up, and he laughed aloud. He took a sip of coffee, thanked Vince, and got back to business. He repeated some of what I had said about the fight, asked me if that was correct. I nodded. Vince went back to leaning on the door.

"Did Frank tell you anything about what he'd be working on today?"

"No."

"Did he call or communicate with you at any time today?"

"No."

"Did you try to contact him?"

"Yes." I told them about the attempts at paging him.

"He didn't call back?"

"No."

"Did he *try* to reach you?"

I looked away. "Not that I know of."

"Didn't page you?"

"I don't carry a pager."

"Nothing on your answering machine or voice mail?" Vince asked.

"No."

"Is that typical?" Reed asked.

"No. But we had been fighting."

"Is this what typically happens when you fight?"

"Look, I don't see what this has to do with anything. I'm not sure Frank would want me to talk about our marriage in this way. In fact, I'm sure he wouldn't."

Vince acted as if he would argue, but Reed made the slightest of gestures to him, a small movement of his fingers, and Vince subsided. Catching this interaction awakened me to the fact that I had been seeing teamwork all along. Reed was playing a role, so was Vince.

"Did you know that Frank planned to go to Riverside today?" Reed asked.

Still smarting from kicking myself, I said, "I'm not saying another word."

"What's wrong?"

"What the hell are you two imagining? That I let someone who might harm my husband know where he would be? That I—that I arranged for this to happen?"

"Of course not. . . ."

"Oh, no," I mocked. "Of course not!"

Reed shifted in his chair. Vince's mouth became a hard line.

"Just trying to help Frank, right, Reed? Who sent the two of you out here? Lieutenant Carlson? What about you, Vince? You come into this house and ask me if I had made my own husband's disappearance a news story?" I was shouting by then.

"Look, we're just trying to learn what we can about the situation," Reed coaxed.

"Get out."

"Listen, Irene—"

"Get out of here. Both of you!"

The dogs were barking, I realized, and wondered if it was because they had heard me shouting. Rachel knocked on the door. "Are you okay, Irene?"

Before I could answer, the doorbell rang again.

I heard Rachel answer it, heard the low sound of men's voices. Vince and Reed exchanged puzzled looks.

A moment later there was a knock on the guest room door. Vince moved away from it, opened it slightly.

"Step back, *Vincente*," she said with a grin. "You boys are in for a surprise."

He stepped back, and Rachel pushed past him. A short, skinny kid in a suit walked in, carrying a brief-case and rubbing his nose with the back of the other hand. He had mouse brown hair and a baby face and moved with the awkwardness of those who are still growing, although I doubted he was. If he was older than he looked, he was starting the second half of his twenties. His eyes, though, were alert and curious, and as he nodded at me I wondered how often he had been underestimated.

He was followed by a big man, a man as tall as Frank—about six four—but lankier. He strolled in with a slow, easy gait. He had a strong face, rough-hewn but not unpleasant. His hair was cut very short. It had been dark once but now was turning gray. His eyes were slate blue.

With Rachel, Vince, Reed, me, and the two new-comers bunched in there, the guest room was crowded. I wanted out.

The big man spoke first. "Mrs. Harriman?" He drawled it out. Pure Texan.

I nodded.

He flipped open a badge holder. "Detective Thomas Cassidy."

Cody ran over and bit his ankle.

3

C ASSIDY GAVE ONLY THE SLIGHTEST WINCE, then picked up the cat and scratched him gently beneath the chin. Cody started purring. Fickle little feline has always been too easy.

"This is Detective Henry Freeman," Cassidy went on, nodding toward the skinny kid.

"Shit. Tex and the Dweeb," Vince grumbled. "We'll never find Harriman alive."

I felt as if I had been kicked. Hard.

"Christ, Vince," Reed said, looking over at me. "Shut up."

"What time is it, Hank?" Cassidy asked the kid, all the while looking at Vince.

The kid pulled back the sleeve of his suit coat and looked at an instrument that appeared to be the Swiss Army knife of watches. Apparently one of the things it could do was tell time, because the kid said, "It's twelve thirty-four, sir."

"Note that as an entry in the AD, would you, please, Hank?"

"Yes, sir," Hank said, grinning as he pulled out a notebook.

Vince took the bait. "What the hell is an AD?" he asked.

"Asshole Diary," Cassidy replied. "Twelve thirty-four A.M. is a little early to make an entry, grant you, but it would have happened sooner or later. I've been keeping track, and I swear I come across at least one asshole a day. The frequency alone is pretty wondrous. Y'all must be breeding with each other. How big is the average litter of assholes, Vince?"

"Screw you, Cassidy."

"Oh, no, thanks. That's finding out the hard way. You know what, Vince? What's really startling is the new and amazing ways y'all strive to perfect your craft. Take that remark you made a minute ago. Insulted at least three people in a few short words. Yep, I'd say you were a perfect asshole."

"You write in that notebook and I'll break your fingers, kid. Call Carlson, Reed," Vince said.

"No need to do that," Rachel said. "He's in the living room. Why don't we all move out there? It's a little stuffy in here."

I wasn't looking forward to facing Carlson. Given all the pressure he had put on Frank lately, I wasn't sure I'd be able to control my temper with the lieutenant. As it turned out, there was an even higher-ranking cop in my living room. Captain Bredloe.

Bredloe stood up when he saw me, walked over, and put an arm around my shoulders. "Irene . . . I got here as fast as I could."

"You have news about Frank?" I asked, scared to hear the answer. What would bring the captain out to my house?

"No, nothing yet, I'm sorry." Bredloe nodded toward Vince and Reed. "These guys treating you okay?" Vince looked a little pale all of a sudden.

"Sure," I said, wondering if Bredloe had heard me shouting at them as he'd walked up to the house.

"That's good," he said. "They won't be able to stay, though." He glanced over at Carlson.

"I won't be able to stay, either," Carlson said, standing up. "I know this must be upsetting for you, Ms. Kelly. We're making every effort to find Frank."

I was just as perfectly polite. "I'm sure you are. Thanks."

"Vince, Reed, let's go outside," he said. Reed followed him, but Vince lagged a little, moving closer to me while Rachel introduced the captain to Jack.

"Thanks, Irene," Vince said. He looked down at his shoes and pinched the bridge of his nose. "Earlier—what I said—that was crap. I don't know what got into me. I'm sorry. . . ."

He was upset, and this time I saw it for what it was. He was worried. Not about the possibility of Bredloe calling him on the carpet, or what I might tell the paper, but about Frank.

"Damn," I heard Cassidy mutter behind me. "I guess I'll have to look for a new one before midnight, Vince."

Vince smiled a little and said, "If anyone can find one, Cassidy, you will."

Vince left, and the rest of us took seats in the living room. Jack and Rachel were apparently going to be included in any discussion. She stayed near the phone. Jack was sitting cross-legged on the floor, petting the dogs, keeping them calm. I moved to my great-grandfather's armchair. It's big and old-fashioned and doesn't match any of the other furniture in the living room. Frank likes to sit in it. I held on to the armrests.

Bredloe cleared his throat. "Irene, I brought Tom Cassidy and his partner, er. . . ."

"Freeman, sir. Henry Freeman."

"Yes, of course. Detective Freeman. I brought them here because they are specialists. Cassidy has worked extensively not only in kidnapping cases, but as a hostage negotiator."

"So you believe Frank is a hostage?" I asked.

"It's the most likely possibility, as far as I'm concerned. Other people in our department will work other angles."

Other angles. Most of which implied that my husband was irresponsible at best, criminal at worst.

There was a snapping noise, and all eyes went to Henry or Hank or whatever he was called. He noticed our attention and looked sheepishly toward Cassidy.

"Hank, you're making more noise than a turkey eating corn out of a metal bowl," Cassidy said. "You setting up?"

"Yes, sir. I'll try to be more quiet."

"Setting up what?" Rachel asked.

"My computer." His briefcase turned out to be the carrying case for a notebook computer.

"What about this informant?" I asked. "The one who got shot out in Riverside. Could he have any connection to this?"

"That homicide is not in our jurisdiction, of

course," Bredloe said. "Riverside has been very cooperative with us so far, and we've tried to share information with them. Normally, I wouldn't be discussing an informant with anyone, but the man is dead—telling you about him certainly won't bring him to any greater harm. Did you bring the file, Freeman?"

"Yes, sir."

Freeman typed something into the computer, then began reading from a screen. "The victim's name is Dana Ross. Address—234 Burnett Road, Riverside. No phone. Aged twenty-eight." He paused, frowning.

"Something wrong?" Cassidy asked.

"Sorry, sir. He looks older than twenty-eight in the photograph. Dissipation from drug abuse, I suppose."

"I expect you're right about that," Cassidy said. "Go on, please."

Freeman rubbed his nose. "Do you want me to read his record?"

"Please just summarize it."

"Several drug arrests, one burglary conviction. Served as an informant on two previous occasions. This would have been his third."

"Three certainly wasn't a charm for the late Mr. Ross," Cassidy said. "And this latest contact?"

"I have my notes from my discussion with Lieutenant Carlson." Freeman tapped a key or two, then read, "Mr. Ross called the Las Piernas Police Department's Homicide Division from a public pay telephone in Riverside at twenty-three hundred hours—"

"Hank," Cassidy said in a low voice.

Freeman colored slightly, then cleared his throat. "He called at eleven P.M. The call was taken by

Detective Matsuda, who was on the homicide desk. Ross claimed to have information on the Novak case, but insisted that he would talk only to Detective Harriman. He was asked if Detective Harriman should be paged, and said no. He refused to talk to Detective Matsuda."

"Novak is one of Pete and Frank's cases," Rachel said. "A junkie in Riverside mentions a case Frank is working on?"

"Yes," Cassidy replied. "But Ross used to live here, so perhaps it's not so strange."

"Did Ross specify a time?" Rachel asked.

"No," Freeman said. "Ross's message was that he would be home between 0900 and"—he caught Cassidy's frown—"I mean, nine in the morning and one in the afternoon."

"Didn't Jake think it was strange that Ross wouldn't talk to anyone but Frank?" I asked.

"It isn't unusual for an informant to have one or two connections to the department and to refuse contact with any other officer. No one questioned Ross's request," Freeman said, "because Detective Harriman was his contact on each of the two previous occasions."

"Frank is the only one who has talked to this guy?"

"Affirmative," Freeman said. I heard Cassidy sigh.

"Pete knows him," Rachel said. "He never told me the guy's name, but he said he knew the junkie that Frank drove out there to see."

"Pete has met him," Cassidy agreed. "And Frank filled him in on anything Ross said. But I noticed that any report on a conversation with this informant had Frank's signature. I talked to Pete just before he left to go out to the scene, and he said Ross would only open up for Frank. Wouldn't give information to anyone else."

"Any reason why?" I asked.

Cassidy hesitated, then said, "He trusted Frank."

"He had every reason to," I said angrily.

"Pardon?" he said, clearly surprised at my reaction.

"Frank would not murder an informant, if that's what you're thinking."

"No one here believes that he would do any such thing," Bredloe said firmly. "I have complete faith in Frank. If he did use his gun, it was with good reason. If he shot that man, it was in self-defense, or to protect another person's life."

I hadn't realized how much I needed to hear someone from the department say they had faith in Frank. I found myself on the verge of tears again.

Jack must have realized I was too choked up to talk. "Of course, anyone who knows Frank knows that," he pitched in, and tried to ask more questions about what was going on in Riverside.

He was politely stonewalled. I listened to the others converse while I tried to calm down. I knew I'd never get the full story from the police about what had transpired at the junkie's house, what they had found there. Pete might tell me eventually, if Rachel and I leaned on him hard enough. Frank was in danger—I couldn't wait for "eventually."

I grew antsy. I needed to act, to do something. The house started to feel too small, too crowded. If I sat around, I'd go crazy.

"Well, I need to get going," Bredloe was saying.

"It was very kind of the three of you to come by," I said.

"Oh, I'm the only one who's going. I'd like to leave Cassidy and Freeman here. Detective Cassidy has a few other things to talk to you about."

I felt a growing sense of panic but didn't say anything. When Bredloe stood I grabbed my jacket and said, "I'll walk you out to your car."

"I'll walk out with you, too," Jack said, making me want to kick him. "I need to get something from my house."

Outside, Jack said a quick good-bye to Bredloe and went next door. I reached in my jacket pocket and felt the comforting weight of my car keys.

"I want to thank you," I said to the captain. "Your faith in Frank means a lot to me."

"Frank earned that faith," he said. "I came out here tonight to reassure you that I'll stay personally involved in seeing that he comes home to you safe and sound."

"Thank you."

"This is not going to be easy on any of us, Irene. We have to respond to what has happened in a number of ways, looking at a variety of possibilities."

" 'Variety of possibilities.' By that you mean Frank may be dead, he may be hurt, he may be—"

"I am going to remain hopeful," he interrupted, "and assume that Frank is a hostage and that whoever has him has nothing to gain by harming him. If so, sooner or later, someone will make an offer." He paused, then added, "Hostage negotiations are tricky. You know that from your own days on the crime beat. Cassidy is good at what he does, but we'll need your trust and cooperation."

I thought of the many times I had witnessed

Bredloe's intervention on Frank's behalf. More than once I had seen his personal concern for the people who worked for him. I didn't want to lie to him, so I said, "I trust you. I'll try to cooperate whenever I'm given any reasonable request."

He smiled. "You phrase that so cautiously. Well, right now, you need to be cautious." He opened his car door and started to get in.

"Captain Bredloe—"

He waited.

"I *have* covered hostage situations. I learned a few things. A group or an individual who takes a cop hostage is likely to be playing for high stakes. If they want to exchange Frank for a prisoner, or ransom, you're not going to meet their demands."

"You can't think about this in those terms—"

"I'm trusting you, remember? The truth."

He drew in a deep breath and sighed. "No."

"I didn't think so."

"Irene, Cassidy has a very high rate of success—"

"None of the hostages were cops, were they? The guy has saved bank tellers, right? I mean, that's great, that's important. But he hasn't ever been in this situation, right?"

He wouldn't meet my eyes. "Right."

"And you can't give in at all in this case, because you can't run the risk that every twisted son of a bitch who watches the nightly news will get the idea that kidnapping cops is a rewarding occupation, right?"

He didn't answer.

"Damn it to hell," I said, and turned away.

• • •

Jack returned just as Bredloe was starting his car.

"When you get back into the house," I said in a whisper, "take Rachel aside and tell her I'm going down to the paper."

"What?"

"I can't stay here, doing nothing. I've got friends at the *Press-Enterprise* in Riverside. I'm going to call them from the office, try to find out what's going on out there."

"Irene—"

"Please, Jack! I need someone to be here in case Frank calls—someone he can trust. Rachel may have to leave, and besides, I don't want to put her in the position of getting Pete in trouble. This way, she can honestly say she had no idea I was going to leave."

"I don't like this," he said. "Call me as soon as you get to the paper, let me know you got there safely."

I got into my car. "Thanks, Jack. Sack out in the guest room if you get tired."

"How long are you going to be gone?" he asked.

"I don't know."

He made some sort of additional protest, but I didn't really hear what he was saying. I had started the noisy Karmann Ghia. I whipped out of the driveway, hoping I'd be at the end of the street before Detective Thomas Cassidy could figure out that I'd left.

4

TRAFFIC WAS SPARSE at just after two in the morning, so even though I wasn't as careful as I usually am when I'm driving near closing time, I noticed the car that was following me. I wasn't exactly sure when the dark sedan had first appeared, but by the time I was within a few blocks of the paper, there was no doubt in my mind that I was being tailed. I tried to get a better look at my pursuer, but when I slowed he slowed. I couldn't make out the color of the car, let alone who was in it.

I made a series of unnecessary turns, cut through the parking lot of the downtown senior center, and turned into a little alleyway near the main library. I doused my lights and waited to see if the sedan was still with me. After a few moments I had the attention of a couple of homeless guys but no one else, so I pulled out and drove on to the paper.

Although the newsroom would be empty, there

were plenty of cars pulling into the parking lot at the *Express*. This was the hour when the drivers from the circulation department arrived. The first copies of the morning paper would already be off the presses; trucks were being loaded. I didn't know any of the people I saw walking toward the building, so it took me a moment to see the man who was just standing outside his sedan, arms folded, staring at me.

"Don't put me in your diary for this, Detective Cassidy."

He moved off the car and walked over to me. "No, Mrs. Harriman—or do you prefer to be called Ms. Kelly?"

"Irene."

"Okay, Irene, just call me Tom or Cassidy—either one will do. I don't think anybody but my mama calls me Thomas these days. Anyway, this doesn't make you an asshole. In fact, after listening to some of the stories the captain told me about you, I would have been disappointed if you didn't try a stunt like this."

"Glad to give you the satisfaction of being right. If you'll excuse me, I'm going into the building."

"Certainly," he said, and started to follow me.

"Wait a minute. The Las Piernas Police Department is not invited to come along."

"You aren't safe here," he said, moving to block my way. "If I could figure out what you were likely to do, so could someone else."

"Frank's the one in danger, not me." I dodged around him, started for the building again. "Why should anyone care if I. . . ."

I came to a halt.

"What is it?" he asked sharply.

"Over there," I said, pointing to a Volvo parked in along the back wall of the building, away from the other cars. "Frank's car. He's here!"

I started running toward it.

"Wait!" Cassidy shouted, grabbing on to me and nearly causing us both to fall to the pavement.

"Let go of me!"

"Irene, please wait." We had drawn some attention by then. A couple of the truck drivers were looking our way. I stood still. Cassidy pulled out his badge holder and held it over his head. "Y'all just go on about your business. The lady's fine."

They hesitated. "I'm all right," I called out. "Really."

Slowly they left.

"Now, let's go take a look," Cassidy said. "I'm anxious to see it, too, but I want us to go about this cautiously. Together. And we aren't going to touch that car. You with me on this?"

I nodded.

"Let's go, then."

The closer we got to the Volvo, the worse I felt about it being there. Frank wouldn't drive to the newspaper in the middle of the night. He would come home. If he didn't want to go to the house for some reason, if he were in trouble and needed my help, this was the last place he'd try to meet me.

"Easy," Cassidy said. "Take it easy. Stay back here a minute."

He crouched down and slowly moved up to the car. He peered inside, then swore under his breath and stood up. He covered his eyes with one hand.

I hurried over, looked into the car.

Empty.

"What's wrong?" I asked, leaning to take a closer look. "Why are you so upset?"

"Don't touch it," he said. Then, standing behind me, he gently took my shoulders and crouched down again, moving me with him. He pointed up through the rear passenger window. "The mirror."

Something was written on the rearview mirror in small, neat letters. It looked as if the writer had used a sharp-tipped black felt pen. The parking lot wasn't brightly lit, but there was enough light to read the words:

HOCUS HAS NEWS. WE KNOW WHERE TO FIND YOU.

"Hocus? Oh, no. No. . . ."

"Shh, shh. Hush. We don't know a thing, really."

I looked at him in disbelief. "We know he's been taken by Hocus! We know he arrested two of them for conspiracy to commit murder!"

"These fools are getting too big for their britches," he said easily. "That's how Frank caught on to them in the first place. Now, we're going back to my car, and I'm going to call for some help."

"Shouldn't we . . . shouldn't we look in the trunk?"

"You have keys to the Volvo with you?"

"Yes."

"Why don't you give them to me?" When I hesitated, he said, "You know that Hocus has used explosives, right?"

I nodded.

"I think we should wait until the bomb squad gets

here and checks the car out first. It would be just like Hocus to think it was funnier than hell to blow the damned newspaper to kingdom come."

"But if Frank is in there. . . ."

"If you're going to get locked in a trunk, a Volvo's one of the better ones to be locked in. They have a hole for skis. He'll have plenty of air. Trust me."

Although I had seen the ski slot in the trunk, I thought he was probably bluffing about the air supply. It didn't matter. "If he's in there, Cassidy, he's dead anyway."

"Don't go talking that kind of talk, now."

"I don't think he's dead. He's alive."

"You got a feeling about that?" he said, steering me toward his car.

I did, but hell if I was going to talk to him about it. "No, logic. Someone went to a lot of trouble today. They lured my husband out to Riverside, to a house the police here knew he was going to. They took him from there, then brought his car all the way back here. They left a message for me in his car, left his car in a place where I was likely to find it. Perhaps not this soon, but by Monday morning." I looked up along the roof of the Wrigley Building, which houses the *Express*. "They undoubtedly knew the security cameras for the parking lot wouldn't catch their faces on videotape if they parked along the back wall of the building. If they were just going to execute Frank for arresting their leader, they wouldn't have needed to go to so much trouble. And they'd be crowing about it by now."

He stopped and studied me for a moment. "Not bad. I'm with you—Frank has value to them as a hostage. On the other hand, the violence by this group has been escalating, and they think of themselves as tricksters. If I think like a trickster, I say the car could be booby-trapped."

When we reached his car I said, "That was you following me, wasn't it?"

"Yeah. Sorry if I scared you."

He called Bredloe at home.

"I'm on a cellular phone, here, sir," he began. "At her place of employment. . . . Yes, we can go into that later, on a land line. Her husband's car is here in the parking lot, with a message from our prankster friends. . . . Yes. . . . I'd prefer not to go into the possibilities on an unsecured line, sir, but thought you'd want to get things rolling. I want to keep an eye on the car so that nobody bumps into it until your brother brings the dogs."

There was a pause.

"Yes, sir. Exactly. . . . Thank you."

As he started to dial another number I asked, "Bredloe's brother is bringing dogs? What's that all about?"

"A little code that we'll have to stop using after tonight, I suppose. . . . The bomb squad is part of the sheriff's department. They use dogs to sniff out explosives. . . ." He spoke into the phone. "Hank? Get everything you can on the pranksters. . . . Yeah, I know. Bredloe will help."

I remembered my promise to Jack and asked Cassidy to pass word along to him that I was okay.

By the time he finished the call, a black-and-white pulled into the parking lot. Cassidy asked the officers to keep everyone away from the Volvo until the bomb squad arrived.

He turned to me. "You all right?"

I nodded.

"Let's go into the building and use a phone in there, okay?"

The night security man was already quite excited because he had seen the cruiser pull into the lot. When Cassidy showed him his detective shield, the guard pulled in his stomach and started hitching up his belt.

Before he could snap a salute or sing the police auxiliary anthem, I told him to expect the parking lot to be besieged by law enforcement. He decided to call the editor, Winston Wrigley III.

Wrigley and I have a strained relationship in the best of times, and between two and three in the morning is never going to rank as one of the best of times. After a minute or two of listening to him bawl me out, I handed the phone over to Cassidy.

"Come on down," Cassidy drawled, a little more heavily than usual, I thought, "but be careful. Y'all might get yourselves launched outta here like a roman candle. Up to you. I gotta get going now. I cain't talk to you and keep your building from blowing up at the same time."

When he hung up, the security man was bug-eyed. "Should I evacuate the building?"

"Probably be a good idea. The bomb squad will be here any minute now. In the meantime, maybe you could ask folks to stay away from that end of the parking lot."

John Walters, who had recently been promoted to managing editor, arrived about the same time as the explosives experts did. His concern that subscribers would be unhappy if their morning papers were not on their driveways before breakfast time did not count for much with the bomb squad. He paced back and forth on the perimeter, where the delivery drivers and press operators waited.

John scowled every time he saw me, but he hadn't spoken to me yet. I took that to mean that even if nothing was found in the car, there was bound to be at least one type of explosion that morning.

Cassidy ambled over to him, spoke with him for a moment, and John stopped pacing. He slumped a little, looking toward his shoes, but I doubted he could see them over the curve of his belly. He glanced back at me, but this time the look was different. Sympathy. An offering I refused by fixing my gaze on the car.

Since the only way to get sympathy from John was to have something really awful happen to you, I preferred seeing him upset. I wasn't exactly cool and calm myself. Although we were some distance away, I could see that the explosives experts had their specially trained dogs out. The two animals worked in a team, cautiously sniffing the exterior of the car. One of the dogs showed some interest in the trunk, but when the handler brought over the other one, the two dogs moved along.

"If the dogs detect any kind of explosive, they signal it very clearly," Cassidy said, now back at my side. "I don't think they found anything just then."

I nodded. As I watched the officers go through other checks, using mirrors on long extensions and other devices, I could feel the weight of each passing moment, every delay seeming to decrease the odds of finding Frank.

"Cut it out," Cassidy said next to me.

"Cut what out?"

"You're winding yourself up tighter than an eight-day clock."

"Forgive me. I'm sure if your wife was missing and the bomb squad was inspecting her car while terrorists did as they pleased with her, you'd just be sitting around whistling Dixie."

For a moment I imagined that I had made him angry. After putting up with his irritating calm, I'd have found it a refreshing change. But I was wrong—he smiled and looked away from me, an expression of private amusement on his face.

"Come on, Ms. Kelly," he said, "they're gonna let us take a look-see."

We moved to the next barrier—yellow police tape surrounding the part of the parking lot where the Volvo stood.

The bomb squad was packing up, and Cassidy was directing the uniformed officers who had been working crowd control to let people back into the building. John was avoiding me for the moment, talking to the production and circulation managers, undoubtedly trying to figure out what this interruption was going to do to press and delivery schedules. Photographs, which had been taken at several points, were now taken from closer angles. A fingerprint technician was already dusting the door handles and other surfaces. Most of the attention was on the open trunk.

As we drew closer, my sense of dread became so acute that the trunk seemed to become a gaping maw, Jonah's whale come to swallow me whole. Police interest of this kind was like John's sympathy—it could not be associated with anything good.

Cassidy took hold of my elbow at some point; I guess I had slowed without realizing it. I heard voices around me, introductions, comments, even Cassidy's drawling version of my name. He was repeating it.

But they were all far away. I was in an incomprehensible world, a world composed solely of the large, dark bloodstain on the carpet in the trunk of my husband's car.

5

I WAS ABLE TO AVOID FAINTING or screaming or going into hysterics, but the tears refused all orders not to fall. Next to the stain, an orderly display of three items caught my eye: a pager, a cellular phone, a gun in a shoulder holster. I knew they were Frank's even before Cassidy steered me away from the car and into the building.

The big marble-and-brass lobby was empty; the security guard was outside, engrossed in watching the police action. Cassidy seated me on a bench and asked for directions to the nearest vending machines. I managed to point the way. I sat there, trembling, hoping I could stop quivering before he came back. I couldn't. He handed me a cup of hot coffee and made me drink it while he watched.

John came in, took in my tearstained face, and snapped, "Get her another cup of that stuff," as if Cassidy were his to command. Cassidy didn't make a fuss about it. The minute he stood up, John sat next to me, even took my hand and patted it in an awkward gesture of reassurance. I wasn't reassured, but it was so weird to have John do something like that, I dried up.

"You going to be okay, Kelly?"

I nodded.

"Can I do anything for you?"

I shook my head.

"Mark's here. I've asked him to cover this."

"Keep him away from me," I said, hating how shaky my voice sounded.

"But, Kelly—"

"I just can't talk to him now, John. Maybe later."

"Before deadline?"

I choked out a laugh.

"You don't blame Mark for this, do you, Kelly?"

Did I? Maybe. It was wrong, I knew. But what if Mark's story had triggered what happened? I thought of the bloodstain. No, I told myself, it's wrong to blame Mark.

I closed my eyes tightly, because that was as close as I could get to being left alone. "Don't make me sort this out right now, John. Please."

"No need to pressure Ms. Kelly," Cassidy said, causing me to look up again as he came back into the room. He handed me the cup of coffee, glanced over at John, and sighed. "I expected more of you, Mr. Walters."

John rubbed a hand over his face. "I'll talk to you later, Kelly." He started up the stairs, then paused. "Are you going to be okay?" he asked again.

"Yes, don't worry. I'll be upstairs in a few minutes."

"Maybe I shouldn't have let you see the car," Cassidy said when John was out of earshot. "Bredloe will probably have my butt for that. I just figured it was easier to let you see the car now—otherwise I might find you breaking into the impound yard trying to get a look at it."

"You were right," I said. I sat up a little straighter, tried to make my voice steady when I asked, "What do you think that bloodstain means?"

"Hmm. If I sit here and speculate, I'm taking up a fool's hobby. We don't know if it's human blood, for starters. Could be blood from a steak, just put there to scare you."

"If it's human. . . ."

"Then we have to figure out how many humans left it there. If it came from one human, then we have to figure out which one it most likely belonged to. When you're worried and thinking that it's your husband's blood, a few drops would seem like a lot of blood. We need to try to measure it, learn how long it's been there, and so on. Lots of questions, Irene, and I'm anxious for the answers, too—but they have to come from the lab guys. Let's you and I concentrate on other questions."

I soon learned that he meant I would concentrate and he would ask questions. Most were similar to the ones Reed had asked me at the house, but the process of being questioned seemed much different with Cassidy. He spoke slowly, softly, and acted as if he were concerned rather than suspicious. He didn't ask for details about my argument with Frank. He wanted to know what credit cards Frank had with him, in case Frank's missing wallet was being used to finance an escape. Most of all, though, he was interested in conversations about Hocus.

"Frank make any comments to you about these people he arrested?"

"Not much. He said he thought they were young, probably in their late teens or twenties. He thought they were from fairly affluent families—said something about demographic studies showing that bombers are often young white males from upper-middle-income households, as I recall, although I might not have that right. He thought they were a bad combination of intelligent and spoiled. And angry, but he wasn't sure why. He was pleased about the arrests, mainly because he hoped Hocus would slow down, maybe even come to a halt."

"He figured Lang was the key man." It wasn't quite a question, but it wasn't a statement, either. Richard Lang and Jeffrey Colson were the two members of Hocus who were jailed.

I hesitated, then said, "No. That conclusion wasn't his, no matter what the story in the *Express* said. Frank didn't deny that Lang could be the ringleader, but he had doubts. Lots of doubts."

Cassidy rubbed his lower jaw, then stared off into space.

I waited for the next question, then realized there wasn't going to be one for a while. "I'm going to go upstairs," I said.

"Sure," he said, still lost in thought.

The newsroom was empty. John was in his office. Mark Baker was still outside. In a couple of hours more of the staff would arrive. I hurried to my desk and logged on to the computer. I asked for all the files on Hocus. Although I had followed the stories about it as closely as anyone else in the city, I wanted a refresher course. I needed to fight the feeling of helplessness that threatened to overwhelm me, and one weapon I had at my disposal was information.

I opened the earliest file and thought back to Hocus's first trick.

We should have seen trouble coming when almost everyone in town got a pleasant surprise on their bank statements. It wasn't the kind of surprise you'd dream about or even specifically hope for—no one had a million dollars irreversibly transferred into their account from a Swiss bank; nothing like the $100 "bank error in your favor" card in Monopoly. Then again, it wasn't the kind of surprise that would give you nightmares. Not one to make you cross your fingers, hoping the payees on your last fifty checks liked just looking at them and wouldn't try to cash them any time soon. No, for the customers of the Bank of Las Piernas, it averaged out to be about an eight-buck windfall.

The message appeared at the bottom of each statement, politely informing the BLP customers that all service charges for that month were waived.

Assuming themselves to be the beneficiaries of an advertising promotion of some sort, the depositors were pleased and looked upon the bank with new regard. "They really have a heart," people were heard to say. Publicly the bank's personnel nodded and accepted their customers' gratitude. Privately there was a panic.

If I hadn't known Guy St. Germain, a vice president at the bank, I wouldn't have been aware that BLP had not sanctioned the fee waiver. He told me what had happened only after I swore six or seven times that I would never write anything about it for the newspaper or tell anyone else. The electronic break-in was a great secret at BLP. In the beginning the bank was unwilling to let its depositors know that hackers had found their way into the bank's computer system.

"You can't follow some sort of electronic trail?" I asked.

"No, *mon amie,*" Guy said in his soft French Canadian accent. "It's not as if they took money. It wasn't transferred from the depositors' accounts into some other place. The hackers just managed to cancel the command that levies the charges on the accounts. Our computer security people have figured out how they got in; they attached a line to one of our executives' computers and listened in on his modem. They were able to record high-level access codes. They used the codes to break in on their own."

"You're sure the executive's not involved?" I asked.

Guy nodded. "This man is not a computer whiz. He has a top level of access because of his position, not his abilities. He wouldn't have known how to change the program."

"But still—"

"He's also a real outdoorsman," Guy continued. "Likes to go rafting, hiking, do all of those things where a person can't be reached by phone. I understand—he has a high-pressure job, and this allowed him to be free for a few days. He was rafting on the Green River in Utah on the days of the electronic break-in, and the calls were definitely local, not long distance."

"Hmm. Perfect timing."

"Yes. Someone was very good at homework, don't you think?"

"No chance that this fellow had a grudge? Maybe hired someone else to do the programming?"

Guy shook his head. "He had nothing to gain. We think it was just a prank."

"A costly one."

"Yes. That is the shame, although few people would see that. No one has much sympathy for bankers."

I understood his point. Most people wouldn't stop to think that the bank counted on those fees for its operations expenses. It wouldn't go broke from this prank, but somewhere the bottom line would be affected; fees would go up, or there would be less money to lend.

"It could have been worse," Guy said. "Much worse. And our security is better now." He paused and smiled. "Who knows? Perhaps we will gain something from the good publicity about waiving the fees."

The second prank was not hidden from the public eye. A few weeks after the bank incident, all street-sweeping ticket records were deleted from the municipal computers. When the city's computer department reached for a separately stored backup file, it was found to be blank, with the exception of one text file: "All street-sweeping fines are forgiven. We are Hocus."

"That's an odd name," Lydia Ames observed when I came into the office with the story. She's the assistant city editor at the *Express* and has been a friend of mine since childhood.

"A perfect name," said John Walters.

"They think of themselves as magicians?" she asked.

"You're thinking of hocus-pocus," I replied. "I made the same mistake, until I looked the word up in the dictionary. Hocus is a verb. It means to play a trick on, to dupe. It may be where the word 'hoax' comes from."

"The cheering will be heard citywide," John said with a scowl. "No one likes parking tickets. But I like tricksters even less."

"I had the same reaction," I said, "right after I decided what I was going to do with the money Hocus saved me on tickets."

The next action came about a week later. All outstanding library fines were eliminated from the city library's computer system. The message "All fines are forgiven, courtesy of Hocus" appeared briefly on the screens one Monday morning. As the city investigated this new breach of security, the bank—given the promise that the information would remain confidential—let the Las Piernas Police Department know that Hocus had taken credit for the fee waiver at the bank.

At first, citizens cheered the news about the library fines as heartily as they had cheered the earlier announcements. No one liked fines. But the library was more forthcoming than the bank or the municipal court—already strapped by budget cutbacks, it couldn't afford the loss of revenue. Libraries would be closed on weekends until further notice.

Parents of kids with homework projects were the

first to howl, and others quickly joined in. A fund-raiser was held, and the library reopened on Saturdays. Now the local citizenry seemed to understand that damage could be done.

The people of Las Piernas began to ask the same questions that computer security personnel had asked all along. Who were these people? How many of them were there? What was Hocus trying to prove? How had they managed to break into these computer systems? And perhaps most important, what would they do next?

In those days all the actions Hocus took had fit with its name. Pranks. No one was taking revenues, they were just preventing the collection of revenues.

Computer experts were called in, and any organization using computers did its best to heighten security. We waited for the next trick.

When it came, we were taken completely by surprise.

An animal rights group was blamed at first. In the immediate chaos that followed the release of every creature in the city animal shelter, the body of the night manager lay undiscovered for over three hours.

If you open a birdcage or two, even let out a couple of snakes, not much is going to happen. Set twenty or thirty cats loose and then release just over two hundred dogs not long afterward, and you're going to see some action. Let a horse be the grand finale, and people will definitely notice.

The birds flew off, and the snakes were never found again. The horse was old and skinny and didn't go much farther than the first open field he came across. The cats apparently had enough lead time to climb trees or make themselves scarce. The dogs were another story.

Social beings that they are, the dogs must have decided these adventures were more fun when shared, and most of them gathered into packs as they set off through the streets. Some packs announced their freedom as they ran.

Most of the police activity in those early hours centered on rounding up animals, especially those dogs that had been quarantined for viciousness.

Two men were on duty that night: the night shift manager and an animal control officer. The animal control officer had gone out on an emergency call that turned out to be bogus. Before he could return, the police were contacting him by radio about the calls they were getting.

For all the pandemonium on the streets nearest the shelter, the shelter itself was eerily quiet. The night manager didn't seem to be on the premises, and a second truck was gone. At first, everyone thought he was out catching dogs. The truck was found much later, abandoned under a freeway overpass.

The shelter actually ended up with more dogs than it started out with—if not necessarily the same dogs—since the previous inmates had picked up some sympathizers along the way. It was only after the dogs had been caught that anyone could spend much time at the shelter itself, trying to figure out what had happened.

A woman LPPD officer saw drops of blood on the ground and followed the trail they made to a building at the back of the shelter. They led to the area where the dogs were put to sleep. The door to one of the chambers used for large dogs was open, but as she stepped closer she saw that the chamber had been recently used. The body of the night manager was inside, along with a note:

HOCUS SET THE CAPTIVES FREE.

Hocus's first murder.

6

THE DREAM HAD BEEN PLEASANT. He could still see her face, feel the whiskey warmth of her skin, her softness. He had already forgotten what had happened in the dream, was not sure if they had made love, but drowsily he thought perhaps they had, as his awakening was the slow, reluctant awakening of the sated.

Moments passed, and still sleep beckoned. He was not without pain, nor was he immune to disturbing thoughts. His head hurt. He was bruised. She was not with him. He didn't know where he was, or with whom, or why he had been taken. He recalled, in fleeting images, a struggle, shots fired.

But in each case—from the aching where the first blow had been struck to the sensation of being lost— no sooner was any discomfort a part of his awareness than a billowing tide of lassitude swept over him, languor robbed him of his ability to react as anything more than a distant observer. Too tired, he thought, closing his eyes—too tired. He smiled to himself. Easier to dream. . . .

Some long-practiced ability to sense trouble urged him awake again, and for a brief moment he opened his eyes. The room caromed wildly above him. He closed them again.

"God, I hate the smell of blood," a voice was saying.

Other words drifted by.

"Pale."

"Not yet. . . ."

". . . make it?"

"Nothing to worry about," someone said.

He thought perhaps there were things to worry about, but they slipped the grasp of his mind and swam away from him.

The conversation between the others went on, but he couldn't concentrate on it long enough to understand what they were saying.

The dreaming began again.

He was standing on the gravel drive, looking at the house.

He remembered coming out this way with his father, back in the late 1950s, in the old blue Buick sedan they had owned then—the one with a metal dash and fierce, toothy grille. From the passenger seat he watched the blur of dark green leaves and smooth, gray trunks of orange and lemon and grapefruit trees go by.

He had been in the area many times since then, of course, but today, standing on the drive, he was remembering a time when his father had needed to bring some papers to Riverside. The girls had had to stay home. "Just boys, this time," his father had said.

It was a long drive from Bakersfield and a hot one. Frank didn't care. His dad was a cop, and they didn't often get this kind of time together.

With the windows down, he could smell the heady fragrance of the groves. They passed dirt driveways that began at the road, marked by tin mailboxes with red flags announcing who had mail, who didn't. And down at the other end of each drive, there was almost always a modest white wood frame house.

The memory came back to him in the dream more vividly than it had in real life. In real life he had stood watching the house, wondering why he was feeling so spooky all of a sudden. Hell, the house looked haunted. The paint was peeling off the trim in large, curling flakes. The house was surrounded by a porch; the porch railing had supports broken out of it, leaving it gap toothed and sagging. Dead vines formed a thick and thorny gray lace that shielded the front door from view. Screens were torn or missing.

The ramshackle house sat on a large lot. Tall, dry grass grew in straw-colored clumps. A gnarled, leafless orange tree held two barren branches up to the cloudless sky as if in a gesture of despair.

He thought of the place as it might have looked thirty years before, of a bright red bougainvillea adding color to a white house surrounded by fruit trees.

He shook his head. He supposed a generation or two of heirs had carved up the original owner's citrus grove and sold it off piecemeal. Nothing else could explain the odd mixture of lots and buildings that made up this street. A handful of trees remained here and there, but the groves were gone. The development that followed had been random. Train tracks ran along the far side of the street, parallel to the back fence of the industrial park that stood on the opposite side of the tracks. All that could be seen of the buildings beyond were windowless concrete walls and loading docks. He wondered if the industrial park had replaced a packing house.

As he stood on the gravel drive, a freight train came slowly rumbling by, horns sounding, echoing loudly off the concrete buildings. He watched it, read the names on the boxcars. AT&SF . . . Southern Pacific . . . Cotton Belt. Where was it going? Where had it been? Conrail . . . Golden West . . . GATX. . . . It slowed, stopped, began backing up, apparently switching or adding cars. As the head end passed him again, an engineer saw him and waved. Surprised, Frank waved back.

When he could no longer see the engineer's face, he straightened his suit and turned back to the house. A mockingbird sang half a dozen verses of a borrowed two-note song, then fell silent.

He paused, listened. Nothing. Gravel crunched and grated as he walked up the drive.

He had never known any trouble from Ross, he told himself. And if Ross had information on the Novak case, he wanted to hear it. The Novak case had been a real pain. Absolutely no breaks in it so far. Probably all kinds of witnesses, but everybody too scared to talk. Nobody knew anything. It angered him. Novak had been a small-time dealer with all the wrong kinds of ambition; whoever executed him had probably saved the state a lot of money by ending his miserable life. But a murder was a murder, and as much as he hated the Novaks of this world, it bothered him more that people would aid a killer with their silence.

The porch steps creaked. When he came to the front door he halted, stepped to the side. It was open. Just a crack, but open.

"Ross?" he called.

"Come on in, Frank," he heard Ross call. "It ain't locked. I seen you comin'."

He thought of every other time he had met with the junkie: the nervousness, the triple-locked doors.

He pulled out his gun.

"Come out here, Ross," he called.

Silence.

"Come out here, or I'm going back to Las Piernas. We'll talk another time."

He heard the porch creak behind him and whirled.

A man in a gold lamé cape and a full set of purple-sequined tails stood on the other end of the porch. He took off his glimmering top hat and bowed.

"Want to see me pull a rabbit out of my hat?" he asked.

"No. Drop the hat and hold your hands—" He sensed a movement behind him but did not quite turn in time to ward off the blow to the back of his head.

He blacked out for a moment, not feeling the fall to the porch until he hit it with his face. His gun clattered away from him, but he could smell powder. Had he fired it? Hit the magician? No, one of the men pinning him to the porch was wearing purple and gold. Dizzy, half-stunned, he struggled beneath them, but they held him down. Soon his hands were tied behind his back.

"You didn't hit him hard enough!" the magician said.

"It won't matter."

He felt fear, cold and real, clearing his head.

"He almost shot me!" the magician complained. "What if someone heard it?"

"Get his gun, goddammit," the other said. The cape lifted.

He struggled again, felt the jab of a needle in his neck.

"Keep wiggling around," the voice said, "and it will only work faster."

He was hauled roughly to his feet and shoved into the house.

Ross was inside, cowering in a corner.

"Oh, God!" he wailed when he saw Frank. "You two are fuckin' nuts! He's a cop!"

"Shut up," the magician said.

Ross started crying but said nothing more.

The pain from his head was not so bad now, but he could feel his own blood, warm and wet on his neck and back, could taste it in his mouth. He was dizzy, but it wasn't so bad to be dizzy, he thought.

"How much time?" the voice behind him asked.

The magician pulled out a pocket watch. "Any minute now," he said, and looked toward the tracks.

A train. Even through the fog that was settling on his mind, he thought of the train. He started to move toward the door. He was yanked back, hard.

He heard the train. These sons of bitches were going to kill him, he thought hazily. Well, screw them. They weren't going to put him down without a fight.

He stumbled forward, pulling his captor off balance, then rolled the young man over his back. A surprised young man, he noted, grinning at him as he lay on the floor.

"Stop it!" the magician yelled, waving the gun.

Frank kicked at the man on the floor but missed him completely. He tried again and lost his own balance, crashing into a lamp and coffee table and God knew what else before the man who had been on the floor was grabbing him again. Frank struggled, but he was growing clumsier now.

"Follow the plan!" the captor yelled. "Kill him!"

Frank fell to his knees, too dizzy, too sleepy, to stand. The magician looked lost.

The captor let him fall to the floor. He marched over to the magician and took the gun.

Frank heard the shot—loud, louder than the train.

Just like falling asleep, he thought. He felt cold. He allowed himself to wish she were holding him. He imagined her arms around him and wondered if she would ever forgive him for getting himself killed.

7

MARK BAKER DIDN'T SEE ME at my desk when he came into the newsroom. He made a beeline into John's office. I'm not sure if it was my chickeny side or my rebellious nature at work, but in either case I wasn't willing to contribute to the story on my husband's disappearance—so I staged one of my own. I slipped out of the newsroom and made my way downstairs.

Cassidy wasn't in the lobby, and I didn't see him among the cops who were still huddled around Frank's car. I looked across the lot and saw him leaning against my Karmann Ghia.

"I'm going home," I told him when I reached the car.

"See you there," he said, an announcement I was less than happy about, but I was in no mood to argue. I got into my car as he watched. I rolled down the window.

"Cassidy?"

"Hmm."

"Should I wait here? This is where they left the message for me. Does that mean they'll call here?"

"I've thought about that. I don't think they'll have any trouble finding you."

"But our home phone number is unlisted. . . ."

"I'll bet you thought your bank account number was private, too."

"Oh." I looked over at the Volvo.

"You okay to drive?" he asked. "I'll take you home if you'd like."

I shook my head. "No, thanks. I'll make it."

"Sure," he said, and sauntered off toward his sedan.

As I drove home I thought of the other information I had gathered on Hocus. The murder of the animal shelter officer had generated a hue and cry for their arrests, but Hocus received less criticism over its next set of targets.

The *Express* received an anonymous call, a male voice saying that Hocus was going to clean up a few neighborhoods. Within a twenty-four-hour period, four houses exploded, killing twenty-one people—a total that was not finalized for several days, because it's hard to count bodies when they're in pieces the size of stew meat. Fifteen of them were at one address, a party cut short.

Normally this kind of terrorism would have resulted in outrage, but this time Hocus actually gained some supporters. It seemed a long list of neighbor complaints had been filed about each of the doomed houses—complaints about drug dealing, noise, and the constant stream of unsavory visitors in and out at all hours. In general, the neighbors of the victims figured that Hocus had done them a favor. If they had any objections, they were only to the occasional peripheral damage done by the explosions—broken windows, pictures falling from walls. Asked about the loss of human life, one man had shrugged and said, "Pest control."

The police, for all their problems with the dealers, weren't so happy with Hocus's solution. Frank had been assigned to what became known as "the party house," the site with the highest body count. He wasn't in good shape when he got home from that one. Sometime after playing with Deke and Dunk, a long run on the beach, and a Macallan on the rocks, he started talking about it. "Going to take a team of forensic anthropologists to figure out how many people were in there, let alone who they were. I'd bet money we end up with half a dozen John and Jane Does. Explosives guys say it was C-4, something in the living room, where most of the people were. Some of the bodies in the outer rooms weren't so badly damaged. There was one that reminded me—" He halted, shook his head. "Just a young girl, high school age. The others were all in their twenties."

My curiosity had been piqued, but I didn't question him. Frank is, on the whole, a quiet man. I get him to lose his temper now and then, but this wasn't one of those situations. It had taken him a while to work up to talking about that day at all, and experience had taught me that what he needed in these times was a listener, not an interrogator. I set aside any impulse to hound him for information.

Later, when the paper ran a photo of the young girl—a soft, gauzy shot from her high school yearbook—I thought I knew why this girl's death bothered him more than others. I had seen the high school graduation photo of his sister, Cassie; if you had dyed her hair blond and updated her makeup, she would have, in many ways, resembled the victim. Cassie was alive and well and married with kids; the woman at the party house might never have made much of her life, but she had been denied the opportunity to try.

While other detectives interviewed the neighbors, Frank and Pete sought the victims' friends and fellow addicts. Fear made some of the small-time dealers a little more talkative. "Any strangers looking to make a buy this past week?" Frank and Pete would ask. "Anyone new come around here trying to score?" They were able to get help in identifying a couple of John Does who had been killed in the party house, but not much more.

I learned details of some of these interviews from dramatic presentations offered free of charge by one of the most natural mimics I know: Pete Baird. Pete loves to gather a small audience and tell stories, gesturing and taking on the parts of all the players. More than once, Rachel and I heard the day's events replayed in this way.

The tenant of record at the party house was a man known as Early—he got his nickname for his ability to score new smoking materials before his competitors, which might have accounted for the number of people at his house on the day it exploded. Early's pals provided a lot of material for Pete's act. Frank served as an instant reviewer. If Pete got it wrong, Frank would grumble or silently shake his head. ("Oh, so you come up here and tell it, then," Pete would say, an offer Frank was too smart to take.) If it was fairly accurate, Frank would smile or laugh. A good way to relieve some of the day's tensions.

After studying the rubble that had once been Early's home, the county's bomb experts were able to determine that the plastic explosives used to demolish the house had probably been packed into a television set. That knowledge, and a discussion Frank had with a space cowboy by the name of Fawkes, led to the first real break in the case.

I recalled Pete's portrayal of that interview:

"So picture this guy. Tall, pale dude, but he hunches his shoulders. Has long, stringy brown hair, parts it in the middle. Pointy beard with a mustard stain in it." That Pete is clean shaven, short, olive-skinned, and bald made no impact on our ability to visualize Fawkes.

"Skinny guy," Pete went on. "Wearin' a black T-shirt and jeans that smell like he's got toadstools growin' in his underwear."

Frank shook his head.

"You couldn't smell that guy? You must have a cold," Pete said. "Irene, reach over an' feel his forehead. Running a fever? . . . No? Hmm. Well, okay, so the jeans don't smell that bad. Bad, but not that bad."

Frank didn't object. The play proceeded. When Pete delivered Frank's lines, his back was straight, his voice low. When he became Fawkes he rocked a little as he spoke, curling imaginary hair along a pair of fingers, gazing off into space. He began with Fawkes.

" 'It's weird, man, I don't know about all those

other people who were at Early's party, that's bad. But Early, whoa—I think it was Early's karma, because of the TV set he stole from my relatives.'

" 'What relatives?' Frank asks him.

" 'Well, you know, Early, like, uh, stole it. Early was always stealing stuff. He ripped me off, man. Stole my backpack.'

" 'Who'd he steal it from?' "

A look of consternation. " 'From me, dude.' "

Frank laughed. Pete grinned and went on.

"Frank stays calm. 'No, I meant the TV. You said he stole it from relatives of yours?'

" 'Maybe. I dunno.'

" 'Why don't you tell me what you do know,' Frank says.

" 'Oh. Well, this guy. He drives a gray van. Musta been a cheap store—only had one of them magnet signs on it. He stops at Early's neighbor's house, and opens up the van. In the neighbor's driveway. The neighbor comes out, asks what's happening. Guy says he's got a TV to deliver. The neighbor says, "I didn't order no TV," so the delivery guy asks, can he come inside and make a phone call to his boss. Neighbor says okay. The dumb-ass driver leaves the van open. And while the dude is in there calling his boss, Early sneaks over and rips off this big ol' TV that's sittin' in the back of the van.' "

Pete straightened his back again to do Frank's part. " 'What did the deliveryman do when he got back?' "

Slouching again. " 'That was weird. He just looks in there, smiles, and drives off.'

" 'You get a look at the name of the appliance store?'

" 'Yeah, 'cause it's my name, man. I mean, not my whole name, just my last name. First name was different.' "

Puzzled. " 'Fawkes?' "

" 'Yeah, only he was Guy Fawkes. I mean, not him, the place. Guy Fawkes TV—hey, you think it's a relative of mine? Maybe they would give me a job. What do you think?' "

I looked over at Frank. He was smiling.

The description of the van matched up with one that had been spotted near one of the other exploding houses. On that street, a member of the local neighborhood watch had seen a gray van pull up. The driver, a young, clean-cut man, left the van open as he walked around the corner, glancing between a clipboard and house numbers as if looking for an address. As she watched, her troublemaking neighbor had come out of his house and stolen a television out of the van. When the young driver came back some time later, she came out to tell him what had happened.

"Would you please call the police?" he asked politely, but drove away while she was making the call.

The police communications computer kept a record of the call, but with no appliance store making a complaint, the matter didn't rate much attention. Frank went back to the neighbor; her description of the driver matched Fawkes's. "Would you like to know the license plate number?" she asked.

He told her he would.

The plate turned out to be stolen off a pickup truck, not a match with a gray van.

Frank called every magnetic sign maker in the county, without luck. On a hunch he called the pickup truck owner, asked if he knew where the plate had been stolen.

"Sure," the man said. "In the El Dorado Shopping Center, in Orange. I was in picking up some signs for a big construction job. Parked in an alley while I loaded them. Young man in there helped me carry them. Took four or five trips. He was the one who noticed it was missing. I had just washed the truck that morning, and I know the plate was on then. That sign place was my first stop, so I know it happened there."

The description of the young man who helped him did not match that of the deliveryman. Still, Frank drove across the county line and down to Orange to talk to the sign maker. As it turned out, he immediately remembered Guy Fawkes TV. The kid at the counter who took the order hadn't studied much history, but his boss, an Englishman, had nearly refused to make the sign. Guy Fawkes, after all, had tried to blow up the British Parliament in 1605.

The young man at the counter had protested that this must be mere coincidence; the order had been placed by a polite man who paid cash in advance. The man had even helped one of the other customers carry several armloads of signs out to his truck.

At Frank's request, the sign maker went through his files. He had a phone number for Guy Fawkes Appliances, one his shop had called when the order was ready. The number was traced to an address down on Bay Shore Drive in Las Piernas, not a part of town you would have figured for housing terrorist gangs. The phone was still connected. The owner of the house and the name the phone was actually listed under were the same: Richard Lang.

Lang hadn't lived in Las Piernas very long. He'd paid cash for the house, which had been for sale by owner. He'd told the previous owner that the cash had come from an insurance settlement he'd received from a car accident. Nobody had questioned that story.

The neighbors claimed that Lang had a live-in girl-friend and a frequent male guest who matched the description of the deliveryman. When, after several days of surveillance, the woman never showed, Frank's boss started pushing for an arrest. Frank wanted to wait, but Carlson didn't want to risk losing a murder suspect. Lang had no criminal record. Carlson figured he would break under pressure and give them the information they needed to arrest any-one else.

Armed with warrants, police searched the house. They found books on explosives and minute traces of C-4 in the van. The two men, Richard Lang and Jeffrey Colson, were arrested without resistance. Like Lang, Colson had no prior arrests. Both had served in the military, though, and had met while in the marines. Lang had worked with explosives during his military career. In lineups Lang was identified by the counterman at the sign shop and Colson by the neigh-bors he had encountered at two of the sites.

Frank wasn't satisfied. "If we had found the com-puter equipment," he told me, "I'd be feeling better. But at least we have part of the group in custody. Maybe the lieutenant's right. Maybe they'll talk."

But Carlson had underestimated the ability of the

two suspects to take the first sentence of the Miranda warning to heart. Lang and Colson had not been willing to talk about their friends. Lang had simply said, "Hocus will take care of me." Although they had made no phone call, a lawyer had appeared. Lawyer or no, bail had not been granted.

When Mark Baker's story appeared, Frank started voicing other misgivings about the arrests. He began to wonder if Lang was a sacrificial lamb. "Maybe the information is coming to Mark from Hocus itself. Lang and Colson don't strike me as leaders. What if they drove out to Orange not to make it tougher to find them, but easier? Maybe they knew the sign maker was British. Knew he'd be someone who'd remember 'Guy Fawkes Appliances.' "

"Maybe," I agreed, "but the sign maker could be a coincidence. There are lots of people who know about Guy Fawkes who aren't British."

"Coincidence?" he asked.

"Okay, maybe not. But I'm not sure Hocus is Mark's source. Maybe it's someone in your department. Maybe someone who would like to make *you* the sacrificial lamb."

I could tell by his face that he had already considered this possibility; the thought obviously depressed him. As if he couldn't accept contemplating that kind of betrayal, he said, "Hocus would prefer the publicity. Makes more sense to assume Mark has been contacted by them."

We were soon too busy arguing about other things to spend much time on whose theory was superior. The biggest argument started after a phone call from his sister, Cassie, who lives in Bakersfield. She called to say that Frank had really been on her mind lately, and she just wondered if he was all right.

"He could use some cheering up," I said. "He'll be sorry he missed your call." I told her about the case and his problems in the office. "This has been tough on him from the moment he went out to the crime scene," I told her. "Fifteen victims at one house. It was pretty grim."

"Yes, we heard about that up here," Cassie said. "In fact, when they showed the photo of the young girl who died, I was hoping Frank didn't have the case. She reminded me of Diana. Didn't look exactly like her, of course, but—"

"Diana?" I asked. "Who's Diana?"

There was a long silence, then she said, "You'd better ask Frank."

"Cassie!"

"Ask Frank," she said. "I'm sorry, Irene. I've got to go."

She hung up.

I waited until after dinner that night. I didn't rush him. He played with Deke and Dunk, worked in his garden. He washed up and came into the kitchen, where I was scrubbing a pan. He put his arms around me and pulled me back against him, nuzzled my ear.

"Who's Diana?" I asked.

I felt the brief tension in him before he relaxed a little and said, "Roman goddess of the hunt. Are you and Jack talking about mythology again?"

"No," I said, turning around to face him. "Not that Diana. The Diana who looks like the girl who died at the party house."

"Shit." His arms dropped away, and he took a step back. He wouldn't look at me.

"Who is she?" I asked again.

"Cassie. Cassie told you, right?"

"Never mind who told me."

"It had to be Cassie. My mother never would have told you."

"Probably not. Your mother doesn't like me—"

"That's not true."

"Not the point, anyway."

"No," he said. He sighed. "Christ. Everything at once."

"Is this another old girlfriend?"

He hesitated, finally looked right at me. He shook his head. "No. Can you give me a minute? I need to make a couple of calls."

"A couple of calls? Jesus, Frank. . . ."

"Please."

Desperate. Under other circumstances I might have been moved by it, responded to him more gently. I was fresh out of gentle. "Go ahead, make your damned calls. But I'm not letting go of this, Frank."

He went into the bedroom to use the phone. That he sought privacy from me only irritated me all the more. I sat in the living room, in the corner of the couch, arms folded. Deke, Dunk, and Cody steered clear of me. I let the dogs out at their request, and Cody disappeared into the guest room. I couldn't blame them. I probably looked like I wanted to kick somebody.

When Frank finally came out of the bedroom, he was holding what I at first took to be a scrap of paper but then realized was a photograph. He held it out to me. More curious than furious, I uncrossed my arms and took it from him.

It was a color snapshot of an attractive teenage girl with honey-colored hair, standing next to a camera-shy younger boy. Nothing about the girl was shy. She was wearing an orange miniskirt with a wide, white belt, white go-go boots, and a lime green sleeveless turtleneck. If that hadn't been enough to place the photo in the late sixties, her pale lipstick, eyes lined doe style, heavy mascara, and ankh necklace would have helped.

I had seen lots of photographs of the boy—it was Frank. And despite a certain resemblance, the girl clearly wasn't Cassie, who's not only dark haired, but younger than Frank. This blond girl was older by several years.

"A cousin?" I guessed.

He shook his head, took a deep breath, then looked right at me as he said, "My sister."

"Sister? You have another sister?"

"Had. She died."

Questions are a specialty of mine, and I had lots of them, but I couldn't seem to get a single one out. Maybe it was sort of a circuit overload, like when everyone tries to call after an earthquake. Zillions of questions trying to be first in line. Shock pushing them all to the back. I sat there gaping at him.

He took back the photo, stared at it. "I wanted to tell you a long time ago, but—"

"You had another sister?"

"Yes. Diana."

"You never told me—"

"Like I said, I wanted to—"

"But you didn't."

"I made a promise. To my mom."

"Your mother made you promise not to tell me about your sister?"

"Uh, not exactly you personally, although . . . well, it's not you. Even before I met you, we didn't talk about her."

"I don't get it."

"Diana had problems," he said, looking at the photo. But the look on his face didn't match the words.

He misses her, I thought. It made me settle down a little. "What kind of problems?"

"Drugs. Alcohol. God knows what else. And her problems became the whole family's problems. It was a strain on all of us. No one ever knew what she'd do next. Dad would tell her to come in at ten, she'd get home at three in the morning. Mom would be worried sick, Dad would be pissed as hell. Cassie and I had to listen to the shouting match that would follow. Diana was rebellious as all get-out."

"You think that's all it was? Teenage rebellion?"

"No, no," he said, lightly rubbing his thumb along the edge of the photo. "That's one of the easy answers. Just like—what is it that people always say? You know, the families? 'Fell in with the wrong crowd.' Well, in part that was true. Her crowd couldn't have been more wrong. Assholes, if you ask me. She was proud to hang out with that bunch, and embarrassed about my dad being a cop. *Embarrassed.*" He shook his head. "She was always trying to prove to her friends that she was cool, even if. . . ."

I waited, but he didn't finish the sentence. "Where were you keeping this photo? I've never seen it before."

"In an envelope, taped to the back of the dresser."

"Hiding it from me?"

"No. From my mom. She doesn't know I have it."

"Shit, Frank. You're almost forty and you're squirreling things away from your mother. You got a pet frog in there, too?"

"Very funny," he said, turning red. "She—ah, Christ, forget it," he said, and stood up.

"Hold on, hold on."

He didn't move. I didn't move.

"Sit down, Frank. Please."

He stayed standing.

"I'm sorry," I said. "I'm just confused by all of this."

He relented then. After a moment he said, "I'm sorry, too." He reached over and took my hand. "I never meant for this to happen this way. I wanted to tell you. But this is something that my family hasn't talked about for years, and I knew I wasn't going to get my mom to give in overnight. My mom set this policy a long time ago, not long after Diana died. 'Don't talk about her. It's too painful for your father.'"

It wasn't hard for me to imagine Bea Harriman choosing this way to protect Frank's dad. Wisely I kept that observation to myself.

"I think it was too painful for *her*," Frank went on. "Diana was her favorite, her firstborn. Cassie and I were closer to my dad. Diana was my mother's darling. Dad always said that when Diana was the only one—before I came along—he spoiled her, too. I never saw it. They were both pretty strict with Cassie and me."

"Diana was how much older than you?"

"Four years. Mom just let her have her way, even then. It was easier than fighting her. Diana was strong willed. By the time Cassie was born, Mom had an infant and a toddler to contend with, and that was more than enough. Everything fell on Mom's shoulders—Dad wasn't home much. He worked graveyard shift for a lot of years. Wouldn't come home until after we were getting ready for school. He'd be asleep when we came back. Trying to make ends meet, he'd catch as much overtime as he could. Gradually he cut back, took on better shifts, but by then Diana was past taming."

"You weren't close to her?"

He lifted one shoulder in a small shrug.

"What happened to her?"

He tensed, took his hand away. But after a while he said, "One night, she wanted to go out with some friends. My dad tried to forbid her to leave the house. Like I said, she was only sixteen, but she had already been through a couple of drug treatment programs. Cost more than my folks could afford, really, but they were getting desperate by then. My mom had convinced my dad to change his shift, so that he'd be home to help deal with her. Didn't really help. Diana would be okay for a little while, then . . . I don't know."

He stared at the picture as if he might find an answer there, some way to explain Diana. Just when I started to wonder if I should prompt him to continue, he started talking again.

"I can remember that night so clearly. It was summer. Our air conditioner was busted, and so we had all the windows and doors open. My mom and Cassie were at the store, and Dad was reading the newspaper, but keeping an eye on Diana. She was angry. She was pacing around in the living room, acting fidgety. I knew something was up, so I tried to distract her. I thought maybe I could keep her out of trouble. So I asked her to teach me to dance. She played along, but the whole time, she was watching for someone. I wasn't much of a dancer. She laughed. I started dancing goofier on purpose, trying to make her laugh more."

He looked up from the photo.

"Useless kid's stuff. Diana's friends drove up and honked for her. They were whooping and yelling, sounded like they were already high or drunk or both. She started to go out the door, my dad stood in her way. She yelled, 'Fuck you, pig.' Screamed it at him. You know, like he wasn't her dad, like he was arresting her at a war protest or something. Her own dad. I couldn't believe she would talk to him like that."

He shook his head, as if he still couldn't believe it. "My dad was furious. I could see it. Whenever you really made him angry, he'd get real quiet."

Just like you do, I thought, but said nothing.

"My dad moved out of her way, and said, 'You go out that door, Diana, don't bother coming back.' It was just something he said because he was hurt, the kind of thing parents say when they're upset. He didn't mean it. She looked over at me, and—I don't know, I guess I've always wondered if she would have stayed if I hadn't been there."

"What do you mean?"

"Oh, just that she had to prove something then, couldn't let her kid brother see Dad face her down. She smiled at me and said, 'Guess you'd better find a new dancing partner, Frankie,' and left." He paused, then said, "It got late and she wasn't home. I was in my bedroom, I heard my mom and dad arguing. I guess my dad was putting on a jacket to go looking for her when the doorbell rang. I heard my dad open the door, and then . . . he made this sound . . . I hadn't ever heard anyone make that sound before. I ran out of my room. My mom was wailing by then, but I was still more worried about him. They were holding on to each other. My dad was sobbing. I had never seen him shed a tear, and here he was, weeping."

He stared off into space for a moment, caught up in his memories. When he spoke again his voice was soft and low, distracted. "A uniform—one of my dad's friends was there. Probably his best friend on the force—his first partner. Gray-haired old guy by the name of Nat Cook. The other guys called him 'Cookie.' Cookie was crying, too, but quietly. He saw me, held out an arm, and I went to him. I was just bewildered. Cookie was too choked up to talk to me. I knew it was about Diana. I knew she had to be dead. If she had been hurt, they would have been rushing off to the hospital, but they were just standing there.

"I was the only one who wasn't crying. I kept thinking that I needed to be strong for my dad. I knew that he was blaming himself, thinking that the last thing he said to her was that she shouldn't come back."

"How did it happen?"

"The car—they were all drunk. Driver, too. I guess they were crossing some tracks, tried to beat a train. Plowed through a lowered gate arm at the railroad crossing, didn't make it across. Killed everybody in the car. Engineer said he didn't even get a chance to try to brake. They all said it was quick, but I don't know. . . ."

This time he fell silent.

"Ever do your crying for her?" I asked softly.

He didn't respond for a moment, then shook his head. "No, not really. I loved her. It wasn't that. It was just that I was a kid and I thought about it the way a kid would, you know? I had to be strong. That was what I kept telling myself. After a while, I *couldn't* cry for her. Not long after the funeral, the whole family was pretending she never existed. My mom gathered up all the photos of her and locked them up in the attic. Even photos of the family that had her in them. I stole this one out of the pile. Never let my folks know I had it. I just didn't want to forget what she looked like." He paused. "I sometimes wonder if Cassie really remembers Diana. Like I said, my mom asked us to promise not to talk about her. I have an aunt that has never forgiven my mother for that, but everyone else just went along with the program."

I took his hand again, gave it a squeeze. He moved closer to me, took me in his arms, and held me. "I know it wasn't right to keep this from you, Irene. But I just couldn't say, 'Hey, by the way, did I ever tell you that I was one of three children, not two?' "

"I think you might have figured out another way to bring it up, Frank. I understand the subject is painful, but I guess it's hard for me to accept that we've known each other all these years without . . . well, you've explained it, but it's still hard to accept."

"I know. I know. I'm sorry."

"When we were engaged, didn't your mom—"

"She made me renew my promise."

I sat up a little. "What?"

"Irene, if you asked me whether this was a healthy way to deal with things, I'd say no, it's not. But I'd also say it's too late. It's the way she chose. Diana was her daughter. I'm her son. I had to respect her wishes. And by now . . . I don't know if she could deal with it. It would just open old wounds. She was upset enough when I told her I was going to tell you tonight."

I found myself unable to argue with him, at least at that moment. But I also felt—rightly or wrongly—pushed outside. That in-law feeling. For that evening, I decided, I could rise above my petty troubles, could comfort him, could see that his problems were greater than mine. Still, the notion that he was keeping secrets from me was not so easily set aside. Needlelike, it jabbed at my nobler intentions, became a small injury that would not heal.

Before we went to bed that evening, I picked up the picture of Diana and handed it to him. "You'd better put this back in its hiding place," I said, avoiding his eyes when I said it.

Avoidance. What a great deal of effort it soon requires.

8

THAT'S THE FINEST DOG I ever did see," Gus
Matthews said, squeezing the boy's shoulders.
"I tell you, Brian, this boy of yours knows
dogs."

Frank's father made a noncommittal grunting
sound, trying to get his partner to drop the subject.
His boy, if encouraged, would bring home every stray
within a ten-mile radius.

"I think she's part Lab and part retriever," Frank
said.

"Is that so? Let me see her walk with you," Gus
said.

Frank pulled gently on the dog's makeshift leash—
a length of his mother's clothesline, cut for the purpose. He'd thought to ask permission to use the
clothesline after the fact, just before his younger sister
finked on him. But his mother had seen his excitement
over the dog and merely said, "If your father lets you

keep this dog, the first walk will be to the shopping center. You'll take your allowance and buy a real leash. And a new clothesline."

The dog, who had followed him all the way home from the baseball field without a leash, needed no encouragement to do his bidding with one. Seeming to know that she was facing some sort of test, she walked perfectly beside him.

"Oh, sure," Gus said. "You really do know dogs, Frank. That is definitely a Lab/retriever. Definitely. Have you named her yet?"

The boy turned red, then looked over to his father, a touch of defiance in his voice when he said, "Dad named her."

"Well, Brian?" Gus asked.

"Trouble," Harriman answered. "The dog's name is Trouble."

Gus's effort to hold back his laughter was doomed. Brian watched his son stand there with the dog while the other man guffawed. The boy's back and shoulders were straight; his eyes never left his father's. One hand stroked the dog's head.

The kid was lonely.

The thought struck Brian so suddenly, he almost said it aloud. The Harrimans had lost their older daughter a few months back. Brian had been miserable with it, and so had Bea, his wife. Cassie, the youngest child, had clung to Frank. Frank had been quiet. Frank was always quiet.

"It's a gift, I tell you," Gus was saying. "Frank, you ought to think about working the K-9 unit. Would that interest you?"

"I want to work homicide," Frank answered.

Both men looked startled. "Twelve years old and you want to work homicide?" Gus asked.

He nodded. "I know I can't start there. But I'm going to be a detective."

"Get a load of that, Harriman. You're raising a suit. Well, Frank, you know what? You'd make a hell of a detective. If they were all like you, we wouldn't have any unsolved crimes in Bakersfield, would we?"

Frank shrugged.

"You can keep the dog," Brian said, and paused as his very quiet son let out a loud whoop of elation. "C'mon, Gus. We're taking Frank and his dog to the pet store. When he makes detective, I don't want you tellin' everybody at work that he used to drag strays around on a clothesline."

9

T HERE IS A PLACE ALONG the stair steps leading
to utter exhaustion that is something like being
not quite drunk enough. On the night Frank
was taken by Hocus, I had reached that point by the
time I pulled into the driveway. I automatically left
room for Frank's car. Cassidy's car pulled up instead,
snapping me out of my musings about Hocus and
Frank's sister and back to the present. I had driven
home on autopilot and at some point forgotten
Cassidy was following me.

I was muzzy-headed, emotionally drained. My
thoughts began to trip over one another. Cassidy.
Thomas Cassidy. Right. And he was walking up to the
car door, probably because I was just sitting there.
Maybe I was putting off going back into the house.
An empty driveway is one thing, an empty bed
another.

He waited for me to step out, closed the car door

for me. We walked in silence to the front door. When I opened it, I saw that Jack and Deke and Dunk were waiting for me in the hall.

"Rachel went home to Pete," Jack said, then to Cassidy, "Your partner is asleep in the guest room."

Cassidy went off to rouse Freeman. I rubbed the dogs' ears, accepted their hovering attention. I told Jack what had happened at the paper.

"Anything I can do?" he asked.

I shook my head. "Rachel angry with me?"

He smiled a little. "No, I think she's quite proud of you."

"That's a relief." I put a hand on his shoulder. "You've been great, Jack, but you're probably almost as tired as I am. Why don't you go home and get some sleep?"

"You'll call me if . . ." He hesitated, looking as though he'd decided against finishing the question.

"If anything changes. Yes, of course." I thanked him again and watched him try to recover his let's-be-brave face as he said good night to Cassidy and a tousled Henry Freeman.

I noticed that Freeman had set up a reel-to-reel tape recorder and headphones and other equipment on the kitchen counter near the phone.

Following my glance, Cassidy said, "Remember, it's not unusual for the takers to wait a couple of days before making contact." He repeated his instructions on what to do if Hocus called, most of which were ploys to keep them talking. As soon as possible I should try to hand the call off to Cassidy. Until then I was to stall and not give a definite yes or no answer to any demands.

"You guys don't have those gizmos that instantly identify the caller?" I asked.

"No. At some point in the near future, we'll be able to do that, but the phone company hasn't installed that kind of equipment in this area yet. Our own computer system can identify the caller and location for calls, but there isn't any way to make it available at a residence yet."

Not wanting to think about what this delay in technology might cost Frank, I told them I was going to try to sleep—it wasn't true, but I needed time to myself. Freeman was already half-asleep when I said good night.

Cody and the dogs followed me into the bedroom. I closed the door behind me. I stood there, leaning my back against it. I thought about calling Frank's mother and sister. It was six in the morning. I'd wait another hour, I decided.

Tired as I was, I still could not make myself lie down in that empty bed. I took Frank's pillow from the bed and moved to the one chair in our bedroom, a wooden rocker. Clutching his pillow to my chest, I breathed in his scent, stared at the bed. Cody, less sentimental, curled up on my pillow; the dogs vied for the position closest to my feet. Dunk won.

I thought of all the times I had watched Frank as he slept, listened to the sound of his snoring. I wondered if he was sleeping now or suffering in some unnameable way. Was he dead—or worse, wishing for death? I was in the wrong damn job. Like doctors, cops, and coroners, reporters know a little too much about the kinds of things people are capable of doing to one another.

I started staring at the clock, wondering if I should ever call Frank's mother and sister, whether I would be cruel enough to bring them with me into hell.

I buried my face in the pillow.

I don't remember falling asleep, but I awakened with a lurch that nearly threw me from the chair. The dogs scrambled to their feet.

The phone was ringing. In the next second Cassidy was pounding on the bedroom door, calling my name. I stumbled out of the chair in a panic. "It's open!" I called toward the door, and snatched up the phone.

"Hello," I half shouted into the receiver. Cassidy entered the room quietly.

There was silence on the other end of the line, then a dial tone.

I hung up. I didn't try to hide my disappointment.

"Too short," I heard Freeman call from the other room.

"Make sure our friends caught that, Hank. Tell them to be ready for the next one."

I looked at the alarm clock. Seven in the morning. The sun was up. I had probably managed to get about forty minutes of sleep. I was so tired, my head felt too heavy for my neck. I realized I was still holding Frank's pillow. I heard Freeman talking to someone else on a cellular phone. I looked up at Cassidy.

"If it's Hocus, they'll call back," he said.

"You don't know that!" I said angrily, but no sooner were the words out of my mouth than the phone rang again.

Cassidy smiled.

I took a breath, picked up the phone. I tried but couldn't keep my voice steady when I said, "Hello?"

"Irene Kelly?" a young man's voice said. The connection was slightly distorted, as if he were holding the phone too far away from his mouth. I heard noise in the background, the sound of cars going by.

"Yes," I said.

"This is Hocus," he said. "Sorry to do this to you on your day off, but you should go into work."

"I've already—"

"We want to talk to you about your husband," the voice continued, "but it's important that you are certain we aren't bluffing."

"I know that you—"

"We'll call you back in three hours."

"Wait—I've already been down to the paper. I know you aren't bluffing. I've seen the car."

He didn't respond, but the background noise told me he hadn't hung up.

"I've seen the car," I went on, giving Cassidy a panicked look. He gave me a thumbs-up sign, motioned me to continue. "I've seen it," I stumbled on. "I saw the car—Frank's car. I know you brought it back from Riverside. I just happened to go into the paper last night. You know, sometimes I have to follow up on a story. I went in last night. I saw the car and what was in the trunk. . . ." I swallowed hard. "Oh, and I read the message on the mirror. I know you're serious. I don't doubt you in the least."

No reply.

"Can I talk to Frank?"

Nothing. Still, he didn't hang up.

"I'd just like to hear his voice," I said. "Will you let me talk to him?"

Nothing other than the sound of a highway.

"Are you still there?" I asked.

Freeman walked in from the other room, holding a cellular phone. "They've got it," he whispered to Cassidy, then left the room.

"Are you still there?" I asked again. "Please, let me talk to Frank. Just to know . . . well, you understand why."

Freeman came in again, handed a note to Cassidy.

"If you won't let me talk to him, would you please just say something?"

I waited, but there was no reply.

"Frank's cousin is going to be out here from Texas," I said, trying to remember the script I had gone over with Cassidy. "He's due in today. They've planned this visit for weeks. He's going to be worried when Frank isn't here. Couldn't I just talk to Frank for a moment, so that I could tell his cousin that he's alive?"

I heard the sound of tires screeching on pavement in the background and, not long after, the squawk of a police radio and a dispatcher's voice.

The police? My panic increased tenfold. If they caught this man, if they didn't just follow him—

"Ms. Kelly?" a voice said. A different male voice.

"Yes?"

"Las Piernas Police. Would you please put Detective Cassidy on?"

"What have you done with the man who called?" I asked.

"He's not here, ma'am. Please, just let me speak to—"

I handed the phone over before he could finish.

I waited impatiently while Cassidy talked to him. I

couldn't make out anything from Cassidy's half of the conversation.

"What happened?" I asked as soon as Cassidy hung up.

"What you heard was a tape being played on a cheap little tape recorder. Phone booth is here in town—gas station near an industrial park. Nobody around this time on a Saturday morning, but of course we'll be checking that out. Caller made sure you were answering the first time, then called back and pushed the play button."

"That whole time—no one was there?"

"Probably not. We'll dust everything for prints, look for witnesses."

"You won't find anything."

"Let's not make any predictions one way or the other, all right?"

I didn't answer.

"I'm going to listen to Hank's tape," he said.

I hesitated, then followed him into the living room. Freeman, whose head made him look as if he were being paid by the cowlick, sat hunched over a recorder. "In spite of being second generation and all the other problems, it's very clear," he said. He played it for us. I listened to myself pleading and cringed.

Cassidy looked at his watch. "Should be getting another call at about ten o'clock."

"What do we do until then?" I asked.

"Why don't you try to get a little sleep?"

"I don't think I can."

"Try."

"The effort will keep me awake. Besides, I need to call his family."

The phone rang before he could respond, and once again I leapt to answer it while Freeman scrambled to monitor the call.

"Kelly?"

"Hold on, John."

I looked over to Cassidy. He motioned to Freeman to turn off the recorder. Freeman hit the button and pulled off his headset.

"You coming in?" John asked.

"No. It's my day off, remember?"

"I know, but I thought you might want to talk to us before you talk to the competition."

"Jesus, how do you come up with this crap? Can you just stop thinking about the front page for a minute or two?"

"I'm not trying to upset you, Irene," he coaxed. "I like Frank, you know I do—"

"Don't"

"What?"

"It's been a long damned night, John. I have no— absolutely no—tolerance for bullshit right now. I've got to get off the phone. For all I know, a busy signal could cost Frank his life. By the way, the line is tapped."

"You let the cops put a—"

"Yes."

"What if one of your sources calls?"

"Not many have this number. I'll tell them not to talk on this line."

"Oh, that will be just great!"

"I can't talk about it now—"

"Listen, you find some other way to call me. Get a cell phone, something—we need to talk."

"Good-bye, John."

Cassidy watched me for a moment, then said, "Perhaps we should discuss—"

Before he could say more, the phone rang again. Once again Freeman scrambled to get the headphones on and the tape in motion.

"Irene?"

"Hello, Mark," I said in resignation. "Don't say anything yet."

Once again Cassidy drew a hand across his neck. Freeman turned off the machine and reluctantly removed his headphones.

"Okay," I said.

"Got a minute to talk?" he asked.

"Did John just tell you to call?"

"I would have called anyway. Will you talk to me?"

Cassidy and Freeman were standing within a few feet of the phone, making no attempt to hide the fact that they were listening to my half of the conversation. "Are you asking me as a friend or are you writing an article?" I asked.

"Both, I guess."

"I don't know, Mark. It's not really a good time—"

"Look, I'm sorry. I asked John to put somebody else on it, but he won't. I would have waited, but it's only a matter of hours before you have other media on the way over there."

"Other media? Here?" I should have thought of it, but nothing was coming to me as quickly as usual.

"So far, we're the only paper that knows what happened last night, because nobody else monitors the scanners down here."

"The police used land lines for anything sensitive," I said.

"Even so, before long, someone in that bomb squad is going to talk to radio or television, and you're going to have microphones in your face."

Mark was saying something about how easy it would be for another reporter to find out where we lived, but I was only half listening. I kept thinking of Frank's mother and sister learning about him from a television or radio broadcast or, worse, being approached for an interview. ("Mrs. Harriman, do you believe there is any hope that your son is still alive? How do you feel at a time like this?") Thought about the number of times I'd seen a television crew broadcast the movements of a SWAT team as they took position in a hostage situation. "I can't talk now," I said to Mark, my self-control slipping. "I'll call you later."

I hung up. Cassidy and Freeman were watching me; I could see they wanted to ask me questions about Mark's call. "Forget it," I said.

Cassidy told Freeman to call Bredloe and ask for help with media control.

That wasn't the answer, either, as far as I was concerned. "I'd rather make my own decisions about whether or not I'll talk to the media," I said.

"I can see why you feel that way," Cassidy said. "And no one is trying to keep you from telling your story at some point down the road. But one of the key elements in any successful hostage negotiation is control of what gets out through the media. Hocus is going to watch television, listen to the radio, read the paper."

I didn't say anything.

"Think about the kinds of things this group has

done so far. While we may never find anything rational behind all this, they seem to be anarchists of a sort. We've got two of them in the pokey, and they seem happy to become martyrs. Don't you think they're on a mission?"

"I don't know. Maybe. Hard to tell."

He looked at me as if I were just being stubborn, which I now admit I was. At the time, I was feeling leaned upon, and stubborn seemed like a good response.

"Look at their possible motivations," he persisted. "You think someone takes a cop for the ransom money?"

"No. I think they want their friends back out of jail."

"Maybe as an immediate goal. But if these folks are making trouble for political reasons, they may be looking for a little airtime. Sometimes the members of these groups are willing to die for their cause—as far as they're concerned, it will be worth it if y'all will help to make them famous."

"If you're about to hint that I'd be willing to let Frank join them on their ride to glory in exchange for a byline, stop now."

"No, ma'am. Not at all. I'll try to make myself clear. I'm telling you that if you want to write about it later, I'm all for it. No one is trying to prevent that. But for now, let us handle it, okay?"

I wasn't sure it was in my nature to make that kind of promise. "You don't know that Hocus is like other groups. Other groups would have published a list of demands. You don't even know what they want."

"I have a feeling, Irene, that they plan to tell us very

soon. Now, I know you want to cooperate with the press. That's only natural, given your line of work. At some point, you'll be able to talk to anyone you want to talk to. I want that to be because Frank is home safe, not because we did something that got him killed."

He was waiting for a reply.

I couldn't give him one. I excused myself and made another small escape. I went into the bathroom and washed my face with cold water. I looked at my reflection in the mirror. Something in that unmerciful glass image fully awakened me.

It was the thought of all the tense and weary faces I had seen over my years as a reporter. I was starting to get that look in my eyes, the one I had seen in theirs. I'd interviewed lots of them.

If you're a reporter, and the victim in your crime story is dead or missing or otherwise unavailable, you do your level best to talk to somebody who gives a damn about that victim. If you fail to do so, nobody gives a damn about your story. So you look for the relatives, the lovers, the best friends. They'll have your story for you. The cops just have what passes for facts.

Facts aren't enough for your readers. Readers want to see that sentence, the one that makes your editor say something like, "Great quote from the widow." No matter how gentle or respectful you are when you're with the people you interview, the truth is, you're after their hearts.

A few of the people you talk to don't have the look. But if the loved one is missing, if there's no body yet— after a while, they almost always do. I've seen it many times—on the face of a father whose daughter had not come home after working a night shift at a college radio station; the face of a wife whose spouse had not returned from a sailing trip; the face of a mother whose son had become separated from the other hikers on a forest trail. It's not just the worry and fatigue that wears them down. It's the helplessness. Knowing that something awful may be happening to someone they love and they can't do a damn thing about it.

"Screw that," I said to the woman in the mirror.

I had some phone calls to make.

10

S O, HOW DID HIS MOM TAKE IT?" Rachel asked me.

Pete and Rachel had arrived not long after he got word that Hocus had called. He wasn't looking so hot.

"Not well," I answered. " 'Hysterics' is too mild a term for it."

"Understandable, I suppose."

"I called his sister first. Have you met Cassie?"

Rachel shook her head.

"Hmm. You'd like her. She was upset, but she took it better than his mom did. She offered to tell her mom, but that didn't seem right to me. I didn't want Bea to think I would tell Cassie and not her. Cassie went over there, though, so Bea has some company. I stayed on the phone with Bea until Cassie got there."

Cassie didn't live far from Frank's mother, and the conversation with Bea Harriman probably didn't last more than twenty minutes. Although Bea Harriman had stoically borne the worries of a cop's wife throughout her marriage to Frank's dad, as a cop's mother she felt no similar need to confine her emotions. Healthier for her, I'm sure, but it had been a long twenty minutes for me.

I looked over at Pete. He was sitting on the couch, hunched forward over his knees, hands clasped in front of him. He was staring at the floor. Every few minutes he looked at his watch. "You've met Frank's mom, right, Pete?"

"What?"

That was how he had answered my last three questions. I asked the question again, as I had the others. It was like listening to a radio that was losing a signal—I had to tune him in again before he could reply.

"Sure," he said. "Yeah, sure, I've met his mom." His eyes widened suddenly. "You told her yet?"

Rachel swore under her breath, but I simply repeated the gist of the conversation he had been too preoccupied to listen to.

"I shoulda thought of calling her," he mumbled.

"Yeah," Rachel said testily. She held out a hand and began counting off his regrets on her fingers. "You should have known something was hinky when Ross left a message asking for Frank. You should've gone out to Riverside with Frank. You should have checked up on him earlier. You should have told Carlson and the rest of the assholes in Homicide to quit riding Frank—"

"That's right, goddammit!" he snapped. He stood up and walked toward the sliding glass doors, then abruptly turned away. I knew what had happened just then—it had happened to me earlier. He had looked through those glass doors and had seen Frank's garden. His fists were clenched now, and he looked like he wanted to punch something. Seeing him pace toward the kitchen, Henry Freeman stood up and made a hasty retreat to the guest room. Cassidy, who had just showered and changed clothes, was leaning up against the counter that separates the kitchen and the living room, drinking a cup of coffee. He didn't flinch as Pete approached.

In a voice that barely reached above a whisper, Cassidy asked, "You get any sleep at all last night, Pete?"

Pete stopped pacing, unclenched his fists.

"I didn't think so," Cassidy said. "Why don't we take a stroll down to the end of the block? I haven't even seen the water yet. I could use some fresh air."

Pete looked at his watch. "They might call. . . ."

"I doubt it. I think they'll be right on time."

Pete seemed to consider the offer, then said, "I can't. They might call."

"Let's just go out front, then, sit on the steps for a while."

Pete looked over to Rachel. "Go on," she said. "I'll run out and get you if the phone rings."

When they had gone outside, Rachel said, "I shouldn't have lost my temper with him. This is so hard on him."

"I know."

"Sorry. Not any easier on you."

"Pete learn anything more out in Riverside?" I asked, wanting to change the subject.

"A little. I didn't want to say anything in front of

Cassidy, because I don't want to get Pete in trouble. It's not much, anyway. The Riverside PD was canvassing the neighborhood, trying to locate anyone who might have seen anything, but it's a pretty isolated area. There's a business park and a railway nearby, but not many houses."

"Do they have any idea when this happened? How long Frank has been with these people?"

She shrugged. "Hard to say. They know roughly what time Frank probably arrived at the house—figuring the time he left here, allowing for traffic, and so on. And they can estimate the time of Dana Ross's death. No one saw the car arrive at the *Express*, so that leaves a big gap between Ross's death and the time it would take for Hocus to bring the car to Las Piernas. And no one knows if Frank was still in Riverside when Ross was shot."

"No one saw anything?"

"If they did, they aren't saying a word. Like I said, it's an isolated area. Riverside PD is doing all they can. You know Pete—he wouldn't have come home if he thought he could pester them into doing more. Several freight trains passed by during the day, and Riverside is even trying to contact the crews, just in case anyone happened to see or hear anything." She paused, then added, "They found a .38 slug in the porch railing; the bullet that killed Ross was the same caliber."

"Frank's gun."

"Maybe—but even if it is, that doesn't mean Frank was the shooter," she said quickly. "And he wouldn't just hand over his weapon. Like I told you last night, there were signs of a struggle—he probably fought them."

I covered my face with my hands, as if that act could block images of what "signs of a struggle" might really mean; the words had not registered in the same way the first time.

"There was blood," she said. "I mean, other than the victim's."

I pulled my hands away and looked at her.

"On the porch and in the house," she said. "Could be Frank's."

I groaned. "Oh, Jesus." I thought of the trunk of the car. If that was Frank's blood . . . and there was more in the house. . . .

"How much blood?" I asked.

"I don't know."

"How much blood?"

Still she hesitated.

"Rachel, if our situations were reversed—"

"Pete thought it could have come from a good-sized cut or gash."

As we grew closer to the time for Hocus's call, conversation died off. I started pacing. Rachel seemed to be staring out into the backyard, but I think she was keeping an eye on Pete. Although she wasn't touching him, she would look at him every time he moved. Pete sat staring at his wristwatch, his expression tight and strained. Henry Freeman kept checking the connections on his computer. Cassidy had positioned himself between Pete and the phone and was reading from a file folder—this one filled with old clippings about Hocus. He was wearing an earphone for a remote extension that Freeman had hooked up. Cody was on the mantel—he barely managed to keep most of his twenty pounds on it. His attempt to appear to be sound asleep was spoiled by the twitching of his tail. The dogs lay near me, heads on paws, brows raised in worried watch.

Ten o'clock. Silence, except for Pete murmuring, "C'mon, c'mon. . . ."

The first ring brought everyone—man, woman, and beast—to their feet. Pete started to move closer to the phone, but Rachel blocked his way. Cassidy said, "You gave me your word, Baird." Pete sat down.

I clasped the receiver, nearly unable to restrain myself from answering until Henry nodded. I picked it up on the second ring.

"Hello?"

"Hello, Irene Kelly," a voice said. A young man's voice, not the same as the one on the tape recording. "Give our regards to Detective Cassidy, too, please. There, that saves you having to resort to any silly business—what would it have been, a brother from Texas?" Before I could answer, he went on. "I suppose Detective Baird is there, also?"

"I want to talk to Frank."

"Of course you do. But we haven't got much time. In fact, let me call you right back."

There was a click and a dial tone.

Henry Freeman made a call on a cellular phone. His face registered disappointment "Not long enough," he said to Cassidy.

"Tell them to stay on the line, we're expecting another call," Cassidy said. He turned to me. "Hank is in contact with the folks who are working with the phone company to trace the call. Notice anything different about this last call?"

"It wasn't a tape recording this time," I said. "The

caller replied directly to what I said. I couldn't hear any background noise this time, and the voice was much clearer." My hands were shaking.

"What did they say?" Pete asked, frantic.

"Hang in there, Baird. I'll go over it with you in just a sec. You all set up, Hank?" Cassidy asked.

Freeman nodded just as the phone rang again.

"Ms. Kelly? Sorry." The same man's voice. "This should work a little better. Cassidy will try to trace all of these calls, of course, so you and I will have very brief conversations."

"You know my name, what's yours?"

"We'll get to introductions later. Now, listen carefully. I'll be speaking rapidly, but you'll undoubtedly have a tape to work from. First, you must learn how we met Detective Harriman. We met him where you met him. Drive out to your former employer's offices there. Go to the library. Talk to Brandon North. He's expecting you to arrive at one-thirty."

"But it takes three hours—"

"Yes, and that's if traffic isn't bad. Mr. North isn't usually there on Saturdays, so he might not wait around. You'd better get going. And don't make Mr. North wait, because that forces us to wait. I'm sure you understand that Detective Harriman's health depends upon your willingness to follow instructions in a timely manner."

"Wait—"

"Oh, we can't wait too long. But you want to talk to him, don't you?"

"Yes—"

"We'll call back."

He hung up again.

"Hank?" Cassidy asked.

"No, sir."

This time the silence began to stretch out longer.

"After we get this next call, I'll let you listen to the tape, Pete," Cassidy said. "Irene, did you—"

The phone rang again.

"Irene?"

"Frank! Oh, Jesus—"

"You sound scared. Don't worry, I'm okay," he said, his speech thick and slow. "God, I had the best dream about you." He started laughing. "I'd better not tell."

Laughing? "Frank?"

"You're not still mad at me, are you?"

"God, no, Frank—"

"So where are you?"

"*Where am I?* Frank, are you—"

The call was disconnected.

"No!" I cried out.

The phone rang again.

"He's fine," the young man's voice came on again. I could hear Frank saying, "Hey, I wanna talk to her."

"He doesn't sound fine. His speech was slurred. What have you done to him?"

"Versed. Just a small dose, a little something to take the edge off. You give it to someone, and later they tend not to remember what happened to them while they were on it. Thought we'd use it this time instead of the morphine."

"Instead of morphine? Why was—"

"He'll be fast asleep in a few minutes. We'll take care of him, Ms. Kelly. As long as you cooperate, of course."

"What is it you want?"

"Let's just take this one step at a time. Meanwhile, I assure you, we sincerely hope we won't be required to cause Detective Harriman any further injury."

"Further injury?"

"Not to worry. We're taking good care of him. He's our hero, after all."

"Your hero?"

"Henry Freeman has probably made some progress by now, so we'll say good-bye."

"Henry Freeman hasn't got a clue where you are. Let me talk to Frank again, I have to tell him—"

A click.

Henry, still on the cellular phone, looked at Cassidy and shook his head.

Pete started shouting questions.

"Play the tape for them, Hank," Cassidy said.

We all listened together. Freeman had made a very clear recording. This time around I was prepared for Frank's laughter, so it affected me differently. He was alive. He could speak to me, he could laugh. He was alive. I felt tears of relief welling up. I needed more sleep, I told myself, and made another grab at a slender thread of self-control.

Focus on the immediate problem. Think about what they said. I glanced at Cassidy. He was studying me. "What's Versed?" I asked.

Freeman opened a black nylon packet and pulled out a compact disc, then slid it into his computer. He typed something, then said, "Schedule Four drug."

"It's a product that's subject to the Controlled Substances Act of 1970," Cassidy translated. "Morphine is Schedule Two, the category for drugs with high potential for abuse; they may lead to severe dependence. Schedule Four has a low potential for abuse."

"What are you reading from, Detective Freeman?" I asked.

He looked up. "The PDR—*Physician's Desk Reference*—I've got it on CD."

"What else does it say about Versed, Hank?" Cassidy asked, then added quickly, "Just the basics."

"Short-acting benzodiazepine CNS depressant," Freeman went on. "Sedates three to five minutes after IV injection, fifteen minutes after IM."

"What the hell is he talking about?" Pete asked.

"It's a central nervous system depressant," Cassidy said, and began reading over Freeman's shoulder. "Looks like they've been around hospital drug supplies—had access to them or stolen from them. Hank, let's make sure we get calls going on that. This isn't something that's popular out on the streets. My guess is, Frank's hooked up to an intravenous feeding device; I'd assume that means his hands aren't free, or they'd have to worry that he could take it out. IM means 'intramuscular'—a needle injection."

"A shot?" Pete asked.

"Yes. Versed has to be given as a shot or through an IV. Isn't available in pill form. Sounds like they started him out on morphine, but gave him this for the phone call. It's something like Valium. When you first give someone a dose of it, he may be giddy and talkative."

"You're saying Frank was high," Rachel said.

"Absolutely. They're clearly sedating him," Cassidy said.

"Is he in danger from these drugs?" I asked.

Cassidy paused, then said, "Any sedative can be

dangerous, especially if the person administering it doesn't know what he's doing. I'm guessing these people know something about medicine, because they've chosen to use a drug that isn't commonly on the street, and knew its effects."

Pete put an arm around my shoulders. "I'm sorry, Irene. I'm so damned sorry."

"Not your fault, Pete. No one is blaming you but yourself. I want to talk to you more about that later, but right now I've got to get out to Bakersfield."

"That's what he was asking you to do? To go to Bakersfield?"

"Yes."

"You used to work for the library there?" Hank asked, regarding me with new respect.

"No, the newspaper. The *Californian*. He means the library at the newspaper—newspapers used to call that part of the paper 'the morgue.' Among other things, it's where you find back issues, file photos, stuff like that. Brandon North has worked there for a long time. We haven't talked to each other for a couple of years now, but we used to keep in touch. I'm sure he'll help if he can."

"Hank," Cassidy said, "start making calls to the other CIT members. Let them know where things stand—start by giving Captain Bredloe a call."

Hank nodded.

"CIT?" I asked

Cassidy turned back to me. "Critical Incident Team. I'll give you the rundown on it later—for now, think about the voices on the calls. Anything recognizable? Maybe someone who used to work with you in Bakersfield?"

I shook my head. "No. Too young. Everyone I worked with would be older. I haven't worked there since I first graduated from college."

"What can we do to help, Irene?" Rachel asked before Pete or Cassidy could ask another question.

"Call Bea and Cassie and Jack, let them know he's alive." Alive. I held on to the word. "I'm going to take a quick shower and change clothes. I've got to get on the road."

"I'll drive," Cassidy said.

"I don't know if they'll—"

"Don't go alone," Pete said. "It could be a trap. Maybe they want to take you as a hostage, too."

"They know I'm involved," Cassidy said. "They don't seem especially concerned about it. I'm sure my ego will recover eventually, but in the meantime, I'm thinking that Pete's absolutely right—you shouldn't go alone. Besides, I'd follow you out there anyway. No reason to take two cars. And I think it'd be easier to get my frail little old granny to climb Mount Everest than it would be to get that old car of yours over the Tejon Pass."

"I hope your granny has fewer miles on her," I said, and heard Pete laugh for the first time all day. I started to leave the room. I stopped and looked back at Cassidy. He was grinning. "Okay, you can drive me out there. Can you make a strong cup of coffee?"

"If we put my coffee in the tank of that Karmann Ghia, it just might make it over the pass after all."

"Thermos is in the cabinet over the refrigerator," I said. "I'll be ready in about twenty minutes."

"And they say Texans lie," he said, but I was on my way to prove him wrong.

11

I DIDN'T DRINK ANY of Cassidy's java-flavored rocket fuel until the trip was more than halfway over, after I awoke with a start while we were somewhere on I-5 between Castaic and Pyramid Lakes. At his suggestion I held off on the coffee before that, sleeping from Torrance to the Tehachapis. I had argued with him at first, insisting on trying to stay awake, but he does, after all, earn part of his living by negotiating, and he won that round. I'm still not sure how it happened.

My awakening was abrupt, but to a pleasant view. The previous winter's rains had been heavy, so the mountainsides were softly covered in a hundred shades of green. Cassidy had turned off his air conditioner—a wise precaution on the steep grades leading up to the pass—and his window was rolled down. I rolled mine down, too. The air was cool and clean, the sky a deep, dark blue. L.A. was out of sight, out of mind.

I stretched, took in the scenery, and shook off the

dream that had awakened me. Cassidy glanced over at me. I was startled to see him looking worried. Mr. Calm, worried? In the next moment I knew what had happened.

I uncapped the thermos, avoiding his eyes. Inhaled the aroma of the coffee, poured it, praying he wasn't glancing at my hands. "What was it this time?" I asked. "Just talking, or did I yell and scream?"

"You didn't scream," he said. Calm again.

"Oh, so just yelling, then. Well! Not bad under the circumstances."

"No need to be embarrassed," he said.

"Who's embarrassed?" I took a sip of the coffee. Strong. Very strong.

"You are. But you needn't be. Fact of the matter is, I'd forgotten your history."

"My history," I said flatly. Held both hands around the cup, held it up close to my lips, felt the steam warm my face. "Now, that's a term used for patients and parolees, isn't it? People who can't be trusted to behave themselves. 'Subject has a history of—' "

"Is that what you think I'm implying?"

I didn't answer.

"By 'your history,' " he said, "I was simply referring to what has happened to you in the past. The fact that you were once held captive."

"I had forgotten that you'd have access to that information. No photos, of course. Did they do a pretty good job of describing it in the police files? The bruises, the dislocated shoulder?"

"More than that," he said quietly.

"Oh, yes," I said, looking out the window. "More than that."

"You have any permanent physical problems?"

I shook my head, not caring if he could see my response.

"Your physical recovery isn't what's remarkable, you know."

"Let's just drop it, okay?"

"You're doing very well. Most people—"

"How well I'm doing isn't what's really important right now," I said. "Do you want any of this coffee?"

"Every hostage has dreams."

"Thank you, Dr. Freud. Mine are of large bananas, snakes, tunnels, and pomegranates. What do you suppose it all means?"

He smiled but didn't reply.

The silence stretched out. "Sorry," I said after a while. "I just don't like to talk about it."

"I didn't get the information from a department file," he said, as if I had invited him to take up where he left off. "Frank talked to me after you came home."

"What?"

"Oh, not very directly, 'least not at first. Stopped by my desk one day, started asking about posttraumatic syndrome in hostages. What was typical, how long did it last, and such."

I just stared at him in disbelief.

"Frank's a quiet man," he went on. "I didn't figure it was too easy on him to bring the subject up. I knew you had been home for a few days. Everyone else was patting him on the back, saying how glad they were that you had been found alive. He was glad, too, but he looked tired."

"Exhausted," I said. "We were both exhausted. For weeks afterward, I rarely slept through a night."

"And now?"

"Better. Much better, for the most part. I wouldn't leave the house at first."

He waited.

"It takes more to trigger a nightmare," I said, giving in. "Some things still bother me—I still can't stand to be in confined spaces for very long. Sometimes, I'll think, Oh, it's all behind me, and then I'll find myself standing in line in a grocery store, and someone is saying, 'Lady? Lady? Are you okay?' because I've let my mind wander, and it's wandered to that time, and I'm remembering."

"But it isn't like a memory."

"No. It's as if I'm there."

"You think about being hurt?"

"No, not usually. If I'm thinking about myself, I think about being scared, afraid of what would come next. Other times. . . ."

"Other times?" he prompted.

"I killed someone," I said. "I think about him. About ending his life."

"What happened?"

"I thought you said Frank talked to you."

"You tell me."

I almost balked again, but there he was, relaxed as ever, and I wanted to shake his complacency. At first, that's what I wanted. But by the time we were over the Tejon Pass and looking down into the San Joaquin Valley, I had confided in him to a degree that I had confided in few others. Usually, recalling those events is an invitation to a certain amount of emotional upheaval, and I found myself wondering not only why I had spoken so freely, but also why I felt relieved rather than devastated. I began to realize that in some way Cassidy's quiet calm had been extended to me, and I had grabbed on to it. It had slowed my reactions, protected me from all the emotions usually so easily aroused when I thought of the time of my captivity.

Cassidy was silent, but there was no uneasiness in it.

He stopped at a gas station in Grapevine even though he still had half a tank, paying an extortionist's price for a few gallons of regular while I went into the rest room and washed my face.

When I came out he had pulled the car away from the pumps and parked it on the side of the station. He was leaning against the car, arms folded, watching the other customers. The wind was gusty, and I had to use both hands to hold my skirt down as I crossed the pavement. When I had dressed that morning I had considered wearing jeans, but when I'd remembered that he was wearing a suit, I'd decided to wear work clothes. I didn't know who else might be hanging around at the *Californian* on a Saturday, but it would be best not to attract too much attention. Now, walking awkwardly to the car, I wished I had remembered about the wind and worn slacks. Cassidy saw me and grinned before he turned to open the passenger door for me.

"You doing okay?" he asked once we were both inside. He hadn't put the key in the ignition yet.

"Yes," I said, self-conscious again.

"Thanks for talking to me about it," he said, starting the car.

"I surprised myself," I admitted. "Frank and Jack are the only other people who've heard the whole story. Unless Frank already told you most of this?"

"No," he said. "No, he hasn't. He really didn't give me too many particulars."

"Are you friends?"

"With Frank?" he asked.

"Yes."

"Well, not exactly. We're friendly, but not close. I do like Frank. Probably because he is one of two people in the whole damned department who never thought it would be a hilarious and original joke to call me 'Hopalong.' "

"Who's the other one?"

"Me."

I laughed. "I'd think the two of you would get along well."

"We do get along. We just don't usually end up handling the same cases. Once or twice he's caught one of the ones that didn't turn out the way I had hoped."

"What does that mean?"

"The CIT—our team—gets called out to negotiate all sorts of critical incidents—suicide threats, kidnappings, hostage takings, and barricade situations—bank robberies, domestic violence, you name it. Much as I'd like to say we're one hundred percent successful, we're not. Over the years, Frank's caught a couple of cases where someone threatening suicide went ahead and did it before I could talk them out of it. Had a domestic barricade situation go bad last year."

"The one where the man was holding his wife and three kids at gunpoint?"

"Yes."

"But you got the kids out."

"Yeah." He didn't say anything more.

"I think I remember the story—something about one of the wife's relatives?"

"Her brother. The brother was with an intelligence negotiator, giving us information on the husband and weapons he might have, and so forth."

"What's an intelligence negotiator?"

"Part of the team—person who gathers as much information as possible on the suspect and anything else relevant to the situation. Ideally, there's a separate, secured area where this person interviews anyone who has information that may be of some use."

"And this time there wasn't?"

"There was, but the intelligence officer got distracted when the kids were released. While the officer was trying to talk to the kids about the situation in the house, the brother decided to play the hero. Snuck off and tried to break through the perimeter we had set up, but didn't make it. We caught him. All the same, there was scuffling and he started shouting. Husband heard the noise and decided we were sending the SWAT team in. He just lost it. Shot her, shot himself."

I stared out the window for a moment. "How old are you, Cassidy?"

"I'm forty-two." He smiled. "Now you know why I'm gray headed—sure as hell ain't the years."

Now I know why you understand people who have nightmares, I thought, but didn't say it.

"I probably shouldn't be talking to you about failures," he said after a minute. "I don't suppose I've inspired your confidence."

"You're wrong." I looked over at him. "You know what? I think you *know* you're wrong. I think one of the first things you learn about anyone is how to inspire his or her confidence."

He laughed. "Hell, Irene, sometimes I really do just talk."

"Sure, Cassidy. Sure."

After miles of hills and mountain grades, we came to the highways that cross the southern end of the San Joaquin Valley, which are flat and waste no time with curves. They practically beg for speed. We took the Highway 99 turnoff and flew past exits for Mettler and Pumpkin Center and Weed Patch. Tumbleweeds skipped across the highway.

"Lordy," Cassidy said, "if it weren't for the palm trees lining that road over there, I'd be afraid I'd died and gone to Amarillo to pay for my sins."

"I like it out here," I told him. "Makes me think of my grandmother's farm in Kansas. Look—there's a windmill." I pointed to one that stood just east of the road. "She had one like that."

"Excited over a windmill, are you? Things must be slow in the Las Piernas newsroom."

I ignored that. "You can see for miles. Crops are growing. There are cattle and—"

"You see a couple of cows and a pumpkin patch, and you get all romantic about it, thinking of your grandma. I see backbreaking work. I moved from our family farm to Austin just so I could keep the bottom of my boots clean."

"Did it work?"

"Nope. Got into law enforcement and I've been stepping in somebody else's BS every day since."

"At least you'll enjoy the music out here. Bakersfield

bills itself as the C and W capital of California."

He grimaced. "Did I ever tell you how I came to live on the West Coast?"

What the hell. "No, Cassidy, even though I've known you for about a dozen hours now, I'm afraid you've never told me."

"Well, I was in Texas, and I had my radio on. All I could tune in was Jesus men and country-western music. So I started driving, trying to get to where I could hear something different. Next thing I knew, I was in California."

I laughed. "And I suppose you had to go to work in Las Piernas just so you could earn gas money to get back home."

"Oh, no. Once I learned I could live some place that had something else on the radio, I never wanted to leave."

"We'd better keep the radio off here, then, and plan on amusing ourselves with conversation."

"A cinch."

"Cassidy?"

"Hmm."

"I've been to Texas—including Austin. I'd swear I heard all kinds of music there."

He just grinned.

"Take a right on Truxtun," I told him. "There are some lettered streets after that—A, B, C, and so on. But when you get to H, the next street is Eye—E-y-e."

"I like that," he said. "Somebody had a sense of humor right from the start."

"Turn left on Eye. The paper's at Eye and Seventeenth Street."

• • •

Built in the 1920s, 1707 Eye Street is a handsome brick edifice. Tall, elaborate columns with composite capitals adorn the front of the building; a turret graces the upper right corner, a balcony the other.

" 'Bakersfield, Californian. Established 1866,' " Cassidy read aloud.

"Bakersfield was a town of cowboys, miners, and railroad workers then," I said.

"So what's changed?"

I smiled. "Oil, for one thing. The business of agriculture, for another. You ought to give the place a chance, Cassidy."

He held up his hands in mock surrender. "Don't mean to offend," he said.

We stepped out of the car. I looked at my watch. One twenty-five. "You made good time. We've got five minutes to spare."

He shrugged, as if to say this was to be expected. "When did you work here?" he asked.

"Right after college," I said. "I interned at the Express, but my first full-time, paying job on a newspaper was here at the Californian."

"Do me a favor," he said. "Don't let your friend know I'm with the police."

Whatever feelings of goodwill I might have been building toward Cassidy were demolished with that request. "Forget it. Brandon is doing me a big favor by letting me into the building. I don't work for this paper now, remember? He's an old friend or I'd be locked out. I'm not lying to him. You'll have to wait downstairs for me."

I rang the night bell before Cassidy could say more,

and a young security guard immediately let us in through the polished brass doors, which were locked on weekends, then went back to his desk to answer a phone. I saw a balding man of medium height waiting just inside the entry. He grinned as we walked in and extended a hand.

"Irene! God, it's great to see you again!"

"Good to see you, too, Brandon," I said, shaking hands.

He looked back at Cassidy. "Are you the fellow who called to set this up?"

"No, I'm afraid not," Cassidy replied. "I'm just Ms. Kelly's ride."

Brandon laughed. "What is this, Irene? You have all the men at the *Express* ready to satisfy your every whim?"

"If only you knew what a disgusting thought that is, Brandon," I said. "No, this is Detective Thomas Cassidy of the Las Piernas Police Department."

I saw Cassidy look up at the room's high ceiling. Fairly certain he wasn't suddenly interested in the patterns on the painted wood beams, I felt smug satisfaction at seeing his armor crack.

"Police?" Brandon was saying. "I'm sorry, but I can't—"

"Detective Cassidy will be waiting right here."

Cassidy, damn him, just smiled.

"Oh, well—"

"Mr. North," Cassidy said in confiding tones, too soft for the security guard to overhear, "I wonder if I might ask you a few questions before you take the ungrateful Ms. Kelly on back to the library?"

Brandon seemed totally confused.

"Cassidy," I warned, my irritation growing.

"I'm out of my jurisdiction, of course," he said. "I could drive on over to the Bakersfield Police Department, which my own department has already contacted. I used my cell phone and spoke to someone there on the drive up here—Ms. Kelly was asleep, so she's unaware that we've obtained their full cooperation."

"Cassidy," I tried again.

"They'd probably be happy to send someone over to question you, Mr. North," he continued, "but then you'd have at least three people connected to law enforcement agencies walking around in your newspaper offices. Might attract attention."

"Three?" Brandon asked.

"Ms. Kelly's husband works with me."

"Husband?" Brandon looked at me in surprise. "You married a cop?"

Hearing Brandon's exclamation, the security guard looked our way.

"Yes," I said. "Look, Brandon, let's step outside for a minute, okay?"

Five minutes later a sheen of perspiration had broken out on Brandon's forehead.

"God, what a mess! Irene, if you had told me what was going on here, I would have understood. You must be worried sick." He paused, then said, "Oh, Jesus—you're saying I talked to a kidnapper!"

"Can you describe the voice of the man who called you on the phone?" Cassidy asked.

"A young man. I don't know why I say that, but—he just sounded young." He started pacing. He glanced at Cassidy, then said, "No accent. I mean, none that I could hear. Seemed well educated."

"When did he call?" Cassidy asked.

"Yesterday. Just before I went home. About three-thirty. Said he was an intern working with Irene, that she had asked him to call. Told me she needed to look through the old files—something on microfilm—wondered would I help her out. I said, 'Sure, tell me what it is and I'll make a copy and fax it to her.' He said she wanted to see me personally and she'd be up in Bakersfield today anyway. If I'd meet her at one-thirty, she'd look it up and then we could go out for a cup of coffee afterward. He got my fax number and said he'd send a list of the things she needed to see." He turned to me. "Why do you think he told you to come to the paper, Irene?"

"I don't know," I said. "I haven't had a lot of time to think about it. I suppose I might have written a story that will have something to do with this. Some similar case, maybe. I was on the crime beat when I worked here."

"Did he send the list?" Cassidy asked.

"Yes, a fax was waiting for me when I came in."

"Recall anything else about him?"

"Oh, yeah. He was very friendly. He sounded polite. He said Irene had told him all about me and my family. That's why I didn't even question his connection to her. He knew I was married. Knew I had five kids. Even knew their names—" He grew pale. "My God! You don't think he'd harm my family?"

"I don't think that's likely at all, but here," Cassidy said, pulling out his cellular phone. "Why don't you check on them? Go ahead, call them."

Brandon looked at him with gratitude and quickly punched in a series of numbers. He bit his lower lip while the call went through, then said, "Honey? Oh, thank God. Thank God. Listen, something's come up. I can't talk about it right now, but *please* take the kids and go over to my dad's house, okay?" He paused. "No, right now, okay? Yeah, I'm fine. This is urgent. . . . Yes. On a cellular phone. . . . No—listen, just do this for me, okay? Right now. . . . No, Dad's fine. I'm fine, too. Just go, okay? . . . Yes. . . . Thank you. . . . Yes. I love you, too. Bye."

He looked like he was ready to cry.

"Use it again," Cassidy offered. "Let your dad know he's about to have a passel of kids over there."

"Thank you," Brandon said. He dialed again. "Dad? I need your help. . . . No, not money. Just listen, okay? I'm worried about Louise and the kids. They're coming over to your place. . . . Yes, I know what Al broke the last time he was there. I'll pay for anything they break, Dad. Listen. Please. . . . Oh, for crying out loud!"

He looked up at Cassidy. "He hung up!"

Cassidy took the phone and pressed the redial button.

"Mr. North? Good afternoon, sir. This is Detective Thomas Cassidy of the Las Piernas Police Department. We have reason to believe that there is a possibility— just a slim possibility—that your grandchildren may be in danger. I'm on an unsecured line here, so I can't go into details, but we asked your son to think of someone who could defend his wife and children until police protection could be arranged. He named you, sir. Your son will probably be calling you to let you know more about all of this, but I wanted to make sure you were up to the job. . . . Well, sir, he seems to believe you are capable, but I would hate to see an elderly gentleman placed in a position of. . . . Well, I'm sure you do know how to use a shotgun. . . . Why, no, that's not very old at all. But you also need to be willing, sir. Sometimes people are not as kind to their kin as you'd expect them to be. . . . Well, no wonder he's so certain of your help, then. As I said, he'll probably be calling, so I won't tie up the line. Thank you, sir. . . . Good day to you, too, sir—and please be very careful with that gun around the children, now. . . . Yes, that's a wise precaution. Good-bye."

He hung up, pressed redial one more time, and handed the phone back to Brandon, who was now looking at him like he was Moses come to take him to the Promised Land. I had known for some minutes that Cassidy was going to get into the library at the *Californian*. Now I was wondering if Brandon would remember to include me.

We went back into the building and headed up to the third floor. At first I thought Brandon was taking us into the newsroom, but he saw my confusion and said, "The library moved since you worked here. It's right next to the newsroom now." We entered a long, narrow room. Painted white and filled with sunlight from the large windows along one wall, it was a more pleasant research environment than our windowless tomb at the *Express*. A long row of putty-colored file cabinets—or, rather, pairs of file cabinets placed back to back—took up most of the room. Newspapers and long, gray metal boxes were stacked on top of the cabinets. Brandon walked to his desk, which was at the far end of the library.

"Let's see, now. Where did I put that fax?" He began shuffling through a pile of papers.

An interior set of windows ran along part of the wall that partitioned the library from the newsroom. I looked through them, wondering if I would see any familiar faces on the other side. But it was Saturday afternoon, and there wasn't much activity. The few reporters who were in the room were busy at their desks, not interested in looking at the library. I didn't recognize any of them.

"Feeling nostalgic?" I heard a voice drawl behind me.

"No," I lied, and kept staring through the glass. A moment later Cassidy walked away. I was glad. He had managed to stick to me like a burr on a foxtail, and I was tired of it. I didn't want him intruding on this particular ground. We all have our sacred places, and I couldn't help it if this part of Bakersfield was one of mine. I had learned to be a reporter at this paper. My college instructors might have taught me how to close my hands around the tools of the trade, but this was where I really learned to use them. I paid my dues here, in this city, in this newsroom. Both had changed, but that didn't matter. Looking through that window, I saw the newsroom not as it was, but as it had been not so long ago.

When I first came to Bakersfield, manual typewriters were giving way to electrics, and a few hotshots had portable computers—although what passed for a portable computer then was a far cry from the notebook computers of today. A newsroom sounded different then. It was a noisy place, filled with the clatter of typewriters and the grinding rasp of carriage returns; the *chunk-chunk-chunk* of the Teletype; bells—real bells, ringing bells on everything—typewriters, Teletypes, and even telephones. Voices.

I thought of a young rookie cop I used to meet for breakfast at a nearby coffee shop at the end of our night shifts.

"I found it!" Brandon said. Then, noticing where I was standing, he asked, "You want to go into the newsroom, for old times' sake?"

"No, thanks, Brandon. Not with a cop in tow." I said it to irritate Cassidy, but it was really for old times' sake that I refused to enter that changed world, with its muted keyboards and paperless monitors and silent wire services.

Brandon handed the fax to me. Cassidy moved closer, read over my shoulder.

Beneath a phony version of the *Express*'s letterhead, a fax purporting to be from me to Brandon listed four dates, all from one year.

June 18
June 19
September 23
October 26

"Mean anything to you, Irene?" Cassidy asked.

"Not offhand. But these aren't my stories. This was the year after I left the paper."

"Let's pull the microfilm," Brandon said.

We followed him out into the hallway and entered to a nearby room, where there were microfilm storage cabinets, each with a padlocked locking bar down the front.

"Why do you lock them up?" Cassidy asked.

"This collection contains every issue of the paper since 1866, except for one missing year. That one walked out of here one day before we started locking the cabinets."

He used a key to unlock one padlock and pulled two boxes from a file. He locked the cabinet again, and we followed him back into the library. He motioned for me to take a seat at the microfilm reader and handed me the June spool. I began loading it onto the reader.

"What's in these files?" Cassidy asked, gesturing to the cabinets.

"Clippings from the more recent years," Brandon said. "Filed by subject."

"You don't have them on computer?"

"Not yet. By the end of the year, reporters will be able to retrieve files that way."

As they talked, I used the fast-forward control on the reader, stopping here and there to scan dates, until I finally came to June 18. I had bypassed the front page and had to back up on the slower speed.

"A Monday," I said, wondering how much of the paper I would need to read before something jumped out at me. For a panicked moment I wondered if there was any point at all in being in Bakersfield that afternoon. Perhaps this was a wild-goose chase, perhaps Hocus had only wanted me to leave the house, to be out of town for a number of hours. . . .

But then the first page rolled slowly into view, and I knew I was looking at the story I was supposed to see. I knew it from the moment I saw the photograph beneath the headline:

FATHER'S DAY TRAGEDY:
TWO BAKERSFIELD MEN SLAIN WHILE SONS WATCH

It was the kind of photograph every photojournalist dreams of taking. Two women, their faces tearstained, mouths contorted in grief, arms outstretched, crouched slightly as they hurried toward two young boys. The boys' faces were scraped and bruised but without expression, their eyes empty—too empty for their nine or ten years. One boy cradled his right arm, which was in a splint, as he leaned his head on a uniformed policeman's shoulder. The other boy held on to the policeman with both arms. The policeman knelt on one knee, his arms around the boys, looking up at the women with anguished eyes.

I knew the officer's name before I read the caption.

Some years after the photo was taken, I married him.

12

VA RYAN AND FRANCINE NEUKIRK, whose
husbands were found murdered Sunday, are
reunited with their sons, who police believe
were made to witness the slayings. Officer Frank
Harriman of the Bakersfield Police Department holds
the boys, Samuel Ryan and Bret Neukirk.' "

I took a deep breath and began reading the story
itself:

A father-son fishing trip ended in tragedy this
weekend, when two Bakersfield men were bru-
tally slain while their nine-year-old sons were
forced to look on in helpless horror. Police say
Dr. Gene Ryan and Julian Neukirk, both 35,
died in the basement of an abandoned warehouse, their throats slashed by an unknown
assailant. Both men also suffered multiple stab
wounds and bore marks indicating they had

struggled with their assailant. No motive has been established for the killings.

Acting on an anonymous tip about a ware-house break-in, Officer Frank Harriman arrived at the scene to find the two boys, Samuel Ryan and Bret Neukirk, chained to a wall in a base-ment storage area, approximately seven feet from their fathers' bodies. The Ryan boy suffered a fractured right arm; both boys received other minor injuries. Blood spatter patterns indicated the boys were in the room when their fathers were attacked. Police say the boys are severely traumatized and thus far have been unable to provide any information about the crime.

Ryan, an emergency room physician, had been looking forward to a week-long fishing trip with the boys and Neukirk, who owns a truck-ing business. Both men grew up in the area and have been friends since childhood.

"They loved one another like brothers," said one family friend, who asked not to be identi-fied. "Bret and Sam are just as close to one another as their fathers were."

The article went on to say that the police were ask-ing any members of the public who might have infor-mation about the case to please contact them immedi-ately.

"On the phone this morning, remember?" I said, looking up at Cassidy. " 'He's our hero.' Which one do you think I talked to, Samuel Ryan or Bret Neukirk?"

"I'll run a check on those names," Cassidy said.

"Mind if we make a couple of copies of this, Mr. North?"

"Not at all," Brandon said.

"I can just print them out from here," I said.

"I vaguely remember this case," Brandon said. "I may even have some photos of the boys on file. I think one of the photographers won an award for that photo."

While Cassidy made a call asking for research on Neukirk and Ryan, I focused the machine as sharply as I could, made two copies of the article, then moved the microfilm to a related story.

The long front-page article included four portraits, the fathers and sons: SILENT WITNESSES: FRIENDS MOURN FATHERS, EXPRESS CONCERN FOR SONS. I skimmed the article, which talked about Gene and Julian's long friendship and how deeply they were mourned.

It also claimed neither of the two boys had spoken a single word to anyone since their rescue. According to the reporter—for this story, a man—the boys seemed extremely frightened of male strangers. With the killer or killers still at large, and the motive for the killings unknown, police were guarding the two households closely. So far, the boys had allowed only one officer anywhere near them—Frank Harriman.

There was a sidebar to the articles. Police were now looking for a brown Volkswagen van that had been seen by several witnesses in the warehouse parking lot over the weekend.

I printed this set of stories, then rolled the film forward to the next issue. Cassidy was looking over my shoulder again. A banner headline jumped out at us: BODY OF RYAN-NEUKIRK KILLER FOUND.

"Hmm. That didn't take long," Cassidy said, moving closer.

"What does it say?" Brandon asked, his view blocked by Cassidy's large frame.

" 'An alert highway patrol officer discovered the body of Christopher Powell, twenty-eight, a man who is now believed to have murdered Dr. Gene Ryan and Julian Neukirk,' " I read aloud. " 'Early Monday, while patrolling Highway 178 between Bakersfield and Lake Isabella, Officer Cecilia Parker. . . .' "

"What's wrong?" Cassidy asked.

" 'Cecilia Parker,' " I forged on, " 'noticed a van matching the description of the one sought by police in connection with the murders. Parker, who is based in Bakersfield, knew of the Ryan-Neukirk case and immediately became suspicious when she saw the van parked on a gravel turnout on a ledge above the Kern River. At first believing the vehicle to be abandoned, on closer examination of the area, Parker spotted Powell's body lying in some brush between the ledge and the river. Powell, who may have stopped at the turnout on his way back to his home near the lake, is thought to have misjudged the edge in the darkness and fallen to his death.

" 'Police said evidence implicating Powell in the Ryan-Neukirk murders had been found, but declined to be any more specific about the nature of the evidence. Sources close to the department say bloodstains not consistent with Powell's own wounds were found on his clothing, and keys that fit locks at the warehouse were on his key ring.

" 'Equally damning was the silent identification given by the only witnesses to the brutal murders—

Ryan's and Neukirk's young sons. Each boy was independently shown a number of photos and asked if he saw the murderer among them. Both boys pointed out Powell's photo.

" 'Although Powell had previous arrests for assault and battery, as well as drug possession, he had never been convicted of any charges.' "

There was a photo of Powell, a mug shot taken during one of his quick visits to the city jail, back in the days when he was breathing. He had one of those fierce expressions that hardcases sometimes adopt for mug shots; he had chosen the one that says, "I call Satan on his private line." He could have been practicing for a Charles Manson look-alike contest. He would have won, if he had been willing to dye his stringy blond hair a few shades darker.

I printed this article, too, then browsed forward. The articles about the Ryan-Neukirk murders grew smaller and began to appear only on inside pages. There was an interview with Powell's mother, who proclaimed her son could not have done all those terrible things they said he did. "Those were just little boys telling lies, like little boys will," she was quoted as saying.

But the other articles revealed that the police had a rather conclusive array of evidence against Powell, from his footprints being found in the blood on the warehouse floor to the victims' skin and hair under his nails. The van was dismantled, and a knife with the victims' blood and Powell's fingerprints was found hidden behind a wooden panel. Even without the boys' identification of him, it seemed clear that Powell had been the murderer.

The motive was not so easily established. Police and hospital records showed that Ryan had treated Powell in the emergency room a year or so earlier. Powell had been brought to the hospital by police after sustaining injuries while resisting arrest. (The charges, which were not specified by the police, were later dropped.) Powell had never complained to anyone about Ryan's treatment of his injuries. No one knew why he would attack both men and their sons or even Ryan alone—but Ryan was the only one of the four who had ever met Powell. The stories disappeared entirely by the beginning of July.

I began to rewind the reel. As Brandon went to look for photographs, I leaned back in the chair and put my fingertips over my eyelids, trying to stave off images.

"Feeling sympathy for them?" Cassidy asked.

"Naturally I am. Nothing like this should ever happen to anybody."

I opened my eyes again just as Brandon brought over a pair of photographs. "We don't hang on to all our old photos here, the way some papers do," he said. "But I found these two. You're lucky they weren't tossed out." He handed them to me. "There were several copies of that first one in the files. I think it's the one that won the award."

It was the one of Frank holding the boys. The photo in the paper had been cropped down from this one, but this print, with more definition than the microfilm could offer, was even more moving.

Brandon handed the second one to me. It showed the boys dressed neatly for school, their arms around each other's shoulders, their faces serious. There was another quality there, one that took a little longer to see. It was in the fierceness with which they held on to one another, in the wariness in their large, dark eyes.

They were scared.

Cassidy took the photos and studied them as I loaded the second reel of microfilm. I moved the film forward to September 23.

There was nothing on the front page. I went slowly through the pages that followed, but it wasn't until I reached the features section that I came across the photograph Brandon had just shown us. WHEN CHILDREN TAKE A VOW OF SILENCE, the headline read. The caption on the photo said, "This week, Bret Neukirk and Sam Ryan return to school after a summer of silence. Speech therapist Regina Szal hopes to help them find their voices."

The article was on elective mutism, a communicative disorder in which a person who is physically capable of speaking refuses to do so. Szal, who was quoted extensively, said that elective mutism should not be confused with shyness. Some elective mutes speak in certain environments, such as the home, or with certain people, such as a parent or sibling. "Twins sometimes refuse to speak to others for a period of time during early childhood," she said. "They've been known to develop secret languages, shared only between themselves. But later—often when they begin to go to school—they form new friendships, establish separate identities. While they may continue to use their secret language between themselves, they will begin to talk to others."

Then, after recapping the stories from June, the article focused on Bret Neukirk's and Samuel Ryan's mutism. Some had expected the boys to begin to talk once they knew Powell was dead. Instead the boys had developed a secret language—including words, manual signs, and written symbols. The language was used only when they were with one another; they continued to be silent when others were present. The complexity of their system of communication was a sign of the boys' intelligence, Szal said.

Szal also said that this type of elective mutism, the result of extreme emotional trauma, required more complex treatment. Counselors, parents, teachers, and speech therapists must work together. "Usually, with a case rooted in trauma, we would be working with an individual child," she said. "In this case, there are two children who, in many ways, consider themselves to be brothers. They've grown up together. Their fathers, though not related, were very close, and their mothers are the best of friends. The boys are the same age and survived a horrific experience together." Asked how the problem should be approached, Szal said, "Gently and patiently. Bret and Samuel are frightened, as anyone would be. We need to help them to feel safe again. Perhaps then they will speak to us."

Looking at the date of the final article, I expected it would be some type of progress report on Szal's efforts. I was wrong.

SLAIN DOCTOR INVOLVED IN DRUG TRAFFICKING, the headline read. Before I could read the first paragraph, Hocus sent another fax.

13

HE HAD BEEN IN A CAR ACCIDENT, he decided, struggling to understand his circumstances. His mind seemed not his own; this one seemed slow and easily distracted.

Something was wrong, and his head hurt. Those two sensations kept returning, although at first he seemed to be able to will them away. Now the sensations were more persistent.

He awakened only gradually, but mindful that he must do so quietly this time. Why did he need to be quiet?

Something is wrong, that's why.

What's wrong?

He couldn't remember. This is what it's like to be stupid, he thought, frustrated.

Recent memory was difficult to hold on to. The car accident memory was an older one, but it helped him to explain the baffling world he was in now.

He was in a hospital bed, with curtains drawn around him. There were muffled voices on the other side. He was wearing a hospital gown. His head throbbed. He tried to reach to touch it and panicked. His wrists were restrained. His ankles, too.

Why?

They were the soft but immovable restraints used in hospitals and psych wards.

Had he gone crazy? Hurt someone? An image came to him, an image of hurting a magician. He could make no sense of it. Another dreamlike memory crossed his mind, of a rolling dive and furniture breaking. Maybe he was crazy after all.

Crazy *and* stupid. Christ, both? Why couldn't it be one or the other?

He was distracted by a tenderness in his left hand. He saw a bandage on it and focused his attention on the back of the hand, which had been pierced by—and still held—an intravenous device, capped off. He tried to remember what it was called and couldn't. There was no tubing now, but. . . .

He was waking up and continued to study the hand. No IV bottle or tubing now, but, yes, there had been one before. He remembered it, remembered that he had awakened and had spoken, and they'd come over with an IV bottle. They'd told him to calm down.

Calm down? While lying here restrained, nearly bare assed, wondering what the hell they were feeding through his veins? Wondering if his slowing breaths were his last?

Calm down?

Yes, it was good that he had been quiet when he awakened this time. At least, he hoped he had been.

Within a few minutes, his memories of the journey to Riverside, the trap, the struggle with his attackers, all became clearer. He remembered dreams, too, but not much more. One thing he knew for a certainty. This was no hospital.

He heard the voices coming closer to the curtain and closed his eyes. Hoped that he would be able to only *pretend* to be asleep, because genuine sleep seemed so ready to claim him again.

Irene said he snored sometimes. Should he pretend to snore?

No. He didn't know what his own snoring sounded like.

The clatter of the curtain rings being pulled back along the rod grated as if they were running along his spine.

"See? Still asleep. You can't predict this to the minute. He could be asleep for another hour or more."

"But he has a head injury—what if the drugs are bad for him?"

"If you weren't so squeamish, you could have seen the wound I stitched up. It's not a very severe injury."

"Don't even talk about it. Please!"

"Okay, okay, I'm sorry. Anyway, the head injury might be making him a little more sleepy. A mild concussion. If he doesn't wake on his own after a while, we'll wake him up, okay? I know you're anxious to talk to him, but he needs to rest. And it will be easier on him if he wakes on his own."

"Can't we untie him? It reminds me of . . . you know."

"We'll untie him later," the other said soothingly.

"He's strong and he thinks we're strangers. We've always known he could be dangerous. Remember what happened in Riverside."

"I remember," his friend said, his voice almost a whisper.

The magician, Frank thought. That one's the magician.

"Are you losing your resolve?" the other asked.

"No," the magician said. Firm. Without hesitation.

"Good," the other said. "Don't become too attached to him."

They closed the curtains again. Hearing their voices drift away, he finally dared to try to move a little. Moving might help him stay awake.

He wished for many things, big (his escape) and small (that someone would scratch the place that itched on the back of his head). He was not one to despair, yet he was so giddy with relief over deceiving them, he soon realized that he must do exactly what they asked him to do the last time he had awakened: calm down.

14

NEXT CONTACT AT FIVE O'CLOCK at Bea Harriman's home," the fax read. "She's expecting you."

"Your mother-in-law?" Cassidy asked as I looked at my watch. It was just after three.

"Yes."

"Where does she live?"

"Here in Bakersfield." I gave him the address. "Brandon, could I use your phone?"

Brandon seemed distracted, but he nodded. Cassidy, in the meantime, started using his cellular phone to call his team back in Las Piernas.

I called Bea Harriman, worried. I could hear several voices in the background, but she said, "Oh, Irene, I'm so glad you're here in town. Your friend at the paper said you'd be here around five. Are you staying overnight?"

"I'm not sure, Bea. I just wanted to make sure you

didn't mind having company on such short notice."

"No, no, not at all. Some family friends have stopped by, and Cassie and Mike are over. We should be together."

"Did my—uh, friend mention that Detective Thomas Cassidy is with me?"

"No," she said, drawing the word out in a sound of uncertainty but recovering quickly. "It's good that you have someone protecting you, though. By all means, bring him along."

As I hung up, I glanced over at Brandon. He was starting to sweat again. Receiving the fax had sent him back into a panic. "Look," he said, "maybe you shouldn't be here. Letting you come here, I might have put other people in danger, too. You should go."

"Brandon—"

"Please! Please just copy the last article and go!"

I looked to Cassidy for help. He was pretending fascination with the index tabs on the front of a file cabinet.

Staying out of it. Fine.

I went back to the microfilm reader, made the copies, rewound the spool. I shut down the machine and took the boxes of film to Brandon. He was seated at his desk, his hands shaking as he tidied papers. He didn't look up at me.

"Thanks for letting us in here, Brandon," I said. "And thanks for coming down here on a Saturday and all. Sorry for the trouble. You're a true friend. When Frank is back home safe and sound, I'll bring him by to thank you personally."

"I'd like that," he said, still not meeting my eyes. "Good luck, Irene."

When we were back in his car, Cassidy said, "You were mighty gracious to him, considering he was giving you the bum's rush."

"No, I wasn't. He's up there feeling guilty."

He grinned and opened the palm of his hand, pretended to write a note to himself. "Lady has a mean streak."

"Keep that in mind."

"Where to next?"

I wasn't quite ready to face Bea, and she wasn't expecting me until five. "A late lunch?"

"Sounds great."

The coffee shop was just around the corner from the paper. We were the only customers, having arrived during those hours between lunch and dinner when sugar packets are replenished and ketchup bottles are refilled.

Cassidy ordered the biggest burger they offered, complete with salad and fries. Although it had been a long time since I had eaten, I didn't have an appetite. I ordered a bowl of chicken soup and left it at that.

I handed Cassidy a copy of the last article and read my own copy while we waited.

According to the article, which quoted only unnamed "sources close to the investigation," new discoveries had been made in the Ryan-Neukirk case. Dr. Gene Ryan had an addiction—not to drugs, but to gambling.

According to the sources, Ryan often flew to Las Vegas in his private plane but engaged in illegal gambling with local bookies as well. The arrest of one of the locals, coupled with several major drug busts, ultimately led to the new revelations about Ryan.

With Ryan's addiction came gambling debts. Big ones. The doctor was making good money, but not good enough to keep up with his losing streaks. He also felt pressure to keep up appearances—in addition to the plane, the Ryans had a large home in an upscale neighborhood, a pair of Mercedes, country club memberships, and other costly trappings.

Ryan sought out investments that could give him quick turnaround and high yields—as well as a guarantee that the IRS wouldn't hear of any profits. Nothing legitimate fit the bill.

Police now linked him to previously unsolved cases of hospital drug thefts, thefts that probably led to Ryan's involvement with his killer—Christopher Powell.

Powell, it had been learned, had been introduced to Gene Ryan several months before their emergency room encounter. Powell was connected to an as-yet-unidentified supplier, a man who needed help transporting drugs. Ryan and his plane were hired, and soon the doctor was able to pay off his gambling debts. In true addict style, though, Ryan returned to the tables, gambling even more recklessly.

Indications were that Ryan had been active in a large-scale drug transportation operation not long before his death. Neukirk and his trucking business may have been involved as well, although that remained unclear.

The waitress served Cassidy's salad. "What do you make of these reading assignments they gave you?" he asked once she had walked away.

"I'm not sure," I said. "Assuming Hocus includes

Bret Neukirk and Samuel Ryan, I guess this lets us know some of their personal history. But why not just ask the *Californian* to fax the articles to me? Why have us drive all the way out here? They can't be seeking revenge—the killer is long dead. And how are the other members of Hocus involved—the ones who are in jail? For all I've learned about these two today, I can't understand why they would take Frank hostage. What do they want?"

"That's what we have to try to get a handle on," he said, "and as soon as possible. I keep hoping they'll state some demands—that would give us a starting point. They haven't even asked us to release their friends."

"And they've let us know their names."

"Right. No attempt to stay anonymous—unless this has been some sort of snipe hunt."

"If they just wanted to get me out of town, they could have told me to go to any number of other cities. Nothing else they've done makes much sense to me—at least, not yet. But Bakersfield fits. Frank has a history here."

"So do you."

"Yes." I looked around the coffee shop. "We used to come here. New reporters often get the police beat. That's how I met Frank—he was a rookie, I was a green reporter. He had late shifts, so did I. His training officer was an old guy they used to call 'the Bear.' Bear Bradshaw. I don't even remember what his real name was. Big guy—guess that's how he got his nickname. Anyway, Bear was one of the few cops I had managed to coax into talking to me. Bear loved to tease Frank. Constantly giving him a hard time."

"In what way?"

I smiled. "You must have been a rookie once. Maybe every TO tries to find out if the rookie has the sense of humor it will take to survive the job."

"Sense of humor and thick hide. You need them both."

"So you live with a little hazing. But to make matters worse in Frank's case, his dad was a cop on the same force. Frank had grown up around these guys. So they went out of their way to try to rile him."

"A chance to get to Frank and his old man at the same time?"

"Right. One time, Bear stuffed a plastic bag full of flour down into the driver's seat of the cruiser—between the bottom and back of the seat. You know how those seats are—made of leather, so every time you sit down on them, air squeezes out. So the seat acted like a bellows, and every time Frank sat down it blew a little flour out."

Cassidy smiled. "I take it they were wearing dark uniforms?"

"Exactly. So Frank ended up with a nice white stripe on his behind. Bear kept asking him who the hell he was trying to signal with it. At first, Frank couldn't figure out what had happened. He'd brush the seat off, brush his pants off, sit down, and it would start all over again. The bag was tucked down deep enough that it wasn't easy to see. One of the other cops took pity on him and showed him what was happening. Bear liked to brag that it was the last time anybody else had to figure something out for Frank."

"Frank get back at him?"

"Oh, yes. Later on, of course. Not while Bear was still his TO. But I was with Frank the day he bought the crickets."

"Crickets?"

"You can buy them at a pet store. People feed them to pet lizards. This group of crickets had more of a fighting chance at survival. They were liberated from their container inside Bear's cruiser. Old Bear learned it was harder than hell to capture all the little suckers. They found their way into all sorts of nooks and crannies. And bred. They sang to Bear for a long time. The other guys learned what happened, and for months, they would see Bear walking down the hall and stop and cock their heads and say, 'Hey, Bear! Do you hear a cricket in here?' Drove him nuts."

Cassidy laughed. "So you met Frank through Bear?"

"Yes. At first Frank was so quiet, I thought he was one of those guys who had vowed never to talk to a reporter. Bear was choosy about who he talked to, but once he decided you were okay, he was quite the conversationalist. Frank would sit there absolutely silent; first two nights he was around me, he didn't say a word. Lots of looks across the table, though, so I decided he was shy, not hostile. Third night, Bear turned to him every couple of minutes and said, 'Shut up, Harriman.' Frank got the hint."

The waitress brought our meals. Her arrival at the table snapped me out of my nostalgia and back into the present.

I wondered how long it had been since Frank had been given anything to eat.

Cassidy dug into his meal, but I pushed aside my

bowl of soup. He paused and said, "You aren't going on a hunger strike on me, are you?"

"I can't eat. It was a stupid idea to come here."

"Why? Because it made you think of Frank?"

I didn't reply.

"You would have been thinking about him anyway. Come on, eat something—you can't get by on two hours of sleep and an empty belly."

"How about you? You must be exhausted."

"I'm used to this. Besides, I'll catch up a little later on today. And I'm eating."

"I'm not—"

"You'll think more clearly if you take care of yourself. I can't do this alone. You've got to work with me, Irene."

I picked up the spoon again, then said, "We never finished our earlier conversation about the media."

He frowned, apparently puzzled that I didn't consider that issue all settled.

"You've got to work with me, too, Cassidy."

He made a noncommittal sort of sound.

"You're going to want the public to be watching for these guys, right?" I asked.

He hesitated, then said, "Yes, I suppose the department will want to have some sort of press conference soon. We do try to coordinate things with the media. Ask your buddy Mark Baker—I've dealt with him before. The CIT doesn't have a history of causing problems for the press. But the department isn't going to give out every detail all at once. That just isn't smart, Irene."

"Do you really believe I'd do anything to further endanger Frank?" I asked tightly.

"Not intentionally, no. You have to understand— under ideal circumstances, even if you weren't a reporter, you wouldn't be this involved. To have a family member this involved is bad enough; to have a reporter is . . . well, never mind. I'm not going to list all of the aspects of this situation that make me unhappy."

"Unhappy. Yes, well, I don't think I'll give you my list, either."

He didn't say anything for a moment. Belatedly I realized his usual calm had briefly slipped away from him—by the time I recognized it, he was firmly back in control of himself. And more withdrawn.

"Forgive me," he said quietly. "What exactly do you want?"

"To bargain."

One corner of his mouth quirked up, but he said, "Let's hear what you have to say."

"The *Express* gets everything first."

He shook his head. "The department can't get away with that," he said. "And it's not safe."

"Not safe?"

"For Frank. Put yourself in your competitor's shoes. The LPPD is denying you access to information that they are spoon-feeding to the *Express*. What do you do?"

"I try to find the information on my own. And, to be honest, I'm going to be angry with the LPPD."

"Exactly."

"I see where this is going. You don't play fair with me, I don't feel obliged to obey your rules."

"Right again."

"Okay, but the problem is, I have to have something to sweeten the offer I'm going to make to the *Express.*"

"You're going to make an offer to your own newspaper?"

"Yes. An exclusive, in exchange for staying off my back."

"An exclusive. Hmm. On what aspects of this situation?"

"I think you can guess."

"Your personal point of view as the wife of a hostage."

I swallowed hard, feeling as though I had just read my own price tag and found myself "marked down."

"It's a story someone else might benefit from," he said. A mind reader.

"Yeah, sure. The marketing department at the *Express,* for one."

"Well. . . ."

"That won't be enough for them, and I know it. So I'll want to write about the CIT, too."

"I'm not sure I'd care to have every barricaded suspect sittin' there with a good idea of what's coming next, thanks to a story in the *Express.*"

"Doesn't have to work that way. We can make it specific to this case. I imagine each case is different to some degree, anyway."

"When would this exclusive run?"

"Not until after I write it. Which will be when everything is . . . over," I said, not liking some of the implications of that word.

"You'll live with our media restrictions until then?" he asked.

I hesitated.

"This isn't bargaining," he said, "unless we each give a little."

"It isn't bargaining if I only end up with exactly what I would have had before we bargained. Or less."

"Beyond the exclusive, what could you offer the *Express*?"

I mulled this over. "Riverside."

"That's the Riverside PD's call, not ours."

"Listen, with Mark Baker's sources in your department, the *Express* probably has more details about what went on there than I do."

"Maybe so." Cassidy hesitated, then said, "Just so you know, I never did believe Frank leaked that story last week."

"That puts you in a group that's just about the same size as the one that didn't like the Hopalong joke."

"No, larger than that, although it might not have felt that way to Frank. Frank's problems with Lieutenant Carlson aren't exactly a secret, you know. Give the others some credit for figuring out that some of the crap Frank got about that story was just political."

I looked away. "That all seems so ridiculously petty now."

"Yeah, I suppose it does."

We ate in silence for a moment. I should say Cassidy ate while I stirred my soup.

"Let's go back to what you want us to do for your newspaper," he said.

"If Mark doesn't know about the Riverside connection yet, let me at least tell them they need to look around out there."

"No problem."

"Second, let them publish any photos we can find of Neukirk and Ryan, any that show what they look like today. Ask for the public's help in learning their whereabouts. Maybe someone saw them driving to Frank's Volvo, or saw them after they left the parking lot of the *Express*. Maybe someone has seen them out shopping for groceries. You never know. This could end up helping you."

"We will most likely be handing the photos out in a press conference anyway—this evening, if I don't miss my guess."

"Okay, but let me give the *Express* just a little more. The other media will assume that the *Express* is going to have some advantage with the great good fortune of having a reporter on the inside."

"All hell is going to break loose out here, isn't it?"

I nodded. "They'll catch wind of this any time now anyway. Brandon's probably calling an editor at the *Californian* while we sit here. But we still don't know what Hocus wants, and I'm not likely to tell anyone other than the *Express*—unless it's to Frank's benefit to do so."

"Why, Ms. Kelly, you surprise me."

He didn't look so surprised. "Do you have any problem with what I've proposed?"

He shook his head. "No, not really."

I realized what I had been sensing in him for the last few moments. "You're disappointed in me, aren't you? You're asking yourself how I could be thinking of writing a story about my own husband's abduction."

He didn't say anything.

"Well, I don't want to write about it. I wish I could just leave the reporting to somebody else. I wish I could believe for a minute that all of the media coverage will only be helpful, that none of my colleagues will do anything that will bring harm to Frank. But that's not the way it works."

"No, I suppose not."

"John Walters won't give up. I've worked with the man for years. He didn't get to where he is today by backing down. He'll be after me every ten minutes if I don't beat him to the punch. I don't need that distraction. I need to stay focused on Frank. The only way I can buy a little breathing room is to make John an offer."

After a moment he said, "Ever hear of the Hickman case?"

I shook my head.

"Took place in L.A. in the late 1920s. One of California's most notorious kidnapping cases, up until Patty Hearst was taken. Hickman abducted a banker's daughter, Marian Parker. When he collected the ransom from the banker, Hickman was in a car, and Marian—she was twelve—seemed to be asleep on the seat next to him. Hickman told the girl's father that he was just going to drive down the street a ways, and then he'd release the girl. He did. But when Marian's father unwrapped the blanket she was in, he discovered she was dead, and that Hickman had amputated her legs."

"This is not the kind of story I need to hear right now."

"I've already told you that we don't always have happy endings in this kind of situation—you need to accept that anything can happen. But that's not my point. There's more to the story."

"Please—"

"Needless to say, there was a great hue and cry, and when Hickman was arrested in Oregon and brought back to Los Angeles, thousands of angry citizens were waiting at the train. For one week at a vaudeville stage in L.A., you could pay to hear the Oregon detectives tell the story of Hickman's arrest. Every paper in the country sent a reporter to cover the trial.

"But one writer who was asked to cover the trial didn't accept the invitation. Will Rogers. He wrote a letter to the *New York Times*. He said he wanted to die claiming only one distinction—that of being the only writer to refuse newspaper offers to cover the Hickman trial. He thought each town ought to be ashamed of the crimes that were committed there. Instead, he said, 'Every town tries to make their murder the biggest one of the year. . . .'"

I looked away from him, then said, "Yeah? Well, I can't do rope tricks worth a shit, either."

He laughed. "I don't know many myself."

I stirred my soup again. "Tell me what's being done—I'm not asking this as a reporter, I'm asking as Frank's wife."

"What's being done? You mean, aside from what you and I are doing?"

"Yes."

"There are several teams involved in this case, some specialized, some doing basic police work—basic, but essential. You only see me and Hank, but there are dozens of other folks working on it. For example, some are working on pinning down Hocus's location,

trying to figure out where they may be keeping
Frank."

"You haven't been able to trace the calls. How can
they be found?"

"They've got an injured person with them—Frank,
or maybe a member of Hocus. We should know more
about the bloodwork soon. In any case, we're checking hospitals and clinics. We've got some time frames
to study—the amount of time that passed from the
last time anyone saw Frank until we found the car
back in Las Piernas, and so on. We know they've been
active in Riverside and Las Piernas, so we'll keep
looking for someone who might have seen them in
one place or another, maybe sold them something—
the tape recorder they left in the phone booth, the tape
itself, anything like that."

"Where would they get the morphine?"

"We aren't assuming they've been truthful when
they've told us that morphine is what they're using to
sedate him—but we've got people checking into every
report of stolen Versed and morphine in Southern
California. There's another angle we're working on—
maybe someone saw a couple of fellows who had a
'drunken' friend with them. A man as big as Frank
isn't easy to cart around. He's six four, right?"

"Yes. Do you know the heights of all the LPPD
detectives?"

"No, ma'am. Starting about ten minutes after the
captain handed the case to me, whenever I've had a
chance, I've been reading about your husband.
Certain questions arose, and even before you were
asked to come out here to Bakersfield, it looked like
Frank was a specifically chosen target, not just a man

who happened to be in the wrong place at the wrong time."

"Because the informant was his, right?"

"Right. Dana Ross. So whatever we learn about Frank helps us to know more about why he was taken. Now, given what we've just read, we have more to go on, even if their motives aren't very clear. We'll be able to look these two up in DMV files and other records, and—as you guessed we would want to do— circulate their photos. We'll have all sorts of folks studying their histories, profiling them, helping us to anticipate how they may react in various circumstances, and so on."

"I can see the advantages of knowing who they are," I said, "but if we don't know where they are—"

"Knowing who they are will help us with that. We can look at their past patterns. People have habits. We won't stop there. The lab guys in Riverside and Las Piernas are going to be turning the car and the Riverside house inside out—soil samples, fiber evidence, all kinds of things."

"That still might make a pretty large circle."

"But a circle all the same. We'll keep tightening it as we go along. We have two people in custody, and we are going to be leaning on them as hard and as long as the law allows. We have psychologists with specialized backgrounds in criminal behavior looking at their profiles, too. We've got people working on building the criminal cases we will bring against Hocus—talking to people who knew the late Mr. Ross, to try to find out who asked him to lure Frank out to Riverside. Maybe Ross talked to someone about his deal with Hocus. And so on."

"What about the police in Bakersfield?"

"We've had total cooperation from them. They've been very helpful—Frank was with this department for more years than he's been with ours. They are just as concerned as we are. They've already got research going on the Ryan-Neukirk case. They will be working on setting up a trace on the call to your mother-in-law's house. The newspaper is a little trickier, but the Bakersfield police will try to subpoena phone company records for Brandon North's phone and fax machine for the calls from Hocus."

After a moment he said, "I should also mention that the department may send more people out here, including another negotiator."

"Why?"

"Relief, for one thing; I may need to catch a little sleep somewhere along the way. Perspective, for another—no one should do this job alone. But also because there are those who think I've already allowed you to be too active in this case."

I didn't want to think about dealing with anyone other than Cassidy as a negotiator. He had irritated me at times, but he was starting to grow on me. "I don't want to work with anyone else," I said.

"I'm flattered. But it may not be your decision."

Conversation dropped off again after that. Cassidy seemed to be lost in his own thoughts, and I was glad for the silence. I tried to go over what I had learned from the articles in the *Californian*.

I took my notebook out of my purse. It was opened to a set of notes I had made while working on two political stories the day before—a millennium or two ago, it seemed now. How mundane the notes were. A quote from a member of the city council on the red-hot issue of permit-only parking for a residential area near a nightclub in his district. A series of questions I planned to ask a restaurant owner who wanted to expand his beachfront patio dining area—over the objections of his neighbors.

This is what you spent your time working on, I told myself, while he was being captured. While Frank bled in the trunk of the car. While someone shot him full of morphine.

Where are you?

I called to Frank from that place within myself where fear and hope were wrestling one another, each fighting dirty. I was willing to become a firm believer in psychic phenomena or a more devout Catholic or whatever it was that God might want in exchange for some timely miracle. ("Cassidy, I've just had a vision. He's in the cellar of a small farmhouse with purple curtains on the kitchen windows. Wait, I also see— yes—they grow okra there.") I've known for a couple of decades that God is not really into these kinds of bargains. I doubted even Cassidy could strike the deal. I didn't really expect an answer, but I silently called to Frank anyway.

I turned to a clean page in my notebook and began writing, using a private form of shorthand I had been taught by O'Connor, my late mentor at the *Express*. To anyone else the notes wouldn't mean much as written, but I could read them as quickly as my native tongue. Samuel and Bret weren't the only ones who had developed a secret language.

Roughly translated, mine read:

Hocus:
Motives—Anarchists? Political? Revenge?
Computer expertise—Hacked into several differ-
ent systems. Common thread in any?
Medical expertise—Used morphine, Versed.
Robbery of hospital pharmacy?
Lang and Colson—Any Bakersfield connections?
Woman seen at Lang's house—Any real connec-
tion to Hocus? Is she now with Bret and
Samuel?

Contact:
Mothers—still in Bakersfield?
Regina Szal—speech therapist

Another name occurred to me, but Cassidy said it
before I could write it down.

"Who's Cecilia Parker?" he asked.

"I've never met her," I said, not looking up from
my notebook.

He waited a moment. I could hear the amusement
in his voice when he said, "Okay. But you know who
she is."

I looked him right in the eye and said, "Frank's ex-
fiancée. She still lives around here, and, yes, we should
probably try to talk to her."

I half expected him to laugh, but he didn't. If anything, he seemed to regret pressing me.

"I'm going to call Jack and Pete. They'll be worried," I said, and reached for my purse.

"Lunch is on me," he said. "First time I ever
bought a woman a teaspoon of soup."

I made the call, did my best to reassure Pete. A hopeless task. Jack, on the other hand, did his best to encourage me, so I guess everything evened out. Cassidy used the pay phone to make a few reports, then let me drive to Bea Harriman's place while he made other calls on his cell phone. Almost all of the calls were requests for current addresses and background information on the people I had on my own list.

"So why did Neukirk and Ryan let us know who they are?" I asked.

"If that's who they are, you mean?"

"Yes."

"They've been a little publicity mad all along, I'd say. They're big on drama. They're leading up to something. With luck, we'll know soon."

I hadn't been to Bea Harriman's home very often, but I remembered the way. I did the driving, while Cassidy tried to coach me in preparation for the call. He would play the role of the caller, I would try to respond in a way that kept him talking and would also gradually allow me to hand off the call to a hostage negotiator.

"Your work as a reporter will help you in one way," he said. "You're used to asking open-ended questions, ones that encourage longer responses. Same thing with silences; you know to let them stretch. But you won't find it easy to stay calm if they start making threats against your husband—and that's very common at first. That's one reason we prefer not to let family members be involved. Your fear for Frank is likely to heighten the tension, which we are trying to lower. More than anything, you've got to try to stay calm, no matter what's said or threatened. And remember—if you keep dwelling on the subject of Frank's well-being, your concern for him may only make him seem more valuable as a hostage. We want to know his condition, but we don't want to focus the conversation on him."

I tried to set aside my fears, to imagine myself behaving just as I should when the time came. I tried not to contemplate the price of failure.

"I'll be right there with you," Cassidy said, watching me. "You won't be alone."

I made the turn onto Bea Harriman's street. The house was a Craftsman, built in the late 1920s on a large lot. It was painted white, as if it intended to provide a canvas for the flowers blooming all around it in a wide spectrum of colors—blues, reds, oranges, yellows, purples, and lush green foliage. The big wooden swing on the front porch was still and empty.

Lots of cars were parked in front of the house, so I had to park a few houses down the street. Cassidy took the keys and opened the trunk of the car, which had a number of hard-shell and soft cases of varying sizes in it. He pulled one out; it was a silver-colored hard-shell case, about the size of a briefcase.

"What is it?" I asked.

"Cassette recorder for the call," he said. "Not as fancy as the reel-to-reel Hank was using at your place, but easier to hook up. If we end up being here for a while, I'll bring in the fax and computer and other equipment. But for now, this will do."

Birds sang as we walked to the house, and I tried to listen to them rather than to the worst of my thoughts.

"Now, that swing makes me think of summer nights back home," Cassidy said as we approached.

At that moment the front door opened, and Bea Harriman walked out. An attractive, dark-haired woman accompanied her. The woman had her arm around Bea's shoulder, and their heads were bent together in a tête-à-tête. They looked up at us and straightened suddenly. As Cassidy and I came closer, the stranger didn't spare more than a quick glance toward him—but her eyes raked over me. Sizing me up, I realized.

I knew in that instant who she was.

Somewhere in the mess of words that was Bea Harriman's stumbling introduction, she confirmed that I could no longer say I had never met Cecilia Parker.

15

"ANY FURTHER WORD ON FRANK?" Cecilia asked without preamble, continuing to stare at me.

"Nothing new," Cassidy said before I could answer. I had been dreading trying to come up with some social nicety if she had said, "So glad to meet you," and now, oddly, I was miffed that she hadn't.

"And you are?" Cecilia said to him, apparently irritated that she had to make eye contact with anyone else.

"Detective Tom Cassidy, Las Piernas Police Department," he said easily. "Now, this has been an extremely difficult day for Mrs. Harriman," he continued, and when Cecilia's eyes slewed to Bea, he put a firm hand on my shoulder. "Oh, for everyone, but especially Mrs. Frank Harriman. So I'll just take her on in while you two say your good-byes."

Bea floundered only for a second. Her own initial reaction to Frank's kidnapping having passed, she snapped into a role in which she excelled—taking care of someone else in a crisis. I could see her home in on me like a smart bomb. "Thanks for coming by, Cecilia," she said, and turned and started to lead the way in.

"Excuse me," I said, halting the parade. Cassidy loosened his grip, and I straightened my spine as I turned back to Cecilia.

She was still standing on the sidewalk, tight-lipped and unmoving.

"Do you really have to leave now?" I asked.

Her eyes widened (long-lashed, beautiful, big brown eyes—damn them). She relaxed out of her combat stance, though, and said, "Yes. I'm sorry, I can't stay."

"Will you be at home later?"

Openly puzzled, she said, "Yes."

"Mind if I call you?"

She almost asked, "Why?" I saw the word begin to form on her lips, but she stopped herself and said, "Of course not. Bea has my number."

She turned and walked away. When I looked back at Cassidy, he appeared to be amused. Bea was holding open the screen door. With as much dignity as I could muster, I walked between them and into the house.

I was met by Mike O'Brien, Frank's brother-in-law who simply said, "Oh, Irene," and pulled me into big, comforting hug; I felt tears well up. When Frank's sister, Cassie, joined us, it was nearly too much. I might have broken down in their embrace had I not heard gruff voice say, "Here, now, don't smother the girl."

When I saw the man who spoke those words,

smiled. I hadn't seen him in years, and he was a little thinner and a little grayer, but I knew him right away. "You're looking good, Bear."

Bea introduced Cassidy to the others, her introduction of Bear Bradshaw reminding me that his first name was Gregory. Cassie said, "Cassie is short for Kathryn—perhaps with the two of us in the same house, Detective Cassidy, it would be easier to call me Kathyrn."

"Heck, no," Bear Bradshaw said. "We'll just call this guy Hopalong."

Bea and Bear enjoyed it, but the rest of us just looked at Cassidy in sympathy. He didn't seem in the least bothered by it. "You could all just call me Tom," he said.

"Actually, I prefer Kathryn," my sister-in-law said. "Only the family and certain untrainable old coots insist on calling me by my childhood name."

"You never told me—" I began.

"I never told you, because you're part of the family," she said with a quick reproachful glance at her mother. "Now, would either of you like some hot coffee?"

We both said yes, and she went off to the kitchen to make a fresh pot. Cassidy asked Bea if he could talk to her alone for a moment.

I glanced at my watch. Eighteen minutes before five o'clock. I moved closer to the phone, which was near Bear Bradshaw, on a table full of knickknacks. Bea was a big believer in knickknacks.

"I wondered if you were going to come over here and say hello to me," Bradshaw said. "I've just had knee surgery, or I'd get up and greet you properly."

"Sorry, Bear. I hadn't noticed the cane. Are you doing okay?"

"Fine, I'll be fine. Just need to baby it a little while it heals. It's a typical cop's problem, I guess. Getting in and out of the car all day is hard on the knees, they tell me. But never mind my puny little problems. How are you holding up?"

"My problems are puny, too. Frank's the one to worry over."

"Frank? No, the boy will be all right. I keep telling Bea, Frank has a good head on his shoulders. Just like his dad did. But Frank's even smarter than Brian was. He'll be okay."

I didn't bother arguing with him, because every word was said as if he wanted to reassure himself.

"You go back a long way with the Harrimans, don't you, Bear?" Mike asked.

"You betcha. Brian was one of my best friends. After my first wife left me, Brian always included me in his family's holiday get-togethers—you know, so I wouldn't be alone."

"You remarried?" I asked.

"Yes, I guess we have a lot of catching up to do. I'm a widower now. My second wife died about a year ago. But I hear my matchmaking finally paid off."

"Your matchmaking?" Mike asked.

Bradshaw grinned at me. "With you and Frank, Irene. Remember?"

"Well, I guess you did get Frank to start talking to me."

He laughed. "Oh, that was priceless! He's always been quiet, but not the tongue-tied type, you know? But when he saw you—oh, God! First night, I kept waiting for him to say something, but not a word until we got back in the car. Then he's *grilling* me. Wanted to know all about you. Now, I've known the boy since he was born. I'd never seen him act like that before. So I made a little wager with Cookie. Couple of times there, I thought I'd lost my money."

"You bet that Frank and I would get married?"

"Yes, I did! Cookie said the boy would never marry a reporter, that the boy knew better than that. And damned if the SOB didn't run around behind my back and load Frank up with a lot of crap about how cops and reporters should never fraternize, and so on. Well, it's true, but you two were the exception, and Cookie has just never learned that there are exceptions in life."

I looked at my watch. Five minutes to go.

"Sorry, guess I'm boring you."

"Oh, no, Bear! Not at all. The call. I'm just worried about the call."

"What call?" Mike asked.

"Hocus—the ones who have Frank. They told me they'd call me here at five."

Bradshaw lost all color in his face. For an awful moment I thought he was going to pass out. Mike rushed over to him, but just as suddenly the Bear seemed to pull himself together. "I'm sorry, I'm sorry," he said, still shaken. "Damn, you don't need that, Irene. . . . Bea—I've got to talk to Bea. . . ." He began to lever himself up from the chair.

Over Bradshaw's growling protests, Mike helped him to his feet, but before he could move forward, Bea and Cassidy came back into the room. Voices rose together. Cassidy calling my name; Bea saying, "Oh,

Greg!" and Bradshaw saying, "Here, now," as he reached out to her with his free hand; Mike trying to respond to his wife's, "What's wrong?" as she came into the room carrying coffee.

The phone rang. We reacted in the way a man walking through the desert alone reacts when he hears a rattle. We all stood stock still, silent.

It rang again, and Cassidy said, "Irene, come with me. The rest of you stay out here."

I followed him as he all but ran to one of the bedrooms, where he had set up the recorder and a telephone headset that would allow him to listen in. Between us were two pads of paper and pens for scribbling notes.

On the third ring, as Cassidy nodded and turned on the recorder, I picked up the phone.

"What happened, Ms. Kelly?" the voice on the other end teased. "Did Detective Cassidy run out of tape cassettes?"

"You know I'm at my mother-in-law's house," I answered. *Speak slowly,* I reminded myself, trying to follow Cassidy's instructions. "There are other people here. I didn't know how private you wanted this conversation to be."

I scribbled a note to Cassidy: "Different caller."

Cassidy nodded.

"Oh, there is no privacy for people in our position," the caller said.

"Your position?"

"Hocus is quite famous now. We're almost as famous now as we were when we were little. Our fathers' murders bought us our first fifteen minutes of fame."

Show empathy. "You survived a horrible ordeal then. People wanted to know more about you."

"Good! You did your homework. We're very pleased."

"Am I speaking to Samuel or Bret?"

"Samuel, at the moment. Our fathers enjoyed stories about the Old West. Bret is named for Bret Harte. I'm named for Samuel Clemens. Detective Cassidy, you do know Samuel Clemens was the man who wrote as Mark Twain, don't you?"

Cassidy pulled the small microphone on the headset down to his mouth. "Well, Samuel, contrary to Yankee propaganda, there are a few literate folks living south of the Mason-Dixon line."

Samuel Ryan laughed; a false, nervous laugh. "What a wit, Thomas! You don't mind if I call you Thomas, do you?"

"Not at all. Tom would be better. You prefer Samuel or Sam?"

"Samuel, please. And Ms. Kelly, would it seem disrespectful if I addressed you as Irene?"

"I'd prefer it to Ms. Kelly."

"Fine. We really think the two of you are well suited for the task we have in mind. Tom is a virtual tower of equanimity. You are so lucky to have him along for the ride, aren't you, Irene?"

"Forgive me if I say I'd rather not be on the ride in the first place."

Cassidy shot me a warning look, but Samuel laughed again.

"Well, I'd love to sit here and chat," Samuel said, "but that would lead to Detective Harriman being even more uncomfortable than he is now."

"Uncomfortable?" Cassidy asked.

"The drugs, the restraints. Being without his own clothes. And of course, as the drugs wear off, there is pain."

My eyes widened. Cassidy held up a hand, motioning me not to talk, obviously aware that I couldn't speak with anything resembling composure. But in the same tone of voice in which anyone else might have said, "Read the funny papers yet?" Cassidy said, "Last time, Bret did mention that Frank was injured."

"You didn't expect him to come along peacefully, did you?" Samuel said defensively. "It's his own fault. He fought us, and he got hurt. But he has received medical attention."

"He has?"

"Yes. I stitched up his head myself."

Visions of infections and fevers and insane medical experiments tumbled through my mind, while the silence stretched. Cassidy had warned me not to be afraid of those silences, but I had not anticipated the course my imagination would take while we waited.

Yet it was Cassidy who broke this silence as he drawled, "You a medical man, Samuel?"

"You've probably already got a whole team of people working on my history and credentials," Samuel said, "so let's not waste Detective Harriman's time. I've been on this call far too long. Bret will be quite upset with me. Everything else you need to know is waiting at a copy shop near Cal State Bakersfield." He gave an address on Stockdale Highway, then added, "It's a twenty-four-hour place. Ask for your fax and mail."

"Can you give us directions, Samuel?" Cassidy

asked. "Irene hasn't been here for a while, and she's already managed to get us lost twice."

"Not my problem. You found your way eventually, didn't you?" he said. "Now, on to business. The reports in the *Californian* are fairly accurate. Wrong in a few places, though. For example, you know that a young officer—our very own Officer Harriman—rescued us from a warehouse. Now here's the problem: How did Officer Harriman know to go to that particular warehouse?"

"I'm not sure I understand, Samuel," Cassidy said.

"Who told Officer Harriman to go to the warehouse?"

"A dispatcher," I answered.

"Yes, but who told the dispatcher about the warehouse?"

"According to the article, an anonymous tipster," I said.

"Ah! That's where the article is wrong. Not the fault of the reporter. That's what the dispatcher told him."

"You believe the dispatcher lied?"

"Maybe. But I think it's far more likely that she knew—well, knew but didn't know—the caller."

"I'm sorry," I said, "I don't understand."

Silence.

"Knew but didn't know," I finally repeated. "Didn't recognize the voice?"

"Exactly."

"Whose voice was it?" Cassidy asked.

"More fun if you guess," Samuel said.

Don't make this into a game! I wanted to shout, but Cassidy simply said, "All right. Was it a relative?"

"No."

"Someone she worked with," I said, trying to follow Cassidy's lead.

"Getting warmer," Samuel enthused.

"A cop," I guessed.

"Yes! I knew you could do this job, Irene."

"This job?"

"You'll have until Tuesday."

"I'll have until Tuesday to do what?"

"Why, to find that cop."

"Which cop? What's his name?" I asked, feeling panic closing in.

"Irene, if we knew that, we wouldn't have needed to go to so much bother. That's why we need you."

"You know the caller was a cop?"

"I'm certain of it."

"What do you mean? How can you be certain?"

Cassidy pushed a note toward me: "Slow down."

"We were there, remember?" Samuel said. "But that isn't much of an explanation, is it? No, you'll need more details if you're going to give us his name by Tuesday. Well, read the fax. Now, this really has gone on too long."

"Wait! Why Tuesday?"

"No special reason," he said. "But we can't be expected to take care of Detective Harriman forever."

"You've started all of this over a weekend," Cassidy said, his tone of voice much more level than mine. "Of course that presents some difficulties."

"Nothing insurmountable."

"Folks go out of town on weekends. Offices are closed. And this all goes back a ways."

"Years," Samuel said bitterly.

"Yes. You've waited a long time to learn this officer's identity. What difference would a few more days make?"

Silence.

We waited.

"Perhaps we will be flexible, Tom. Perhaps not. You'll just have to see how we feel on Tuesday."

"I just figured you'd want her to be sure she had identified the right man."

"How would you know what we want, Tom?"

"Why don't you tell me?" Cassidy asked, but we could already hear the drone of the dial tone.

16

YOU DID FINE," Cassidy said. "You let him get your goat a couple of times, but that's what he was aiming to do." He paused, then said, "They're a little unusual. They've studied the Las Piernas Police Department."

"What do you mean?"

His cellular phone rang before he could reply. He answered the call, listened for a moment, and said, "Well, it will be helpful whenever it does come through. Thank you. . . . Yes, we may be receiving other calls here."

He hung up and said, "That was Bakersfield PD. The phone company says it's going to be at least a couple of hours before they can get back to us with the trace. The call came from out of the local area. That's no surprise. He talked too long—he was probably fairly sure it would take us a while to trace it."

He explained that a telephone call made within a

local area could be traced fairly rapidly; but a call made from outside areas, or one that crossed phone company service areas, might take much longer to trap—two days or more.

"So at least one of them—Samuel—isn't in Bakersfield."

"Right."

"And they don't seem to have anyone following us around, or he would have picked up on your lie about getting lost."

He smiled. "Right again."

"You took a chance there, didn't you?"

"Not much of one. I was more worried that you'd get angry and deny it than I was that he'd make a fuss over it."

"Now you're *trying* to make me angry. What were you saying before—about Hocus studying the department?"

"They've got all kinds of information that takers don't usually have. They were expecting me to be here with you. They've done some research on how our department handles these situations, who they send out for crisis negotiation."

"You don't like that, do you?"

He shrugged. "Not the way I'd prefer it to be, but not the end of the world."

I looked toward the door. "I guess I'd better let the others know what's happening before we go to pick up that fax."

"Hold up a minute," he said. "I'd like you to listen to the tape while I play it for Hank. Sometimes, the second time through, you learn things, pick up on things you missed while you were feeling the pressure.

Just let me make a couple of quick calls, then we can go and talk to the family together."

He called Captain Bredloe, gave him a synopsis of the call, mentioned I was still in the room with him. After a brief pause he said, "Yes, sir. I'll call back a little later." He then called Henry Freeman, told him he would have a modem set up soon and would be sending a report for Freeman to distribute. He played the tape, and I tried to learn from his part of the conversation while wincing over my own mistakes. He was right about the second time through, though.

"I noticed something," I said when he finished his call. "They wanted to call us by our first names, but they keep calling Frank 'Detective Harriman.' They aren't—what do you call that? When the hostages and hostage takers bond with one another, start to worry about each other—"

"Stockholming," he said. "Or Stockholm syndrome. Gets its name from an incident in Sweden. Some hostages were held for six days in a bank vault by two escaped convicts. When they were released and the takers were arrested, police there noticed something kind of odd—both the takers and the hostages had developed a kind of sympathy and affection for one another.

"Hard to say why it happens," he went on. "Maybe it's because of the dependency of the hostages on the takers; others say that under stressful conditions, as time passes, the hostages and the takers are more likely to begin to see each other as individual human beings."

"So you're saying it's too soon for Samuel and Bret to form that kind of bond with Frank, then?"

"It may not happen at all. I'd warn you not to count on it happening here."

"Why not?"

"There's been a lot of publicity about Stockholming, especially since the Hearst case, so people mistakenly believe the Stockholm syndrome is a given. It's not."

"But you seem especially doubtful about it in this case," I pressed.

He sighed. "Like I said before, these takers know who goes out on a crisis call in Las Piernas. They know how long it takes to trace a phone call. We have many examples that show they are intelligent and that they plan ahead. My guess is they know all about the Stockholm syndrome. They'll do their best not to succumb to it—you can see signs of it already. Calling him 'Detective Harriman' instead of 'Frank'—that will help them keep some emotional distance."

"But how can they have emotional distance from the man who saved them from that cellar?"

"How could they injure him?" Cassidy countered. "How could they put their 'hero' in the trunk of a car? Drug him? Use him as a pawn? Do any of the other things they may have done to him?"

"It has something to do with his being a cop, doesn't it? They have some problem with cops."

"Maybe."

"They never once mentioned Lang and Colson. Never once proposed an exchange."

"No, they didn't. Odd, isn't it?"

"Yes. They don't seem to want an exchange, but

they do want me to find a Bakersfield cop who made an anonymous phone call to a dispatcher. Why?"

"It doesn't make sense to me, either," Cassidy said. "If an officer made the call, there was no reason for him not to identify himself to the dispatcher."

After a moment's thought I said, "But if a cop *did* make the call to the dispatcher, he had to know that something was going on at the warehouse."

"Right," Cassidy said. "Let's say he drove by and suspected something, then didn't do anything about it until it was too late. Maybe they resent him for it. Maybe they believe he could have saved their fathers' lives."

"No, he had to have done more than drive by the place," I said. "Otherwise they wouldn't be aware of his existence—how would they know he had seen anything in the first place? They must have seen him or heard him themselves. Samuel said they were *certain* the caller was a cop."

"So he showed up, left, and didn't save them—"

"Or was actually involved in the murders," I said.

Cassidy rubbed a hand over his hair. I could see him resisting that theory, trying to come up with another explanation.

"They were afraid of policemen, remember?" I went on. "What reason would the cop have for fleeing from the scene? Even if he didn't want to go in on his own, he could have radioed for backup."

"Let's go get that fax," he said.

"I want to talk to Frank's family. They've been waiting out there." I stood up.

Cassidy stayed seated. "This fellow, Greg Bradshaw—he's the one you were telling me about earlier, right?"

"Yes. He's the Bear."

"Former Bakersfield Police Department?"

"Yes."

"You going to tell the family everything we talked about just now?"

I thought it over. "No, probably not. It's just a theory."

"Even if they ask you to tell them what Samuel said?"

"I don't know. . . ."

"Better if you don't," he said.

"I don't want to lie to them."

"I'll make it easy on you. Let me talk to them."

"You mentioned Bradshaw," I said. "Bear's the problem?"

"I didn't say that."

"You're starting to believe it, aren't you? You think a Bakersfield officer was involved in the Ryan-Neukirk murders."

He shook his head "Not necessarily—but it's possible. Don't tell me that just as it's starting to make sense to me, you're moving on to some other theory."

"No, but even if it's true—not Bear. I know Greg Bradshaw. He was a good cop."

"You knew him when you were in your early twenties?"

"Yes."

"Have you grown any less trusting of people since then, Irene?"

"Yes, but I'm willing to bet he was a good cop even by my present cynical standards."

"Willing to bet Frank's life on it?"

I bit back the reply I wanted to make, not ready to have my mother-in-law hear that end of my vocabulary under her own roof. But Cassidy must have read it on my face, because he said, "Simmer down."

"If you want me to simmer down," I said, "quit turning up the heat."

He smiled, which doubled my irritation. "Fair enough," he said.

They were still in the living room, silent and tense. Bea sat next to Bear, her face full of worry. Mike paced with his hands in his pockets. Cassie sat on the couch, elbows on her knees, her forehead resting in one palm. Cassidy was behind me, so I was the first one to walk into the room. They all looked up at me at once, the way people in a hospital waiting room look up when a surgeon comes out to talk to them. I was no surgeon.

"They say Frank's okay," I said, "but they're keeping the calls short. I didn't get a chance to talk to him this time—"

"Will y'all forgive us if we keep you waiting for another twenty minutes?" Cassidy interrupted as he walked in the room. "I need to borrow Irene for a little while, but I'll bring her right back. I'd love to explain, but for the moment, I can't. You know how that goes, don't you, Officer Bradshaw?"

"Sure, sure do—only I'm retired, so just call me Greg. That's good enough. Mike, here, now he's an officer. He works for the highway patrol."

Cassidy smiled at Mike and said, "Forgive me. Irene neglected to tell me you were in law enforcement."

"I'm sure she's had other things on her mind," Mike said.

"Yes, well, we'd better get going, Irene." He handed a card to Bea. "My cell phone number's on that card, Mrs. Harriman. Please call me immediately if Hocus makes any contact with you or if you need to reach me for any other reason."

"We'll be right back," I said even as Cassidy walked toward the front door.

"Well, that didn't go very smoothly," I said as we headed toward the west side of town.

"I'll try to do better next time," he said, not even attempting sincerity. "Especially now that I have a little more information about the family."

"Sorry. Mike was right, I've been distracted. But the real reason I didn't mention it is that I think of him as Mike, not Mr. CHP."

"No real harm done, I suppose. Don't worry about it. And don't worry about not telling the family everything there is to tell. It's best if they understand right away that they aren't all going to be included in everything that goes on—much as they might like to be. They do strike me as the type of folks who might have a curious nature."

What he said made sense. The more I thought about it, the more uneasy I became. "You have the tape with you?"

He smiled. "Why? You think your in-laws will listen to it while we're gone?"

"No, of course not," I said, shifting a little on the car seat.

"Of course not." He laughed.

"Cassidy—"

He reached into an inside pocket on his suit coat and pulled out a cassette. "Why tempt fate—or anybody else, for that matter?" he said, and slipped it back into his jacket.

The copy store was busy. There was a long line at the order desk, and all of the self-service copiers were in use. The place was noisy and smelled of toner. The help was all under the age of twenty-three.

Students were preparing term papers, job hunters were copying résumés, businesspeople were printing newsletters and flyers. Normal life.

Fortunately more people were placing orders than picking them up. I walked up to the cashier, who had a name tag that read SHAUN, and asked if they had a fax for Irene Kelly.

"Just a moment," he said. "I'll have someone check."

He turned around and shouted, "Suzanne! Is there a fax here for Irene Kelly?"

"I don't know," Suzanne shouted back. "I'm with a customer." That didn't stop her from shouting in turn, "Heather!"

Heather, who was on the phone, shrugged when Suzanne shouted the question to her.

Cassidy hooked two fingers in his mouth and whistled like a drover. I'd swear it nearly broke the windows. All conversation ceased. Except for the soft *shuck-shuck* of the collator on a large, automated copier, the room was still. "Pardon me," Cassidy said in a low voice, "but we can't wait for y'all to holler your way around to everybody workin' on first shift.

Would one of you please just look for Ms. Kelly's fax? It's important."

I don't know how anyone found the fax, since all eyes seemed to be on us, but somehow they managed it. By the time Shaun handed me a manila envelope, the noise level was nearly its old self again, even if I hadn't stopped feeling acutely embarrassed. I opened the envelope and saw a good number of pages. I pulled out the first one and turned to Cassidy. "Look."

It was a cover sheet, which had the usual sort of information on it:

To: Irene Kelly
From: Hocus
Pages Including Cover: 21

It also gave my home phone number as the number to call if pages were not received. But at the very top of the page, the copy shop's fax machine had printed the time the fax was received—eleven A.M.—and a phone number in my area code, a number that was not mine. Cassidy immediately took out his cell phone.

"That will be $11.13 with tax," Shaun said.

Paying for the fax rankled, but I had bigger concerns.

Still the subject of a lot of attention, I decided to read the other pages outside. It was then I remembered Samuel Ryan's exact words. "There was also supposed to be some mail here for me, too," I said to Shaun.

"Oh, right!" he said. "You're the one. We do have a package for you."

"A package?"

"Well, an Express Mail envelope," he said, reaching below the counter and handing me a brightly colored cardboard mailer.

I stared at the Express Mail address tag. My name was on it, printed in neat block letters. The return address was labeled "Mr. John Oakhurst," with a Las Piernas address, on a street I didn't recognize. I doubted it was a real one. After all, I realized, the package had to have been mailed the day before—when only Hocus knew I would be in Bakersfield to receive it.

"Do you usually do this sort of thing?" I asked. "Hold mail for customers, I mean?"

"No, but my manager said this John Oakhurst asked us to do him a favor, because he'd be sending a big fax later and you needed this to go with it. But the fax didn't have his name on it, so I guess they were held in separate places."

I pulled on the tab that would open the cardboard envelope.

"Don't!" Cassidy shouted, but it was too late. The package was open.

Nothing exploded.

The inside of the envelope had been lined in bubble wrap. Within the lining there was a small object and nothing more.

"Please don't reach in there," Cassidy said, sounding as if he might actually be on the verge of becoming upset. "And please don't go opening any other gifts from Hocus."

I didn't answer him. I was staring at the object.

It was a vial of blood.

17

T HE ROOM STARTED CLOSING IN ON ME. I
shoved the envelopes toward Cassidy and hurried outside. It was a while before Cassidy
came out of the store, carrying the faxes and the
package. He found me leaning my folded arms
against the roof of the car, resting my forehead on
them, trying very hard not to let this be the moment
when every impulse that had been urging me to
become hysterical won.

"Irene?"

I looked up at him.

"You look a little peaked," he said. "Want to sit
down in the car for a while? We don't have to go anywhere. We can stay here until you're feeling better."

I stepped away from the door and let him unlock it.

"I'm okay," I said.

"Sure," he said.

He rolled down the windows and pulled out of the

parking lot. I didn't talk to him, and it was a while before I realized that we weren't headed back to my mother-in-law's house.

"I'm sorry," I said. "You need me to give you directions, don't you?"

"Naw, I remember the way back," he said.

"Where are you going?"

He smiled. "I guess I don't know the exact answer to that question. But I think the general plan will do us some good."

He made a turn, and soon we were on a road that led to an orange grove. He pulled over. "Take a deep breath," he said, turning off the engine.

The delicate fragrance of orange blossoms filled the car. Not as exotic as what might be found at a department store's perfume counter, perhaps, but no less enticing for its sweet simplicity.

In the midst of this grove of bright green leaves and small white blossoms, inhaling a scent I associate with cleanliness and innocence, I said, "I want to kill those assholes."

"I see the shock has worn off," Cassidy said. "Take another deep breath."

"What is this? Aromatherapy?"

"Sure," he said easily. "You can work through all five stages of grief, one breath at a time."

"Great," I said. "These twisted sons of bitches may be torturing my husband while we sit here. Or maybe they're just draining his blood and mailing it to me one vial at a time. But the important thing is that I'll be in perfect mental balance because I've taken time to 'stop and smell the flowers.' "

He didn't say anything. I ranted at him for another

ten minutes or so, at which point I finally caught on, said, "Oh shit," and shut up.

Cassidy stayed silent, just looking out at the trees. Finally he said, "Abductions are always triangles. Lot of folks think about the taker, or the taken, but not about that third side of the triangle, the person who waits and worries and—maybe worst of all—wonders. Wonders what the takers are doing to the person they love."

I felt a tightness in my chest.

I must have looked bad, because Cassidy waited. After I had calmed down a little he said, "The takers know you care. They know you're going to worry. It's in their best interest to keep you worried. So they do things like this, to ensure your compliance. Truth is, Frank probably doesn't even know he's missing this little vial of blood. They probably took it from him while he was loaded up with morphine or Versed. They've got control of him. They want to take control of you as well."

"So you take me to an orange grove so I can blow off steam, get back in control of myself."

"They'll keep you going twenty-four hours a day if you let them. They'll exhaust you. Later on, when we find them, you may not have the luxury of fifteen or twenty minutes in an orange grove." He looked out at the trees. "Scent is one of the strongest psychological links to memory we have, and you need to be able to remember to stay calm—so the next time they try to rile you, you think of orange blossoms, Irene."

"You said, 'When we find them.' You think we will?"

"Yes. They're starting to make little mistakes."

"The Express Mail package was one, wasn't it? There's a cutoff time for next-day delivery. If that's Frank's blood, then it had to be mailed yesterday, after they took him and yet before the cutoff time."

"Right. Usually that's five o'clock, if the person wants any kind of assurance that it will get to its destination by the next day."

I studied the Express Mail label more carefully. "The date and time of acceptance is written on the package by the mail carrier who picks it up," I said, "so even though it was probably dropped in a roadside box with a stamp already on it, we know it was mailed before"—I looked at the place where the carrier had initialed the label—"four thirty-five P.M."

"Yes."

"And the zip code of the accepting post office is noted," I said. "This is a Las Piernas zip code."

"So we know the general area where they mailed it," Cassidy said, "and just about when. Once we find out which carrier those initials belong to, we'll be able to find out which box they mailed it from. But we're getting a time frame at the very least. When I called Hank about this package, he told me that we've had another piece of luck."

I looked up at him. He pulled out a notebook and flipped it open. "A fellow by the name of James Washington saw Frank in Riverside yesterday."

"What?"

"Riverside PD had people interviewing rail workers, showing them photos of Frank. Washington remembered seeing Frank. He said Frank waved to him from the driveway of a run-down house—and described Dana Ross's place. Working with the railroad people, Riverside has narrowed the time down to about eleven, eleven-fifteen. That fits within the general time frame of Ross's death."

He paused, and I saw his brows draw together a little.

"Go ahead and tell me, Cassidy. Your face doesn't usually give much away, but for about two seconds there, you were easy to read."

"No kidding. I must be slipping."

I waited.

"The gun that shot Dana Ross was definitely Frank's gun," he said.

"Proving almost nothing."

"I agree. Except that Ross had to be killed after Frank arrived. Some of the blood at the scene matches Frank's blood type—which is different from Ross's. The blood in the trunk matches Frank's blood type. More definitive tests will take longer, but for now we'll assume the stain in the trunk is from Frank. We know he was injured, probably in a struggle out in Riverside. He was then placed in the trunk of the Volvo and driven to Las Piernas. He was drugged at some point, probably early on. So we're getting a clearer picture of events.

"Hank had other news," he continued. "They used one of Frank's credit cards yesterday."

"Where?"

"At a gas station in Riverside." He consulted his notes again. "At a little after one o'clock. Used it twice—filled up two tanks."

"Two vehicles? Frank's and the one they used to get to Riverside?"

"Probably."

"Were they caught on camera, by any chance?"

"No luck there," he said. "There are cameras, but they only cover the area near the cashier, not the outside at the pumps. The pumps are self-serve only, the type that have credit card readers built in. The customer can pay the cashier, or use his card right at the pump. Hocus used Frank's card at the pump."

"One o'clock," I said. "That means they drove back to Las Piernas in time to take Frank's blood from him, pack it up in the Express Mail envelope, and mail it, all before four-thirty yesterday."

He nodded. "One more item. Hank told me the number on the fax you received is from a public fax machine at the Las Piernas Airport."

"A copy center at the airport?"

"No, an unattended machine—sort of like a pay phone, only it's a fax. You have to use a credit card. The card was stolen, but we've got folks out there now looking for prints and trying to find witnesses. Hank's already got photos of Neukirk and Ryan."

"I'm surprised they didn't just send the fax by computer."

"So am I," he said. "It would easily have been within their capabilities."

"That fax was sent not long after the second call to my house—when they told me to go to the *Californian*—right?"

"Almost exactly an hour later," he said. "You talked to Frank then, so unless they've moved him since the call, he's probably no more than forty-five minutes away from the airport. That's allowing for time to park at the airport, walk in, and set up the fax. The fax man was careless. I don't think he knew the number was picked up by the receiving fax."

"So it begins to look like they've stayed in the Las Piernas area."

"Yes. And with the photos circulating, we may get a better fix on them."

"If Frank is in Las Piernas, I don't want to be here in Bakersfield!"

"Nothing is certain right now, Irene. When we're able to locate him, we'll let you know right away. But we don't know where he is, not yet. Even if we learn where he's being kept, we've only changed some of the dynamics of the situation—that's not the same as freeing Frank."

I was silent for a moment. "Why would they be so careful for weeks, and then suddenly grow careless?"

"I don't know. After working in law enforcement for a time, I started to learn what every cop learns—that every criminal is bound to do something stupid sooner or later. I've been amazed by some of them."

"I don't know, Cassidy. It bothers me. They have to know that they're wanted for capital offenses, but they told us who they are." I swallowed hard and said, "Maybe they're suicidal."

"Maybe," he agreed.

I wondered if I really did want him to be so honest with me. "What's on the fax pages?" I asked.

"Here," he said, and handed me the pages.

"You've read them?"

"No, just skimmed them. I'll read them again more closely as you finish them."

I pulled the pages out of the envelope, set aside the cover page. Two words formed the title of the pages that followed:

Father's Day.

FATHER'S DAY

THEIR FATHERS AWAKENED them at two-thirty that Saturday morning. It was still dark outside, and the air was cool. Sleepily the boys dressed in jeans and flannel shirts. The car was already packed, waiting in the driveway in front of Bret's house. They were on their way by three. "We'll beat the traffic," Bret's father said. "Besides, we have to get there while the fish are still hungry for breakfast."

The boys had stayed up late the night before, giggling and telling ghost stories, too excited about the prospect of spending a week at Lake Isabella to fall asleep when they were supposed to. They would stay at the Neukirks' cabin. The cabin was small, but most of the time would be spent at the lake, in the Ryans' boat, which would be ready and waiting in a nearby storage area. Sam's dad didn't get much time off, but he had promised everyone the week of fishing. Sam had confided to Bret that he had been afraid his father would cancel at the last minute. Gene had worked very late that night, and even Julian had been looking at the clock a lot. But Gene showed up. He was tired and worn out, but ready to go fishing.

In recent months something had been bothering their fathers. Sam and Bret had worried over this, talked about it again and again. The boys still saw each other every day, but sometimes Gene just dropped Sam off and left for the hospital. That wasn't like him. He usually wanted to see Julian. But whatever had come between the grown-ups seemed to be over, and now the men were doing things together again. The boys were especially happy, because the rift had scared them.

Now they were tired, and almost as soon as they were in the backseat of the Ryans' car, they fell asleep. Julian drove.

They didn't know how long they had been sleeping when they awakened again. It was still dark outside. The car had stopped. The inside of the car was bathed in red, pulsing light. "It's all right, boys," Julian said, seeing their worried looks in the rearview mirror. "I was just going a little fast and now I'm going to get a ticket."

"Mom's going to be mad!" Bret said.

"We don't have to worry about that for a week, now, do we?" Julian said.

He rolled down his window. "Is there a problem, Officer?" he said, trying to shield his eyes. The policeman was shining a bright flashlight into his face.

The boys could not see the policeman's face, because he didn't lean over at all. But they saw the dark blue of his uniform. They heard him say, "Would you please step outside the vehicle, sir?"

Julian did what the policeman said to do. As he stepped out, though, the policeman hit him hard with the grip of the flashlight. He fell to the ground.

The boys screamed, and Gene shouted, "Julian!"

The front passenger door flew open. A man grabbed Gene and held a gun to his head. The man was dirty and had strange eyes. Later they would learn that his name was Christopher Powell.

"Oh, Christ, the cop . . . ," Gene murmured.

"That's right," Powell said. "You just met your boss. Now tell them kids to sit still and shut the fuck up or I'll blow your fucking brains out!"

The boys stopped screaming before Gene had to say anything. They had never been so afraid.

"Chris," the policeman said, "you are using foul language in front of children. And why are there children here, Chris?"

The policeman was facing away from them, but his voice carried. It was a calm voice, but there was a meanness in it. They could not see his face, but they saw his back as he bent over Julian's prone form. The policeman was big, bigger than their fathers, bigger than Powell. He had silver hair—it showed beneath his cap, above the dark blue of his collar. They could see a word on the patch on his sleeve: Bakersfield.

It made Powell angry when the policeman asked him why they were there. The boys were watching Powell now and saw him look at the policeman as if he wanted to shoot him. "It's a trick, boss. The doc here don't think you'll hurt him if kids are around."

"Tape all three of them," the policeman said, and they heard him move away.

Powell grinned. He reached into his jacket and shoved a roll of tape at Gene. It was duct tape, wide and silver. He made Gene tape the boys' eyes. They were crying, and Powell made them wipe their faces before Gene put the tape over their eyes. "Not just once. Wrap it again and again."

Gene obeyed. Next, at Powell's command, their hands were taped behind their backs.

"Their mouths, too," Powell said.

But the policeman was closer again now, and he said, "No. You'll be quiet, won't you, boys?" They nodded.

"Put your hands behind your back!" Powell said to Gene, and they heard Gene grunt with pain. Powell was angry again; they could feel it, even with their eyes taped shut. The policeman made Powell angry, and Powell took his anger out on one of them at the earliest opportunity. It was a pattern that would be repeated.

"Ready," Powell said when he had finished.

"Please keep your eyes forward, Gene," the policeman said.

"Don't you try to look at his face in the mirror, neither!" Powell added.

The boys could not see anything now, but they heard the car door next to Bret being opened.

"Not the boys," Gene begged. "Please—"

"Shut up!" Powell said.

"Of course nothing will happen to the boys," the policeman said. "Did you hear me, Chris?"

"Yes," Powell said sullenly.

There was a silence, then Powell said, "Yes, sir, I heard you," in a nervous voice. "Nothing will happen to them boys."

They heard movement outside the car.

"Oh, Jesus!" Gene said. "Oh, please, don't hurt Julian—"

"I really don't want to hear protests from the good doctor," the policeman said. "This is all his fault, anyway. Tape his mouth, Chris."

They heard the tape being pulled off the roll, Gene's pleas for mercy stilled midsentence.

"Scoot over, boys," the policeman said. "Toward the other door."

They obeyed, huddling together.

"Wait," he said. "Chris, tape their hands in front of them, not behind. It's a long ride back." But the policeman was the one who gently reached for them, cut the bonds, moved their hands forward, and retaped their wrists. The skin on his hands was rough, but when he touched them he was almost as gentle as Gene had been. "There, that's better now."

Next they felt him move off the seat, and soon after, another weight replaced him. Julian. Julian's head was laid across their laps. Bret was unable to prevent himself from making a small sound of anxiousness, but otherwise their terror kept them silent. They lightly moved their fingers over Julian's face and hair in a blind quest for reassurance. Bret could feel Julian's breath, the warmth of his skin. His eyes were taped, but not his mouth. He was alive.

"There now, he's fine," the policeman said. "Everyone will be fine very soon, right, Gene?"

Gene made a muffled sound.

"I know you are frightened by all of this, boys," the policeman said, "but I promise you won't be hurt." He paused. "Do you understand what I'm saying, Chris?"

"Yes, sir."

"My dad . . . ," Bret dared to say.

"Your dad got a little bump on the head. He'll wake up soon. Now, Chris, cut the tape from Gene's hands so he can write the information for us. Eyes front, Gene. . . . Thank you." They heard the sound of tape being cut. A rustle of paper.

"You didn't mean to delay taking our payment to our suppliers, did you, Gene?" the policeman asked. "No, I didn't think so. And it won't ever happen again, will it? No. Now, Chris is just going to keep an eye on everyone until I'm satisfied that you haven't done anything foolish, Gene. Anything else foolish, I should say. Because, Gene, forcing me to deal with you directly like this is very, very foolish. So think carefully before you write."

They could hear Gene scribbling.

When the scribbling stopped, the policeman said, "Now, before you hand that piece of paper over your shoulder, make certain it will be very easy for me to find the money. . . . You're certain? Fine, then." He paused, then said, "This mushroom-shaped rock—is it easily recognized?"

They heard Gene's frantic sounds.

"Good. I would hate to have your children terrified—not to mention leaving you and your friend so very uncomfortable—while I searched every last boulder in the gorge. Close your eyes now, Gene, and keep them closed. Chris, tape his hands again, please. His eyes as well."

The car door closed.

"A word with you when you've finished, Chris," he said, his voice now coming from the driver's side window. "Oh, one other thing, Gene. Your gambling friends haven't seen any of this money yet, have they? . . . No? I'm so happy to hear that. For your sake."

Christopher Powell closed the car door. "Don't cry, Daddy," Sam whispered as they heard Gene Ryan trying to conceal the sobbing sounds he was making behind his gag.

They heard the police car drive off. When Powell came back to their car, he quickly taped the boys' mouths shut.

"Fuck that old bastard," Powell said. "I ain't listening to no kid's bellyaching."

Powell drove them to the warehouse. The boys tried to figure out where they were being taken, like kidnap victims did on TV, but they couldn't keep track. Every time the car would turn, Julian would start to slide off their laps, so they spent most of their time trying to hold on to him.

The car stopped, and they heard the sound of a big metal door sliding open. Powell got back into the car and drove it into the warehouse. He got out again and closed the big door behind them.

First he took Gene. This brought new terror to the boys. Julian started to rouse, though. They heard him groan. He struggled for a moment, then seemed to realize that he was being held by the boys.

"Bret? Sam?"

The boys tried to let him know they heard him, patting him.

"Oh, God . . . Gene?"

Their hands stilled.

"Gene!" he called out.

Bret moved his fingers over his father's lips, trying to warn him to be silent. He tried to pull the tape away from his father's eyes, but soon he heard Powell's angry steps crossing the room.

"I heard you yellin'," he said, "so I know you're awake. That's good. Easier if I don't have to lift you. Don't mess around, or I'll have to shoot one of these little boys." Julian was hauled off them. "Stand up," they heard Powell say.

They heard Powell taking Julian away. Bret tried to pull the tape away from his own eyes but was making no progress. There were too many layers. He felt Sam nudging him, pushing him with his hands. As clearly as if Sam were speaking to him, he knew that Sam was urging him out of the car, wanting to escape. Bret was scared, but Sam, as always, was brave.

So without knowing with any certainty what was beyond the car, Bret scooted along the seat until he felt his feet hit the wooden floor. He staggered, then turned toward the back of the car, feeling his way along it. Sam was soon behind him.

Bret remembered the door being shut behind the car. He kept moving toward the back of the car, then tried reaching out with his hands. Nothingness. He crouched down. The whole building reeked of old oil and grease, but this close to the floor, the smell was almost overwhelming.

He came to a wall—no! It was the door. He could

feel the cold air coming in from beneath it. He straightened again, tried to call to Sam. But Sam was moving away from him.

"Hey!" Powell's voice called. "Come here, you little son of a bitch!"

Sam stumbled. Bret heard him fall. Sam made a sound in his throat. Bret knew what Sam meant to tell him. "Run!" he was saying. "Run, Bret!"

Bret fumbled along the door, trying to find a latch, a handle. He pictured himself in the car, hearing the sliding sound. Right to left. Now, from the inside, it would be left to right—the handle would be on the left. He heard Powell laughing.

"Come here," Powell called, but Bret realized that he was talking to Sam. Bret found the handle and pulled. Nothing. He heard the sound of tape ripping, Sam crying out in pain. He stopped, tried to turn toward the sound.

"Run, Bret!" Sam cried. "Run!"

Bret found the hasp. Miraculously, it seemed to him, no lock was on it.

"Come back here now or I'll hurt your friend," Powell said.

"Go, Bret, don't worry, just go!" Sam commanded.

Powell started laughing. Bret unlatched the door. He felt sick to his stomach, worried about what would happen to Sam and their fathers, but he pulled on the door with all his might. It budged only about an inch.

He heard Powell running straight at him. He tried to duck, but Powell caught him, grabbed him with bruising strength. Powell pulled at the tape around Bret's eyes, which in turn tore at Bret's hair and skin.

Bret blinked and looked up into Powell's dirty, wild-eyed face, which was glowing red. Taillight red. Belatedly Bret realized Powell had left the car lights on. Alone, those lights might not have been enough, but because the car doors were open, the dome light was on—just enough of a soft glow came from the car to illuminate the area near the warehouse door. Had the boys shut the car door, they might not have been seen.

Except for the area illuminated by the dome light and headlights of the car, it was dark in the cavernous brick building. Later they would learn that the building had been used for many purposes, its design changed for each tenant. Most recently it had been used to store surplus machinery; the greasy smell came from lubricants that had drained out of the old machines and soaked into the building's wooden floor. The warehouse had been abandoned for at least five years.

Powell dragged Bret to the place where Sam, still blindfolded, had been tethered to a post. Powell was hurting Bret, pulling his arm up hard behind him. Bret made a whimpering sound behind the tape over his mouth. Sam heard it and shouted, "Leave him alone!" Powell slapped Sam hard. Sam stopped shouting, but he refused to cry. Powell untied him and made Bret lead him along.

Powell took them to a doorway. It opened onto a set of wooden steps that went into a dimly lit basement. He told them to go down the steps. He shut the thick wooden door behind them.

Gene and Julian were each tied to a post. The posts were about six feet apart in the center of the room, and the men were tied so that they faced one another. Their faces were no longer taped.

When the boys came down the stairs, Bret saw both fear and relief on the faces of their fathers. Gene was crying. Julian tried to smile at Bret, but it didn't look like a real smile.

The boys were taken to a wall. Leather bands with thick iron rings attached to them were fastened tightly to the boys' slender wrists and ankles; each iron ring was padlocked to a heavy chain. The other end of each chain was fastened to an eyelet in the wall. Only when all the padlocks were snapped closed did Powell pull the tape off Sam's eyes and Bret's mouth. The chains were just long enough to allow some movement, but the boys staggered under their weight. Sam immediately pulled at his, tried to reach his father. Although Gene was tied to the closer of the two posts, the chains were far too short to allow that.

"These were gonna be on you," Powell said to the men, laughing. "Bought 'em at a sex shop and rigged 'em up myself. Long time ago." His thoughts seemed to wander, then he smiled at Gene. "Figured it would bother you more to see these two little weasels in 'em than to be in 'em yourself. And I see I'm right."

Powell began pacing back and forth across the basement. There was a sleeping bag on a cot against the far wall and a small wooden table. A portable, battery-operated lantern sat on the table, along with a rumpled canvas bag and wadded-up paper sacks from a fast-food place. The lantern light cast long, strange shadows. This room didn't smell like oil. It smelled like sweat and old hamburgers.

"Daddy, why is he doing this to us?" Sam asked.

Powell laughed again. "Tell him, Gene. Tell him what a great guy his old man is."

"It's all my fault, Sam," Gene choked out. "God forgive me, it's all my fault."

"Gene—" Julian said.

"Shut the fuck up, Neukirk," Powell said. "Let the doc make his confession."

But Gene was silent. Powell went over to the canvas bag and exchanged his gun for a long knife. He moved over to Julian and, before anyone knew what he was planning, made a small cut on Julian's arm.

Bret started screaming. Gene and Sam were shouting.

"Shut up!" Powell yelled, moving back toward Julian with the knife.

They were all silent.

"It's okay, it's okay," Julian said, but his face was pale. Sam moved over to Bret, held on to him.

"Now, Gene, I asked you to make your confession," Powell said. "Tell these little faggot kids of yours what you did."

"No one should ever call anyone a faggot," Sam said, repeating—verbatim—one part of a lecture they had received not long ago.

Bret, who had not been able to take his eyes from his father's bleeding cut, was terrified that Powell would slice at Julian again because of Sammy's remark.

But Powell just laughed. "You admit being faggots, huh?"

"No. We're just like brothers," Sam said, still holding Bret. "Brothers don't have sex with each other. But even if we were gay, you shouldn't say the word 'faggot.' It's bad manners."

Powell howled with laughter. "Man, you are a piece of work, kid."

"I'm very proud of you, Sam," Gene said quietly, attracting everyone's attention. Bret realized that Gene's voice was different. He sounded stronger, as if being proud of Sam had made him braver. "But I'm not so proud of myself. You're right. You and Bret are like brothers, just as Julian and I are like brothers. It's also right that it's my fault we are here—partly because I didn't confide in Julian."

"It doesn't matter now," Julian said.

"It's the only thing that matters," Gene said. "Boys, I want to tell you a story—a true story. Julian knows some of it, but not all of it."

Powell backed off from the men and sat on the cot. "I'm gonna enjoy the hell outta this," he said.

Julian looked over at Bret and Sam. He mouthed the words, "Be brave."

So Gene began to tell them about gambling and losing money. He talked about being afraid of the men he owed money to, of what they might do if he didn't pay them back. He talked about Powell approaching him with the chance to make easy money.

"Chris knew a man who wanted something flown to the United States from Mexico," he said.

"What was it, Daddy?" Sam asked.

Gene hesitated.

Powell jumped to his feet, knife in hand. He swaggered over to Gene. "What was it, Daddy?" he mimicked.

"Cocaine," Gene whispered.

Bret saw Sam's eyes widen in disbelief. Bret shouted what Sam had wanted to say. "You're lying!"

"Bret!" Julian said sharply.

Gene was shaking his head. "No, Bret, I'm sorry, I'm not."

"Boys," Julian said quickly, "this is a secret. You understand? No one ever hears about this. No one! Not ever."

Powell turned and slashed him again, the other arm this time. In the next instant, he cut Gene.

"You two are pissing me off!" Powell shouted. "Now get on with the story, Gene. Or next time, I cut one of these little babies over here."

Shakily Gene went on. He told of flights to Mexico in the Cessna 210—flights the boys thought were missions of mercy to help people too poor to pay for doctors. Yes, he really did help the poor, he told them when Sam asked. But while the other doctors were there only to help, he was also doing illegal business on the side. That's why he always went on his own, alone, and the others went in groups. If he met up with other doctors, he told them he flew alone because of his insurance, but that wasn't true.

He picked up the drugs—marijuana or cocaine or heroin—in Mexico. He would then fly the plane to the Kern Valley Airport, near Lake Isabella, and drive down to Bakersfield from there. Powell would unload the drugs and leave money for Gene in a special locked box. It was a lot of money. It helped him get out of debt quickly.

Although at first he did not handle any payments to the suppliers, eventually Gene was entrusted with taking large sums of cash to Mexico.

Now he was no longer afraid of the men who had tried to collect his gambling debts. He was afraid of Powell and Powell's boss. He was being asked to make more and more frequent flights. Between the flights and his schedule at the hospital, he was never home. He was always fatigued, unable to enjoy time with his friends or family. He was worried that he would be caught. He began to see how foolish he had been.

He went to seek help from the man who had always been his best friend. Julian said that no matter what happened, he would always stand by him.

"And I will," Julian said when Gene reached this part of the story.

"And I'll always stand by Sam," Bret said, because he knew his friend was feeling bewildered and ashamed.

Julian smiled at Bret. Gene began weeping again.

"Very fucking touching," Powell said, "but you ain't finished."

Julian had suggested he take some time off, Gene said. Julian had seen that Gene was exhausted, not able to think clearly. It was a complex problem. They could spend some time talking things over once Gene got some rest.

So they planned the fishing trip, and as the day grew closer Gene found himself excited at the prospect of spending time with his friend and their sons. He worked a long shift at the hospital, trying to make sure everything would go smoothly while he was gone for the week. Then his pager went off; the code on it signified a call from Powell. It meant Powell wanted a flight.

Gene drove up to Lake Isabella, to the airport, but

as he sat in the plane, weary in more ways than one, he changed his mind. He shut down the engines and was going to leave the money on the plane, but he realized his "false start" had attracted some attention. He took the money, put it in his car, and drove to Powell's house. He planned to tell Powell that he wanted out but Powell wasn't home. He tried calling him but only reached the answering machine. He left a message, saying he hadn't gone on the flight, that he needed to talk to Powell. He headed back to Bakersfield, but began to feel afraid and confused, unsure of what to do.

"Forget all the excuses," Powell said. "You did a dumb-ass thing."

As he drove, Gene said, he decided he didn't like the idea of having this kind of money near his family, where someone might hurt them in order to take it.

Powell laughed over that.

"I decided not to take the money home," Gene said. "But I was more than halfway to Bakersfield and too tired to drive all the way back to Lake Isabella and wait for Powell, so I pulled off at the side of the road and buried the money."

"I go to this plane," Powell said, "thinking maybe he's left the money there. And what do I find, huh? What do I find?"

"An empty plane," Gene said. "But—"

"Fuckin' A, an empty plane!" Powell started pacing.

"I called you again when I got home and told you where I'd left the money!" Gene said.

"Not so's I could find it."

"I didn't know!" Gene said. "Would I be driving

toward your house if I thought you hadn't found the money? Would I have my children in the car with me? I wasn't trying to escape!"

"Shut up!" Powell raged. "I ain't stupid! You fucked up!"

He began pacing again.

As time went on, Powell became more restless. The tempo of his pacing increased. He said it was taking too long for the boss to get there. Something was wrong. Maybe Gene had never hidden any money there after all. In time he convinced himself that Gene had set a trap.

That's when the killing began. He cut the men loose, but he didn't give them a real chance to fight. They had been tied up for hours by then, and the circulation had gone out of their hands and feet. And each time Powell inflicted a wound, he became more excited, more frenzied.

Julian died first, then Gene. The boys were screaming. Powell turned on them. He dropped the knife and shook them, but still they screamed. He picked up a piece of pipe, was going to hit Bret with it. But at the last minute Sam shielded Bret, who was smaller. That was how Sam's arm was broken.

Sam yelled, "You promised the policeman you wouldn't hurt us!"

Powell stopped then, as quickly as he had begun. He looked around the room in surprise, as if a stranger had done this terrible work. He hurriedly mounted the stairs, closed the basement door. Faintly they heard the sliding metal door open. They did not hear it close.

The boys screamed for help until they were hoarse.

The lantern batteries, already weak by the time Powell left, dimmed rapidly; the room grew darker and darker, until it was pitch black.

The boys held on to one another.

They settled into a state that was almost like being asleep, dreamlike and distant, only Sam's occasional moan of pain bringing Bret back to the present. They did not know how much time had passed when the basement door opened and a flashlight shone into the dark. They stayed silent.

"Powell?"

The policeman.

The chains made a rattling sound. They were both shaking.

The light glanced onto the floor and then into their faces. They were too exhausted from standing on their feet for hours in the heavy chains to raise their hands to shield their eyes from the light.

The policeman made a keening sound, a sound not unlike the ones they had made when they'd still had voices to cry out with. Then he was gone.

Bret felt as if he had been awakened again. He could feel the cold of the room, smell the blood, feel Sam shiver. He began to wonder if anyone would ever find them. It was then that the door opened and another policeman came in.

His name was Frank Harriman. He left them only long enough to radio for help, which was long enough for the boys to decide that no one would ever believe the truth.

When Frank Harriman came back he tried to free them, but the swelling in their hands and feet had made the leather too tight to cut. When he saw he couldn't free them without hurting them, he stayed with them, there in the cold darkness, with the stench all around, waiting for help. He braced his back against the wall and lifted them carefully onto his lap, cradling their arms so that the strain of holding the chains was finally relieved. He didn't mind that they were silent or that they had blood on them.

He was young, younger than their fathers. And he was taller. But something about him reminded Bret and Sam of Julian. That's why the boys let him hold them until their mothers could be there. They did not let any of the other men take them from him, even after they were able to leave the basement—not even the one who put a splint on Sam's arm.

Frank Harriman wouldn't let anyone separate them. When the others saw that the boys wouldn't answer questions, the others were upset. He made the ones who were upset leave the boys alone. He knew they were tired and weak and afraid. He didn't complain. He held them. Frank Harriman, and no one else.

They didn't trust him completely, but they trusted no one else at all.

18

THE DARK-HAIRED YOUNG MAN stood with his left arm extended to the side, his open left hand palm up. In his right hand he held a pack of cards. In one smooth, even movement he spread the cards from the palm of his left hand up the length of his arm to his elbow. With a grace that belied his quickness, he lifted his left arm, rolled his palm downward, and turned his body to the left. For a brief instant the cards stood in the air as one unit, then cascaded in an improbable, fluid motion to his waiting right hand, where he caught them perfectly.

Dressed less outlandishly than he was when Frank last saw him—on Dana Ross's porch—the magician wore jeans and a blue T-shirt. He repeated the catch again and again, never failing to spread the pack smoothly, never dropping a card, never seeming to use the concentration that must have been required.

Frank watched silently from the bed. His headache

was less sharp now, not nearly as sharp as his disappointment in realizing that he had slept again. The magician's card flourishes had drawn his eye when he first awakened, but now he spent time taking in all that had changed during his most recent drug-induced nap.

The curtain that had surrounded the bed was gone. The room beyond it was an odd one, of soft bending walls. As he awakened more fully, he came to the conclusion that although he was in the same bed, he was, inexplicably, inside a large tent. He had been rolled onto his right side. The IV bottle had been attached again but seemed to be clamped shut—he couldn't be sure. His hands were still tethered, but he could move his legs. As he did, he saw that he was no longer dressed in the hospital gown. He now wore a set of surgeon's scrubs.

Without looking at Frank, the magician said, "Please don't bother trying to fake sleep again. You have too much trouble staying awake to pull it off. At this rate, we'll never get to talk to one another."

Frank didn't reply, but he kept his eyes open.

The young man stopped, set down the pack, and turned toward the bed. "On my tenth birthday, you gave me a magic kit. Do you remember?"

"Bret?" he asked in utter disbelief. He saw the young man flinch at that disbelief, and his long-carried sense of protectiveness toward Bret Neukirk made him sorry for not hiding his reaction. But confusion soon overran regret—he could not reconcile what was happening to him now with his memory of the silent young boy.

I'm still dreaming, he told himself. The drugs—

"Yes," the young man said, "I'm Bret. I'm sorry about all of this, Detective Harriman. I really am."

"Sorry? Bret, for chrissakes—"

"I'm afraid you're our hostage, sir."

He could only repeat numbly, "Our?"

"Samuel. Me. Hocus."

Frank shut his eyes. Clenched them shut. This isn't happening, he told himself. This isn't happening.

"Are you in pain?" Bret asked worriedly.

Oh, yes, Frank thought. I'm in pain. Not Bret. Not Sam. He opened his eyes. "Why?"

"I made a promise," he said. "Samuel and I promised something to each other. We would see justice done, no matter how long it took."

"Justice? But Powell is dead—"

"Yes," Bret answered, watching him closely. "But not the policeman."

Frank tried to read Bret's expression. "You want to kill me?"

Bret smiled, then looked away quickly. His voice— a voice Frank had never heard speak more than a few words—was full of emotion. "I *knew* you wouldn't know. I knew it. I told Samuel, but Samuel is less trusting—not that I blame him."

"Wouldn't know what?" Frank asked, his headache suddenly fierce.

"A little later on, I'll give you something to read— our story. It explains everything. It's the one we sent to Irene."

"You've talked to Irene?"

"Yes. You have, too, actually," he said. "I know you find it hard to believe," he added quickly. "In your position, I would feel the same. When you spoke to her, Samuel had given you a drug that often makes people forget what has happened while they are under its influence."

Calm down. Calm down.

"This is a lot to take in all at once, I suppose," Bret said. "But I assure you, we will not harm Irene. She's not a target. We didn't want to hurt you, either. I want you to be free when this is all over."

"And Sam? Does he want the same thing?"

Bret hesitated. "Well, of course, that's the ideal situation."

"And if things don't work out ideally?"

"You shouldn't think about such things."

"Forgive me, Bret, but it's hard to think about anything else."

"I'm going to do everything I can to get you out of here alive."

He could find no real comfort in that. He began to take comfort instead in the sharp aching of his head, reasoning that this much pain meant the drugs no longer had so strong a hold on him.

To survive, he knew, he needed information. And he needed to make sure Bret remained concerned about him.

"Where is Sam?" he asked.

"With his girlfriend. He doesn't like to be called Sam, by the way. He goes by Samuel now."

"Okay, I'll try to remember that. 'Detective Harriman' is a little formal. Why don't you call me 'Frank'?"

Bret hesitated. "Maybe when it's just the two of us here," he said.

Frank shrugged one shoulder, as if it didn't matter.

But he thought of the implications of Bret's statement even as he said casually, "I'm more comfortable here on my side. Are you the one who moved me around?"

Bret nodded. "It's not good for you to stay in one position. And I thought you would like these clothes better. I—I hope that doesn't embarrass you."

Having his clothes changed while he slept? It humiliated him. But he said, "No, not at all. The other outfit was embarrassing. I didn't like the gown much."

"I knew you wouldn't!"

"You were right."

"I know you don't like being restrained, either . . . Frank." He said the name timidly, trying it out.

"You're right, Bret. I know you understand why."

He nodded. "I do, Frank. I don't like to see anyone tied up. I don't even like to see dogs tied up. Or animals in cages."

"Was the animal shelter your idea?"

"The shelter," he said, "but not the killing." Anxiously he added, "Do you believe me?"

"Yes," Frank said quite truthfully. He remembered the hesitancy Bret had shown at Dana Ross's place. Samuel had been the one who did all the rough work.

"Maybe later, I'll be able to convince Samuel that you should be allowed to walk around. He thinks we'll be in danger from you if you aren't restrained."

"What do you think?"

"Oh, you can't leave this building unless we let you out, so it would be foolish to try to harm one of us. And we have some devices that we could put on you that would discourage escape attempts, or violence, but that would allow you to move about." Seeing

Frank's eyes widen, he added quickly, "I wouldn't put them on you without your consent, of course. And you would know the penalty for breaking the rules beforehand."

When Frank didn't reply, Bret added, "I don't really like the idea myself—but as an alternative to being tied to the bed?"

"Yes, you're right."

A silence stretched between them. Frank said, "So Samuel has a girlfriend?"

Bret nodded.

"It's hard for me to realize that you're both men now. It's been a long time."

"Yes."

"What's the girlfriend like?"

Bret shrugged. "He doesn't love her. She's just someone to have sex with."

"You don't like her?"

"I don't like or dislike her. She doesn't really matter. I feel a little sorry for her, if anything, because I think she really cares about Samuel."

"Are you sure he doesn't care about her?"

"Oh, he cares, but only because he likes having sex with her."

"Do you have a girlfriend?"

"No. But it doesn't matter. I mean, I think I would have pursued it before now if it did. I've been attracted to women, but I didn't want a relationship to just be something . . . *passing*. Do you understand?"

"I think so. But why would it have to be passing? Maybe it would last longer."

"No, it couldn't. But let's not talk about that now."

He looked at his watch. "We only have another hour before I have to start the drip again."

"Please—I don't need the drugs—"

"Let's not talk about it."

Frank was silent, trying to fight a sense of panic. Awake, he stood some sort of chance. With the drugs. . . .

"Tell me about your life," Bret was saying. When Frank hesitated Bret said, "I mean, what's happened to you since we last saw you?"

"You seem to know a lot about me already," Frank said, hearing the anger, the resentment, over his captivity come to the surface. He knew he should not show it. But it was there.

Bret shook his head. "No, those are just facts."

"You want lies?"

"No," Bret said, turning red. "I mean, facts don't tell a person anything. I know you moved to Las Piernas. I know you are a homicide detective and that Pete Baird is your partner and that your wife is named Irene and that she's a reporter. So what? It's like reading tombstones in a graveyard. 'Born.' 'Died.' 'Beloved daughter of . . .' So what?" He paused, then said, "Are you thirsty?"

"Yes," Frank said, surprised by the question.

"I'm sorry, I should have asked earlier." He moved to a small table near the bed, then brought a water glass and a straw over to the rail, helped Frank to take a drink. It was cool and good.

"Now," Bret said, setting down the glass. "We aren't going to have much time together, and when this is over, we'll never see each other again. I've wondered about you, Frank Harriman. Are you happier in

Las Piernas than in Bakersfield? Do you like what you do? Does it bother you, working in homicide? Is Pete Baird your favorite partner, or do you wish you worked with someone else? Are you glad you married Irene? Do you miss your father?"

Frank stared at him a moment, then said, "Yes. Yes, I do miss him. I think about him often."

And he began to talk to Bret about his father and Las Piernas and even about Irene, not noticing when Bret reached over and started the IV again, until he was feeling far too drowsy to fight it. The water, he thought belatedly. The water was drugged.

He was not sure if the voice was within the dream or not. He heard a door close and thought it strange that a tent would have a door that closed just like a metal door. He was thinking about that when the voice said, "What the hell have you done?"

"You've been wrong about him," Bret said.

Everything after that was most definitely within a dream.

19

THE LAST PAGE OF THE FAX contained only a few brief sentences:

As for the contents of the package you received, just remember—there is more where that came from.

It may help you to know that Julian Neukirk was six feet tall; the policeman was taller.

When you learn the identity of the policeman, place an ad in the *Las Piernas News Express,* in the personals, to read: "John Oakhurst, come home."

Detective Harriman will receive increasing amounts of morphine over the next few days. He will stop receiving the morphine when we are satisfied that you have correctly identified our enemy. We suggest you hurry.

"Let's go," I said to Cassidy. "There's a lot to be done."

He started the car. "What do you think of the story?"

" 'Father's Day'?"

"Yes."

"I think they were trying to tell the truth—at least as they remember it. They didn't try to apologize for Gene Ryan. Other than that . . . well, I'd say Bret wrote it."

"Why Bret?" he asked.

"Even though it's in third person, everything is from his point of view."

Cassidy nodded. "Any idea who John Oakhurst is?"

"No, although the name seems familiar."

"To me, too," he said. "I just can't remember where I've heard it."

"Maybe it's just a made-up name."

"Not with this group."

"No. No, I suppose not . . . I understand why they want me to find this cop. But it's so hard for me to understand how they feel about Frank."

"I'm not sure they understand that themselves. Remember the last line? About trust? If nothing else, we can learn a lot about them from this story."

I went ahead and asked the question I was afraid to hear answered. "How long do you suppose it will be before they're giving him a fatal level of morphine?"

He shrugged. "They could do it in one injection if they set their minds to it. But if they go slowly enough, he'll build a tolerance."

My mind snagged on the words "one injection" as surely as if they had been made of barbed wire.

He picked up his cellular phone and dialed Bea's number. "Mrs. Harriman? Tom Cassidy. Sorry to keep you waiting so long, ma'am. We're on our way back to the house now." He listened, then said, "I'm sorry to hear you were troubled. Yes, ma'am. Couldn't have handled it better myself."

He hung up and said, "You guessed right about the *Californian*. They've already sent a reporter out. Your mother-in-law slammed the door in the man's face. Surprised it took the paper this long. I guess your buddy the librarian must have struggled with his conscience for a while."

"Conscience? Yeah, right. Brandon just spent the afternoon wondering which would make his boss angrier: his admission that he let us into the library or getting beat by an out-of-town paper on a story he had a jump start on."

"Did he choose right?"

"I'd say so. Is Bea upset about this?"

"Not really. Greg Bradshaw called one of his friends on the Bakersfield PD, and they've got someone watching the house now, making sure the family isn't disturbed."

Cassidy's cellular phone rang. He answered with his name, made a few noncommittal sounds, then said, "That's great, Hank. Yes, I'll have the fax set up, too. I've got quite a bit of new information to send you." He told Hank about the *Californian*'s visit to Bea Harriman's house. There was a pause, then he frowned. "Sure, put him on." Another pause. "Yes, sir." He glanced at his watch, listened for some time. "Yes, I'll tell her."

He hung up. "Bret Neukirk—no surprise—is a

computer wizard. Something of a wizard in any case—he's an accomplished magician. And Samuel Ryan is an EMT—emergency medical technician. He's been working as a paramedic."

"That explains how he had access to drugs."

"Made it easier for him to steal them, anyway," Cassidy said. "One other thing. Captain asked me to tell you that the press conference is set for a little later this evening—eight-thirty. Supposed to give the electronic media time to fit it into the late evening news."

I glanced at my watch. "That's only a couple of hours from now. I've got to call John. What information will the department be releasing?"

"Not much. We'll announce that Frank was taken hostage. We'll release descriptions of Bret Neukirk and Samuel Ryan and announce that they are wanted by police. We'll say we believe they are in Southern California, probably the Las Piernas area, but they could be anywhere. That's about it."

I looked at the envelopes on the front seat between us, then stared out the car windows for a few minutes. It was dusk now, the last of the setting sun reflected in the west-facing windows of some of the buildings that lined the street ahead of us. I watched the cars moving alongside ours, in the other lanes of the Stockdale Highway. Families. Couples. Singles. I wished them all a perfectly ordinary, boring evening. Somebody ought to have one.

"I need to find a phone," I said.

"I don't suppose you want to use mine?"

"No, thanks." I told him what I was planning to tell John.

He sighed. "I guess almost all of that will be coming out in the paper here or in Riverside. But—hell, I hope the captain has a good breakfast before he reads the *Express* tomorrow."

After a moment he asked, "You covered Bakersfield PD when you were a reporter here?"

"The crime beat. It's not exactly the same as reporting on the department itself. I was just covering the blotter for the most part."

"Ever hear any rumors of somebody in the department doing better than they should on a cop's salary?"

I shook my head. "No. Nothing that reached me. I was here when things were starting to look better after a long history of problems."

"What kinds of problems?"

"Oh, that goes back even to the city's early years— one of my favorite stories about Bakersfield is that the early citizens once voted for disincorporation in order to get rid of a local marshal."

"Disincorporation—you mean they stopped being a city?"

"Officially, yes. Apparently, this marshal considered himself king—had a habit of harassing anybody and everybody. That was back in the 1870s. They reincorporated later on, but there were constant problems between the police and city hall. Frank once told me that not long after his dad joined the department—in the late 1940s—the chief of police was suspended and charged with taking vice payoffs. He was found not guilty. A lot of people will tell you that although there was real corruption back then, the chief was just the victim of politicians."

"Anything more recent?" Cassidy asked.

"By the time I started working here, the department

had a new chief. He once said he had the 'dubious privilege of arresting more police officers than any other chief.' "

"There was some housecleaning going on?"

"Exactly. Complaints had been made against the department, just as there are against almost all police departments—some deserved, some not. But this new chief made a real effort to clean up the Bakersfield PD, and during his years, there weren't charges of corruption at higher levels, as there had been before."

He pulled into a gas station and waited while I used the phone. I tried John's office number, on a hunch that he would still be in. It paid off.

"I wondered if I'd be hearing from you," he said angrily. "You talk to Mark yet?"

"You know damned well I haven't. I've got an offer to make."

"Talk to Mark."

"The paper undoubtedly sent Mark to cover the press conference. Now, we can sit here and play 'come to the principal's office' on the phone, or you can listen to my offer."

"I do have other options."

"Yes, you can fire me. Want to fire me right now, John? To be honest, it would probably be a relief. I could stop thinking about Will Rogers."

"Will Rogers?"

"Never mind. Am I fired?"

I suppose the silence was supposed to make me nervous. It just made me furious.

"No, you aren't fired. Not yet."

"Then I've got some information for you now, and an exclusive for you later, in exchange for as much breathing room as you can bear to give me."

"Do I have a choice?" he groused.

"Not really," I said, "unless we're back to square one."

"What's the information?"

"We have a deal?"

"Yes."

"This all started in Riverside. That's where things went bad. No one else has that."

"Is that where you are now?"

"No."

Silence, then, "Any possibility of an exchange for Lang and Colson?"

"I can't answer that, John, but you probably don't need me to tell you what the policy on hostage exchanges is."

"I'm sorry, Irene," he said, his voice low, as if all the anger he had been burning up with a moment before had gone out of him. My own anger abated, replaced by a sense of guilt. I didn't feel good about withholding information from John; I knew that Lang and Colson seemed to be of no consequence to Hocus, that their interests seemed to lie elsewhere. When I didn't say anything, he added, "You know . . . well, you know I like Frank."

"Yes, I know." I took a deep breath. "The press conference will tell you a lot, but the radio and TV folks will be able to make use of most of it before the paper comes out tomorrow morning. But you've got the information on the car, which is strictly yours at this point. If you get someone out to Riverside, you'll have an angle that's all your own. And one other thing—"

He waited.

"One other thing, but when I tell it to you, promise me—I'm begging here, John—promise me you won't crowd me. If I see a reporter from the *Express* in my rearview mirror just once, I swear to Jesus I will give this story to someone else."

"There are times, Kelly, when you sorely try my—"

"A deal, remember?"

"All right, all right."

"People in Bakersfield are going to recognize the names of the hostage takers."

"Bakersfield?"

"I'm fairly sure the *Californian* is going to have someone digging all of this up soon. I was in their library this afternoon, and here's what I learned." I told him about the Father's Day murders—as they were reported in the *Californian*. I didn't mention Hocus's claims about Powell's accomplice, or the fax, or the vial of blood. I gave him only what I was sure would be revived in the Bakersfield media.

"Whew," he said. "So what's the connection? If Frank rescued them. . . ."

I didn't answer.

"You know more than you're telling me, Kelly."

"Breathing room, John."

"Shit. When do I hear from you again?"

"I don't know. Maybe not until this is over."

"Kelly—"

"Gotta go, John. Bye."

Cassidy didn't try to talk to me when I got back to the car. I appreciated it. As we made our way to Bea's house, I wondered if she'd like to slam the door in my face, too.

I tried to remember what orange blossoms smelled like.

I was wrong about Bea. She was fussing over me from the moment I walked in the door. "I hope that reporter parked out front didn't bother you," she said, putting an arm around my shoulders as if I were not of the same genus and species as the fellow from the *Californian*.

"No," I said, "he didn't make it out of his car in time to question us."

"Mike and Cassie went home," she said. "They've got two little ones," she explained to Cassidy. "I invited Greg to stay for supper."

I watched Cassidy, who had warned me, just before we got out of the car, to follow his lead where Greg Bradshaw was concerned. Cassidy had his hands full of cases from the trunk of the car, but he nodded toward the Bear.

"Glad we'll have a chance to get to know one another better," he said.

Bradshaw smiled. "Yes, me too. Need help with those cases?"

"Oh, I'll manage, thanks. Mind if I set up camp in that back room, Mrs. Harriman?"

"Not at all—Oh, that reminds me. Irene, Rachel called. She's bringing some overnight things up here for you. I told her to plan on staying over, but I think she wants to get back home to Pete."

"I can understand that," I said. "Need any help in the kitchen?"

"Oh, it's just roasted chicken. Won't be ready for about another forty minutes."

She sat down next to Greg again, and he took her hand. I wondered briefly about the gesture, then decided not to read too much into it. She was worried, I knew, and I regretted making her wait so long to hear more about what had happened to her son. I asked her to catch me up on news of her grandchildren. It made better than average small talk.

Cassidy came back into the room and wandered over to the mantel, picked up a photograph. Bea had family photographs everywhere, but the one he held was my favorite. Frank's favorite, too, I remembered. In it Frank stood next to his father, whom he strongly resembled. They were both in uniform. Brian Harriman's arm was around his son's shoulders, his pride evident.

My thoughts wandered for a moment to the missing photographs, the ones that might have included his sister Diana.

"The people who have Frank didn't choose him at random," Cassidy said, gently replacing the father-son photograph, bringing my attention back to Bea and Greg. "He was deliberately targeted."

Cassidy did his best to prepare them for the upcoming press conference, although he provided them with only a little more information than I had given John.

When he first mentioned the Ryan-Neukirk murders, only Greg seemed to recognize the case by name. But the moment he said "two young boys in a warehouse basement," Bea drew a sharp breath.

Although he talked about the Ryan-Neukirk case, Cassidy never mentioned the possibility of a cop's involvement. Apparently sure of my cooperation, he didn't try to cue me to keep my mouth shut about that. No quelling glances, no phrases with double meaning, no hand signals.

If you surveyed everyone who's ever known me, friends and enemies alike, and asked them to write down ten words that describe me, "obedient" wouldn't make anybody's list. So why, I wondered, was I quietly listening to Cassidy deceive people I cared about?

The easy answer was that Frank's life was at stake. The harder one was that Cassidy's seed of doubt about Greg Bradshaw was taking root. Greg was silver haired by the time I first met him; he was easily over six feet tall. For the moment I was going to trust Cassidy's judgment. If he was wrong, though, and we were wasting an opportunity to get the Bear's help, would I be able to forgive myself?

I watched Cassidy, grudgingly admiring his ability to win their confidence. He sat there, speaking in that soft and slow drawl, his voice and demeanor lulling them into matching his own calmness at a time when panic and dismay beckoned. Nothing in those slate blue eyes gave away worry or anxiety or even the weariness he must have been feeling after a long, demanding day.

I saw their tension easing as he spoke. Here was someone in command of the situation, their faces said, someone who knew what was best.

"I retired not too long after those murders," Greg said, breaking into my reverie. He was speaking to Cassidy, his voice gruff with emotion. "Within the next year or so, Gus and Brian left, too."

"Cookie retired then, didn't he?" Bea asked.

"No, he was already retired." Greg frowned. "At least, I think he was. But you know Cookie—he kept up on things. Brian was the same way after he left."

"Forgive me," Cassidy said. "Brian is—?"

"Frank's dad," Greg said. "He's in the picture you were holding. Passed away about four years ago. Cookie's real name is Nat. Nat Cook."

"Our extended family, Detective Cassidy," Bea said. "Along with Greg, Gus Matthews and Nat Cook were my husband's closest friends. They all worked with him on the Bakersfield Police Department."

"We all hated the Ryan-Neukirk case," Greg said. "Those kids—it was one of those things that just made you feel too old and tired for the job. I was thinking of retiring anyway, but I still wasn't sure I wanted out. Afraid retirement would be too dull for me. There would be action somewhere, and I wouldn't be around to see it, you understand?"

Cassidy nodded. "Sure."

"Then the Ryan-Neukirk case came along, and I just said, 'Okay, that's it, I've had enough.' It was like that."

"I can see how it would be," Cassidy said. "It was hard to just read about it in the old newspaper articles. Must have been pretty rough to be there."

"It was," Greg said. "I knew that was going to be a bad one from the beginning. I don't remember where I was exactly, but I was out in a patrol car somewhere. What I remember so clearly is—I heard Frank making the call from this warehouse—and my God, his voice—I don't think I'll forget Frank's voice on that call as long as I live. Frank's quiet, you know?"

He looked at Cassidy, who nodded.

"The boy's a cool one," he went on, "like you. He wasn't panicked. He reported it perfectly. But . . . I don't know . . . it was in his voice. He just sounded like he was . . . like he was . . . *wounded*. You know what I mean?"

"Yes," Cassidy said simply, but there was something different in the way he was looking at Greg now.

"I went right over. Frank had gone back down in that basement, to stay with those kids. Even after we got the detectives and a doctor there, those boys wouldn't let any of the rest of us near them. They were terrified of everyone except Frank. They held on to him for dear life. Frank was down there with them until they could get the chains off them. Down there in that damned basement.

"He had tried to get the chains off with a bolt cutter, but that didn't work. He told me later that he had only gone to his car once, just long enough to make the call, get the bolt cutter and a first-aid kit. Before he went to the car, he told the boys that he'd be right back, but they started crying. They hadn't been crying before then. So after he got back, he told them he wouldn't leave them again until their mothers came for them. And he didn't. But Lord Almighty. . . ."

"Their mothers? Did Frank know the dead men were their fathers?" I asked.

Greg shook his head. "Not right away. The bodies were cut up so bad, I don't blame Frank for not seeing a resemblance between the boys and the fathers. And the boys didn't speak—they would nod or point—that's all. Frank asked them if they knew the men, they nodded yes—went on like that. So before too long, he realizes they've been in there with their own fathers' bodies—blood everywhere—and I don't know, I guess it just—it just hit him hard. It would have done the same to anybody."

"I'm so glad Frank had you there to help him deal with it," Bea said. "Brian felt so bad later."

"Frank's dad wasn't around that day?" Cassidy asked.

"Not until later. I don't even remember now where he was, but Greg and Cookie called here, trying to find him. When Brian realized what had happened, he was very upset that he hadn't been there."

"Probably better that he wasn't, really," Greg said.

"What do you mean?" Bea asked.

"Frank was on his own, and he did fine. In fact, he really proved himself that day. He moved up to detectives not long after that. For the first time, I think a lot of people saw him as somebody who was more than Brian Harriman's son."

Seeing Bea bristle, I said, "Frank is so proud of his dad, I don't think he would have minded anyone thinking of him as Brian's son."

Bea looked at me gratefully. She stood up. "I'd better check on dinner. It's nothing too fancy, Detective Cassidy."

"Ma'am, my mouth has been watering since I walked in here this evening. Heaven can't smell any better than whatever you're cooking in there."

"Just chicken," she said.

"Don't let her fool you with that 'just chicken' stuff," Greg said. "Bea's a fantastic cook."

The momentary tension between them was gone. "I'll help you," I said to Bea, and followed her into the kitchen. Cassidy offered his help as well and was politely refused. He began talking to Greg about his years on the local force.

I was thinking ahead by then, about what I needed to do before that "one injection." In order to help Frank escape, I might have to plan one of my own.

"Bea," I asked after setting the table—the only interference she would brook—"mind if I use your phone?"

"No, go right ahead."

I thumbed through the telephone book and found a listing for Regina Szal, speech therapist. I called and got voice mail. How appropriate, I thought.

The outgoing message presented several options, including "If you would like to mark this message for urgent delivery, please press the pound sign before you hang up." I left my name and Bea's number and added, "This is an emergency. Please call me as soon as possible." I pressed the pound sign, got an automated, "Thank you," and a click.

Figuring Bakersfield couldn't be overrun with unrelated Szals, I called the other listing for that last name, a Bernard Szal. When a woman answered I asked for Regina.

"This is Regina," she answered in a voice so sultry, I figured I'd pay a tidy sum if she could teach me to talk like that.

"My name is Irene Kelly. I need to talk to you about two of your former clients—Bret Neukirk and Samuel Ryan."

I was expecting her to immediately respond with a speech about confidentiality. Instead she said, "Yes, I know. I've been expecting to hear from you."

"You have?"

"Yes. Bret and Samuel wrote to me a couple of weeks ago. They said you would have questions about them. They also said you would be in a hurry."

"That hardly describes it. I need to see you as soon as possible."

"Hmm. All right. When?"

"How late will you be up this evening?" I asked.

"Oh, until about three in the morning."

"Three?"

"Bernard's an amateur astronomer. We're both night owls. Fortunately, I'm able to schedule my clients late in the day. In any case, you're welcome to come by this evening. I'll give you my address, and if we don't answer the bell, just come through the gate and into the backyard. You'll see the tower. That's where we'll be."

"Thanks." I wrote the address and directions. "You're outside the city."

"Away from the lights," she said.

"You'll forgive me, but I wasn't expecting this to be so easy."

"Bret and Sam were favorites of mine. And they very wisely enclosed signed releases. But do you mind telling me what this is all about?"

"Perhaps that would be best explained in person."

"What time should I expect you?"

I thought this over. "Do you watch the eleven o'clock news?"

"Sometimes."

"Watch it tonight. I'll be over sometime after midnight."

"How very mysterious. But all right, we'll see you after midnight."

• • •

I checked the phone book for a listing for Eva Ryan or Francine Neukirk. There were no Neukirks at all and, although there were plenty of Ryans, nothing for Eva. On a whim, I looked for John Oakhurst. Zero.

I wasn't surprised to discover that Cecilia Parker's number was unlisted. I turned to Bea. "Could I get Cecilia's phone number from you?"

"Just autodial number seven from the kitchen phone," she said.

Autodial? I thought. I tried not to let myself get too steamed over that.

Cassidy came into the kitchen then, so I didn't make the call.

"How you doing?" he asked.

"Fine," I said.

He smiled. He knew I was up to something. I knew he knew. I was hoping he was going to be sleepy before midnight.

20

A FTER DINNER, while Cassidy was busy preparing a report to send to Hank Freeman, I again asked Bea for Cecilia's number. "I need to make the call from a pay phone," I explained, not wanting Cassidy to be able to overhear—or tape—the call. Belatedly I realized he could have taped the conversation with Regina Szal, although I didn't think he had.

When Bea raised her eyebrows I said, "Cassidy will need to use the phone line for his fax. And I don't want to tie up the line here."

There was no loss of skepticism in her expression, but she wrote down Cecilia's number, then went to her purse. She came back with the car keys and handed them to me. "Be careful," she said.

Surprised, I hesitated.

"A down payment on an apology," she said. "But that's something we can talk about later."

"I'll be right back," I said.

Although the patrolman from the Bakersfield PD was waiting outside, I didn't see the reporter. I got into Bea's Plymouth sedan, adjusted the seat and mirrors, and started the car. As I turned the corner I saw Cassidy coming out onto the front porch.

I drove to the second-nearest pay phone, hoping Cassidy would look for me at the nearest. The one I chose was at the dark end of a gas station parking lot. I dialed Cecilia Parker's number.

Once I had identified myself she said, "Have they found him?"

"No. But we know who has him. I'll get to that. Look, I may only have a few minutes here, so I'm going to make this quick. Are you working tomorrow?"

"No," she said. "I have the day off. Why?"

"I'd like to meet you for breakfast."

She hesitated. "Look, I'm not sure this is such a great idea. . . ."

"This isn't about your relationship with Frank," I said. "But for his sake, I need to talk to you."

"I don't see what good it's going to do him to have the two of us talk," she said.

"What are you afraid of, Cecilia?"

"Not you, if that's what you're asking."

"Then meet me at the Hill House Cafe at seven o'clock."

"Seven o'clock? On my day off?"

"Under the circumstances, I don't have a lot of free time. Besides, we may need to do some traveling together."

"Now, wait a minute—I don't get it. Frank is missing and you want to waste time meeting with me?"

"Because I think you might be able to help me save his life. If that wasn't true, I wouldn't have gone sneaking out of Bea Harriman's house to make this call."

She was silent.

"Please," I begged.

"Okay, sure," she relented. "No harm in it, I suppose. Now tell me about Frank."

I looked up and saw the cruiser that had been in front of Bea's house pulling into the gas station.

"Oh, hell. Look, I've got to go. Watch the news tonight—Las Piernas is holding a press conference about Frank. Or turn on an all-news radio station in about twenty minutes. It will explain who has him, and you'll probably be able to figure out why I want to meet with you."

"What's going on?"

"Cassidy sent the locals looking for me. I'll see you tomorrow morning."

I hung up just as the patrolman spotted me. He pulled up, rolled down his window, and said, "Ready to go home now?"

"If I'm not, what happens?"

"I follow you all over town."

I got into Bea's car and drove back.

Cassidy was sitting on the swing, arms folded, long legs outstretched. When I pulled into the driveway, he stood up and went into the house. By the time I got inside he was asking Bea to turn on the radio. He didn't look at me. When he took a seat in the living room, he stared at the radio as if it were a television. Bea and Greg kept exchanging anxious glances.

"Can I get you anything, Detective Cassidy?" Bea asked.

"No, thank you, ma'am," he said, his eyes never leaving the radio.

"Cassidy—" I began.

"Oh, please don't bother, Irene. You come up with some cock'n bull story about how you ran out of here because you had a sudden hankerin' for a NeHi strawberry soda, you'll just end up insulting my intelligence."

Before I could reply, the news announcer on the radio said, "Our top story this half hour: A Las Piernas homicide detective has been taken hostage, apparently by Hocus, the anarchist group that is blamed for recent terrorist acts in that city. We now go live to a press conference in Las Piernas, where police are expected to give further details. . . ."

A statement was read by a public information officer. He was joined at the podium by Frank's boss, Lieutenant Carlson. Carlson did not speak. The statement was just as Cassidy had predicted it would be: Frank Harriman had been missing since the previous afternoon, was now believed to be the hostage of the group calling itself Hocus; Neukirk and Ryan were wanted for questioning; anyone with any information on their whereabouts or the disappearance of Detective Harriman should call the LPPD.

Once the statement was read, a barrage of questions were shouted from the reporters. All but one of the questions were answered with, "We have no further comment at this time." The one exception was, "Do you believe Frank Harriman is still alive?"

The answer was, "We remain optimistic."

The conference was ended. The on-scene reporter, obviously reading from a release, described Samuel

Ryan as being twenty-two years old, five eleven, muscular build, with reddish brown hair and brown eyes. Bret Neukirk was twenty-one, six feet tall, slender, dark brown hair and eyes. He described Frank in this same, spare way. It seemed unlikely that anyone would recognize any of them from these descriptions.

The anchorman recapped the information in a sentence, then cut to a commercial for a roofing company.

The phone started ringing. Each time, I thought it might be Hocus, but the callers were friends of Bea Harriman. By the sixth call, her own nerves worn thin, she turned over the task of answering the phone to Cassidy, who again and again said politely that Mrs. Harriman appreciated the concern but needed to keep the phone line free.

Pete and Rachel arrived with an overnight bag— and a package for Cassidy. I was surprised to see Pete—but realized quickly why Rachel hadn't left him behind. He hadn't shaved, his eyes were bloodshot, his shoulders were drooping, his gait was tired and slow. He had the look of a man who had been holding long, unpleasant conversations with himself.

"Pete Baird," Cassidy said from behind me. "Dang, I'm glad to see you. I really could use your help."

"Sure, Cassidy," Pete said, straightening. "Anything you need."

Cassidy clapped a hand on Pete's shoulder and walked him back to his makeshift office.

Rachel stared after them. "Amazing."

"What?"

"It took Tom Cassidy less than two seconds to figure out exactly what Pete needed."

"What was that?"

"Something to do."

I suddenly realized that if Hocus hadn't decided I could find their enemy, I would have been in the same position Pete had been in over the last several hours. Waiting. Only waiting.

Bea began to lobby Rachel to stay overnight. "I've got three extra bedrooms here," she said. "Two are spoken for, so you might as well grab the last one."

Before long, Bea was feeding them at the kitchen table, convincing Cassidy and Greg to join them for dessert. I eased out of the gathering and went back to the bedroom Bea had set aside for me. The room held good memories for me; Frank had proposed to me there. I set the alarm for ten-thirty P.M. and went to sleep.

I awoke just before the alarm went off, no recollection of a dream, but my face damp with tears.

"Don't start this shit," I said to myself, blew my nose, and tried to pull myself together.

There was a soft knock at the door, and when I opened it Cassidy stood leaning against the jamb. He studied my face just a little too long to carry off his pretense of not noticing the tears. "Got a minute?" he said. "I'd like to talk to you."

I nodded.

"Let's go out back," he suggested.

We walked through a side door to the backyard, avoiding the crowd in Bea's house. Cassidy told me that my sister-in-law had returned; Mike had stayed home with the kids.

I heard motors running and saw that the front yard was bathed in light.

"Local TV news," Cassidy said. "Hoping to get a reaction from the family. I think they're going to have to be satisfied with a shot of the outside of the house. Ol' Bea is pretty tough."

"Yes, she's had to be."

He waited, and when I didn't say more, he kept walking. We sat down on a couple of chairs on the back porch.

He stretched out his legs and sighed. "So how are we gonna work this out, Irene Kelly?"

"Work what out?"

"You seem to be feeling a little fenced in," he said.

"More than a little. But I understand. You've got your job to do, I've got mine."

"As a reporter?"

"No. As Frank's wife."

He tapped the tips of his fingers together, then said, "The conversation with Mrs. Szal was recorded, you know."

"Don't you think she should have been made aware of that?"

"Probably," he agreed. "Why don't you tell her that you knew we were legally recording calls on this line, but you failed to tell her?"

The truth was, I had thought only in terms of incoming calls, although I should have known better.

"Well, now you know why I had a 'hankerin' for a NeHi," I said.

He smiled. "You wake up cranky, don't you?"

"You haven't even seen the free preview for cranky yet," I said.

"A chill just went down my spine," he drawled lazily. "Look, how about letting Pete go out there with you? He doesn't have to go inside the house. Just let him go along. That way, I don't get shot at dawn for letting you wander all over Bakersfield on your own."

"I'm supposed to be in mortal danger from someone who teaches people how to stop stuttering?" I asked.

"Someone who has been in communication with Ryan and Neukirk. Who speaks of them as her 'favorites.' "

I sighed. "What's the alternative? A patrol car tailing me?"

"Yep."

"You're a devious son of a bitch, Cassidy. You know I won't refuse Pete a chance to feel useful. And you know I won't try to give him the slip, because you know I won't want him to . . . well, right now, he doesn't need to feel like he's failed at anything."

The smile built up to a full-fledged shit-eating grin.

An hour later Rachel, who had come along for the ride, was laughing and congratulating Pete, who was gleefully ditching the last of the handful of reporters who had tried to follow us away from Bea's house.

I was wondering what it would take for me to do the same to Cassidy.

21

THE SZAL HOUSE WAS OFF a small rural road, near a vineyard east of the city. It was a modest stucco home on a large lot. Pete pulled into the gravel driveway, took a look at the darkened house, and said, "Looks like they've turned in for the night."

"No, they're night owls," I said. "They told me they might be in the backyard."

"Cassidy said to let you go alone," Pete said, "but I don't know. . . ."

"She'll be fine," Rachel said.

"This may take a while," I said, not for the first time.

"We'll find something to do. Don't get worried if the windows are steamed up," Pete said.

Rachel laughed.

"I'll pound on the hood before I open the car door," I said. I got out and walked to the front of the house. No one answered the doorbell. I walked to the back gate. Peering over it, I couldn't see anyone, but softly glowing solar yard lights lit a path between the house and fence. "Hello?" I called.

There was no answer, but the gate was unlatched, so I opened it.

I followed the path, and when I reached the back of the house, I saw a softly glowing pink globe across the yard—a Chinese lantern hanging from a wooden post near a tall, rectangular building. The lantern light did little to illuminate the yard. I could not see the building very well, nor much of what lay between me and it. But the building was the tallest structure nearby—easily two stories tall. This, then, must be the tower Regina Szal spoke of.

I stood still, trying to let my eyes adjust to the darkness. The lantern bobbed gently in the warm breeze. The same breeze carried soft laughter from that direction. Wishing for a flashlight, I walked with uncertain steps along a paved path toward the sound.

As I went farther into the yard and my eyes became more accustomed to the darkness, I saw that the building was an odd wooden structure, about the width of a two-car garage and a little longer. Its roof was pitched like a house's roof but seemed to cover only half the building. The other half was open and I could hear the murmur of voices through it, a woman's laugh. There were no windows on the first floor, but the path led to a door. I reached it and knocked.

The conversation above me stopped. "Ms. Kelly?" I heard a woman call from above.

"Yes," I shouted.

"Oh, darn! We missed the news! I'll be right down,

Irene," she said. "Bernard, hit the switch so she doesn't trip and fall."

I heard the clumping sound of someone hurrying down wooden stairs, her voice calling up, "Well, I don't want her to think she's come across vampires out here."

A light came on at a high window, then at the porch where I stood. I blinked in its sudden brightness. The door was thrown open by a woman wearing a plain white cotton shirt, straight-legged Wranglers, and dusty cowboy boots. She had straight strawberry blond hair cut bluntly just above her shoulders, and long, lean legs. She had eyes the color of brown sugar and a warm smile that carried just a hint of mischief in it. She extended a hand. "Hi, I'm Regina."

"Irene," I said, taking it. She had a firm handshake.

"Welcome to the Szal Observatory," she said, grinning more broadly when a man's voice complained, "Regina. . . ." She glanced up and said, "Come on in, I'll show you around."

I entered a plain room with a concrete floor. There was a large concrete pillar at one end of the room; near us, the wooden stairway. On either side of us were other rooms. "That was going to be the darkroom," she said, pointing to the room on the left. "But it's just storage now. Bernard wants to get a CCD system." Seeing my puzzled look, she said, "He could tell you more, but basically, it's a way of using computers for astrophotography." She pointed to the pillar. "The telescope rests on that, to keep it level and still." She turned and pointed to a small, darkened office area, "That's where the computers are. Come on upstairs. I'll let you catch a glimpse of my husband before he makes us turn all the lights out again."

She hit switches as we passed a landing, darkening the space below.

Waiting patiently above us was a big man holding a ginger-colored cat. The man had an athletic build, one that suggested he didn't have a desk job. He was wearing loose trousers and a T-shirt that was stretched tight across big shoulders. The shirt had Chinese characters on it.

He wore a close-cropped beard and had tied his straight black hair into a ponytail. He stood on an elevated platform in the open-roof area, next to a large white telescope.

"This is Bernard," Regina said, introducing her husband. He had gorgeous green eyes and a face that was otherwise made up of imperfect features—a slightly crooked smile, a nose that had been broken at least once in its lifetime, a small scar just below one cheekbone—features that nevertheless made an appealing combination. I decided it was the smile—he didn't look as though he had to work hard to find it. I smiled back and shook his hand. I glanced down and was amused to see he was barefoot.

"Glad to meet you," he said. The cat wriggled loose and headed downstairs. "That was Stanley," Regina said. "Stan for short. We used to have another one named Livingstone. Poor Stan outlived his partner in exploration."

"Sorry we lost track of the time and missed the news," Bernard said. "We've got great viewing tonight—better than anything you could see on TV, anyway." He snapped out the lights. "Give your eyes a few minutes to become dark adjusted."

I let my gaze travel upward and saw a sugar-brushed sky. A city dweller, I had become estranged from this bright and shimmering canopy.

"Have a seat, Irene," Regina said, turning on a flashlight that gave off a red light. She guided me to a chair along a window-lined wall. Sitting in it, I could see for miles in several directions. The warm night air felt good. I looked back at the half roof.

"It's a sliding roof," she said. "It's sort of a large, rolling skylight. We pull it closed when we aren't up here."

"You picked a good night," Bernard said, keying some numbers into a handheld device that was about the size of a calculator. The telescope moved. He looked through the eyepiece. "Air is nice and dry, so the city lights aren't reflected up very far from the horizon."

"She didn't come out here to see M objects," Regina said, laughing. She opened an ice chest, reached in, and pulled out a Budweiser. She twisted off the top and handed it to me before I could decide if I wanted it. "One for you, Bernard?" she offered.

"Sure."

"What's an 'M object'?" I asked.

"Messier object," Bernard answered without looking away from the telescope. "Messier was a French astronomer. He started making a list of unusual blurry objects he saw through his telescope—this was back near the time of the American Revolution. Eventually, he compiled an astronomical catalog of over a hundred objects. He really was a great observer—his list is still used. M one, for example, is the Crab Nebula. M thirty-one is the Andromeda galaxy. Some of the most exquisite objects in the sky are Messier objects."

Regina was looking at him as if he had recited love sonnets. "Bernard built this telescope," she said proudly.

"Assembled," he said, taking the beer she offered. He smiled at her and said, "Builders make the parts—including the lenses." He bent to the eyepiece again. "This is a Maksutov-Cassegrain telescope," he said. "It's a reflector. Not as much resolution as a refractor, but better for deep sky objects."

Deep sky. Maybe Regina was hearing poetry after all.

He beckoned to me. "Take a look, Irene."

My eyes now adjusted to the darkness, I moved back to the telescope and bent to look through the L-shaped portion of the eyepiece. I saw what appeared to be a bright mound of light, concentrated at the center, blurring at the edges. Other, single round objects—stars—were nearby.

"What is it?" I asked.

"A spiral galaxy in the constellation Virgo. It's called the Sombrero galaxy."

I smiled, now seeing its resemblance to a hat.

"Didn't expect to come out here and get a science lesson, did you?" Regina asked.

"No," I said, straightening, "but I appreciate it all the same. Thanks, Bernard."

"You're welcome," he said, already back to watching the sky.

I moved back to my chair, picked at the label on the beer. How to begin?

Regina began it for me. "How are Bret and Sam these days?"

"I'm not exactly sure how to answer that question," I said. "Why don't you tell me about them—back when you first met them?"

She tilted her head to one side as she studied me, then shrugged, as if deciding I could have things my way.

"Do you know how they came to be my clients?"

"I know what happened to their fathers, yes. And I've read the article in the *Californian*."

"The one about elective mutism?"

"Yes."

"So you know that I tried to get them to talk again, with the help of a team of people that were concerned about them. A school psychologist, a doctor, the boys' teachers, their mothers, and so on."

"When did they begin speaking again?"

"Not for a long time."

"How long?"

"Three years."

"Three years?" I repeated.

"The boys were—are—very bright. We tested their IQs. Sam's scores were much higher than average—he's definitely gifted. Bret scored even higher, very gifted. I rarely see scores as high as Bret's. Kids who are as bright as Sam and Bret can be a handful. Given the severe emotional trauma they had experienced, their intelligence, their closeness as friends, it's not too hard to see how they could sustain elective mutism over that period of time."

"So how did they communicate?"

"With others?" she asked.

"Yes."

"Pointing, signs. . . ."

"Formal signing? Like ASL?"

"No, these were very crude by comparison to American Sign Language, which really is a complex language of its own, with its own idioms and so forth. I'm not speaking of signs or language in that sense. But the boys had a secret code, we'll say. Signs and a spoken secret code they used with one another—words they made up and understood perfectly."

"Something like pig Latin?"

"Beyond that. Not just rhyming or mixing syllables. Out-and-out new words."

"Didn't other people grow frustrated with this?"

"Oh, they drove everyone nuts at first. Eva Ryan had no patience at all with it, and neither did Sam's stepfather."

"Stepfather?"

"Yes, didn't you know? She remarried not long after Gene Ryan's death. Another doctor. Gene left her with a pile of debts, so I guess she was lucky to land on her feet."

"Was the stepfather . . . cruel to Sam?" I asked.

"Not at all. Sam basically left the family, joined the Neukirks."

"I don't understand."

"You might say the boys decided it. They didn't want to be separated. No one could blame them, especially in the beginning—the boys were so withdrawn and terrified in those early months. The mothers were friends, and had been widowed at the same time, so they stayed close at first."

"What do you mean, at first?"

"Well, I think friction started arriving with the reversal of their circumstances."

"The mothers' circumstances?"

"Yes. Everyone always talked about what a great guy Gene Ryan was. His best friend in grade school was a poor kid. Gene's family wasn't the richest one in town, but they were upper middle class. Compared to Julian's folks—who had moved here during the Dust Bowl migrations—the Ryans lived like kings. Gene was an only child, and he sort of adopted Julian as a brother."

"But Gene went on to college, right?"

"Yes. Gene's family could afford it, Julian's couldn't. So everyone talked about how kind Gene was, because even when he came back here to set up his practice, he was hanging out with his old buddy Julian."

"Julian was a trucker?"

"He started out as a driver. To tell you the truth, I think he was the smarter of the two of them. He was making more money than Gene when he died."

"As a truck driver?"

"He owned his own trucking company by then—and was managing it very well. He didn't spend the way Gene did. He had a different attitude toward money."

"So when the men died, Eva found herself poor—"

"And Francine found herself rich. Julian had a huge life insurance policy, all sorts of investments, and she got the trucking company to boot. She ran it for a few years, then cashed out and moved to Las Piernas."

I sat up straighter. "Las Piernas? Why?"

"The boys wanted to go to school there. They were pretty young—too young to live in a dorm, as far as Francine was concerned, and I think she was right. Bret graduated from high school when he was fifteen. Sam was sixteen. I'm not sure why the boys picked Las Piernas, except that Sam was accepted by the community college and Bret by the university there."

"The boys," I repeated. "Let's go back to that—you said Sam left his family?"

"Yes. Francine—Bret's mother—was the more nurturing of the two women. Sam started staying overnight at Bret's house. Soon he was living there. Later, Eva was so embarrassed by the revelations about Gene, and so involved in her courtship with her second husband, I think she was happy not to have Sam around. And Francine loved Sam."

"But was it good for them to be together so often?"

"I was against it, but Eva and Francine were the ruling parties in that case. They kept saying that the boys had already suffered enough loss and separation. A speech therapist can only exert so much pressure. And the boys proved quite obstinate. Neither one of them would give you any cooperation if they were alone."

"Did they ever talk to you about what happened to their fathers?"

She shook her head. "No, that was taboo. Even when we got them to talk again, they made it very clear they wouldn't discuss it. Bret once told me that their fathers' murders had made them freaks—that even if they hadn't been mute, the other kids would have looked at them differently. And Sam—until those articles about his father came out, I thought we were making progress. If not for Bret's loyalty to him, I don't know what would have happened to him."

"So Bret was the leader of the two?"

"No, actually, I think Sam was. They had a remarkable lack of discord between them, though, and I wouldn't say that Sam bullied Bret. Bret can assert himself. They each had different skills, and they weren't jealous of one another."

"How did you get them to start talking again?"

"Well, it didn't just happen all at once. At first, we were just trying to get them not to be so frightened of the world around them. They were so scared. Francine told me that except for their secret language, the only time she heard their voices was when they were having nightmares. They didn't have as much trouble with women as with men. Bernard stopped by the office one day to take me to lunch, and the boys ran and hid. Bernard felt so bad. Fortunately, the only man they ever allowed near them came by just then, and he was able to coax them out. He even got them to shake Bernard's hand—you don't know what a breakthrough that was. But this man was very patient. He was a police officer—the one who found them in the basement."

I was glad for the darkness. I leaned back into the shadows. "The boys liked him?"

"Oh, yes. His name was Frank Harriman. He came by fairly often at first, until the news about Gene. He busted the guy who gave the police the information on Gene's gambling problems. Sam—he was pretty upset. He started leaving the room when Frank came over. Bret must have reasoned with him, though, because that passed. Pretty soon Frank was helping him with homework again, playing catch and. . . ." She frowned. "But I don't know. For some reason, it seems to me that Frank saw less of them after that."

"You've got it all mixed up, Regina," Bernard said, coming over to us. "It wasn't the news about Gene that caused the problems, it was that witch he almost married."

"That's right! I must have blocked her from my mind."

"I don't know how you could have." He turned to me. "This woman called me at work, said the reason Frank came by to see the boys was to hit on Regina. I told her she was full of crap. I guess she didn't know I had met Frank. The guy is working with Regina, spending time outside of work trying to get these kids to talk—I mean, I had seen how the kids responded to him. But this woman must have had him by the short hairs, because he stopped coming by not long after that."

"I had forgotten about her," Regina said. "Bernard's right. It was just after Bret's tenth birthday. Frank bought Bret a magic kit, and I thought, This is going to be it. Bret loved it. He was such a smart little boy. He didn't have to talk to perform the tricks, but the other kids started to admire him. He came out of his shell."

"He started talking because of that?"

"No. Sam wasn't coming out of his shell yet, and Bret wouldn't leave him behind."

"That's when I came into the picture," Bernard said. "Regina brought them over to my studio."

"You're an artist?" I asked.

"He's a martial artist," Regina said, smiling. "He teaches aikido."

"Sam and Bret became experts in aikido?"

"No, Bret never tried it," Bernard said, "he just watched. And Sam didn't stay with it, but he made a start, and it improved his self-confidence."

"And his trust extended to Bernard," Regina said. "That was a giant step forward. A lot of what we tried to do all along was build their trust, to help them feel safe."

Not an easy task, I thought, given their experiences.

"The next thing we tried was a computer," she continued. "A friend of mine had an Apple II+. She let the boys play on it. They absolutely loved it. They did their first 'talking' by writing things on the computer."

"They weren't writing before then?"

"No, they were writing in school—school assignments. Well . . . unless the teacher assigned anything personal, I should say. But if it was a history lesson, or an essay on another country—whenever they didn't have to tell about themselves or their families—they completed it. Got A's, usually."

"What about answering questions in class?"

"The teachers soon learned that they just wouldn't do it. In fact, the other kids started to sort of band around the boys, to protect them from adults. They'd learn the boys' sign language, speak for them. We had to sit them all down and ask them to stop making it easier for the boys to be silent."

"The boys were well behaved otherwise?"

"Yes," Regina said. "Sam got in trouble once or twice defending Bret from bullies. But that went on before their fathers were murdered. They were both good students, earning A's, studying quietly. Teachers didn't find it hard to cope with that."

"Were they in the same classroom? I thought Sam was older."

"Yes, he is, but Bret skipped a grade. When he started talking again, he did even better. They both finished high school early."

"So they started communicating with a computer, you said."

"Yes. On the first day they used that old Apple, Bret wrote a note to me: 'Can we do this again?' It was the first time he had communicated directly with me in English. I was thrilled. So I typed a message back to him. I asked if Sam wanted to come back, too. I expected Bret to answer for him, but he looked at Sam and motioned to him to come over to the keyboard. Sam typed, 'Yes, I like it.' It was all I could do not to start crying."

"How long before they started speaking?"

"Not too long after that. About three months later, as I recall. Francine bought them computers. They each said, 'Thank you.' Aloud. She *did* start crying. Not that I blamed her."

"And they just started talking after that?"

"No. It was still very gradual from there. Sam talked to Bernard before he talked to me."

I looked at Bernard, who had taken a chair nearby.

"He asked me to teach him to dance," Bernard said. "Regina wouldn't believe me at first."

"Oh, only because you tease me about so many other things!"

He smiled. "Once I convinced her that it was the truth, she was mad that he hadn't talked to her first."

"You are such a liar," she said. "I was thrilled. Besides, Bret walked into my office the next day and said, 'Sam has a girlfriend.' "

Bernard laughed. "She's not telling the whole truth. What Bret said was, 'Sam has a girlfriend, but she's not as pretty as you are.' "

It was too dark to actually see the blush on her face, but I could hear the embarrassment in her voice when she said, "Don't you have a comet to discover or something?"

"He had a crush on you?" I asked.

"Not really. Bret was just feeling a little lonely, I think. Sam wanted to start talking to other people—the girl he wanted to dance with. Bret was a little younger, a little more reluctant to step out of this cocoon they had built around themselves. Once he saw that Sam wasn't just going to abandon him, though, I think he was all right."

"You still saw them after they started speaking?"

"For a time, yes. And we stayed in touch."

"Did they ever talk to you about what happened when their fathers died?"

"No," she said, then frowned. "Well, one day Bret stopped by, just before they moved. He was upset, shaky. I asked him what was wrong. He told me that while they were packing things for the move, Sam had cut his hand, started bleeding. Bret had passed out. He said Sam was fine—Francine took him to an emergency room and got him stitched up. Bret turned so white telling me about it, I was worried he was going to faint again. He kept saying it made him think of the basement. I didn't need to ask which one. He calmed down, but just before he left he said,

'I haven't forgotten anything about that day. Not one single thing.' I asked him if he wanted to talk about it, and he said, 'You should be grateful we never did.' "

We sat in silence for a moment, then I asked, "Did they resent Frank Harriman for not visiting?"

"I don't think so. He didn't just cut them off, he just gradually stopped seeing them. They seemed pretty understanding about it. And they were spending more time with Bernard by then."

I looked up into the sky, tried to quiet my sense of despair. The Szals were good-hearted people, an active, intelligent couple with wide-ranging interests—people I would have liked to form a friendship with under other circumstances. But that night I felt as though I had wasted my time talking to them. For all I had learned about Sam and Bret, I could see nothing in it that would help me gain Frank's freedom.

"What's your connection to Bret and Sam?" Regina asked.

"Frank Harriman is my husband," I began.

They both exclaimed happily over this but quickly noticed I was having a hard time responding appropriately.

"How is Frank?" Bernard asked cautiously.

At another time I might have faked an answer. I couldn't. "Not well," I said. "He's a hostage."

At their looks of utter astonishment, I realized that anything else I might say would destroy their memories of two young boys they had helped. I set my untasted beer on the deck and said, "I should leave."

"No," Bernard said. "You can't just say something like that and leave! Please tell us—Frank's our friend.

We haven't seen much of him since he moved to Las Piernas, but my God—a hostage?"

"Sam and Bret's hostage."

Regina sat stunned in wide-eyed disbelief, but Bernard moved over to my side, caught my attention by taking my hand. "Tell us what happened," he said. "Maybe we can help."

"Yes," Regina said, recovering quickly. When I hesitated she added with unerring insight, "I care very much about Sam and Bret, but I'm not blind to the fact that they were troubled. I won't protect them at Frank's expense. Bernard's right. Frank's our friend—a good man. Let us help. Please."

So I began to talk, and they did all they could to make the telling easier. There was no point, I realized, in hiding anything from them. If they knew how to help, they would need to know about the policeman.

Regina sat silently. When I was finished she said, "It makes me so angry that they are using all of us like pawns!"

"Yes," I said, "I'm angry about that, too."

"Tell Detective Cassidy what I've told you," she said. "And tell him to call us if he wants to talk to us about the boys. If he ends up negotiating with them, maybe it will be of use."

"Do you know how to get in touch with Francine?"

"Francine died a year ago," Regina said.

"Unless something drastically changed her financial circumstances," Bernard said, "Bret has come into a lot of money. Maybe Sam, too, depending on her will. That's what's financing them—the Neukirk fortune."

"Sam will know medicine, and he's probably the

one who recruited the fellows who knew about the explosives," Regina said. "He was much more interested in that sort of thing than Bret. Bret could never stand any sort of violence—which is why it's hard to understand how Sam might have convinced him to go along with this."

"You think Sam came up with the idea?" I asked.

"Certain portions of it would be Sam's way of doing things—the blood vial—Bret wouldn't go near blood if he could help it," Regina said.

"Sam's always been the more dominant of the two," Bernard said.

"Yes, but Bret's not without a will of his own," Regina said. "And the computer security breaches—that's Bret. He did an internship at a company that supplied computer security systems."

"Any idea who the woman might be?"

"Sam's girlfriend," Bernard said without hesitation. "Bret is more of a loner."

"That's true," Regina said. "Sam can be very charming when he wants to be. Bret's charm is more genuine, more a part of who he is. Sam can turn it on and off."

"The last time we saw Bret," Bernard said, "he complained about Sam's attitude toward women. Said Sam didn't really care about the women he dated, that he just wanted sex."

"Do you think Bret was jealous of them?" I asked.

"No," Bernard said. "I don't think he has a romantic attachment to Sam. He talks about Sam the way one brother talks about another. And they knew we would have accepted them, gay or straight. That's not an issue with us."

"Any idea who Sam was dating lately?"

They considered, then Bernard said, "Didn't he send us a picture from a ski trip?"

"Yes!" Regina said. "Wait here!"

She went downstairs, and I heard her go into the office below.

"Sam wrote to us around Thanksgiving," Bernard said. "He had gone skiing with some friends. Regina kept the photo."

"How often do you hear from them?"

"Not too often. Once or twice a year they'll send us a card or a letter. Last time we saw them in person was about four years ago."

She ran back up the stairs, trailed by Stan the cat, who apparently enjoyed the activity—he continued to run around the loft. Regina handed me a 4 x 6 photograph.

"Turn the lights on," she said.

Bernard complied, and I found myself staring at a group shot of four young skiers.

"I don't know who the others are, but that's Sam," Regina said, pointing to a young man in a blue ski cap. He looked more relaxed in this shot than he did in the driver's license photo that was shown on the eleven o'clock news, but he was easily recognizable as the same person. There was a dark-haired woman standing next to him. I didn't recognize her, but I knew the faces of the other two men in the photo.

"Lang and Colson," I said.

22

IT WAS AFTER TWO IN THE MORNING when we
pulled into Bea's driveway. The reporters were
gone, although once the story broke in the
Californian, I expected them to be back before I left to
have breakfast with Cecilia. I wasn't too surprised to
see Cassidy sitting on the front porch swing.

He was reading through some papers, apparently
the latest faxes from Hank Freeman. Pete and Rachel
murmured, "Good night," and went inside. I sat on
the swing and handed the photo to Cassidy.

"I think Lang's and Colson's neighbors might recognize her," I said. "The Szals think she might be
Sam's girlfriend."

Cassidy studied the photo. "She fits the description
the neighbors gave us all right. This is terrific. What
else did you learn?"

"What an M number is," I answered, ignoring his
puzzled look as I went on to tell him what the Szals

had said about Sam and Bret. Not long after I started, Cassidy took out his notebook and began making notes—lots of them.

"This is great," he said, far too enthusiastic for the hour. "This is the kind of information we can only get from people who know them. We can predict Bret and Sam a little better because of it—especially the info about how they work with each other. And this photo—these folks you talked to have done us a world of good." Then he sobered and added, "I suppose it wasn't too easy on them."

"No," I said "But it seems to be in their natures to be helpful. And they care about Frank. Fortunately for us, that prevailed over their loyalty to Bret and Sam."

"Yes. I'm going to take them up on their offer for a talk." He stood up and stretched. "Well, I better get this off to Hank while it's fresh in my mind."

"Don't you sleep?"

"Had a short nap while you were working. I'll be fine. You look like you're all tuckered out, though."

"I am," I said. "I just don't know if I can sleep."

"Give it a try," he said, and we walked in. I said good night as he went into his room, which was across the hall from mine.

I fell asleep almost as soon as I lay down but awakened at four-thirty. I could hear Cassidy talking, and although I couldn't make out what he was saying, there was an urgency in his voice that was unmistakable. I put on a pair of jeans and a T-shirt and was reaching for my socks when I heard him fall silent. I listened and decided to forgo footwear when I heard him stumbling down the hallway at a hurried pace. I opened the bedroom door but could not see him. I heard the front door open and rushed to follow. By the time I reached him, he was standing on the front porch, gripping the railing, taking deep breaths.

"Cassidy?"

He whirled to face me, his eyes wild and unseeing, his face covered with sweat. My own eyes widened— Cassidy, frantic? What god-awful news had he received?

In the next moment, though, I understood what was happening. "Wake up, Cassidy," I said quietly but firmly. "Wake up."

He looked at me, and I could see the change in his eyes when he focused on me as something more than a voice invading a dream. Those eyes were quickly lowered in shame.

"God damn," he said with feeling.

"Somebody once told me that you shouldn't be embarrassed about having nightmares," I said.

"That guy is more full of horseshit than a rodeo wheelbarrow," Cassidy said, still not looking at me, sounding none too steady. "Everybody knows that."

"Yeah, but they like him anyway. Let's sit on the swing until you get your land legs back."

He went along with the suggestion, maybe because he wasn't in any shape to move much farther. It takes a lot of energy to have a really horrific nightmare. They wear you out.

I set the swing in motion, and we rocked back and forth in it for a time.

"I don't want to talk about it," he finally said, still not making eye contact.

"Who asked you to? You think I give a crap about your problems?"

He looked at me then and abruptly started laughing. Doubling over, wheezing laughter. He did his best not to wake the household, but it looked like the effort was going to give him a hernia.

"What?" I asked, too punchy from sleeplessness to keep myself from laughing in response.

Tears were rolling down his face. "Your hair," he choked out.

I looked over the back of the swing into a picture window, where I saw my admittedly ridiculous reflection. I had slept on my hair funny, and now, on each side of my face, it spiked out in fantastic angles from my head. I looked like I had hired my hairdresser after a layoff at the circus.

"Glad you like it," I said, trying to smooth it down. Hopeless. As hopeless as not laughing about it myself.

Eventually we wound down from it. I felt suddenly ashamed.

"You think Frank would resent you for laughing?" he asked, his accuracy annoying the hell out of me once again.

"You're full of horseshit, remember?"

"Yeah," he said, starting the swing in motion again.

After a moment he said, "I have this dream sometimes—about an old, old case. An early-morning bank robbery. There were three employees inside, but two got out while this one woman distracted the robbers, told them she was the only one there. They kept her hostage. In real life, they shot and killed her in the bank. In the dream, she's alive again. Instead of shooting her, they've taken her with them to a hiding place. I've got another chance to find her, and I'm out looking for her. Sometimes, that's all there is to it—I just search in vain. Wake up frustrated. Other times, like tonight, I find the hiding place, but no matter what I say, they shoot her."

We sat in the swing for what seemed like a long time.

"Thanks," he said at last.

"You'd do the same for one of your friends, right?"

He looked at me and smiled. "Sure would."

A little later he said, "If we're friends, then—"

"Uh-oh," I said. "Here it comes."

"If we're friends," he repeated, "why don't you tell me what you have planned for the day?"

"Why should I?"

"Why not?"

I thought about it for a moment. "I guess I've never been too hot on getting permission. I like to be able to work independently."

"So you're feeling hemmed in."

"But you can see what my concerns are? Not just for your safety, but for Frank's?"

"Yes," I admitted. "And I understand—it's a police investigation."

"Well, as far as that goes, if a case requires me to get someone outside of the department to work with me, I don't get too fussy about it if they don't have a badge. I've got bigger problems to solve. But I also have to keep a handle on things, so I can't just let everyone who wants to help go haring off in any old direction they please."

"I have a feeling you have a compromise in mind."

He smiled. "You do, huh? Well, you're right. How about this—you go on and tell me what your plans are. You tell me what you're going to do today, and unless I've got a reasonable objection, you do it. But you talk to me before you talk to anybody—I mean *anybody*. That includes friends, family, editors, Pete, Rachel, reporters—you name it."

"And your part of this bargain?"

"I don't have you tailed or hound you or force you to stay around here just so I know where you are—all of which I can easily do, you understand. But I prefer it this way. I trust you. You trust me. That's it. You don't waste your time trying to sneak around, I don't waste mine keeping a leash on you."

I thought about it. "All right," I said. "I'm meeting Cecilia Parker at seven. Then I'm going to the library."

He raised a skeptical eyebrow.

"Yes, the library, Cassidy. Not as direct as going to the Bakersfield PD, but it won't set off as many alarm bells if our man has friends in the department."

"You don't believe they'll protect someone like this, do you?"

"No, I don't believe the department is crooked, if that's what you're asking. But if word gets around that you're asking for personnel files, don't you think we'll give this guy a head start?"

"I haven't asked for any yet."

"Why not?"

He sighed. "For the reasons you just mentioned."

"I'm thinking of asking Bea to invite Brian's old friends over for dinner. They're the right age group. Maybe we can pick up a few leads from them. I'll tell Bea that we need to talk to people who were around at the time, who know about the case."

"Sounds good, but I don't understand what you're going to be doing at the library."

"On a Sunday, it's probably the fastest way to get a look at photographs of the Bakersfield PD."

"Photographs of officers in the library?"

"City annuals. They'll have them in the historical collection at the Beale Library on Truxtun. At the very least, they'll include a group photograph of the department. And while I'm doing that, there is something you can do for me that might not raise much suspicion."

"What's that?"

"Get Powell's arrest records."

Cassidy smiled. "The records are in storage, but Bakersfield PD has promised me they'll have them for me this morning. Along with everything they can find about the Ryan-Neukirk case."

"Sorry. Of course you would have thought of that already."

"No, don't apologize," he said. "I'm spread pretty thin here, so I might miss something along the way. Keep making suggestions."

"I don't know about you," I said, "but right now my best suggestion is to try to catch a little more sleep."

"Sounds good," he said, and we walked into the house. Just as I turned to go into my room he whispered, "Irene?"

I looked back at him. "Yes?"

"Careful you don't muss your do."

I flipped him the bird and shut the door. I could hear him laughing as he shut his.

●　　●　　●

I woke up in a good mood, in spite of little sleep and big worries. Maybe it was that I had tamed my hair or that I had Cassidy's assistance in escaping the encampment in front of Bea's house. Cecilia Parker, who now sat across from me in a booth at the Hill House Hotel Cafe, did not seem nearly so chipper.

She wore jeans and a yellow T-shirt. Not everyone can wear yellow without looking as though they've got liver problems. She looked good in it, I was disappointed to note. She kept her dark sunglasses on until the waitress innocently asked her if we'd like to be seated where the light wasn't so bright.

Cecilia refused to order more than a cup of coffee. I ordered coffee and a breakfast roll and hoped she was hungry.

"So what's all this about?" she said, apparently not in the mood for small talk.

I had a copy of the "Father's Day" fax in my purse, and the easiest thing to do would have been to give it to her to read, but I didn't know if I could trust her.

"You watched the news?" I asked.

She nodded.

"Have you read the *Californian* this morning?"

"Yes. Is this a media quiz?"

I ignored that. "So you know that Frank was taken by—"

"The boys he rescued. Some thanks, huh?"

"You remember them?" I asked.

"Yes, of course. They gave me the creeps back then."

"Why?"

"Don't misunderstand me. I felt sorry for them, just like everybody else. But even if they had a reason to be messed up, they were still messed up. You know what I mean?" She gave a dramatic shiver. "The silent treatment got to me. They could be in a room and not say a word to each other and communicate with just a look. Almost like they were psychic."

The coffee and my roll arrived. She looked at it and said, "Maybe I'll have one of those, too." The waitress shrugged and brought one. I realized how petty I had been in wanting her to covet my breakfast roll as much as she coveted my husband.

"So, you think the boys were psychic?" I asked.

"No. I don't believe in any of that crap. They must have given each other very subtle nonverbal cues, that's all."

I thought about saying something like, "I hear they had a good-looking speech therapist" but thought better of it. I needed her cooperation.

"They've only made one demand," I said.

"Free their buddies who got caught." She said it in a bored tone.

"No." I savored her surprise, then said, "They want me to find someone who was involved in their fathers' murders."

"What? They *are* completely nuts, aren't they? Everybody who had anything to do with their fathers' murders is dead."

"Everybody?"

She gave me a narrow look. "Everybody."

"Who do you mean?"

"Powell. I mean Powell."

"Just Powell?"

She hesitated only slightly before saying, "Of course just Powell!"

"But why use the word 'everybody'?"

She shrugged. "I'll go home and brush up on my grammar. Right after I get some sleep—which I didn't get last night, worrying about Frank."

I studied her for a moment, during which she studied me right back. "You really *are* worried about him, aren't you?" I said.

"Yes," she said, a little less hostile. Then, almost as if she'd caught herself backing off, added, "Maybe more than you are."

"We can come up with some contest about it later."

"Doesn't really matter now, does it?"

"Look, Cecilia, right now, I just want him to live. To do that, I've got to try to meet the kidnappers' demand."

"Well, best of luck to you."

"I need your help."

"I've told you—"

"Take me to the place where you found Powell."

"What?"

"The place where you found Powell."

"I heard you. I just don't— What makes you think I remember it?"

"Think of Frank Harriman and answer truthfully—"

"All right, all right, I remember it. Of course I remember it. First time I found a body outside a car—first one that hadn't gone through a windshield, anyway."

"Take me there."

She looked at me for what seemed like a good forty-eight hours before saying, "Oh, what the hell. But let's get going—I've got other things to do with my time."

She got up and left me to pay the bill. Well, it was my invitation, and the bill wasn't steep—but a person with manners would have waited before walking outside. As I went back to leave a tip on the table, she honked the horn of her car in impatience. Several times.

Frank, I thought, if we both survive this ordeal, I've got some tough questions for you.

She was driving a dark blue T-bird. The sunglasses were back on. She drove with the expertise of a person who lives behind the wheel. It was a warm morning, and we rolled the windows down.

We traveled the first few miles in complete silence, driving north to Highway 178 and then heading east. As we went past the Ant Hill Oil Field, I asked, "Was this your regular patrol area?"

"This highway? One seventy-eight?" she asked.

"Yes."

"It wasn't the first time I drove it."

"But it wasn't your regular assignment?"

She checked the rearview mirror, adjusted it a little, and said, "No, but I offered to take it that day."

"Why?"

She shrugged. "I had my reasons."

If we hadn't passed a big citrus grove just then, I might have started to lose my temper. Cassidy's trick worked like a charm, though, and I stayed silent, if not calm. I looked out the window and saw the Greenhorn Ranger Station, which marked this entrance to the Sequoia National Forest.

"Bakersfield CHP office patrols this highway all the way to the lake?" I asked.

"Bakersfield CHP only has the lower portion of

this highway. The upper portion is patrolled by the Kernville office. Ours goes up to where it becomes a divided highway."

"So you found him on the lower portion, where it's two-lane?"

"Yes."

Soon we came to the signs saying "Route 178 to Lake Isabella Open," "Falling Rock—Road Not Maintained at Night," and the big death toll sign. The Kern River flows with often brutal force along a rocky canyon; while there are relatively safe places to raft or stick your toes in the water, close to two hundred people had drowned in the Kern since they started the tally in 1968.

We could see and hear it now, its white rapids pounding between steep, boulder-strewn banks. The narrow road climbed in sharp curves, between the river on the left and a steep, sheer cliff to the right. We passed an old Edison plant with a corrugated tin roof and continued to climb.

Cecilia's continued silence and the barren landscape gradually unraveled any remnants of my good mood.

You're wasting your time, an inner voice accused. *You're on the wrong track. Frank could be dying while you screw around up here.*

"You don't get carsick, do you?" Cecilia asked.

It snapped me out of thoughts that were as dangerous as the rapids below us.

"If I do," I said, "it will be a first." And it will be my pleasure to barf all over your fancy upholstery.

"You don't look so good," she said nervously, as if hearing my unspoken thought. "I'll pull over if you're going to puke."

"It's not car sickness," I said.

"Pregnant?"

"No," I said, unable to conceal my irritation. "I'm not sick, I'm not pregnant, and I'm not going to puke!"

Smirking. She was smirking.

I knew damned well we were miles away from any orange blossoms. I took deep breaths anyway. If I so much as clenched my fists, she would notice, and I wasn't going to give her the pleasure of seeing that she had angered me—not a second time. I looked away from her, pretending fascination with the less scenic side of the road.

To my surprise, she didn't try to goad me. I did calm down. The road was a little wider, and there was more chaparral. We passed Live Oak Picnic Ground and Upper and Lower Richbar. There were signs warning of cattle crossings, reminding me that there were ranches in the hills to the right. We began to see trees, and the canyon grew deeper and broader.

"Look," Cecilia said, breaking the silence. She pointed out a pair of eagles circling above the river, looking for breakfast. "Nothing like this in Las Piernas," she said.

"No, there's not," I said, not wanting to quibble so soon after regaining my temper. Besides, she was right. Las Piernas had its own attractions, but no eagles or fifty miles of rapids or other Kern River wonders.

"I didn't fit in down there," she said.

When I didn't comment she added, "People seemed so phony to me down there. I guess I belong out here with roughnecks, rednecks, and the *raza*. You probably didn't like it out here."

Ignoring the implication that I was phony, I said,

"It was a big change at first, but I was looking for a change. I didn't leave Bakersfield because I disliked it. I liked the people and the place just fine."

"Why, then?"

"My father was ill. I didn't want to be away from him."

She focused her attention back on the road. "Not far from here," she said as we passed a sign for Democrat Hot Springs. The canyon was steep, the river far below. She slowed cautiously, then pulled into a turnout on the right side. She watched for traffic, then made a sharp U-turn, doubling back and pulling into another unpaved turnout, this one on the opposite side of the road.

"This is it," she said. "Right here between the Democrat Hot Springs and China Garden."

"This exact turnout? Are you certain?" I asked, my mouth suddenly dry as I looked not at the river or cliffs or trees, but at the object that held her gaze.

"Yes. It's because of that rock. Every time I drive past it, I think of Powell."

It wouldn't be difficult to remember the spot. The large, mushroom-shaped rock was quite distinctive.

One Father's Day weekend a policeman had asked Gene Ryan about that same rock, not realizing that Christopher Powell would remember that part of their conversation or that two young boys would remember it still. No, at that moment he was probably more concerned that Gene Ryan was lying to him.

Ryan hadn't lied.

I had the feeling that every time a certain Bakersfield cop drove past it, he remembered Christopher Powell, too.

23

I GOT OUT OF THE CAR and walked to the edge of the turnout. Although there was a slope beyond it, the ground was not especially steep for the first few yards. It was flat and fairly open, only a few low shrubs nearby. But beyond that first thirty feet, the earth fell away sharply. If you wandered beyond the first slope, especially in darkness, you could easily take a fast and bumpy fall. Because of trees and boulders and chaparral, your body might not reach the river—far below—but you'd travel quite a ways before the landscape slowed you down.

Off to the right, upriver some distance but in plain view, I saw a footbridge and what seemed to be trails. I could also see a campsite.

Cecilia was leaning against the T-bird, arms folded, watching me.

I turned to her and said, "Tell me what you saw that day."

"Just the van. I didn't see the body until later."

"Any sign of other cars?"

"Of course. It's a turnout."

"Goddammit, Cecilia, you know what I meant."

She smiled. "No, there were no other vehicles parked in the area. It was June. No rain. Very dry conditions. No fresh tire marks in the mud or anything like that. Nothing more stupendous than that brown van, leaking oil."

I looked up the road again.

"Doesn't make sense for him to have pulled in here, does it?" I said.

"Why not?"

"He lived in Lake Isabella. Northeast of here, up the road. First, why is he going home? He's fleeing a double homicide where he's left two living witnesses. Why head for a known address?"

"The guy was a druggie, and never famous for being brilliant—never."

"Maybe that's it. But let's say he does have a reason to go home. He's covered with blood—he wants to clean up, change clothes, grab some provisions, and take off again."

"Sure, why not?" she said impatiently.

"So what the hell is he doing on this side of the road? Why stop at a turnout on the downhill side?"

"Maybe he was headed back to Bakersfield," she said, standing up straight now, starting to pace.

I shook my head. "When you found him, he still had the bloody clothes on. He hadn't been home yet."

She threw up her hands in exasperation. "So he stopped to take a leak! Big deal!"

"Why change directions? Why not relieve himself on the other side of the road?"

"Hell, I don't know," she said, half shouting. "You had me drive all the way up here to talk about why Powell crossed the road?"

"No, I already know why."

She pulled the sunglasses off and gave me a look so fierce, I thought she might hit me. My own anger was all that kept me from cowering.

"You know, too, don't you?" I said.

"I sure as hell do not," she said, stepping closer.

"I thought it was a little strange—the woman who happened to find Powell's body is the girlfriend of the cop who discovered the Ryan-Neukirk murders. That could have been coincidence, but it bothered me."

She made a sound of derision. "You're way off base."

"Then this morning," I went on, "you tell me that you handpicked this route that day. I've got to ask myself what led you to change your routine, to do something different on that day of all days."

She was silent, still glaring at me, her fists clenched.

"I think someone made a suggestion to you," I said.

"I don't have to listen to this," she said, breaking off her stare.

"I think someone told you to come up here."

She turned on her heel, started walking toward the car.

"I think that someone was a Bakersfield cop."

She stopped. She murmured something I couldn't make out.

"What did you say?"

She turned back to me. The anger was gone; she looked shaken. "I said, 'Frank will never forgive me.' "

"Forgive you for what? Not telling me the name of that cop? Believe me, he'll thank you. His *life,* Cecilia. For God's sake, what do I have to say to convince you that Hocus follows through on its threats?"

As she had from the moment she met me, she studied me. This time with much less hostility than before. "You're a member of the family now. Is that important to you?"

"Of course—"

"You know how much Frank loved his dad?"

"Yes. Loved and admired him."

To my complete surprise, she started crying. Not with loud sobs, just with big, silent tears. She looked away from me, down toward the river.

"Cecilia? What has this got to do with—" But at that moment I understood what she was saying. "Oh, no. I don't believe that for a minute."

She wiped the heel of her hand against her eyes. "Believe it. It was Brian."

"I don't. I don't believe it."

"Well, too damn bad! It's the truth."

"It doesn't make sense," I said, my mind reeling. "Brian Harriman?"

She wiped at the tears again. I rummaged through my purse and found a packet of tissues. "Here," I said, offering them to her.

She took them, said, "Thanks," and walked away from me. Toward the river.

Frightened that she might be more despondent than I had guessed, I followed her, but she merely sat on a rock. "If one of the guys in my office sees my car—I don't want them to see me like this," she explained, crying harder now.

I sat next to her. "Cecilia, tell me the whole story."

"I got a call from Bea on Father's Day—Sunday morning. I hadn't been seeing Frank for very long."

She stopped for a moment and said, "Look, I want to get something straight with you. Bea and my mom are friends, and I think half the reason Frank and I started seeing each other was because of them. We were always—on again, off again, you know?"

"Cecilia—"

"I know Bea calls me Frank's ex-fiancée, but technically that's not really true. We were never formally engaged. When one of us wanted to get married, the other didn't. We moved down to Las Piernas to get out from under the pressure our families and friends were putting on us, see if the relationship could stand on its own. We didn't last long."

"Look, you don't have to talk to me about this."

"Yeah, I do. Frank is—Frank is—just one of the best friends I've ever had, that's all. I—I just can't talk to anyone else the way I can with Frank. Not anybody. He's never been anything but good to me. And I know that even if he's released unharmed, this is going to hurt him . . . it's going to hurt him so bad. . . ." She couldn't talk for a while.

She blew her nose and said, "Shit, I never cry."

She drew a deep breath and went on. "Father's Day. It was Father's Day. Bea called, saying that she was worried about Frank, because she had word from one of Brian's friends—I don't remember who—telling her that Frank had found these kids in the basement and all. Brian's not back from a fishing trip, and she's worried about Frank, 'cause whoever called her said he was a mess."

She paused, took another tissue out of the pack. "Well, I go down to the hospital where they've got these kids, because everybody at the scene tells me that Frank went with them to the ER. He went with them all right. He didn't leave those kids for a minute. Unless Frank was with them, they were freaked out. They were giving the doctors fits. The docs wanted to sedate them, but naturally, Bakersfield PD was trying to get some kind of description of the killer out of them before the docs knocked them out."

"You were there when they were questioning the boys?"

She shook her head. "No, I had to stay in the waiting room. I heard about it from Frank, later. But while I'm sitting there, Brian gets there, and he has to wait in the waiting room, too. We've met, but this is the first time we have a chance to talk, to get to know each other. Frank finally comes out, and apologizes to us for the wait. He's a wreck, but he's also excited, because the kids have drawn pictures of the killer. Pretty good ones, too, considering their age. Between that and a lot of gesturing and nodding by the boys, they've got something to go on.

"That night, I had dinner with the Harrimans. My own dad kicked a long time ago—I don't even remember him, but I'm supposed to look like him—my stepfather used to refer to him as my mom's 'Latin lover.' Called me her little taco."

"Your stepfather sounds like a real gem."

"Ah, nothing worse than schoolkids could dish out. And he wasn't much smarter than a schoolkid. He was the Parker—that marriage didn't last too long. So anyway, with the Harrimans that night—this is the first time I've ever been to a Father's Day dinner. It was kind of a late supper, on account of everything else that was going on.

"The Harrimans get a call just as dinner is ending, somebody wanting to talk to Brian—one of his pals from work, I think. Frank says he's going to turn in for the night, which I understood—he was just completely wrung out by then. But Brian gets off the phone and asks me to stick around. What the hell, it's Father's Day, right?"

She looked down at the river again, then back at me. "We go out on the porch, on that swing. Brian is sitting there, and I'm thinking, This is what Frank will look like in thirty years. And Brian says, 'Every rookie needs a break, and I'm going to give you one. I know who killed those men, and I'd swear to God I saw his van today.' He goes on to tell me that there's a scumbag named Chris Powell, not worth the spit it takes to say his name, and that the pictures the little boys drew remind him of this guy.

"Then he tells me that one of his friends just called to say they're looking for a brown van—and that has absolutely convinced him that the killer is Powell. He tells me he watched the van for a while, drove past it a couple of times, but he thinks Powell abandoned it. He tells me not to be a hero or anything—just to go up and see if the van is still where he saw it earlier. If it is, radio for backup—I'll make a good impression on my bosses just by finding it.

"I ask him why doesn't he just report it? He tells me that there's been a lot of bad blood between him and this guy, and it would be better if someone else called it in. Besides, it's out of Bakersfield's jurisdiction, but within CHP's. He tells me to come right up here. I mean, exactly here."

"Did he say how he knew Powell?"

"The story he gave me was that Powell was a dealer, but he was slippery. Brian couldn't figure it, because Powell didn't strike him as being very bright. He arrested him a couple of times—even got rough with him once. Brian said the guy resisted, but Powell ended up in the emergency room and Brian got in trouble over it. He told me he still kept an eye on Powell after that, but he didn't dare hassle him too openly."

We heard a car pull into the turnout and she stopped talking. We were too far down the slope to see the turnout itself. After a moment the car left.

"Probably just letting traffic pass," she said.

"Did Brian tell you Powell would be dead when you got here?"

"No. He wasn't even sure that the van would still be here. At least, that's how he talked it up to me. Brian told me to see if I could switch with the guy who was scheduled to patrol this stretch. That was the easy part. I started out at six in the morning. I tried to keep a straight face when they briefed us on the van before the watch. The truth is, I figured this guy was going to be long gone, but I wanted to make Brian happy—you know, please the boyfriend's dad.

"So I head up to the spot he mentioned, and lo and behold, here's the van. I call it in. The dispatcher starts doing handsprings, because the Ryan-Neukirk case was big news—I mean, *everybody* wanted a piece of this son of a bitch—and the CHP has found the guy's van."

"And quickly," I said. "The CHP must have looked like the most efficient law enforcement agency in Kern County."

"Yeah, the whole office was pretty proud." She said it quietly, as if she were anything but proud.

"What made you go looking for Powell himself? Weren't you afraid?"

"Hell, no. Well, maybe a little. At first, I had my weapon out, and I wasn't going to approach the van until I had backup, but gradually, I felt less worried—pretty certain that he had just left it here. But then something caught my eye—up in the sky, above the river. Vultures. Turkey vultures. This canyon is full of them in the summer. At first, I just figured they'd found some dead livestock or something. Some of them had already come on down for a closer look—I hear this nasty squawking sound coming from them. I peer over the edge of the slope, and I can see them fighting over some piece of meat. I got my binoculars out, and I could just make out what they were competing for—Powell's body. Made me sick. I couldn't reach him, though. I just had to sit and wait for help to arrive. Even the rangers had to rig up special equipment to pull him out of there—what was left of him."

"Did Brian ever talk to you about it again?"

"No. And I never told Frank how I happened to find the van. He was so wrapped up in those kids, I didn't see much of him in those first few months anyway."

"You think Brian killed Powell?"

She hesitated, then said, "No. I know it might look that way, but I don't. Did you know Brian?"

"No, I'm sorry to say. No, I didn't."

"It just wasn't something he would do. I don't think he was sorry to see Powell go. Good riddance. But Brian wouldn't kill someone in cold blood."

I reached into my purse again.

"I don't need any more tissues," she said. "I'm okay now."

I handed her the folded fax.

She took it warily and opened it.

"I haven't even shown that to Bea," I said as she began to read. "So I guess I don't have to tell you that this is absolutely confidential."

She nodded. " 'Father's Day'?" she read aloud.

"Yes. I think Bret Neukirk wrote it."

When she had finished she looked as though she might cry again after all.

"I can't believe it!"

"There's nothing to believe," I said, "except that Brian wasn't the one responsible for what happened on Father's Day. But I think he had a friend who was."

"Don't you understand? Brian fits the description of this man!"

"Physically, yes. But Brian Harriman would never be involved in drug dealing."

"He did hate dealers with a passion," she said, then frowned. "Or said he did. What if that was all for show?"

So Cecilia didn't know about Diana. If this woman—whose new phone number was on Bea's autodialer—wasn't privy to the family secret, Frank's older sister surely was well hidden. As much as I disliked the notion of helping them continue to hide her, I owed Frank my silence on the subject for now. "It wasn't for show."

"How the hell can you be so sure?" she asked. "You said you never met him."

"No, but Frank talks about him."

"Frank hero-worships him," she said.

"I don't know if I'd go that far. Look—I can't say anything that will convince you. Convince yourself. Think about Brian—you knew him for what, about ten years?"

She thought a moment. "Eight. Eight years."

"Would he have worked with Chris Powell? Would he encourage someone like Powell to take two ten-year-old boys and their fathers to a basement prison?"

"No, but . . ." She looked back at the fax, then simply said, "No."

"What are you doing tonight?"

She looked puzzled, then said, "If you want me to chauffeur you all over Kern County—"

"No, I was thinking of asking Bea to extend an invitation to a dinner party to you." I explained the situation.

"Greg Bradshaw, Nat Cook, Gus Matthews," she said. "Those were his closest friends all right. There were a few others in that age range, though, and Brian was well liked. You're smart to check at the county library."

My God. A compliment. "I could use your help tonight," I said. "I need someone who has worked around here, who knows these men better than I do, who's observant. You might be able to pick up on something that will go right past me or Cassidy."

"Okay, sure. I'll be there."

We got in the car and headed back to Bakersfield. We didn't talk much, but this time the silence was companionable. As she pulled into the parking lot of the Beale Library, she said, "Why are you so sure about Brian?"

"Are you having doubts again?"

"No, not really. But you never met him. How can you know what he would or wouldn't do?"

"I know his son," I said. "And while I've found the man can be remarkably mule-headed, I've never seen any cruelty in Frank. If Frank had been raised by a drug dealer or a murderer, he still might have somehow managed to be a decent fellow. But if he had been raised by a man who knowingly made the call that sent Frank walking into that basement? Forced his own son to be the first one on the scene?" I shook my head. "If Brian Harriman had been a father that cold-blooded, Frank wouldn't have grown up to be the man I know."

Cecilia sighed. "You're right."

I got out of the car and was almost to the sidewalk when she honked and made me jump half out of my skin.

I turned around and glared at her.

She laughed and drove off.

24

MANY OF BAKERSFIELD'S public buildings were constructed after the summer of 1952, when two severe earthquakes struck within a month of each other, changing the look of the town, making it seem younger than it is. Although the older buildings haven't all disappeared from Bakersfield, the city apparently got used to the idea of changing its look every so often, for Truxtun Avenue is a mix of architectural styles that range over a hundred years— by California standards, a respectable length of time.

On Truxtun at Q Street, next to the Kern Island Canal, the Beale Memorial Library is one of the more contemporary structures in the civic center area: a library of light and open spaces.

The local history collection for Kern County is housed in one corner of the building, enclosed in a room of its own. The materials there are noncirculating; a reference librarian is there to help, but she's also stationed near the door, not far from a sign-in sheet.

The room has slightly different hours from those of the rest of the library and had just opened for the day, so I was the first one to sign in. I entered my name and wrote only "Las Piernas" under the address heading. For "area of interest," I put "Bakersfield history" and left it at that.

The librarian gave me a smile as I walked back into the section of the stacks that housed information on the city of Bakersfield. I saw a couple of other people walk in, a middle-aged woman in a floral-print dress and an elderly man who was hunched over, walking with the help of a cane. Each browsed in other rows.

The section I was in covered a wide range of subjects, including stagecoach lines, railroads, ranching, mining, and oil. High school yearbooks and local magazines were on these shelves. Someday, I decided, I'd come back and look up Frank's senior picture. That thought led to another temptation, to look up Diana's high school photos. The lady in the floral dress turned down my aisle and seemed to be waiting for me to move along. It served to remind me that there was no time now for high school yearbooks.

The city annuals were lined up together. I discovered the one I was looking for and pulled it out. I took it to one of the round wooden tables that are lined up in front of the librarian's desk and began to look through it.

The woman patron left. But her perfume seemed to linger. After a moment I realized that I hadn't smelled any perfume in the aisle. The heavy scent was coming from the table behind me. It was the elderly gentleman; he has apparently doused himself in some sort of after-shave. I turned to look at him; he was bent over the book, his face close to the page, humming to himself as he read—no particular tune, just humming. I turned away and tried to concentrate on the task at hand.

I pulled out a pen and my notebook from my purse and opened the annual; I soon found the section I was looking for. It was two pages long. One page was devoted to the chief of police, half taken up with his portrait and half with a message from him; the latter was pretty standard rah-rah fare. On the page opposite were the ubiquitous K-9 unit photo, crime lab photo, and patrol car (with door decal in the foreground) photo. You could see similar photos in city PR publications just about everywhere; if the city had been working with a bigger budget that year, no doubt it would have included photos of a mounted police unit riding palominos in a parade and a couple of schoolkids smiling up at a public safety puppet show. They had, of course, sprung for the equally ubiquitous put-everyone-in-their-dress-blues-and-line-them-up-on-the-front-steps police department photo.

It was this last that I was most interested in.

The good news was that the photo was in color and the men were all standing with their hats off—tucked into their arms military style, but off. The bad news was that the photo was taken from too great a distance—I'd have trouble getting a very close look at any of them.

"Pardon me," a low, gravelly voice said. I turned to see the old man standing beside me, leaning on his cane. "Perhaps you could make use of this." He reached into one pocket of his too large suit coat and pulled out a large red handkerchief. He wheezed a little laugh and said, "Oh no, ho! Not that." He sniffed and reached again and this time produced a magnifier. He set it on the table next to me. "At my age, it's impossible to get by without one," he rasped, chuckling and putting away the handkerchief.

"Thank you," I said, "I'll only need it for a moment."

"As long as you like, honey. As long as you like."

He picked up his book and cane and shuffled back toward the stacks. That, I thought, was what I liked about people out here—their courtesy and friendliness.

Using the old man's magnifier, I went to work looking over the group photo. I could not resist going to Frank's photo first. Standing at the end of a row, young and smiling, but not so very different from the Frank I knew now. His posture was no longer so ramrod straight, and over the years his eyes had come to reflect more wisdom, if not cynicism. But the photo made me feel his absence more acutely, and I quickly moved to scan the other faces.

Many were familiar to me; I had met them when I worked the night shift crime beat. But the next one I studied was of a man I often wished I'd met—Brian Harriman. I stared at his image for a long time, just to make sure I wasn't trying to see something that wasn't there. When I thought of the picture on the mantel in Bea's home, I realized that I should have known what to expect. In that photo, taken when Frank graduated from the academy, Brian had a little gray in his hair. He was far from completely gray then, and now, looking at this photo, I could see that he was still a long way from it two years later. He wasn't the man Bret had described in the fax.

Some of Cecilia's doubts about Brian must have bothered me more than I had acknowledged to myself, for I felt a sudden relief that could have no other origin than dispelling those doubts.

I found Bear Bradshaw next. Unmistakably gray. The same was true of Gus Matthews and Nathan Cook. I started making a more orderly search of the photo then. There were not all that many older officers. I found two others.

The next feature to consider was height. I knew Frank was six four, his father a little shorter. I put my notebook next to Frank's photo, marked on the paper the distance from the top of Frank's head to the step where he stood. Now I had a rough scale and held it up to the photos of Bear and Cookie and Gus. Not easy to judge, but they were all nearly the same height as Frank, Bear being the shortest. The other two silver-haired cops were shorter than Bear, but were they too short to fit Bret's description? In Bret's memory the cop had been bigger than Julian—but it was the memory of a terrified child seeing his father attacked.

I wrote down the names of the two older cops, men I hadn't met when I'd worked in Bakersfield. The caption gave only initials for their first names.

M. Beecham and Q. Wilson.

I sighed and stretched. I looked for the old man but didn't see him. The room seemed empty, except for the librarian. She saw me looking around and said, "Can I help you find something?"

"Someone, maybe. The elderly gentleman who was in here a moment ago?"

"Oh, he left."

"Oh, no. He loaned this magnifier to me. He must have forgotten."

"Well, perhaps we can page him before he leaves the library. Let's look on the sign-in sheet." She reached it before I did and started laughing. "Well, I guess he didn't want us to know his name. This is a character in a short story."

I stared at the signature in disbelief.

The name on the sign-in sheet was John Oakhurst. He gave his address as Poker Flat.

"I guess he's a fan of Bret Harte," she said. " 'The Outcasts of Poker Flat.' "

"Call the police!" I said, running to the door.

"For goodness' sakes, it's not that serious," I heard her say behind me.

I stopped and turned back to her. "That man is wanted by the police. Call them!"

As I entered the open area beyond the local history collection, I heard my name paged. I looked back at the librarian, who was watching me as if my next move would help her decide whether I was a harmless lunatic or a dangerous one. No phone in her hand.

I ran to the main information desk. "Please call the police."

This librarian was studying me, but not as if I were crazy. "Are you Irene Kelly?" she asked.

"Yes!" I said, starting to run out the door without thinking about how she knew my name.

"Stop!" she called out.

I turned back.

"It's right here, with me," she said, and to my amazement she held up my purse.

"How . . . ?"

"An old man found it and turned it in. Didn't you hear me page you just now?"

"An old man . . . which way did he go?"

"Are you all right? If you'd like to check it to see if anything is missing. . . ."

"Which way did he go?" I shouted.

Her eyes widened, but she pointed toward the front doors.

"Call the police," I said again, and ran outside.

I looked for any sign of someone pulling out of the parking lot, frantically scanned the area in front of the building for any sign of him. Not a soul. I ran all the way around the building, to P Street and back. It was on the return trip that I saw something red.

It was the old man's handkerchief, tied to the canal fence. As I walked toward it, I heard a train whistle, saw a freight train on the tracks behind the library. The rumble of the train blocked out all other sound, even the water flowing swift and sure through the narrow channel below. I touched the handkerchief, saw that something was knotted within it. With shaking hands I loosened the handkerchief, then the knot that held the weighty object.

A folded piece of paper and something made of shiny metal fell out into my hand.

Frank's watch. An old-fashioned watch—his father's retirement watch—the kind you have to wind. Unable to stand, I sat on the sidewalk next to the fence. I unfolded the piece of paper.

It was a page from a desk calendar. Next Tuesday. In block letters the words "Time is running out."

The information desk librarian was outside then

and walked over to me. "Here's your purse," she said gently. "Are you all right?"

"Did you call the police?" I asked.

"Yes."

"Then I'm all right." I held the watch to my ear, listened to it tick, and wept.

25

"WHAT'S THIS?" Cassidy asked.

"A tampon holder," I answered, then snapped out of my state of numbness as if I'd been slapped. "What the hell are you doing going through my purse?"

The officer driving the police cruiser that was taking us back to Bea's house was smiling. She caught my attention and rolled her eyes in sympathy.

Cassidy set the holder between us, on the seat, and was already pulling out my wallet. But at my question he looked up and said, "Feeling any better?"

I nodded. "While you're rummaging through my belongings, see if there are any tissues in there. I've used up all the ones the librarians gave me."

Instead he reached into his shirt pocket and handed me his neatly ironed and folded handkerchief.

"I didn't think anybody carried these anymore," I managed to say as I took the soft cloth from him. "Christ, it even has your initials on it."

"Hell, yes. I want it back."

"I'll wash it first."

He laughed. "I'd appreciate that."

The first police officers had arrived almost immediately—the Bakersfield Police Department is just down the street from the library. The moment I mentioned "Ryan-Neukurk" they were on the radio.

I went back into the local history room to gather my notebook and put away the annual when Cassidy arrived; the Bakersfield officers were already searching the building and surrounding area. The local history librarian, who had been apologetic, had also done a better job than I of observing the man.

A gray wig and dark clothing, reeking of aftershave but found in a neat bundle, were retrieved from a rest room waste bin. But despite an intensive effort to find him, there was no other sign of the person who had played the part of the old man.

Cassidy convinced the local police that it would be best to let me go home with him while it was still possible to evade the reporters who were waiting outside. My fellow journalists had shouted questions, but I simply let Cassidy silently maneuver me into a waiting patrol car.

"I decided to let Officer Brewitt do the driving when we got the call," he said as he closed the car door, then got in and asked her to take the long way back to Bea's house.

•   •   •

The circuitous route had given me time to regain some of my composure, but now I realized it had also given Cassidy time to search my purse.

"Cassidy," I said more insistently now, "give that back to me."

"Just making sure there aren't any new items in here," he said. "Here, you go through the wallet. Don't just look for things that might be missing. Look for things that might be added. He took your purse for a reason."

I was noting that Hocus hadn't left me any poorer or richer when Cassidy said, "Bingo."

He handed me a little slip of paper. "I take it this wasn't already in here?"

It was a note that said "Progress report scheduled for midnight—H."

"No, no, it wasn't," I told him. "So they're calling at midnight?"

"Looks that way," Cassidy said. "Officer Brewitt, would you please be so kind as to ask your dispatcher to patch me through to Detective Ellie Sledzik?"

"Ellie?" the driver asked.

"Excuse me. Detective Eleanor C. Sledzik."

Brewitt smiled and made the call.

When Detective Sledzik came on, Cassidy merely said, "Next one at twenty-four hundred." She acknowledged the information and they signed off.

Cassidy did a little more rummaging, then handed the purse back and said, "Keep checking for me, Irene. I might have missed something still."

"Who's Eleanor Sledzik?"

"She's our liaison with Bakersfield PD. She's also been working with the phone company on the tap on your mother-in-law's phone line. Besides being damned smart and a pleasure to work with, she has a gift for getting judges to see when they ought to hurry up and act on a request for a warrant."

"I'm surprised you haven't tried to recruit her down to Las Piernas."

"She's considering it," Cassidy said, making Officer Brewitt laugh. Brewitt hadn't been around Cassidy long enough to know he wasn't kidding.

As we climbed the porch steps Cassidy said, "Boy, when old Frank is home safe and sound again, I've got to be the first one who gets to talk to him."

I looked up at him. He was grinning.

"Oh, yes," he said. "I'm dying to tell him that his wife got into trouble just going to the library."

"Maybe I won't wash that handkerchief."

Once inside the house I was fussed over by Bea and Rachel and Pete.

"If y'all will excuse us," Cassidy said, "it's important that I have a few minutes to talk to Irene."

Reluctantly they allowed me to follow him back to his temporary office. I told him what I had learned from Cecilia and at the library.

"Well," he said, "I was considering Brian Harriman myself. Powell's arrest records show that Frank's dad arrested Powell twice."

"But Brian couldn't—"

"Hold your horses, there's more to it. Both times, Powell was right back out again. First time, the substance they found on him was not illegal—at least, it wasn't by the time the lab looked at it. Second time, key witness came in and said he was coerced into making false statements. When I looked at it a little closer, either problem could have been caused by Harriman's partners."

"Which partners?"

"Different one each time—Bradshaw, then Matthews. But Cook had a connection to Powell, too. He was the first one to arrest Powell. He was assigned to Vice at the time."

"He was a detective?"

"I asked Ellie Sledzik about it. She looked up Cook's records and found out that Cook spent three years as a detective—blew something on a big case and ended up back on patrol." He paused, then added, "I asked for information on all three officers— and Brian Harriman, too."

"What?"

"I know you wanted a 'head start,' but the brass in Las Piernas told me to reconsider; they thought I should be talking to Bakersfield about this, and they were right to get on me about it. But just so you don't blame the department, I have to say I was having second thoughts anyway—I think I would have asked for Ellie Sledzik's help even if my boss hadn't pushed for it. We don't have a hell of a lot to go on, and we need more information than we can get from a dinner party."

I was silent. He waited.

"It makes sense, I suppose," I said. "We don't really have the luxury of a delay, do we?"

"No. Glad you understand. I'll have these other two names—Beecham and Wilson—checked out, too."

"So what did you learn about the original group?"

"Not much yet. It will take her—Detective Sledzik—some time to get all of the records. All three of them were respected, thought of as good cops—although Matthews was something of a maverick. All had been Brian Harriman's partner at one time or another. All had some contact with Powell. Cook was on the force the longest, then Matthews and Bradshaw."

I thought for a moment, then said, "I have a favor to ask, Cassidy. It's about Bea. I want to tell her what's going on tonight. I mean, what's really going on."

"Feeling guilty?"

"Yes, as a matter of fact. She's gone out of her way for us, put people up for the night, even agreed to invite these guys over for dinner. All at a time when her only son is missing. I don't like the idea of deceiving her. It's her home, and we're scheming to snare one of her friends under her own roof."

"She's too close to Bradshaw."

"Her son, Cassidy—her son's life is at stake. Bradshaw won't mean anything to her by comparison."

He hesitated, then shook his head. "We'll tell her as soon as we can, but not yet."

I crossed my arms and looked at the toe of my shoe. "Okay."

"Don't even think about it," he said.

"Think about what?"

"Telling her anyway."

"I said, 'Okay,' didn't I?"

"Yes, but you lied."

"How the hell can you know that?"

He laughed.

"Shit," I said. "I need more sleep. What I meant was—"

"Oh, let's not compound it with another lie."

"So answer the question."

"Neurolinguistics," he said.

"Body language?"

"Basically, yes. But it isn't as easy as some first-year psych students believe it is."

"Nothing about human behavior is. So what did you see me do?"

"Why should I tell you? You might just become a better liar."

"Well, they say imitation is the highest form of flattery, Cassidy, so—"

"For some reason, I doubt teaching you to be a better liar will make my head swell. But, okay, I'll tell you what you did this time. You folded your arms—mere resistance. Then you avoided my eyes, suddenly looked away. So I took a guess, provoked you, and got an admission of guilt."

I sighed. "All right, I won't say anything to Bea. Honest. I'm not giving any hidden signs or gestures now, am I?"

"No, you're cranky, but truthful."

"What is it you have against Bradshaw?" I asked.

He moved over to the desk, picked up a file folder, and opened it. He pulled a photograph from it and handed it to me.

It was the photo of Frank holding the boys after their rescue.

"Oh, shit, Cassidy. . . ."

He lifted a brow.

"You stole this from the *Californian!*"

"Borrowed."

"Stole!"

"Mr. North handed it to me," he drawled, "and didn't ask for it back. They have other copies. And I believe he said the newspaper should have thrown them out long ago, so it's not as if they would expect to find it still in their files."

"Not expect it? After Brandon had been showing it to us that afternoon?"

"We can sit here and bicker over that, or you can take a look at the folks in the background—in the part that got cropped out of the newspaper version."

I scowled at him but did as he suggested. I immediately saw what he wanted me to see. "Bear. . . ."

"Yes."

I looked up at Cassidy. "He's not wearing a uniform."

"No, he's not."

"So he couldn't have been in a patrol car when Frank's call came in."

"No."

"Well, hell." I handed the photo back to him.

"It doesn't mean he's the one," Cassidy said.

"No, but he lied."

"Listen, we have a long way to go yet, Irene. I haven't even had a gander at Cook or Matthews. Let's see what we can learn tonight."

I sighed.

"You like him," Cassidy said.

"Yes."

"That's going to make it a rough evening, I suppose. Maybe you should try to get a little sleep," he said.

I shook my head. "I'm not leaving Bea with all the work. Besides, I haven't really had a chance to talk to her. Don't worry, I won't—"

"I know you won't. By the way—what you learned from Cecilia Parker this morning is a big help. Thanks. I know that couldn't have been easy on you. You sure you want her over here tonight?"

"Oh, my God, I forgot to tell Bea that I've expanded the guest list. Are we done here, Cassidy?"

"For the moment, anyway." He yawned. "I may try to catch a little sleep myself."

I needn't have worried about Bea as far as dinner arrangements went—Rachel and Pete were in the kitchen with her, having somehow managed to take over the preparations without excluding her. If Cassidy hadn't said he was going to try to sleep, I would have awakened him for the lesson in negotiating.

Bea wasn't the only one who was surprised to hear Cecilia was coming to dinner. Rachel sent Pete a quelling glance, or I'm sure we would have been treated to his analysis of the situation.

"You aren't inviting her because of me, are you?" Bea said.

I wasn't sure I understood all that was implied by that question, but I said, "No, I enjoyed the time I spent with her today." I was very careful not to cross my arms or break eye contact.

"Oh, good," she said.

I kept watching her as we set the table together. While she was brave faced when Pete and Rachel were near, when we were alone, there were moments when she failed to hide her fear—the moment when the dishes rattled because her hands were shaking as she took her good plates from the china cabinet; the moment when she simply stopped in the middle of setting a spoon next to a knife, stood frozen in distraction, her face despondent. She caught me watching her once, and her tears welled up before she could dash them away. I moved over to her and held her, and she made a sound that brought Pete and Rachel hurrying from the kitchen and then—seeing us—hurrying back again.

"I'm sorry, I'm sorry," she said, but I shushed her and held on.

"You get your turn, too," I said. "Cecilia and I have had ours today."

She looked up at me. "Cecilia? Cecilia cried?"

"Not because I said anything mean to her," I added quickly, wondering if that was strictly true.

"Oh, Irene," she chided, "I didn't think you were mean to her. It's just that I've never seen her shed a tear over anything."

She straightened then and went to wash her face. I finished setting the table, wondering if this dinner party scheme was going to demolish an opportunity to grow closer to her.

26

H E WAS WAKING UP AGAIN. A wonderful thing, waking up. He was starting to appreciate it more than he ever had before. Awareness. Blessed awareness.

Awareness meant that Bret was back. Bret would allow him to awaken.

He stretched, took the inventory that was now a part of every return to consciousness. He was facing the other direction, lying on his left side now. The scrubs were still on. His feet were not restrained. He could move his legs. The IV catheter was still in but capped off; the bottle and tubing were not within sight.

Facing this way, he could not see them. He waited for sounds, sounds that would tell him where they were, if both of them were here. Bret was here, though. Bret preferred him to be awake.

Samuel, on the other hand, preferred control, and the drugs gave him that.

These were the kinds of things he had learned about them over the last few hours—were they hours? he wondered. His watch was gone with everything else. They had left him his wedding ring, at least.

Samuel paid less attention to him than Bret did, was less interested in him. Samuel was worried about other things, things outside this tent.

This lack of attention could prove to be an advantage, of course. Frank knew that if he could clear his mind enough to grasp an opportunity to escape, he was better off being ignored.

Still, he was uneasy about Samuel. It was not just the capacity for violence in the young man that disturbed Frank, it was the sense that the future meant nothing to Samuel—meant nothing, not in the way of the young—of disbelief or lack of ability to imagine it—but in the way of the very old or dying, who have simply accepted that it is not to be theirs.

Bret was the stabilizer. Samuel listened to him. Although he might be angered to some degree by Bret's suggestions regarding Frank, he generally gave Bret his way.

And Bret was curious about Frank. No, there was something more than curiosity at work here. He was not asking questions just out of idle curiosity.

Indebtedness? For the rescue from the basement all those years ago? Maybe, but that did not explain Bret's . . . how to name it? Concern? No, more than that.

It seemed important to him to know this, to name it. But as he considered and rejected word after word, he heard a voice behind him.

"Would you like to sit up?"

Bret's voice.

"Yes," he answered.

A different voice said, "All right, but I've got a gun pointed at you, Detective Harriman, and I'm quite willing to use it."

Samuel.

Bret came around to face him, smiled, and unlocked Frank's left wrist. Frank knew Samuel probably did hold a gun, and that if he did, Samuel was willing—perhaps even hoping—to use it. He knew the drugs would slow his reactions too greatly, knew this was not the opportunity he sought. Still, he found it nearly impossible to resist the urge to try to free himself.

Bret paused, and Frank looked into his face. As clearly as if he had spoken words, Frank knew Bret was telling him not to struggle, not to resist.

He was puzzled, unsure how Bret had conveyed this to him, but Samuel was saying, "He doesn't have our understanding, you know. You have to speak out loud to him. Go ahead and warn him."

"I don't need to warn him," Bret said, motioning Frank to lie on his back. "You're the only one who expects the worst of him."

The simple act of moving to his back sent Frank's head spinning. He closed his eyes as Bret reattached his wrist to the opposite bed rail, waited for the dizziness to pass. He berated himself silently. *Useless. Useless. Useless.*

"Are you nauseated?" Bret asked.

"No," Frank said, opening his eyes, seeing that Sam was indeed holding a gun on him. "Not sick, just a little woozy."

"He's thirsty," Samuel said. "Give him something to drink."

"No," Frank said quickly, hearing the rasp in his own voice. "No, I'm all right."

Samuel laughed, but Bret said, "We'll give you just plain water this time. But let me move you up first, so that you can sit."

He heard the whirring of the motor on the bed, felt it angling him up. A little more dizziness, but not as bad as before. Bret brought the glass of water to him, but he turned his head away. Spinning, spinning.

Move more slowly, he told himself.

When he turned his head back, very gradually, he saw that Bret still waited with the water.

He felt a primal rage, a blinding fury building up within him, a fierce, sudden anger that made him want to pull free of the goddamn railings and attack them both. Let them shoot him! Let them! His rage would keep him in motion, like a matinee monster. Bullets couldn't stop him.

"You see?" Samuel said. "His fists are clenched. I think our hero wants to kill us."

"Of course he does," Bret said softly. "Don't you remember how it feels, Samuel?"

There was silence. Bret said, "Samuel—"

But Samuel was already walking away. "Do what you want. If I come back and find you dead, I'll kill him, and then myself. I'll open the valve, then—bang. Right through my own head. Bang. I won't care about anything then. You hear me? Not anything."

Frank heard the outer door slam shut.

Bret still stood with the glass of water, but he was not looking at Frank. His face was solemn.

"I'm sorry," Frank said. "That was my fault."

"No," Bret said, coming out of his reverie. "No, none of this is your fault."

"I'm sure he didn't mean to—"

"Oh, no, Frank. Don't make that mistake. He meant every word of it." He offered the glass. "It really is just water."

What the hell, Frank thought, and took a sip.

"You have a choice," Bret said. "You can allow me to give you a chance to survive, or you can die with us."

Better able to control his panic now, he was more cautious. "There's no reason for you to die."

Bret smiled. "Ever watch any airplane disaster movies? Some panicked person on the plane always screams, 'We're all going to die!' Well, truer words were never spoken. Most of us don't know when we will die, and many of us won't believe there is any reason for our deaths. When and why. Samuel and I have a reasonable approximation of the former and a certainty of the latter. We have that."

"But still—"

"No, Frank, Samuel and I won't live through this set of events we've set in motion. We are rather good amateurs, but time and experience is on the side of people like Detective Cassidy."

"Cassidy isn't a killer," Frank said. "He'll do everything he can to end this peacefully."

"It won't be up to Cassidy, I'm afraid."

"I don't understand—"

"No, I'm sorry. You are still at a great disadvantage. I promised you a story. Now, would you like to get out of this bed and sit at a table and read it yourself?"

Confused, but seeing that—for the moment—Bret would discuss matters only on his own terms, Frank said, "Yes."

"All right, then first let me explain a few things. Samuel and I went to a great deal of trouble to refit this building to our own needs. Right now, we are in a tent within a room within a room. One door to each, no windows. Soundproof. The tent is similar to tents used for fumigating buildings, made of the same material. There is a security system to which I must respond before anyone can gain entry. Without going into the sort of details that will give you a little too much information, I'll tell you that opening the valve Samuel referred to starts the flow of a gas into this tent. The gas will asphyxiate anyone in the tent. In other words, if he wanted to, he could open that valve now, and we would be suffocated."

Frank thought of the mood Samuel had been in when he left and closed his eyes.

"I see you begin to understand. I can free you if I become a prisoner within the room with you. Should I need to leave the room, you will have to return voluntarily to the bed and will be restrained as you are now. Samuel will not come in here unless you are restrained. If you refuse to be restrained, Samuel will receive a signal from me to start the flow of the gas."

"You'd die with me."

"If your only goal is to kill me, I'm giving you that opportunity. But if I die, Samuel starts the gas. If you injure me, prevent me from restraining you, or prevent me from giving the proper entry signal to Samuel, then we die together. I suppose I'm counting on the fact that you are probably less reconciled to death than I am."

"I don't understand this," Frank said, knowing he should be calmer, should be trying a different approach, but unable to manage it. "I don't know why you want to die."

"I don't. I'm *willing* to die. That's different. I don't want you to die with me, but I'm willing to allow that to happen, too. I'd prefer you live. I'd prefer we passed our very limited time together with the more pleasant pursuits of meals and conversation. Conversation with you, the opportunity to get to know you. . . ." He smiled again. "It's a sort of going-away present to myself."

"We can talk and eat while I'm still in this bed. Why go to all this trouble to let me roam around the room?"

"You know the answer to that."

After a long silence Frank said, "Because you've been chained."

"Exactly."

"The drugs—"

"Are a necessity, I'm afraid. I'll do my best to keep them at a minimum. That's largely up to you. If you're uncooperative, you'll probably spend most of your remaining time with us in a state of unconsciousness. If you prefer that, I can start the IV again now."

"No—"

"I didn't think that would be your choice. Shall I untie you now?"

"Yes."

"I have your word—you'll accept our conditions?"

Miserable. He felt goddamned miserable and angry

with himself for it. He tried not to let any of this show as he said, "Yes."

"Good," Bret said, but he was frowning, watching Frank's face. He lowered his head in concentration as he began to unfasten the restraint he had so recently attached to the rail.

There it was again, Frank thought. Bret, attuned to his moods, watching for little cues.

He would need to be more careful. Yet here was his hope, perhaps his only hope—Bret's concern for him.

"Bret—"

Bret looked up at him.

"How does Samuel feel about this?"

Bret smiled, now working to take the restraint off the wrist itself. "He dislikes the idea intensely, but we humor one another. He knows this will make me happy, and so he gives in."

"And what did you give to him in return?"

His hands stilled. "We don't have a tally sheet."

Frank made no other comment as Bret finished removing the left wrist restraint. His impatience to be freed was nearly unbearable now, and he immediately reached to remove the one on the right wrist, only to grow dizzy again. But Bret did not try to interfere; he waited, let Frank free himself, first from the rail, then from the restraint itself. He did not say anything when Frank threw the strap hard to the ground like a hated thing.

Frank blew out a breath, tried to control the rush of emotion he felt as the strap made a satisfying slap on the floor.

He rubbed his wrists as Bret lowered the rail, slightly embarrassed now at the display of temper. But that passed with the anticipation of another measure of freedom.

"Careful now," Bret said, and helped him from the bed.

He was ridiculously wobbly and dizzy as all hell, but he was on his own two feet. He didn't know how long he had been here or how long he would remain, but at least he wasn't tied to the damned bed.

"Thank you," Frank said, and saw that Bret had some idea of how deeply he meant it.

He walked like an old man to the table, leaning on Bret for the first few steps, then on his own. He eased into a chair, rolled and stretched the stiff muscles of his shoulders and back. He looked at the bed.

"Don't think about being back there," Bret said, following Frank's anxious line of thought. "We have time now, and we should make the most of it. Are you hungry?"

"Yes," Frank said in the tone of one making a discovery. He felt awkward, unsure of how to proceed.

"Just sandwiches this time, I'm afraid," Bret said, going to an ice chest.

"You said you have something for me to read?" Frank asked as Bret arrived with paper plates wrapped in plastic wrap, a sandwich and fresh fruit on each. He did not doubt that all of his food would be of a kind that could be eaten without utensils. No makeshift weaponry.

"You can read it after we eat," Bret said. "Do you remember the Szals?"

"Bernard and Regina? Yes, of course."

They talked of the Szals and telescopes and aikido. Bret politely steered the conversation away from any potentially touchy subjects, such as the years of silence. Still, Frank could not deny that it was a genuinely pleasant exchange. Bret had come alive, had been enthusiastic, was always eager for Frank's thoughts and opinions.

After eating, Frank stood and walked slowly around the tent, which was roomy but sparsely furnished. Barefoot, he was fairly certain the floor beneath the tent was wooden. There were several locked trunks of various sizes along one side of the tent; he was curious about them but decided against asking about them now.

His head itched. He reached back to scratch it and felt the shaved and slightly tender skin around the stitches.

"God, it feels good to be able to scratch that damned itch," he said.

Bret's face fell. "I'm so sorry. I should have thought of that."

You try hard to anticipate what others are feeling, Frank thought. Aloud he said, "It wasn't so bad. I probably shouldn't be touching it, anyway."

"There shouldn't be much of a scar," Bret said. "Your hair will cover it, I'm sure."

"You put in the stitches?"

He couldn't fail to notice Bret's sudden pallor. "No," Bret said. "No, Samuel did."

"I'll have to thank him," Frank said. "I seem to remember bleeding." He touched the slightly puffy place on his upper lip. "My lip?"

Bret was looking away now. "Your lip, your nose. Your head. It was terrible." He shuddered. "Let's talk about something else."

"Sure."

He made his way back to the table. He was still plagued by dizziness and weakness, but they seemed to be lessening: the drugs clearing from his system, no doubt. He tried to keep from touching the IV device.

"Here," Bret said, handing him some papers as he was seated. "I think it's time you read this."

While the title—"Father's Day"—came as no real surprise, almost everything that followed did.

27

I DIDN'T EAT MUCH, even though the food was terrific. The cooks didn't take it personally. Pete, for one, was too busy glaring at Cecilia.

I had forgotten that Pete—for reasons he had never confided in me—disliked her intensely. He did little to disguise that fact at dinner. Rachel kept muttering things to him in Italian, while Cookie—as I was learning to refer to Nat Cook—was doing his best to distract Cecilia. He needn't have bothered.

Cookie was the oldest of the three. Bear was next, then Gus. Gus was still brawny, while Cookie appeared to be quite frail.

Bea suggested we adjourn to the living room, but Rachel agreed only on the condition that she and Pete would clear the table and do the dishes. I could see Pete's rebellion forming, but not in time to save himself—she all but grabbed him by the ear. Cassidy took in all of this with amusement.

Before the trio arrived, Cassidy had taken me aside and asked me not to jump in with any questions of my own until he asked one about the Ryan-Neukirk case. From there, he said, I'd be asking most of them, at least in the beginning. "And don't go convicting Bradshaw just yet," he added sternly. "You've got to act as calm and natural as you can tonight. I'm depending on it. Don't let me catch you giving him the evil eye or fidgeting like you've got a bumblebee in your drawers. You think of him as the man who brought you and Frank together—that guy you talked about when we had lunch the other day."

I tried to heed his warnings but still felt nervous as we sat down to dinner. Early attention and talk, fortunately, was focused on Greg Bradshaw's knee surgery. By the time I had calmed myself enough to look up from the first course, I realized Cassidy had somehow taken control of the conversation. He seemed to set some silent ground rule: no one would discuss Frank's captivity or, by extension, the Ryan-Neukirk murders. He did not announce this; he merely started several discussions that were obviously not about our great concern. Everyone picked up on this cue, probably certain that he was doing this to keep Frank's mother or wife calm during a meal he called—despite Pete's constant corrections—our "Eye-talian supper." I think he was getting back at Pete for harassing Cecilia, since Rachel seemed to be suppressing a laugh every time he said it.

Once Cassidy got the ball rolling in the direction he wanted it to go, he spent most of his time listening to the three older cops argue with one another over who told the true version of whichever war story was under discussion.

The stories began to have similar themes. If they were about Gus, they were wild-man exploits: Gus diving and tackling an armed suspect in an alley after his own gun had jammed; Gus climbing a water tower (while drunk) because he saw a pretty girl on it, only to discover it was a long-haired young man who was contemplating suicide—managing to talk the young man out of it; Gus hearing other cops call him "What's-your-twenty-Matthews"—a reference to the dispatchers' frequent efforts to locate him. These were the stories about Gus: often heroic, more often foolish.

It was clear that Gus thought nothing of bucking authority, had put in some drinking years, had paid a price for both by never managing to hold on to a promotion for long. But he seemed untroubled by that fact, and whenever Bear or Cookie alluded to it, he smiled and said, "What the hell? I enjoyed my work. It was a good ride. I never had your finesse, is all. You two were a couple of sneaks."

He was right; while tales were told in which Bear and Cookie were heroes, these almost always involved outwitting criminals rather than Gus's brute force or action. Within the department, both were pranksters. Bear's pranks were on a relatively small scale. They were similar to those he played on Frank as a rookie—putting a penny in a patrol car hubcap to make a maddening rattle, putting shoe polish on the rim of a motorcycle cop's goggles.

Cookie's pranks involved more strategy. One summer the sound of church bells was broadcast over all the department radios. Bells ringing at midnight, twelve long tolls. When it was heard every night for three nights in a row, the infuriated chief put detectives on the task of discovering the culprit. They compared bell sounds to recordings of the midnight broadcasts. The bells had a distinctive sound, and their most likely source was a certain church. The minister gave permission for police to search it. Nothing was found. Undeterred, the chief ordered the building surrounded and watched. As on previous nights, bells marked midnight and were heard over the radios, although clearly not being transmitted by anyone present.

"Because," Bear said, "Cookie is a dozen miles away, parked up on a hill, with a little cassette deck in his car playing a tape of those bells!"

Cassidy also told a few anecdotes from his own law enforcement career, with the same flair for humorous storytelling he had demonstrated during our drive to Bakersfield. They took to him, accepted him as one of their own. That, I began to see, was the point.

Now, as the dinner guests were seated around Bea's living room, Cassidy gave me a smile that was undoubtedly seen as a gesture of reassurance by the others, but that I knew to be a warning.

Get ready.

He stayed on his feet, leaned against the mantel. "Irene, were these old farts this decrepit when you were working here?"

They smiled good-naturedly. "Come here, Tex," Gus joked, "and I'll show you what decrepit can do."

This was met with cheers by Bea and the other two.

"Well, Cassidy," I said, "not decrepit, but they *were* a little gray headed." I looked pointedly at his hair. "You know how that can be."

He smiled at their laughter and ran a hand over his

hair. "Well, some men just look more handsome in gray hair, right, fellas?"

"That's right, that's right," Bear said. "Looks distinguished. Remember, Cookie, when old Brian went Grecian Formula on us?"

This brought on more laughter, while Bea turned red with embarrassment. "Greg Bradshaw," she muttered. "Honestly! The things you are liable to say."

I sat stunned, quickly reminding myself that Brian Harriman's hair color was only one reason to believe in him. Cecilia caught my eye, smiled at me. It was enough to calm me down again.

Cassidy, meanwhile, reached over and picked up the photo of Frank and his dad. "By golly, I just might try some of that hair-coloring stuff. Looks damned natural to me."

"He wasn't using it then," Cookie said.

"Yep, Cookie's right," Gus said. "Having Frank on the force is what turned poor ol' Brian gray."

"It is not!" Bea protested. "He was very proud of Frank."

"Oh, of course! Of course he was," Bear soothed, shooting Gus a dirty look. "Hell, everyone knows that. We're all proud of him. Frank is a damned fine cop. He's never given anyone any reason not to be proud of him."

The room fell silent.

"As far as I'm concerned," I said, trying to steer the conversation back on course, "Frank isn't going to be any less handsome when he turns gray. How old was Brian when his hair changed?"

"It wasn't long after Frank joined the department," Bea said, then added pointedly, "But it wasn't because he was worried about Frank." Gus didn't see her glance or seem to notice her tone of voice. He was bent forward, elbows on widespread knees, hands clasped, looking down at the floor. His facial expressions were hidden.

"Aw, Bea," Bear said, suddenly caught between loyalties, "nobody is knocking Brian. It was just something funny, that's all. Brian laughed about it himself. He only used it for a little while, until we gave him so much grief over it, he figured it was easier to be gray. Truth is, he looked fine either way. Right, Cookie?"

"Right. We scared everybody else off of trying to color his gray, though."

"I vaguely remember a couple of other guys who were going gray," I said. "A Wilson and . . . Beech, maybe?"

"Beecham," Cookie said. "Manny Beecham. And if the Wilson you're thinking of was gray haired, it was Quinn. Wilson and Beecham were motorcycle cops. Boy, I tell you—that was tough duty. Cold in winter. I knew men who would stuff newspapers in their jackets, trying to stay warm."

"We weren't much better off in the cars," Bear said, watching Gus. "Right, Gus?"

Gus looked up. His eyes looked a little red. "Yeah, Bear, the cars were cold, too."

"Irene, we didn't get heaters in our cars until 1958," Bear said, more animated now that Gus had joined in again. "Brian and I used to turn the spotlight on and aim it into the car just to heat ourselves up."

"Everybody did that," Cookie said. "We were supposed to ride with our windows down in the winter, so we could hear what was going on outside the car."

"I reckon that would make things a little chilly," Cassidy said.

Gus suddenly got to his feet. "I can't stand this! We're sitting in here talking about the fucking weather!"

Cookie stood up, too, and said, "Have a seat, Gus."

Gus didn't move. "It ain't even today's weather, for God's sake!"

"Have a seat, Gus," Bear said quietly. "For Bea's sake."

Gus sat.

"And watch your mouth," Cookie added. "This is Bea's home. You think if Brian were alive, he'd let you talk like that in front of his wife?"

"He didn't mean anything by it," Cecilia said, drawing all eyes. "Gus is just upset, worried about Frank, right?"

Gus said nothing, looking down between his feet again.

"Yes," Bea said, "that's all it is. Nathan?"

Cookie said, "Of course. I'm sorry, Gus. I guess my nerves are on edge, too." He sat down.

Cassidy glanced at me, then moved to sit in a chair near Cecilia, across from Gus and Cookie.

"Gus," he said quietly, "I don't blame you. We've avoided the topic that's been on everybody's mind all evening. You've always been close to Frank, right?"

He nodded.

"And you know who has him?"

"Those boys," he said to the floor.

Cassidy glanced at me again, leaned back.

"Do you remember that day?" I asked Gus.

"You mean when the boys were found?" he said, looking up at me now.

"Yes."

"Sure. Never forget it. I got there last. Cookie and Bear were there. Not Brian, though."

"Brian had gone fishing that day," Cecilia said. "He was off that weekend."

"That's right!" Bea said. "I had forgotten. That's why he got back so late. He used to go fishing with some friends of ours in Bodfish."

"Bodfish?" Cassidy asked. "I never heard of a fish called a bodfish."

"It isn't named after a fish, it's named after a person," she said. "His name was George Homer Bodfish."

"I guess he didn't want to have to live alone with it," Cassidy said.

"Brian was in Bodfish that weekend?" Cookie asked.

"Just Saturday," Cecilia answered. "He was back here by Sunday night."

"How do you know?" Pete asked, coming in from the kitchen.

"It was the first time I'd been to a Father's Day dinner. The Harrimans invited me. When Frank got the call that day, Brian hadn't come back from fishing. Our plans got changed a little."

I gave Pete a look that said "Lay off." I guess he got the message, because he took a seat and didn't say anything more. Rachel came in and sat next to him.

"I'm sure anyone who was a friend of the family would remember that Father's Day," I said. "All three of you went to the scene?"

"Yeah," Gus said. "I don't think anybody who was there could forget those two kids. Or Frank, the way he was that day. Oh, man. I felt so bad for him, you know, because he caught that call."

"How did you hear about it?"

"I was working. . . . I had just come on for my shift, so it must have been . . . let's see . . . around six-thirty. That's right—I was on days for those last few years before I retired. Brian had also been on days, but he had been on them for a long time." He glanced at Bea and then up at the photos on the mantel. He shook his head sadly.

"Six-thirty?" I said. "You must have been there pretty early on, then."

"Naw, the call had been in for at least half an hour. I didn't hear about it until I reported for work. We had started working tens then—ten-hour shifts. Seven A.M. to four P.M., five P.M. to two A.M., eleven P.M. to eight A.M. You'd come in about thirty minutes before and stay about thirty minutes later for the shift changes, but those were the shifts. Frank and Cookie worked graveyard shift. What'd you have then, Bear?"

Bear was frowning. "I must have been mixed up about something yesterday. . . ."

"When I met you, I think you were working afternoon shift," I said. "Bars would be closed, we'd go to one of the all-night coffee shops—you and Frank and I. We'd talk until everyone wound down, until about four in the morning."

"That's right," he said, but he still looked puzzled. "Afternoons . . . I must have been on afternoons."

"Frank switched to graveyards after you left, Irene," Bea said. "Cecilia worked days. He'd sleep while she worked, and they'd go out in the evenings."

Cecilia seemed uneasy with this talk. "It cut every evening short," she said quickly.

"Well, Frank was lucky to have y'all there for him," Cassidy said, pulling the conversation back to that day. "I understand he took it pretty hard."

"Yeah," Gus said. "Those kids—they just wouldn't let go of him. Even after their mothers got there. We wanted to talk to Frank, but any man came near 'em, they freaked out."

"Now I know!" Bear said. "The scanner!"

The rest of us looked puzzled, but Gus started laughing. "Oh, goddamn—excuse me, Bea. Oh, oh—I'd forgotten about that, you were such a—!" He looked at Bea again, couldn't seem to come up with a clean word, and contented himself with laughing.

Bear was turning red. "Gus, it's not *that* funny!"

"Cassidy," Gus said, "you have never met anybody whose blood is so blue. Blue, blue, blue. The guy works ten-hour shifts, spends all his time off with other cops, and when they can't stand him anymore and send him home, what does he do? Listens to his scanner. Remember how much sh— uh, what a hard time we used to give him about that, Cookie?"

Cookie, who had been silent for some time, merely said, "I remember."

"You were there that day, too?" I asked him.

"Yes. I was there. As Gus said, I worked nights. But I wasn't working that Sunday, the one when Frank found the boys. I had come in on Friday night, and worked until eight on Saturday morning. I was off on Saturday night and Sunday morning."

"How did you find out about it, then?"

"Bea called me, said Brian was out of town, asked if I could go over to the warehouse."

It seemed a little odd to me that Bea, who must

have heard about the incident from Bear or Gus, would call in additional reinforcements. But this may have been the way their "extended family" operated—all for one, one for all.

"So you were there fairly soon?" I asked Bear.

"Yes. I tried to go down to the basement, to talk to Frank, but by the time I arrived the crime lab was there and not letting anyone near him. Once they came up out of that basement—as Gus said, the boys became very upset around any other man. I thought it was just me, at first. But they reacted that way to any other male."

"Do you have any idea where they're holding Frank?" Gus asked.

"Not at present, no," Cassidy said. "But we believe it's somewhere in Las Piernas. Folks down there are working hard to locate him."

"What are you doing out here, then, if you don't mind my asking?"

"Ryan and Neukirk—the boys—contact us here. They tell us they have some task for us to complete before they'll release Frank. Something to do with the murder of their fathers, I'm sure. Any of you have any idea what it could be? If you did, it could sure help us—help Frank most of all."

No arms crossed, no nervousness, no eyes averted. Yes—Cassidy was a cool liar.

"Something to do with the old case?" Gus was asking. He grew thoughtful. All three men were silent, seemed to be considering the question.

"I don't know what it could be," Bear said. "The boys know the killer is dead, right?"

"Yes," Cassidy said.

"Cecilia," Cookie said, "you discovered the body of the killer, didn't you?"

"Yes," she said.

"Were there any signs that he might have had a partner, an accomplice?"

"No," she answered. "Not a thing. Of course, I didn't get involved in the forensics—just made the call."

"Wait," Gus said. "Cookie—man, they never should have kept you out of detectives. You were born to be a suit, I tell you."

Nathan Cook colored red from his neck to the top of his head. "Really, Gus—"

But Gus was continuing, in a tone that seemed—at least to me—to be slightly sarcastic. "You see how he is, Cassidy? He can think ahead like that—"

"Gus—" Cookie tried again.

"No, I mean it. We used to say it that way, 'one smart Cookie.' Remember, Bear?"

"Yeah, he's right," Bear said, looking nervously at Cookie. "But I don't—"

"Gus, Bear. Please," Cookie said.

"You're brilliant," Gus went on. "The rest of us always assumed it was just the one guy doing the killing down in that basement, but Cookie here thinks differently from the average cop. I mean, that's a hell of a suggestion. Maybe there was more than one person involved—"

"Sorry, Gus," Cassidy interrupted. "You're right, ol' Cookie here is smart. But I've read the reports from that case, including the labwork. Other than the victims, there was only one man in that basement. There were several indications that it was only one man, but one piece of evidence was almost undeniable proof."

He turned to Cookie. "You see, there was quite a bit of blood on the floor, and anybody who went all the way down those stairs couldn't miss stepping in it. Until Frank went out to his car to make the call, no one had walked in and out of that basement except the killer."

"Hmm," Cookie said. "I suppose that rules out an accomplice."

"As I said," Cassidy continued, "spatter patterns and other evidence back that up. Those boys were just damned lucky that someone called the department about the suspected robbery. If not, who knows how long they would have been down there?"

"Those boys," Bear said. "I mean, it isn't too hard to understand that you might not be quite right after something like that, is it? Sitting down there for hours and hours. . . ."

"Let's not get morbid," Cookie said. "I'm sure Bea didn't want us to come over here just to make her think about such gruesome things."

"I'm all right, Cookie," she said. "You know I'm tougher than that."

"Yes, well, I'm not so tough myself," Cookie said. "I'm older than the rest of you. If you'll forgive me, I've got to be going."

Everyone stood, and the good-nights began. Cecilia left right after Cookie. Gus and Bear had driven over together and left soon after her. We waved good-bye from the front porch.

Bea and Rachel and Pete went back into the house, leaving me on the porch with Cassidy.

"I guess we both know who it is, now," I said.

28

CASSIDY RAISED A brow. "Oh?"

"It's Cookie, isn't it?" I said.

"Now, what makes you think so?" he asked, although nothing in his voice indicated he disagreed.

"Bret Neukirk's version of events that night may or may not be completely accurate, but there are certain parts of the story that he's unlikely to have invented or misremembered."

"Such as?"

"Such as what time of day they were traveling to Lake Isabella. He said they left the house at three in the morning and were pulled over by a patrol car. The Bakersfield department wasn't so big or poorly managed that you could just drive a cruiser off the lot without anyone noticing. So they were probably pulled over by a car that was already in use."

"Okay, I'll buy that. We'll assume it wasn't a stolen cruiser."

"Gus worked days," I said. "He would have finished his shift by four in the afternoon. Bear would have been off by about two-thirty in the morning. Only Cookie would have been in a patrol car after three in the morning."

"Yes, but if Bret had the time wrong by an hour or two, it could have been Bradshaw."

"Maybe," I said, "but he would have been pushing it—he would have been at the very end of the shift, planning to take two men hostage. But Nathan Cook had plenty of time."

"Powell was there to help him—might not have figured on needing much time. It's clear the boys were an unexpected complication," Cassidy said. "I'm not arguing against your notion about Cook, though. He mentioned he had worked that shift."

"Which is another thing that bothered me about him. This happened a dozen years ago. His memory is almost too good."

"A dozen years ago for everybody," Cassidy said.

"Sure. Every one of them seems to remember *something* about that day. There are reasons for them to remember it—Frank was important to them, for starters. Second, the Ryan-Neukirk case was so disturbing. And they have a memorable date to tie it to—because the bodies were discovered on a holiday. Boys and their fathers on Father's Day."

"Okay, so it made an impression that could last a dozen years."

"Right. Gus can remember working that day," I went on, "because like most people, he remembers where he was when he received shocking news. He first heard about the murders when he reported for work."

"And Bradshaw?"

"Bear was a little less sure—when we first talked to him, he thought he was working, but that was because he remembered hearing Frank's voice on the call. For him, the first memory of that day is an auditory one. It's not surprising that he connected a call on a scanner with being at work. But even though he was mixed up about where he was, he clearly recalled the part of the memory that made the strongest impression."

"But you think Cook 'remembers' too much?"

"Exactly. He said he was off that Saturday night and Sunday morning. He said he got a call from Bea on Sunday morning. Maybe, maybe not—we may never know. If he had stopped there, no red flags would have gone up. But then he tells us that he remembers coming into work on Friday night and working until about eight on Saturday. Why? Why should he remember that?"

"You think he was lying?"

"No, Mr. Neurolinguistics. I think he was telling the truth about working that graveyard shift. He worked it all those years ago, and remembered it. Do you remember which nights you worked and which ones you had off ten or twelve years ago? No. You remember the nights when something extraordinary happened. So does Cook. That was a night he probably won't ever forget. He pulled Julian Neukirk's car over, and set hell in motion. Yeah, I think it was a busy night for him—knocking people unconscious, taping up children's hands, going treasure hunting. Saturday night was busy for him, too, since that's probably when he gave Powell a shove."

"I think he was doing his treasure hunting that night, too," Cassidy said. "You said you thought that slope was visible from the campground during the day, right?"

"Yes. The campground is on the same side of the canyon, but upriver."

"This was Father's Day weekend," he said. "Mid-June. By the time Cook ended his ten-hour graveyard shift, turned in a car, and drove up to the place where X marked the spot, it would have been midmorning."

"You're right. There would have been plenty of sunlight at the turnout by the time he arrived. And he probably took time to change clothes—I don't picture Nat Cook being the kind of guy who would wear his uniform to do that kind of work."

"No," Cassidy agreed, "even if he was willing to get it dirty, he wouldn't want to attract that kind of attention. So with all those delays—Cook might have been able to take a look at the turnout by Saturday afternoon, but probably couldn't have done any digging until Saturday night, after traffic settled down. That was just too many hours for Powell."

"Right," I said. "Powell got restless, and by the time Cook showed up at the warehouse, Powell had killed the men and left. And my guess is that Cook knew Powell well enough to figure out where he was headed. Cook might have been concerned about the boys, but he would have been out-and-out terrified that Powell would be caught, covered with blood, and raving about his good buddy Nathan Cook."

"Yes, he'd take care of Powell before making a call to the dispatcher—otherwise, Bakersfield PD might find Powell first. That would explain why there wasn't a call until Sunday morning." He thought for a moment, then nodded. "It's all possible."

"There were other things that bothered me," I said.

He smiled. "Namely?"

"What's so funny?"

"Oh, nothing. Just wondering if old 'smart Cookie' had any idea of what he was up against."

"When Gus said that about him—called him 'smart Cookie'—did you get the impression it was meant as a dig?"

"Yes, and I think Cookie saw it as one. I'm pretty sure Bradshaw did, too. I'm hoping Gus and your friend the Bear stay out of this now."

"Hmm. Why do I have the feeling you're already planning something in connection with Cookie?"

"Surveillance only, at this point."

"He was followed from here?"

"Yes. Now what were the other things that bothered you?"

"He asked Cecilia if she had found any signs of an accomplice. Why would he mention the area where they found Powell's body, instead of the warehouse?"

"Probably a slip, but he could always claim that he already knew they hadn't found signs of an accomplice at the warehouse, and was just confirming information from a scene outside Bakersfield's jurisdiction."

"Yeah, right," I said.

Cassidy smiled.

"It won't work for him to claim that—tonight he tried to pretend he was hearing the warehouse information for the first time."

"Anything else?" Cassidy asked.

I hesitated. "The other stuff isn't so. . . ."

"Isn't so what?"

"Objective, I guess."

"Try it out on me anyway. Half of what I have to work with most of the time is impressions. They're important."

"Okay, I tried to get an impression of this cop from Bret Neukirk's fax. He seemed to be an uptight kind of person, rigid. He's also careful, able to hide things. Gus is a man of action, but he isn't very careful. Bear—can you picture Bear hiding anything? And he's just too easygoing. Cook—he's more cautious. In those stories you got them to tell, Cook was the one who could make long-term plans."

"I don't know that I got them to tell—"

"No time for false modesty, Cassidy."

"What other impressions?"

"The man in Bret's fax goes ballistic over foul language," I said. "Did you see Cook's reaction tonight?"

"You're probably glad you didn't say anything to set him off first."

"Hilarious. Does any of this make sense to you, Cassidy?"

"Absolutely. I think you're right, by the way."

"You do? Great!" I started pacing. "I know this isn't the kind of thing you could take to court. Not that we have anything even remotely resembling admissible evidence at this point, but—"

"Irene," he said quietly, "I'm afraid I may have misled you."

I looked up at him.

"I am very rarely interested in the same thing a district attorney is interested in," he said. "It's part of why I like my job. I'm almost always trying to help somebody stay alive. I have never had any real hope of seeing this rogue cop convicted for his part in the murders."

"What?" I said. "I don't believe this! What have we been trying to do all this time?"

"You want to hear my goals? I want to keep Frank alive. I want him to be located and freed—ideally, unharmed. I want Samuel Ryan and Bret Neukirk and any other members of Hocus to surrender—ideally, peacefully. If they won't surrender, then I've failed, and this becomes a job for the tactical folks on the CIT. The people you know as the SWAT team."

"But—"

"If I do my job right," he went on, "and everything goes well, people are alive at the end of the day. That's it. The DA isn't saying, 'Yes, we've got enough evidence to go to trial.' The trial is over. Court is adjourned, one way or the other."

"Forgive me if I'm missing something," I gritted out, "but it seems to me that bringing Nathan Cook to justice is going to go a long way toward freeing my husband!"

"Not really."

I stood there gaping at him for a second before my anger kicked in. "Damn it, Cassidy, what the hell has this been? Busywork? Some project to keep Frank Harriman's nosy reporter wife out of the way?"

"Now, Irene—"

"Don't 'Now, Irene' me! What have I been running my ass all over Bakersfield for? What would you have done if Tuesday came along and we had no idea who that cop was?"

"I would have lied," he said.

"Shit."

"You would prefer that I tell them, 'Sorry, fellas, Irene can't figure it out, you win—so feel free to go ahead and kill Frank'?"

I felt a rage so pure, I went deaf, dumb, and blind. I knew my hand hurt before I had calmed down enough to realize what I had done. It was a good, hard slap. My palm and fingers had a thousand needles in them. I was breathing hard, panting, as if I had gone ten rounds with him.

He was rubbing his face with his left hand, but he hadn't lifted either hand to defend himself. He could have, I realized. He had proven hours ago that he could anticipate my reactions.

"You knew that was coming," I said, the rage nearly gone, despair ready to step in.

"Yes," he said, still rubbing his cheek, "but I'll admit I misjudged your speed and strength. And most women wind up a little—you know—raise their hand up by their shoulder."

"I shouldn't have hit you," I said.

"Was that an apology?"

"Not exactly, was it?"

"No." He laughed. "I'll start. I'm sorry I provoked you." He rubbed his face again. "*Real* sorry."

I was shaking. I didn't give a damn.

The anger was subsiding, going out like a tide. I didn't like the sense of despair it was leaving behind. My lower lip quivered, and that was enough to scare me, so I thought of Cassidy letting me spend my morning listening to Cecilia honk her fucking horn, just to make that tide come in again.

But once you've hit high tide, the waves never reach the same point on the beach.

"Tell me you won't say that again," I said.

"That I'm sorry?"

"No, Cassidy," I said, feeling an almost pleasant return to being irritated with him.

"Oh, you mean don't ever suggest that Frank might be killed?"

"Don't say it," I said quietly. "I know what might happen. I know."

"Do you?" he asked, sounding weary. "I was convinced a moment ago that you thought we were almost home free. That if we gave up Nathan Cook to them, they would send Frank out, and that would be that."

I almost denied it but couldn't.

"You're right. I just wanted to believe—Never mind, it was foolish."

"No," he said, "just human. And I really do apologize for making you so angry. I would have picked another way to get the point across, but midnight is getting closer, Hocus plans a call, and this seemed like it might be a fast and sure method to get you to change gears. Anyway, I didn't want you to say anything to them about Mr. Cook just yet."

"Couldn't you just ask me not to?"

"Because you're noted for doing as you're told?"

I had no answer for that.

"I thought so," he said.

Frank's alive, I told myself. Hold on to that. Hold on. If he can put up with whatever they're doing to him, you can deal with one lousy Texan.

But it was a mistake, thinking of what might be

happening to him. I swallowed past a lump in my throat. "Yeah, well," I said, "sorry about slapping you."

"Irene."

"What?" I said, not looking at him.

"What you've been doing—that hasn't just been busywork."

I sighed. "Don't lie to me, Cassidy. I might look like I need a lie, but I don't."

"I'm not lying. If you think about it, I've told you the truth. You don't always want to hear it."

I didn't reply.

"Not that I blame you," he added.

"Thanks for that, anyway."

"Listen to me now. It's always better for us to know as much as we can about the takers. Knowing who, in all likelihood, took them that night—that gives us something to bargain with."

"You just told me you could have bargained with a lie."

"Better if we can bargain with the truth. Much better."

Somehow I just couldn't work up any enthusiasm over that. I felt as if I'd spent precious hours hunting for a lost key, only to come back home and find out all the locks had been changed.

He put a hand on my shoulder. "Let's go in."

"I'm tired, Cassidy."

"I know you are," he said. "I know you are."

I looked up at him. He looked sad. I was going to apologize again for slapping him, but his cell phone rang.

Everything began to change with that call.

29

S O WE'RE ALL SET?"
It was Samuel's voice. He tried to listen, to pay
attention. It was better than thinking about the
restraints, about being back in the bed. Better than
thinking about the curtain being around the bed
again, cutting off his view.

Bret had drugged him again, given him something
mild in a drink that made him less upset about being
placed in the restraints again. But now, awake, he had
nothing to take the edge off. Better to be alert, he told
himself.

He was marveling at how easily he had awakened
this time. He did not feel nearly so groggy. And the
dizziness was not so severe. Had Bret cut down the
dosage?

"Of course we are, Samuel." A woman's voice.
"Don't you trust me to do anything right?"

The stranger's voice startled him. He felt a deep

sense of shame that yet another person would see him like this, then set aside those feelings. Pay attention, he told himself again.

"No, Faye, as a matter of fact, I don't." Samuel. "Especially not after you broke that bottle of after-shave."

"I wasn't the one who broke it!"

"You were the one who didn't pack it right," Samuel said.

"It doesn't matter. Thanks for making the arrangements, Faye." Bret's voice, placating.

"The only one who has made any kind of mistake so far is you, Sammy boy," Faye said.

"Don't call me that," Samuel said. Couldn't she hear his anger? Frank wondered.

"Did he tell you?" Faye went on. "He screwed up the fax yesterday."

There was a silence.

"Bret doesn't care," Samuel said. "You think you can divide us, but you can't."

"This isn't about division. Bret's not interested in me. But he's interested in knowing how you really sent that fax. I can see it in his face."

"No," Bret said. "Samuel doesn't have to tell me anything he doesn't want to."

Another hesitation. "She's trying to make a big deal out of nothing!" Sam's voice, exasperated. "I couldn't get the computer to work with the pay phone at the airport. So I used the hard copy you gave me and sent it on an actual fax machine. Big deal."

"Sorry you had problems," Bret said. "Must have been frustrating."

"It was," Samuel said. Frank could hear him gloating, heard his belief that Faye hadn't caused the trouble she'd intended.

"Where was the fax machine?" Bret asked.

"There in the airport. A commercial one. Self-service."

"Oh, so you didn't have to hand it to anyone else." Frank heard the relief in Bret's voice.

"No," Samuel said. "I wouldn't do that."

"Well, Faye, he didn't make a mistake. He ran into unforeseen difficulties and found a creative way around them. Which is what an intelligent person does when he encounters the unexpected. A lesser person would have given up."

"You still haven't heard just how creative this greater person was. How do you suppose he paid for the fax?"

Silence.

"He stole a woman's wallet," she said.

"Faye, I removed one credit card from a wallet and returned the wallet and everything else that was in it to the woman's bag—all before she even knew it was missing. The charges for the fax are so small, she'll never have to pay them herself. So try some new way to make trouble."

"Faye, did you have some problem with the contractor?" Bret asked.

"None," she answered quickly. "Now, when do I get to take a peek at our guest?"

"You don't," Bret answered. "It's very difficult for him to be in this situation. It would make him feel ashamed to have others see him as a hostage."

"But he's asleep! He'll never know!"

"Doesn't anyone's dignity matter to you, Faye?" Samuel asked.

"Honestly! As if a guy who's knocked out on morphine is going to know who looked at him."

"People aren't exhibits," Samuel said. "This isn't a zoo or a carnival. Right now, I feel a greater affinity to that man than I do to you. I know what it's like to have someone else view you as a curiosity. It stinks."

"We have a lot to do," Bret said. "We should get to work."

Faye seemed to understand that it was time to drop the subject. Frank kept listening, but most of what he heard was the sound of the trunks being moved.

He listened and lay wondering why Bret had allowed this wakefulness. When he wasn't thinking about that, he was thinking about the cop in the story that Bret had given him to read, and Bakersfield, and men who had always made him proud of being a cop, men who had always treated him like a son.

Again and again he thought of Irene, and things he wished he had told her more times than he had.

30

I WATCHED AS CASSIDY'S FACE CHANGED, from weary to suddenly alert. He didn't say much to the caller. He listened, looked at his watch, and said, "Great. I'll call back just as soon as I can."

He put the phone away and smiled. "I don't want you to get your hopes up, but our luck just might be changing. That was Hank. We've had a couple of breaks.

"First, seems a fellow who just got back in town picked up his newspapers from his neighbor's house and saw a familiar face on the front page of the *Las Piernas News Express*. It was Samuel Ryan's photo that drew his attention. Seems he was hired by Ryan—who was using a different name—to do some peculiar unpermitted work on a building. So after wrestling with his conscience and calling his lawyer, he's on his way down to the department to have a little talk. But from the sounds of it, there's a possibility that this man can lead us to where they're holding Frank."

"What kind of peculiar work?"

"No real details on that yet," he said.

"Cassidy—"

"A soundproof room of some sort."

"Oh, Christ. . . ."

"Don't think like that. It won't help."

"No, no—of course not," I said. "You're right. Any minute now, we could know where he is. That's what's important."

I was trying hard to convince myself, and he knew it, but he was kind enough not to point it out. He went on to say that the other break had been here in Bakersfield. Detectives had spent time checking out rental car agencies, asking if anyone recalled customers who smelled of aftershave. They'd come across one agency that said no customer smelling of aftershave had been in, but one of their vans had come back reeking of the stuff.

They had been a little surprised, because the van had been rented and returned to them by a woman—who matched the description of the woman in Hocus. The detectives had the van at the crime lab now, but the fragrance had definitely matched the scent on the abandoned "old man's" clothing.

Her name, according to their records and her driver's license, was Faye Taft. She had given an address and a credit card number. The rental car agency was near the airport—and Bakersfield PD had learned that Faye Taft also had a pilot's license. Her flight plans had been to Torrance, and she had left just after the incident at the library. The Torrance Airport confirmed that her plane had been there, but she'd then flown on to Las Piernas.

"Do you think it could have been a woman who approached you?" Cassidy asked.

"Maybe, but for reasons I can't exactly name, I'm fairly sure it was a man. Besides, if the person who approached me showed up at the rental counter, they would have smelled the aftershave."

"Well, the fellows at the airport did say she had a large trunk with her, so maybe our magician friend Bret was with her. In any case, between information that's coming in on Ryan and Neukirk and now this, everybody is pretty busy back in Las Piernas. I think I'm going to have to send Pete on home."

Pete was happy to go, antsy to get on the road. Rachel was more reluctant. "I don't want to leave you here alone," she said.

"I'll be all right," I said. "And I'm not alone."

"You know what I meant."

"Yes. Thanks. I'll be coming home soon. Maybe you could help Jack to hang in there."

"Sure," she said, and gave me a fierce hug before she left.

The call from Hocus came in right at midnight.

"Good evening, Irene, Tom." Samuel again.

"Evening, Samuel," Cassidy answered. "Bret still on his way back from Bakersfield?"

I looked over to him in surprise, then realized what he was doing.

"Now, Tom, that's the sort of question you know we'll never answer."

"I just figured he was the magician in the family. The master of disguise and all that."

"I have talents of my own," Samuel said.

"Really? I mean, I'm not surprised, but I guess I supposed the medical training would take up a lot of time."

"It did. But as it so happens—perhaps Irene will recognize this." Matching his voice to that of the old man's, he said, " 'As long as you like, honey.' "

"So it was you," I said.

"Yes," he said, laughing. "And since you were expecting this call, you must have discovered our note. Now, what we'd like to know is, how are things coming along?"

"Well, as I mentioned, it's tough getting things done on the weekend," Cassidy said.

"And yet Irene has narrowed the field, hasn't she? She's even gone to the place where Powell died. If she's willing to sit around and talk to the woman her husband was once in love with, she's making a real effort, isn't she?"

"Yes," Cassidy said. "I think that shows you that we're doing our best here. She's been through a lot today, trying to find out who this man could be."

"Irene, you're being very quiet," he said.

"Sorry, Samuel, I'm just tired."

"Poor Irene. Cassidy is a man of great endurance. Did you know that? In high school, he was a miler."

"A miler?" I asked.

"In track and field," Samuel said. "I could name some of his times, and the races he won. It's how he got to college. On a track scholarship."

"I'm flattered," Cassidy said. "You must have made a real effort to find that out. You interested in track, Samuel?"

"No, Cassidy, in you. You've become a specialty of

mine. I know all sorts of things about you. I know the name of the little town in Texas where you grew up. I know your high school. I've been there. People are very friendly there."

"Yes, they are," Cassidy said, but he shifted in his chair. His forehead furrowed with tension.

"Why'd you go into law enforcement, Cassidy?"

Cassidy relaxed a little. "Oh, like a lot of people who get into it, I wanted to make a difference. Is that why you got into medicine?"

"No. I'm not really in medicine, of course, although I know as much as any doctor. I didn't become an EMT because I was into the humanity of it all, Cassidy. I'm not very fond of most of humanity, for one thing. But it takes a lot to hold my interest—I had such a thrilling childhood, you see. Being a paramedic is far more exciting to me than working in a hospital would be. All except the emergency department. But I like my job better. I like racing to the scene, hearing the sirens, finding everything in chaos—saving them or not saving them. It's up to me. Just me. We're alike in that way, aren't we, Cassidy?"

"There are definite similarities, Samuel," he said.

"We even have rather tragic beginnings to our stories," Samuel said.

Cassidy was silent. I was startled to notice he was gripping the phone cord. Cassidy—tense. I watched his face. In the past forty-eight hours, almost constantly in his company, I had not seen this look. He was shaken.

"Yes, that little town in Texas," Samuel went on. "That's as far as anyone looks, isn't it? Thomas Cassidy, track star, likeable guy, very popular. They don't ask who you dated in high school, do they? They don't find out that you didn't date the girls from the local school, do they?"

I saw Cassidy's gaze wander. I wrote a note: "Cassidy? What's going on?"

"They do the background checks, but they don't ask the right people," Samuel went on. "The jealous women. You met her at a track meet, I hear. From a rival school. But her town wasn't too far from yours, right?"

Cassidy was ignoring the note. He had closed his eyes.

"What's the point to all of this, Samuel?" I said.

"You, of all people, should be interested in this, Irene. Your husband's life is in his hands."

"So he dated someone from a rival town. Not something that exactly rocks my world, Samuel."

Cassidy opened his eyes now, seemed to come back into focus. "Not much to that, is there? How's Faye doing?"

Samuel laughed. "Who cares?"

"Well, you seem to depend on her quite a bit."

"She isn't important. Women are not important, Cassidy. Even the beautiful ones. Especially them. Now, the young woman you loved was—you'll forgive me, Cassidy—she was rather plain."

"She's not our concern at the moment," Cassidy said, but the tension was back in his voice.

"She is if I say she is. *And I say so!*" Samuel shouted. When he spoke again, his voice was soft and low. "I say she is, and that she was plain."

"You get that from those jealous women you talked to?" Cassidy asked. Something was still not right.

"No, I saw her picture in her high school yearbook. She wasn't even Miss Personality or any of the other things they give to the ugly girls."

Nothing.

"Look," I said, "as fascinating as this is—"

"Shut up!" Samuel said. "No one is talking to you. No one. Cassidy, aren't you going to defend her?"

Silence.

"I don't need anyone to defend me," I said.

"Once again, Ms. Kelly, you are butting in. No one is talking about defending you. I meant Johnnie."

"Johnnie?" I asked. Cassidy was pale, and a fine sheen of sweat covered his forehead and upper lip.

"Yes, isn't that delightful? A Texas name. Johnnie Lee Meadows. Can you believe someone would force a girl—an ugly girl—to go through life with that name?"

"She wasn't ugly," Cassidy said. There was steel in his voice now.

"Plain. Totally unremarkable."

"No, there you're wrong."

I felt panic rising. If I spoke, I angered Samuel, which might in turn cause him to harm Frank. My only hope seemed to be to get through to Cassidy. I wrote another note: "Come back to me. Please. I need your help."

He read it, seemed to snap back out of whatever spell Samuel was weaving.

"You surprised me, Cassidy," Samuel was saying. "I thought you'd have your pick of the girls."

"I did," he said. "Tell me, how did you meet Faye?"

"I can't seem to make you understand that she is no longer of interest to me."

"Well, we're even, then. Johnnie Lee is dead, and she's been dead for many years."

"It still hurts, doesn't it, Cassidy?"

"Of course it does, Samuel. You still feel sad about your father, right?"

"Yes, but to be very honest, Julian was the greater loss. My father betrayed us. All of us. But Julian didn't deserve what happened to him."

"You knew Julian pretty well, I guess."

"Yes. And I look forward to seeing him again."

Cassidy hesitated only slightly before saying, "Tell me about him."

"He's dead, and soon we will be, too. Perhaps Detective Harriman will be joining us. That's up to you. Good-bye, Cassidy. I've enjoyed knowing you."

"Samuel—"

But Samuel had hung up.

The cell phone rang before I could ask Cassidy what the hell had happened.

"Yes, sir," he said. He listened, smiled broadly. "I was hoping that would be long enough," he said. "That confirms the address, then. I'm on my way—"

He paused, listened again. He lost the smile. "Sir. . . ."

He glanced over at me, then looked down. "Certainly. I understand. Yes, I'll explain."

He hung up, and it was a moment before he looked up at me. "Samuel talked long enough to let us trap the number," he said. "Between that and the information from the contractor, they've got an address. They're already getting set up down there. There's a plane waiting at the Kern County Airport. It will get you home faster than driving will. An officer will meet you at the Las Piernas Airport and take you to the site. I'll warn you that they probably won't let you close, but—"

"Cassidy," I interrupted.

"I won't be going with you," he continued.

"What?"

"I'm off the case."

31

THE OLD MAN PEERED cautiously through the blinds, angled so that he could look out at the cruiser across the street. The officer in the car was watchful, but well past the point where boredom had set in. Would he fall asleep?

The old man wouldn't. He slept little now. He was fully dressed, waiting. He was always waiting. For almost twelve years now he had waited. He had thought of them each day when he awakened, each night, until exhaustion overtook memory. It was worse during the month of June. In June he hardly slept at all.

He had waited on that Father's Day for the boys to identify him, to at least mention a policeman.

But the boys hadn't spoken. Even their drawings had never included a policeman. He knew, because he'd asked Frank Harriman about them.

He had almost confessed everything to Frank.

More than once. But each time, he'd thought of Diana Harriman, thought of the cruelty of telling Frank of his betrayal. It should be someone else, he told himself, but never sought another priest.

Instead he waited. He woke up every morning, wondering, Will this be the day?

Three years of hell went by. Silent hell. When the boys started talking, he was sure the first words out of their mouths would be his name.

Instead they didn't speak of it at all. Did they know then? Did they know how their silence punished him? Made his nights sleepless? Left him wondering when he did sleep, if he had shouted the truth in dreams?

Now this surveillance. He looked back out at the cruiser. Had Cassidy asked them to wait in plain sight, knowing how it would chafe at him?

There was a soft tapping at the back door.

He glanced at his reflection in a hallway mirror, straightened his tie.

"It never hurts to look your best," he could hear his mother's voice say, somewhere deep inside his head.

The tapping came again.

He opened the door.

"You," he said, mildly surprised.

"Us," came a whispered voice, as others stepped out of the shadows.

32

I T WAS TOO DARK INSIDE the small plane to read the business card I held in my hand, but I skimmed my fingertip over the print, over the embossed insignia of the Las Piernas Police Department and the name Thomas Cassidy. I didn't need light to know what it said; I had looked at it a dozen times before takeoff.

"Detective," it said, along with all the other official humbug. On the back of the card, nestled against the palm of my hand, in bold, blue strokes, he had written his home phone number. "Say hello to Frank for me," he had said as he'd handed it to me. "Tell him to give me a call when he's up to it."

I had taken it, not nearly so able to pretend I had faith that I would be able to give it to my husband. "I'll let you know what happens," I had said, knowing that for Cassidy, giving me his card was a way to stay connected to the case. For me, the card was a talisman, a protection from panic.

Bredloe had decided that Cassidy needed a few hours' sleep. That was the story. They needed someone in place in Las Piernas, Bredloe said, needed someone who could take over immediately. It would take Cassidy about three hours to drive back, about an hour and a half to fly. Too long either way. And Cassidy sounded tired, he said.

That was the official line, but Cassidy didn't buy it. He figured Bredloe had listened to that tape and worried that his negotiator was not in control, had shown a lack of judgment. Worries Cassidy couldn't blame him for, not with the life of one of his officers on the line.

"Who was Johnnie Lee?" I asked.

"The woman of my dreams," he said dryly. "Literally. The dream I had this morning."

"She was the teller? You knew her?"

"Yes. The negotiation part of the dream—that never happened. I was just a kid, just out of high school, trying to decide if I would survive my first year of college without her.

"That summer, I tried to see her every chance I got. She worked in the bank. She'd get a fifteen-minute break at ten-fifteen in the morning. I'd go over there, spend her little break with her, cool my heels until lunch, show up again, and take her to lunch. I did that every day, waited around that damn town for every minute I could spend with her."

He paused and swallowed hard. "Except—that last morning, when I showed up, the bank was surrounded by cops—wouldn't let me near it. Local sher-

iff was a hothead," he said. "Went in with guns blaz-
ing. Used to brag that thanks to him, the robbers
didn't get a dime out of that bank." He took a deep
breath, let it out slowly. "She was a remarkable young
woman," he said, but nothing more.

"I'll talk to Bredloe," I said.

"No," he said.

When I abandoned arguments he simply would not
respond to and began to plead frantically with him to
fly back with us, he said, "I'd appreciate it if you
didn't make this any harder than it already is."

Calm.

I went into the kitchen, talked to Bea, and made a
phone call to Cecilia. I gathered my belongings and
waited in Bea's car while she gave Cassidy instructions
on locking up.

I should have been glad to know that they had
located Frank, but I was filled with uneasiness. He
was still in the hands of Hocus. The man who best
knew Hocus, who was best prepared to meet them,
was left behind, packing up his gear in Bakersfield.
Our disagreements meant nothing. I trusted Thomas
Cassidy, would trust him with Frank's life.

Now I was sailing off without an anchor.

"When do you suppose you'll get around to telling
me what this evening's performance was all about?"
Bea asked, snapping me out of my self-pity.

Leaning close so that I could be heard over the
engines, I told her all I knew about why her son was a
hostage.

We were met at the airport by a black-and-white and
rushed to the scene or, I should say, the outskirts of

the scene. The only people who were kept farther away were media and the public. We were only slightly closer than the media. Very slightly.

All attention was focused on the windowless face of a warehouse about a block away from us, all four sides of the square building lit up by police arc lights. A dull, ocher-colored building, hardly worthy of any notice, it now stood front and center, a solo act on a dilapidated stage.

The whole area hummed with the sound of generators, truck motors, voices.

We were in an older part of town, on a stretch of wide boulevard that was once a commercial district but was now falling into ruin. Easily a quarter of the buildings on this same block were abandoned. There were a couple of old hotels turned into low-income apartment buildings; almost all the other doorways had locked grating pulled in place. From where we were stationed, I could see two or three other warehouses mixed in with a storefront church, a pawnshop, a thrift store, and a used-record shop. Not much new merchandise for sale.

The Las Piernas Police Department had apparently reacted swiftly. The phone call from Samuel had ended just two hours earlier, and the neighborhood surrounding the warehouse was clearly under police control. On the inner perimeter a command post and primary negotiators' area had been set up, and SWAT team members were already in position. Nearby, there were ambulances, a fire truck, a HazMat vehicle—for the hazardous materials team from the fire department—a bomb squad truck, and a number of other specially equipped vehicles. Some belonged to SWAT, others obviously contained communications devices.

All buildings adjoining the warehouse property were evacuated. Not many folks were displaced.

Pete, Rachel, and Jack were waiting for us in our area, one set aside for Frank's close friends and family. Guarded by a pair of uniformed officers—whose job it was to keep us separated from press and action—I found it difficult not to feel that we were hostages of another sort. Forbidden to take part in the activities, Pete was distraught that Cassidy would not be handling negotiations. When I asked him who would be taking Cassidy's place, he said, "Guy by the name of Lewis. He's good, but. . . ."

"Cassidy's better."

Pete nodded.

Henry Freeman came over to our area. He was looking tired.

"Hi, Hank," I said.

He smiled. "You've been around Detective Cassidy too long. How is he?"

"Not too good, last time I saw him."

"Don't let Captain Bredloe know I said this, but I think he should have given him another chance."

"Me too. But I guess we'll have to accept Detective Lewis. You work with him, too?"

"Yes. If this lasts much longer, they'll get someone to give me a break. That's all they needed to do with Detective Cassidy."

"Think Lewis will come back here to talk to us?" I asked.

Freeman ran a finger around the inside of his collar. "Not really," he said.

"Well, I won't second-guess him," I said. "I'd prefer he stays busy helping Frank. Can you tell us anything about what's going on?"

I heard a voice shout, "Freeman! Get your ass over here!"

Freeman turned red.

"Lewis?" I asked.

He nodded quickly and left.

Thirty minutes passed, with no apparent change in the activities. Feeling penned in, I told the others I was taking a walk over to the media corral and started to leave, only to be halted by one of our keepers. A little testy, I fished press credentials out of my purse, flashed them under his nose, and told him to live with it.

I approached the press gathering cautiously, thankful that attention was on the building, where a helicopter had moved in and was hovering overhead. I felt strange, maybe like the first salamander or whatever it was that originally ventured onto dry land. The water would never look the same.

Taking the plunge all the same, I walked up to Mark Baker, who, to my great fortune, was near the back of the pack. I tapped him on the shoulder—a reach—and he turned to look at me.

"Can I talk to you for a minute?" I whispered.

He frowned, but nodded and followed me. When we were beyond the outer perimeter, he said, "Look, I can't get too far away from the action."

"What action?"

"There's a rumor that the roof is soaked with gasoline. SWAT team could smell it from other rooftops. Building was built in the 1930s, has a tar-paper roof. They're saying the place could go anytime."

I stared at him.

"Sorry—sorry. I didn't mean to just say that—"

"You're stealing my lines, Mark. I came over to offer you my humble and abject apology. My sincere and humble and groveling—"

"Stop," he said. "Just stop that nonsense."

"Let me say it, Mark. I'm sorry I even thought of blaming you for what's happened. It doesn't have anything to do with you or your story, and never really could have. I guess I wanted to find some reason for it, and before I had one—I'm sorry. It wasn't right."

He sighed. "Irene, you think I didn't understand that? I wish to God that John had put someone else on this story—"

"I don't. No one else would tell me what's going on without trying to pry a quote out of me."

He smiled. "No quote? Why the hell did I follow you over here?"

"Hope springs eternal, I guess."

He looked toward the building, solemn now. "Got to have hope."

"What's happening in there?" I asked, trying to sound braver than I was feeling.

"The police have cut the phone lines and power, had SWAT deliver a throw phone. But the takers aren't talking on it yet. There's some kind of backup generator that's supplying power to some of the floors. The team in the helicopter has used a FLIR—forward-looking infrared devices—you know about them?"

I nodded. "Thermal sensors, right? The devices that can pick up body heat?"

"Yes. They're also called thermal imaging devices.

They can pick up anything that gives off more than two degrees of heat."

"The building is about five stories high, though—"

"Doesn't matter. They've got them so sensitive now, multiple stories are no problem. You'd have to go to some extreme measures to defeat them."

"What have they picked up?"

"Two people in the building, on one of the upper floors—third floor." He hesitated, then added, "One lying prone. Hasn't moved much."

I bit my lower lip. He put a hand on my shoulder.

"These guys are the best," Mark said. "I've seen them pull off some amazing shit."

"Thanks for telling me, Mark."

"I wasn't sure I should. I figured I'd want to know, if it was my wife in there."

"Yes."

"Look, I've got to get back over there. You want me to walk you back?"

I shook my head. "No, I'll be all right. Go on ahead."

Reluctantly he started to go. He paused, then turned back. "That other business—I just want you to know, Hocus wasn't my source. I won't say who it was, but it wasn't them. I didn't want you to think . . . well, it wasn't them."

"Thanks," I said. "It wouldn't matter to me anyway."

"No, I guess not. See you."

He hurried off.

Slowly I walked back. The cop who had hassled me had been replaced, and I hoped I hadn't caused him to get in trouble. The new cop apparently recognized me, because he didn't keep me from walking into the roped-off area.

Jack took one look at my face and said, "My God, what's happened?"

I didn't have to answer. We were distracted when everyone who was watching the building gave a collective shout—as the roof burst into flames.

33

W E STOOD IN A HUDDLE, clutching one another, looking and not wanting to look, as flames spiked up into the building's smoky crown. Black and billowing clouds rose from the roof, carrying ashes that fell on us as swirling, papery rain. The helicopter pulled sharply away. Over nearby police radios, we heard the crackle of voices raised—the staccato of urgent commands.

Get him out of there, I prayed silently. Please, please, please.

"Why aren't they going in?" Bea asked angrily.

"SWAT team has to clear the building," Pete said. "Can't risk the firefighters' lives. If they can't get the taker out of there, they may just let it burn."

To our horror, for long moments it seemed that was exactly what would happen.

The roof suddenly collapsed with a loud boom. The walls of the upper story gave way—bricks flew outward, plummeting to the street in a hot and deadly rain. At the top of the building sparks outdistanced flames, rising orange and bright even as the fire fell. More smoke followed as the blaze began to devour the next floor of the building.

Apparently a signal was given by the SWAT team soon after the roof collapsed, for a great rush toward the building began—orderly but rapid movement by men dressed in yellow slickers and masks, carrying heavy hoses and equipment.

As the interior fire-fighting team went in, another group worked from the exterior of the building. The streets below became slick and shiny with water. Sirens sounded as more trucks arrived.

At one point a set of television lights turned our way, and others soon followed, stark and bright. We turned from them like cave creatures, unused to the sun. Lewis barked some orders and the police moved us out of range. Denied the treat of capturing our tense faces, cameras and lights swung back to the building.

The fire burned for over two hours. Bea and Pete were in bad shape by the end of that time, both weeping openly. As the rest of us tried to shore them up, I found myself outwardly numb, unable to display my emotions. Within, I was not far from collapsing like that roof.

Firefighters were still moving in and out of the building when I saw one of their officials walk up to Captain Bredloe, glance at us, and turn his body so that we could see only his back. I recognized the signs.

"No," I said aloud as I watched Bredloe cover his eyes. "No. . . ."

The others followed my gaze. Now Bredloe was talking to someone in a blue jacket, a man who used his radio. The man turned toward the building, began walking toward it. The bright yellow letters on his jacket said "Coroner."

Bredloe began walking toward us. Bea grasped my hand. I wanted Bredloe to stop, to never reach us—but he kept drawing closer, and now I could see his face was drawn into a terrible frown.

"We don't know where Frank is," he said. "I want you to understand that before you hear anything else. Do you understand? We don't know where he is."

We all nodded.

"There's a body in the building," he said. "We don't know who it is. Coroner is going in there now."

I felt myself sway. Jack moved closer, let me lean on him. Bea was trembling.

"It's not Frank!" Pete half shouted. He walked off, reached the limit of the police tape around us, and began pacing, swearing to himself in Italian. Rachel watched him in silence.

"Perhaps we should all sit down," Bredloe suggested. Pete and Rachel stayed standing; everyone else moved to a chair. Bea began crying quietly again.

Think, I told myself. Think. You'll have all kinds of time to panic later, hours and hours to fall apart. Right now, just think.

"Only one body?" I asked.

"Yes—so far. It may take us a day to sift through the debris. But we were watching the building with thermal sensors before the fire broke out, and there were only two people in the building—one who moved about and one who stayed stationary. What's more, the body is in the part of the building where Ryan and Neukirk had special construction done."

"The soundproof room?"

He nodded. "We asked the fire department to try to get to that area first, because we assumed that might be where they were keeping Frank."

"And that was the area where. . . ."

"Where the remains were found," he finished for me. "Yes. The fire department believes a separate fire was started in that room—using an accelerant, perhaps gasoline—that's what was used on the roof. The chemical analysis will take time. And while it will take some time to make any final determination, they believe the fire in that room may have started after the roof fire. It fits with the last thing the helicopter saw— the person who was moving around in the building left that area not long before the rooftop fire started. Otherwise, the men in the helicopter would have detected the fire in the room before they had to pull out."

"Any sign of that person?" I asked. "The one who was moving around?"

"No," Bredloe said. "But we're searching the area."

"The arithmetic is all wrong, isn't it?"

"What do you mean?" Bea asked. She had stopped crying, was wiping at her face.

"There should have been four people in that building," I said. "Frank, Bret Neukirk, Samuel Ryan, and a woman—Faye Taft—Samuel's girlfriend."

As I said her name, I thought of Samuel's voice as he'd spoken to us during the last phone call, of his chilling lack of regard for her.

"Yes," Bredloe said. "Two of them were out of the building before we arrived."

"And at least one of the other two knew you were coming."

"Why do you say that?" Bredloe asked.

"They were ready with the gasoline on the roof, and had some method of igniting it without going up there, right?"

"Yes. The arson investigators will find the ignition device, I'm sure."

"Unless it leads them to Frank, I'm not sure I care."

He didn't reply.

"There are other signs that this was all set up in advance," I said. "Ryan and Neukirk have contacted me by phone several times in the last few days. They never once allowed themselves to be traced—until now. I think they wanted to be traced. Ryan picked a topic that was bound to elicit an emotional reaction from Cassidy. Maybe they even wanted you to do just what you did—remove him, at least temporarily, from the case."

"Why would they want to do that?" Bredloe asked.

"I'm not sure. Maybe because Cassidy is getting a feel for them, is starting to anticipate them to some degree. Maybe if he had been here, he would have reacted differently from Lewis. I don't know."

"The negotiator was never really allowed to get involved in this one," Bredloe said.

"No, I guess not." I reconsidered. "Maybe it wasn't to get Cassidy off the case. Maybe it was a distraction—they knew you'd be concerned with Cassidy's reaction—and might not stop to think about the length of the call, about the fact that they were letting you trace them."

"You underestimate the ego of this type of taker," a voice said.

I looked up to see a balding man of medium height standing nearby. He was thin, wearing a brown suit that looked a little too big for him. He had a pleasant enough face.

"Detective Lewis," Bredloe said, and made introductions all around.

"Takers tend to fit certain profiles, Ms. Kelly," Lewis went on, even though no one asked him to. "Paranoid schizophrenic, psychotic depressive, antisocial personality, or inadequate personality. We've already seen that Neukirk and Ryan are not true political terrorists, as are their friends in jail. Lang and Colson believed all along that they were part of an anarchist organization. Neukirk and Ryan gave them an outlet for their needs."

Pete, who had moved nearer and listened to this, made a snorting sound. "Didn't take you long to figure everything out, did it?"

"How do you know what Lang and Colson's motives are?" I asked. "Have they talked?"

"No," Lewis said, "but—"

"Have you checked Lang's and Colson's family backgrounds?" I asked. "Or did you stop once you knew where they learned to work with explosives? Anyone look back beyond their years in the military?"

Bredloe looked uncomfortable. "We haven't had much time. We've concentrated on Ryan and Neukirk."

I decided not to mention that Lang and Colson had been under suspicion days before Hocus took Frank; decided against suggesting that perhaps Lieutenant Carlson had been too busy hassling Frank to allow time to thoroughly investigate his prisoners. I didn't say it, but the anger was there all the same. "No matter which one of Detective Lewis's four categories Ryan and Neukirk fit into," I said, "we already know how the damage was done. We also know they are masters of the art of distraction."

The next bit wasn't so easy to say, but I swallowed hard and went on. "I don't believe the body in that building belongs to Frank. They still need him as a bargaining chip. Making *you* think it was Frank was important, though. I think they've kept most of your resources busy while they were up to something else. Exactly what, I don't know, but I'm fairly certain they just got rid of someone who had outlived her usefulness to them."

"*Her* usefulness?" Bredloe asked. "The young woman?"

Before I could answer, his radio squawked.

"Bredloe," he answered. "Hold on a minute, Carlos."

He stood up and walked away from us, put an earphone in his ear. But he watched me the whole time.

Lewis was saying something about leaving things to professionals, but no one was listening. We were watching Bredloe.

He walked back over to us. "It's not Frank," he said.

"Oh, thank God!" Bea said, then clasped her hand over her mouth. "I don't mean to sound happy about whoever—"

"It's okay, Mrs. Harriman," Pete said. "We all feel the same."

"Coroner says the pelvis indicates a female," Bredloe said.

"Pelvis?" Lewis said. "You mean they only had bones—"

"Yes," Bredloe said, cutting him off. "Lewis, why don't you wait for me over at the command post? I'll be along shortly."

"Yes, sir," Lewis said, apparently not in the least perturbed by the dismissal.

"How did you know?" Bredloe asked me once Lewis had gone.

"I didn't. I hoped."

He was silent.

"No," I said, "that's not true. There were reasons I hoped—the ones I gave you. And remembering that last phone call, the way Samuel sounded whenever we talked about her. Remember? He said, 'I can't seem to make you understand that she is no longer of interest to me.' "

"Hmm. Yes, I remember."

"A couple I talked to—the Szals? They said that even Bret Neukirk disliked Samuel's attitude toward women—Bret thought he simply used them."

After a moment he said, "The firemen found some gas tanks up there. You know anything about that?"

"No," I said. "Sorry. What kind of gas?"

"Nitrogen. They think it might have been hooked up to the room somehow. Enough to asphyxiate someone, they said."

We sat in silence, Bredloe's thoughts seeming far away.

"Put Thomas Cassidy back on this case," I said. "Please. He understands Ryan and Neukirk."

"He undoubtedly does understand them," Bredloe said. "That's what he specializes in—understanding what drives people, what they want. But Hocus also knows what drives him, I'm afraid."

"Just because—"

"I heard that tape, Irene," he interrupted. "Even you would have to admit that the man is exhausted."

I couldn't argue with that.

"Don't underestimate Lewis," he said. "When he's under pressure, he's a different man. After SWAT moved in, the intense pressure Lewis has been under for the last few hours was suddenly off, and what you just saw was as close as he gets to a hysterical reaction." He turned to Pete. "A reaction no one need discuss outside this group. Understood?"

"Yes, sir," Pete said.

"Shall I have a car take you home?" Bredloe asked me.

"I'll take them," Jack offered. "I've got a van here."

At home, the dogs and Cody gave me an exuberant greeting that went a long way toward holding off my own hysterical reaction. I got Bea settled in and went into the kitchen. Hank Freeman's equipment was still set up. I supposed he would be back soon. I wasn't sure what all of the equipment did, but I could figure out which line led back to the recorder. I unplugged it, looked at the clock, and made the call anyway.

"Cassidy," he answered.

"You're awake."

"Yes. Tape recorder on?"

"No, Hank's not back yet. But I suppose they'll know I called you?"

"Yes, but I wouldn't worry over it."

I told him what had happened, only leaving out most of my conversation with Bredloe.

"You all right?" he asked.

"Hanging in there," I said. "And you?"

"Tuckered out, I'll admit," he said. "But if you hadn't called to let me know what had gone on, I'd be about as restless as a toad on a griddle. Maybe now I'll sleep. Thanks for calling."

I reconnected the recorder just as Hank Freeman came in the door. He sleepily checked over the equipment, then looked puzzled. He pressed a button on one device, which made a phone number appear on a display. He smiled.

"How is he?" he asked, obviously familiar with the number.

"Fine," I said.

"I thought he'd be . . . let's see . . . 'nervous as a long-tailed cat in a room full of rocking chairs'?"

"No, I got the toad—"

"On a griddle," he finished for me.

I smiled. "Couch okay for you tonight?"

He nodded, yawning. "Don't bother folding it out. I'm so tired, I could sleep on the floor."

He was asleep before I turned out all the lights.

Cody, who considered sleeping on the bed itself to be a cat privilege extended to certain humans as a courtesy, would usually not allow the dogs to come too near it. This night he magnanimously let them curl up on the rug within reach of my hand. He snuggled up to me, near my heart, and purred loudly.

I lay awake for a long time.

It was good to be home, just not quite good enough.

34

H
E AWAKENED, first noting the darkness, the cotton gag over his mouth. He couldn't move more than a few inches. Something was right above him—silky, padded. He was in a close-fitting, satin-lined box.

A coffin! They've put me in a goddamned coffin!

The last of his self-control shattered. He began screaming, beating his bound hands against the lid.

But almost instantly the lid was lifted, and he squinted in the sudden brightness. Bret's pale face appeared above him. "I'm sorry!" Bret said anxiously. "I'm sorry! I thought you'd sleep longer!"

Frank was terrified, knew he looked it. Didn't care. The gag was too much at this point. He tried to take in breaths of air as Bret continued to apologize, helped him to sit up. Dizzy again, he made a growling sound of frustration. Bret stepped away from him.

Gradually the room stopped spinning. He was in a

trunk, he saw then, a magician's trunk. Not airtight—breathing holes, in fact. Not a coffin.

It didn't matter. He was shaking.

Bret still did not approach, and Frank realized that even bound and gagged he probably looked like he wanted to kill somebody.

Don't frighten Bret, he told himself. You may need his help. Even if you don't, the last thing you need to do is make him wary of you.

Still, it took a while to calm down.

He looked around. He wasn't in the tent now. This was some kind of cellar. That thought nearly brought another round of panic, but he fought it off.

His hands were tethered together at the wrist, the IV catheter—tender after his attack on the lid of the trunk—still in. Now, he noticed, his ankles were manacled as well.

Once he was fairly sure he could do so without appearing ferocious, he looked over at Bret. Made the unspoken request, knew Bret understood it.

Bret stepped closer again, moved behind Frank. Hesitated only slightly before he removed the gag.

Frank stretched his jaw, rubbed his tethered hands against his face.

"Thanks," he said. "Where are we?"

Bret shook his head. "I can't tell you that, of course. But we've moved. I should warn you that it would be as dangerous for you to harm me or to try to leave this place as it was to leave the tent."

"Where's Samuel?"

"He'll be along later. He'll be bringing his friend, Faye." He paused, then said, "Would you like me to help you step out of there?"

More than just about anything, he thought, but simply said, "Yes, thanks."

Awkwardly, unable to move his legs freely or use his hands for proper leverage, he climbed out of the trunk with Bret's help. He saw other trunks stacked along one wall, although not as many as he had seen in the tent. The IV bottle and pole stood in one corner, near a folded bed. He decided he must have awakened while Bret was still in the process of setting up after the move.

His gaze traveled to a steep staircase that led up to a closed metal door. At the foot of the stairs there was an alarm keypad, its lights red—indicating it was armed.

He moved slowly, still dizzy from the drugs, weakened by the long hours under their influence. Bret watched him but did not prevent him from walking a few paces, dragging the chain as he moved. There was a small bathroom with a single shower stall, a few simple furnishings. The walls were brick lined, the floor concrete.

There were no windows, but the room was brightly lit. A panel of electronic equipment had been installed on one wall, including a phone, four small television monitors, and what seemed to be videotaping equipment. None of the monitors were on. For all this modern equipment, the building itself appeared to be old.

How much time had passed? Was he still in Las Piernas? In California? In the U.S.?

He turned to see that Bret had picked up a deck of cards, was idly shuffling, bridging, fanning, and moving them through his fingers with a dexterity that Frank found fascinating. Watching Bret distracted him from his fears, allowed him to relax a little more.

"You're very talented," he said as Bret completed a particularly complex series of flourishes.

Bret shrugged. "An amateur, really."

"I'd like to see you perform magic someday."

For the first time in all the time Frank had watched him practice these tricks, Bret dropped a card. The young man bent to pick it up, then set the deck on a small table. "That would have been nice—letting you see what I've learned," he said. "Perhaps I'll show you how a few of the tricks are done. We won't have an opportunity for more than that, I'm afraid."

"Why not?" Frank said.

"You already know," Bret said patiently, without any sign of irritation. "I'll be dead. We've been over this before."

"What's the rush? You can always die later," Frank said. "That's something any of us can do—all of us will do."

Bret picked up the cards again but held them still in his hands. "Not the way we will."

"You don't really want to die, do you? This has to do with Samuel."

"Do you know the story 'The Outcasts of Poker Flat,' by Bret Harte?" he asked, shuffling, fanning, then extending the pack to Frank—an invitation to participate in a trick. "I'm named for him, you know."

Frank shook his head, tried to hide his frustration. Every time he approached this topic, Bret changed the subject.

But Bret didn't tell the tale, as Frank thought he might. Instead he folded the deck again and said, "Samuel is damaged. So am I, even if it's not so readily apparent to you. We aren't whole, Frank. We don't fit in."

"No one fits in, Bret. Not completely. Not the way you imagine it. No one."

"You do."

Frank laughed. "When you took me from Riverside—at Ross's house?"

Bret flinched at the memory but nodded.

"That morning, I had a huge argument with my wife—part of a fight that had been going on for a couple of days—my mother wasn't speaking to me, and I was happy to get out of the office, where I was being shunned after you planted that story in the paper—"

"What story?" Bret interrupted.

"About the arrests of Lang and Colson."

"That wasn't us."

"But the details of the arrests—"

"No," Bret said again. "We didn't have anything to do with that story."

Frank stared at him in disbelief, then quickly realized Bret had no reason to lie to him.

"What's wrong?" Bret asked, setting down the cards.

"If you didn't leak anything to the paper, then someone in my department did."

"And everyone else assumed it was you?"

"Not everyone," Frank admitted, "but I was definitely getting the cold shoulder."

"You were betrayed," Bret said.

"I don't know if I'd put it like that—it's not that serious," Frank said, but Bret was lost in his own thoughts.

Frank heard a beeping sound. Bret moved to the keypad, entered some numbers. The door at the top of the stairs opened. Samuel walked in, dressed in dark, damp clothing, carrying a bundle. The bundle was wrapped up in what appeared to be a yellow slicker. "LPFD" was stenciled on the slicker in large red letters. Samuel was covered with soot.

"What's he doing up?" he asked, looking at Frank.

"Where's Faye?" Bret asked.

Samuel laughed. "She had to go to a barbecue."

Bret was silent, his mouth drawn tight in a line of disapproval.

"She was dead before I started the fires," Samuel said.

Still Bret said nothing.

"She said she was willing to die with us, remember?"

"But she didn't, did she?" Bret said in a low voice.

"I almost didn't get out of there," Samuel said, but no one gave him any sympathy. Sulking, he walked over to the keypad, punched in some numbers, and said, "You forgot to rearm it."

Bret shrugged, made a show of closing up the trunk Frank had been in.

Samuel turned to Frank, pointed at him. "You cause trouble," he said, stabbing the air with his blackened index finger as he said each word. He turned and walked into the bathroom, slamming the door shut behind him.

Frank began pacing again, thinking not of Samuel's tantrum, nor lamenting the dead woman, but trying to recall the pattern of movement of Samuel's hand on the alarm keypad. He drew close to the keypad, glanced at it furtively. He memorized the numbers with black smudges on them, thought again of Samuel's sooty hand moving—upper right, lower left, lower right, middle, upper left.

Maybe, he thought, I *will* cause trouble.

35

I'M GOING FOR A WALK," I said to Henry Freeman as we finished breakfast the next morning. Bea, who had been completely exhausted when we had arrived home a few hours earlier, was still asleep.

"But if Hocus calls—" Hank protested.

"Tell them I went for a walk."

He handed me a lightweight cellular phone. "Take this, please."

It might come in handy, I thought, and thanked him for it. I put it into the back pocket of my jeans.

"Where are you walking?" he asked.

"I'll be down at the beach. I'm taking the dogs."

It wasn't a lie—I did what I told him I would do. I took the dogs for a walk on the beach. Dunk—Frank's dog—wouldn't allow Deke or me to lag behind or rove ahead but kept shepherding us into a close pack.

Several times the dogs looked back at the stairs that led up to our street. Watching for Frank.

The ocean air was good for me, as was my time alone with the dogs. I mentally sorted through the last few days, all that had happened, all I had seen and heard and felt.

Over breakfast that morning I had asked Hank Freeman for ownership information on the warehouse, knowing the police would have not only that, but any architectural drawings they could lay their hands on. Hank told me the building had been purchased by a company four years ago, a business police had just this morning traced back to Francine Neukirk. The late Mrs. Neukirk, Hank said, had owned most of the buildings on that side of the block. They were sold to her as a unit—the warehouse, it turned out, had once been connected to two other buildings, both now vacant. Basement passageways that building plans had shown to be sealed off had been reopened.

I had asked Hank if anyone had been in the passageways that night.

"Only firefighters and SWAT," he said. "We were all over the place. Even if the taker had tried to leave that way, he would have been seen by one of us."

Hank also told me that outside of the recent construction work on the soundproof room—which had been completed about six months ago—none of the few neighboring business owners had seen anyone entering the building.

As I approached the house when we returned, I went to our backyard gate and let the dogs in through it, but I didn't follow them, much to Dunk's consternation. I took my keys, got in the car, and drove off.

I wasn't around the corner before the cell phone rang. I answered it by saying, "Leave me alone, Hank."

"I'm responsible for you," he said.

"No, you're not," I said. "You're responsible for Frank. I'm not under arrest, am I?"

"Of course not, but—"

"See you later, then. Please apologize to Bea for me when she wakes up." I was at a stop sign. I hung up, studied the phone, found the power switch, and turned it off. I took the long way to the newspaper. It was about nine-thirty when I pulled into the parking lot. I walked past the space where Frank's car had been left just a few days before, ignored the sudden queasiness those memories brought on, and entered the building.

Avoiding anyone associated with the newsroom, I quickly ducked into the downstairs office of classified advertising. Following Hocus's instructions, I paid for an ad in the personals section that read "John Oakhurst, come home."

Geoffrey, the day shift security guard, had never failed to do me any kindness he could manage, and he kept his record at one hundred percent when I asked him if all the pool cars were spoken for. He didn't answer yes or no, just handed me a set of keys and said, "Drive carefully."

"Thanks," I said, and started to leave. I stopped at the front doors and turned back. I handed him the cellular phone and said, "When the Las Piernas Police Department comes looking for me, please give them their phone."

He laughed his wheezy laugh and said, "Sure."

• • •

I parked the pool car several blocks away from the burned-out warehouse, not even driving past it, although the temptation was great. But I knew there would still be some activity there, investigators sifting through the rubble, so I avoided it. Frank isn't there, I told myself. Prayed to God it was true.

I got out of the car and started walking. The night before, as we had stayed penned in our enclosure, I had thought about this neighborhood. Now, walking through it, I was fairly certain that Hocus was still nearby.

Whether or not they had been seen entering it, Hocus had been in the warehouse. I was betting they hadn't moved far. First, Frank wouldn't be easy to move. If he were awake, he might escape. That meant he was probably still doped up on morphine, all the more likely if they were sticking to their plan of increasing his dosages.

As I had told Bredloe, I didn't think the arrival of the police at the warehouse had been a surprise—they had been beckoned there. Only two people were in the warehouse when the fire was set; Faye Taft was very likely the "prone" person in the warehouse. So Frank had been moved and had had to be watched by Samuel or Bret.

Bret, most likely, I decided. Faye was Samuel's girlfriend. I couldn't be sure it was Samuel who stayed there to make sure she burned up with the building, but there was something in the way he had spoken of her that made me believe he was capable of it. And I remembered Regina Szal telling me that Bret had passed out at the sight of blood. Bret, I had decided, made an unlikely killer.

Samuel had to have left on foot. Any escape in a vehicle would have been impossible. Either he disguised himself as an official—a firefighter or SWAT team member—or he had left by some concealed exit.

When I was about a block north and two blocks east of the warehouse, I slowed down, started paying more attention to the neighborhood. I walked past a shoe repair shop with a faded cardboard sign in the window that said "We closed Mondays." There was a comic book store next to it. I glanced in, saw five or six customers, all who seemed to be men in their thirties. I kept walking.

When I reached the row of shops directly behind the warehouse, I began to get the distinct impression that someone was following me. Paranoia required no effort on my part at this point, so I ducked into a small café. All the tables were covered with plastic-coated, red-and-white-checkered tablecloths. There were dusty plastic vases with dusty plastic flowers in them. I sat at a table in the back, only to glance down and notice that a large fly was in final repose on one of the red checkers.

"We don't open for lunch for another hour," a voice called from the back.

"I'm in luck, then," I said under my breath, then stood up and walked toward the voice. A large, rough-faced man in a dirty apron filled up most of a narrow hallway. His arms were covered with tattoos. He was lighting a cigarette.

I looked back toward the street, just in time to see Reed Collins peer in through the window. After seeing nothing but empty tables, he walked on.

"You want something, lady?" Mr. Culinary Arts asked.

"Could I use your rest room?"

"Look, we're closed."

I reached into my jeans and pulled out a buck. "Could I use your rest room?" I asked again.

He looked skeptical. "A lousy buck?"

"Even pay toilets used to only cost a nickel," I said.

He took a long drag on the cigarette. "So did a candy bar. Stop or you'll make me cry."

After glancing back at the window, I pulled out a second dollar. He snatched the bills from my fingers and said, "Make yourself at home."

The bathroom was past the kitchen, and judging from the sweltering heat in the tiny room, the ovens were on the other side of one wall. I flipped on the light switch, which also turned on a fan that sounded like a tank battalion crossing a metal bridge but did nothing to cool the room. The switch also apparently signaled an air freshener dispenser to have multiple orgasms—it found its release again and again. The toilet and sink were rust stained, the floor was sticky, and toilet paper seemed to be on a BYO roll basis.

Thank God I didn't have to go.

Trying not to touch *anything,* I waited. I started wondering if I was going to end up with some disease late in life, an illness that would be traced back to overexposure to that air freshener. The scent must have been named "Yes, Bears Do."

When I couldn't take it any longer, I stepped out.

"He turned right at the corner," the cook said.

"Who?"

He crossed his arms and leaned against the wall. "The cop you're avoiding. Plainclothes guy."

"He came in here?"

"No. Like I said, went around the corner to the right."

"How could you tell he was a cop?" I asked.

"Folsom, class of 1989. Fully rehabilitated, of course."

"Of course," I said. "What makes you so sure I'm avoiding a cop?"

He started laughing and pulled the two dollars back out of his pocket. He handed them to me and said, "Sister, you earned it," as he walked back into the kitchen.

As I started toward the front door, I heard him say, "Hey!"

I turned around.

"You in some kind of trouble?" he asked.

"Not really. Someone else is."

"Yeah? Well, go over to the little bookstore across the street. Guy over there will let you out the back way."

"Thanks," I said.

The long, narrow store sold used books. The owner was at a counter in the back, talking on the phone. He was tall and thin and looked as if he had been selling books since the day the Gutenberg Bible was hot off the press. There was a closed door marked EMPLOYEES ONLY behind him. I decided not to make a scene by rushing through it and passed the time browsing—not an unpleasant diversion. I found a paperback copy of a collection of short stories by Bret Harte and pulled it from the shelf. A penciled notation on the title page said it was mine for a quarter—a deal.

Deciding I needed to move toward the rear of the store in case Reed Collins came back, I moved closer to the counter and started looking over the eclectic collections on the back shelves, which yellowed tags identified as books on gardening, bicycling, architecture, military history, and other subjects. While most sections were crowded with titles, there was a noticeable gap on one of the upper shelves, and I stood on tiptoe to read its tag.

"Magic and Magicians," I read aloud.

The store owner had just finished his call. "Magic?" he repeated. "Not you, too. Is this some new craze or something?"

"You've had a lot of people in here buying books on magic?"

He shook his head. "No, just Mr. Messier, the fellow that bought the theater."

Something was familiar about that name, but I couldn't place it. "Which theater?"

"Oh, it's just down the alley from here. The Starlight. Long time ago, it was quite a grand place, but then it went broke. Church group had it for a little while. Called it the Starlight Chapel. Then the church went broke. Hasn't operated as a theater in years, but Mr. Messier's restoring it."

The Starlight. I knew where I had heard the name, then. "Would this be Mr. Charles Messier?"

"Why, yes!" he said, smiling. "Do you know him?"

"We've spoken on the phone," I said. "Is he a young man?"

"Yes, but don't let that fool you. He's well off. And

smart as a whip. And I'm telling you, he showed me a couple of card tricks—he should be in Vegas, he's that good."

"Sounds like you've taken a liking to him."

"I have, I have. Mr. Messier is a very charming young man. And he's put a lot of work into that theater."

I paid for the Harte stories and said, "I have a favor to ask."

The owner looked up at me.

"The cook at the café across the street said you might let me out the back door, into the alley."

The old man smiled. "Ray said that? Well, sure, go right ahead."

"How well do you know Ray?" I asked, curiosity getting the better of me.

"You mean, do I know he's an ex-con? Sure I do. He worked here for me when he first got out, then went to work over there at the café. He keeps an eye out for me, though. Neighborhood's a lot tougher than it used to be—heck, they tell me the SWAT team was all over the place last night. A warehouse burned down. Anyway, Ray doesn't let anybody give me any trouble. So if he wants you to see our lovely alley, go right on through that back door. But I'll warn you, that back door will lock behind you, so once you're in the alley, you have to walk to the end of it to get out."

"Thank you—and please thank Ray again for me." I started to leave, then paused and asked, "Do you know where the nearest pay phone is?"

"Local call?"

"Yes, but—"

"Go right ahead and use mine."

"Thanks."

I dialed Cassidy's number, got an answering machine.

"Cassidy, this is Irene. There's an old theater between Twentieth and Twenty-first Streets, off. . . ."

"Denton," the old man supplied.

"Denton," I said. "It's owned by Mr. Charles Messier, whom you may remember from our conversation with the Szals. I think he has our package. The Starlight Theater. I'll call back in a few minutes."

I hung up, stood wondering if I trusted such an important message to an answering machine.

"Go ahead," the old man said, "make another call." At my puzzled look he added, "You're still hanging on to the phone. Squeezing it half to death, I'd say."

I looked down at my hand, embarrassed to see he was right. "Thank you," I said again.

As the phone rang, I started to lose my courage. Hank was probably going to follow the rule book and call up Bredloe or Lewis. Or maybe ignore everything I had to say and try to charge me with interfering with an investigation.

He answered with a nervous, "Hello?"

"Hank, it's Irene."

"Oh, thank God!" he said. "Uh, just a minute."

"No stalling, Hank. Page Cassidy. Tell him to check his answering machine." I hung up.

I thanked the bookstore owner again and left, hoping Freeman wouldn't be able to trace the call.

The alley, as it turned out, was a blind one, ending at a brick wall not far from the bookstore. Luckily the open end of the alley was in the direction I would have taken anyway—to my left, opposite the one Reed Collins was last seen traveling. It was fairly wide, as alleys went—wide enough for a truck. All the same, with only one way out, as the bookstore door closed behind me, I felt cornered.

The alley was not much to look at. Brick walls, metal doors, and trash bins. A few high, barred windows and some roof access ladders. One or two fire escapes.

A scruffy cat slept on one of the fire escapes. He didn't look as if he had ever let anyone call him a pet. He was one of the few things in the alley that didn't have a layer of soot on it.

The day was starting to warm up, and the odor from the bins, already sharp, was going to increase with every degree of heat.

I started walking down the center of the alley, but soon that sensation of being watched returned, and I moved closer to the wall on my right. I looked up at the rooflines of the buildings on the left. No one. I was about to edge closer to the other side when I heard a loud metallic rattling sound. I shrank back against the wall, hiding behind a bin. The sound, I realized, was that of a large, metal roll-up door being opened. I heard a motor start up, and a brown delivery van slowly pulled out into the alley. Fading paint on the brick above the doorway said "Starlight Theater."

In the van's side mirror I saw the reflection of the driver. Another old man, except I knew this one. I had seen him in a library in Bakersfield.

He honked the horn of the van, and the door started to roll shut as he drove off.

Frank was nearby. Either in that van or in the building.

I ran around the bin, flattened myself to the ground, and rolled beneath the door just as it closed.

I was in total darkness.

36

I COULD HEAR FAINT SOUNDS coming from somewhere inside the building. I started to crawl forward, feeling my way along the concrete floor.
Suddenly the room I was in was filled with bright
light, and I heard a high-pitched whistling sound.
Panicked, I jumped to my feet and looked for a place
to hide. The room was a delivery bay, absolutely barren, with three doors leading off it. The one farthest to
the left had an alarm keypad next to it. Several of the
lights on the keypad were blinking.

Certain that someone was going to come through
one of the other doors at any moment, I tried the middle one. Locked. The door to the right, however, pulled
open. I shut it behind me. I was again in darkness, but I
could hear someone entering the delivery bay. I turned
to flee and immediately stumbled. I reached out and
caught myself between the narrow walls of the space
ahead of me. A stairway, I realized. Hurrying, but mov-

ing as quietly as possible, I climbed the stairs, waiting for lights to be turned on above me or to find myself stepping off into some void. I reached a landing, but there were more stairs above it. I continued upward.

The stairs went on forever, it seemed, finally ending at another doorway. Cautiously, bending low, I turned the handle, pushed open the door. There was low light here, most of it coming through windows that faced the stage. I was, I realized, in a projection booth.

The small booth was unoccupied. A lighting control console was on, a computerized system with monitors and a keyboard added to a variety of other controls. Sitting on a sleek black desk, the console appeared to be the only new fixture in a room that was otherwise musty with age. A pile of discarded equipment stood in one corner. A ladder attached to one wall rose into a recess in the ceiling. I wasn't sure what it led to, but the door in the recess appeared to be locked.

Staying low, I crept to the largest of the windows in the booth. I gradually raised up to look down on the stage below.

My eyes were drawn immediately to a figure lying on a draped table. His hands and feet manacled, he was dressed in what appeared to be pajamas. One hand bandaged. Face pale beneath three days' growth of beard, but maybe he only seemed pale because of the bright stage lights. He didn't move, but perhaps he was asleep.

Frank.

I put a hand over my mouth to keep from shouting out his name. As if he heard me anyway, he stirred slightly.

Tears began running down my cheeks. I wiped them away. Nothing to feel so all-fired relieved about yet, I told myself, but to no avail. He was alive. I could see him.

In addition to the draped table, there were several other objects on the stage. Some long, freestanding mirrors, trunks, a colorful set of boxes, and a large cylinder. A mechanical lift stood at one side of the stage, its platform extended up into the ceiling. I only glanced at these objects; Frank held my attention. I wondered how long I could keep myself from running to him. If anything happened to him while I watched from a distance. . . .

He opened his eyes, seemed groggy, disoriented.

I tried to force myself to look at the situation logically. As much as I wanted to be with Frank now, doing anything that might let Hocus know I was here would be madness—dangerous for both Frank and me. It would give Hocus two hostages instead of one. If, instead, I could stay hidden until Cassidy arrived, maybe we would both survive.

As foolish as it may have been to enter Hocus's lair, I had no regrets at that moment. I had answers now to at least two of the questions that had tortured me since Friday night. I knew where Frank was, I knew he was alive.

Another figure appeared on the stage, a young man dressed in a shimmering white cape and black top hat, wearing white gloves. Bret Neukirk. I drew back from the window, though I doubted he could see beyond the stage lights.

"How are you feeling?" he asked Frank. Hearing his voice so clearly, I gave a start, then realized the sound was coming through a speaker in the booth.

Frank was looking around, obviously confused by his surroundings.

"You're on stage," Bret said, and Frank's face turned red. "No—no," Bret added quickly. "No one is out there. I know you can't see past the lights, but the theater is empty. Don't move too much to one side or the other, by the way. You're on a platform, not a bed."

Frank tried to lift himself up, but Bret put a hand on his shoulder. "Stay here for a moment. You can watch while I show you how to levitate. Can you see yourself?"

"Yes," Frank said, looking at one of the several mirrors. His expression changed then, to one of dismay.

"Oh, no—I'm sorry. Perhaps this was a mistake," Bret said, reading that change of expression as clearly as I did. "I didn't think about . . . well, I just didn't think."

"It's all right," Frank said. "My reflection surprised me, that's all." He studied Bret and said, "That's a different cape from the one you were wearing in Riverside, at Ross's house. The other one was purple."

"Yes," Bret said. "I got rid of that one." He looked a little pale.

"Because it had blood on it," Frank said gently.

I was a little puzzled by Frank's tone of voice.

Just above a whisper, Bret said, "Yes."

"Go ahead and show me the trick," Frank said, obviously trying to distract Bret from troubling thoughts.

Bret, seeming to come out of a reverie, said, "I'd

take your chains off, but Samuel is already upset with me, and he should be back soon."

"It's all right," Frank said again—as if comforting Bret.

I was confused by that. Was this the "Stock-holming" Cassidy had spoken of? Or was Frank trying to get Bret to drop his guard? Perhaps there was something in the drugs they were giving him that made Frank docile.

I was soon distracted by the implications of what Bret had just said. If Samuel was returning, I would need a better hiding place. But if I went down the stairs, I ran the risk of walking right into him. I looked at the pile of equipment in the corner. I might be able to hide behind some of it.

"I stand here," Bret said, drawing my attention back to the stage. He moved to a center point behind Frank. "The audience sees me lift this drape—usually, I'd cover you with it. But since you need to see what I'm doing, I'll remove it for now." He pulled the drape from the front of the platform with a flourish.

Frank was on a long board, it seemed, not a table, as I had thought. The board was supported by two folding chairs. It looked pretty unstable, and I wondered if Bret was planning to injure Frank in some way.

"Watch the mirror at the front of the stage," Bret said, then suddenly pulled both chairs away.

I drew in a breath. Frank was floating in midair.

And smiling.

"Oh, if you were part of my act, I'd ask you to be more serious than that," Bret said, obviously enjoying himself. "This is levitation, and if my concentration is broken, you'll fall!"

Wires, I thought, trying to see them.

Bret picked up a large hoop, passed it completely over and under Frank's body, then, putting it over Frank's legs, brought it to Frank's waist. He laid it almost flat in one direction, then the other; he repeated this motion from the other direction, brought the hoop over Frank's head and shoulders to his waist. So much for wires.

Frank was starting to laugh.

"Do you know what's holding you up?" Bret asked.

"No," Frank said.

"Here, give me your hand."

Bret helped Frank to stand up. As Bret moved I could just make out some object near the platform. Frank was studying it. "Here," Bret said, "I'll turn the lights up."

For a moment I feared he would come up the stairs, but he changed the lighting from the stage. In the brighter overhead light I could see that a sturdy pole was planted into the floor of the stage. The pole rose straight up, about thirty inches from the floor, then bent forward toward the audience at a right angle, forming an arm that extended parallel to the floor. This horizontal arm connected to the platform.

"See this S-shaped bend?" Bret asked, pointing to a curve in the arm.

"Yes," Frank said. "What's it for?"

"The hoop pass. This pole is called an S-suspension. From the audience's point of view, when the trick begins, the platform is draped. So I move up to the pole and straddle the arm, keeping my feet together and hiding the vertical part of the pole behind my legs. As I said, usually, the drape is pulled upward and over you."

"But once the drape is pulled up, you can't move from the center of the platform, right?" Frank asked.

"Right. I have to stay where I am to hide the pole. So the drape is pulled up, and the chairs removed. Naturally, with the support beneath you apparently gone, the audience believes you are suspended by wires. So I pass the hoop, first from one end and then the other, using the S-bend to lay it almost flat when it's in front of me. No wires! When I do the trick in front of an audience, I replace the chairs, then allow the drape to drop back over the front of the platform. Only then can I move away from the pole. There's another version of this trick, where the pole is behind a curtain. In that version, I can move around. But I like this version better. I think a curtain that close to the platform is too obvious—makes the audience suspicious."

He began showing Frank other tricks, how they were done. Although Frank was slowed by the chains between his ankles, he seemed to be enjoying the conversation. Under other circumstances they would have appeared to be friends. Frank made no attempt to overpower him, although I was fairly sure he could have.

At one point Frank said, "Why are you showing me all of this? Isn't there some code of silence among magicians?"

"Not really. Otherwise, all the secrets would have died out with Houdini or Thurston." Bret smiled. "Or Merlin."

"But I'm not exactly a sorcerer's apprentice," Frank said.

"This isn't really magic. It's illusion. It requires skill and showmanship and no small amount of mechanical wizardry. And it works best if you believe in real magic."

"Do you?" Frank asked.

"Of course. What if someone else had found us that day?"

Frank was silent.

"I want this to be a children's theater," Bret said. "With magic shows."

"Then make sure you get what you want," Frank said.

Bret shook his head.

A door burst open and Samuel came onto the stage.

"The alarm was tripped," he said to Bret.

"I know," Bret said.

"What do you mean?"

"It was nothing. I checked the building. No one."

Uneasy with this discussion, I moved back to the pile of equipment.

"What do you mean, 'no one'?" Samuel asked.

"I mean, it went off not long after you left. The point of entry was the delivery area. The entry door was secure. All the doors leading from it were locked."

"I just checked the videotape," Samuel said angrily.

I felt sick to my stomach.

"And?" Bret said calmly.

"And you erased part of it."

"Yes. The lights went on in the delivery area. The cameras rolled—and recorded absolutely nothing. Is there some special reason you'd like to save a tape of an empty concrete room?"

There was a brief silence, then Samuel said, "Did you check the other parts of the building anyway?"

"Of course."

There was another lull in the conversation, then Samuel said, "What's he doing up here?"

"I was teaching Frank something about magic," Bret said, then added, "You are being impossibly rude."

"Shhh," Samuel said suddenly.

At first I didn't understand what was happening. Frank said, "What's wrong?"

"Shut up!" Samuel snapped, then, in sarcastic tones, said, "Forgive me. Please listen."

Soon I heard it, too. The unmistakable sound of a rotor blade slapping the air. A helicopter was hovering overhead.

"They've found us!" Samuel said. "Let's move it."

I heard a scrambling sound, Frank's chains rattling. Then Bret said, "I'll go up to the control booth to turn the board off. You take Frank." He paused, then said, "And, Samuel—"

"I won't hurt him, for chrissakes. Not unless—"

"Samuel!"

"Just go. He'll be fine. Hell, if you're that worried about him, I'll go up to the booth."

"No," Bret said, and even I heard the quickness of the reply.

There was another brief silence.

"You've run all the errands," Bret said. "I can't make you do everything for me."

"I don't mind," Samuel said, all the heat gone out of his voice. "I like staying busy. You know that."

"Yes," Bret said. "I know. But you have plenty to do right now."

"Don't take too long!" Samuel said.

I waited, listening, until I heard approaching footsteps. I broke out in a cold sweat, my heart hammering. I have problems with claustrophobia to begin with, but admit my fears at that moment were strictly of humans, not confined spaces. I held my breath as the door opened.

Carrying a flashlight, Bret walked quickly to the console and turned it off. The room was pitch black except for the light from the flashlight. He left it on, setting it on a corner of the black desk. He opened a drawer, pulled out a key, and left it next to the flashlight. Leaving the flashlight on the desk, he walked across the room in the darkness with sure steps. At the door he paused, listened, then said, "This is not a good hiding place. Don't try to leave the building now, though. The exterior doors are armed." He was so quiet after that, I thought he might have left. But then I heard him say, "Sorry we didn't get to know one another."

The door closed, and I heard the rapid fall of his footsteps as he raced down the stairs.

37

"FOUR." Cassidy swore under his breath. "He's certain?" he asked, already knowing the answer.

Henry Freeman spoke into the headset, listened, then looked up at Cassidy and nodded. "Four. Three just moved out of sight. He thinks they're in a room with a thick metal ceiling or some other shield to prevent thermal readings. Fourth is at the other end of the building."

"Moving?"

"Yes."

He sighed. "At least they haven't found her yet."

"Sir, maybe it isn't Ms. Kelly."

"You still hanging your stocking by the chimney, Hank?"

"No, sir."

"How are we doing otherwise?"

"The phone company has already moved to deny

origination, so they don't have a dial tone on their phones. New line will be established any minute now."

"We have building plans yet?"

"No, sir, but they're on the way."

Cassidy picked up his binoculars, stared at the old theater. The metal doors were new, but everything else about it spoke of another era—the big marquee with star-shaped neon lights ascending from it; the etched glass on the box office windows; the colorful, fan-shaped entry mosaic. The word "Starlight" was spelled out in brass-outlined letters in the mosaic.

"Which end of the building did they see her in?" he asked.

Freeman called the helicopter, repeated the question.

"This end, sir. Up high."

"Up high?"

"Yes, sir."

"Near the projection booth, then," Cassidy said. "Is this a movie theater?"

"No, sir," Freeman answered. "Although it may have been at one time. The gentleman from the bookstore said there were plays performed here until the church owned it."

Cassidy dropped the binoculars but kept watching the building.

"Sir?" Freeman said.

"When are you going to figure out that you don't have to call me that?"

"I don't think I can break the habit now, sir."

Cassidy smiled. "I guess not. What's the trouble, Detective Henry Freeman?"

"No trouble, sir. I just wanted to say that I'm glad Captain Bredloe is allowing you to handle this one."

"Why, thank you, Hank. But we've got a long way to go before we feel glad about anything."

A few minutes later Freeman said, "The phone is ready."

"You all set up?" Cassidy asked.

Freeman nodded.

"Let's give them a call, then."

The phone was answered on the second ring.

"Hello, Tom. Nice to have you back."

"Hello, Samuel. How's it going?"

"Well, we're not too happy. We're cooped up in here with Detective Harriman. Our phone doesn't work unless you call."

"Oh, you can call me now, Samuel. It's just that you can't call anyone else. By the way, how did you know it was me?"

"We can see you, of course. These high-pressure tactics are upsetting us. We don't have the man we asked for, and time is running out."

"Our work finding your man was delayed a little. But we've made progress."

"Not enough, I'm afraid."

"Oh?"

"You've pushed us now, Tom. We would have waited until Tuesday, but you've pushed us. We'll just have to give Detective Harriman a little larger dose of medicine."

"Why rush things, Samuel?"

There was a long silence. "You talk to him," he heard Samuel say to someone else.

There was muffled conversation, then he heard a

door closing. He wrote a quick note to Freeman, who radioed the helicopter.

"Hello?" a voice said on the phone line.

"Hello," Cassidy said.

"This is Bret."

"Hello, Bret. We haven't spoken much. I'm Tom. How are you doing?"

"I need to convey some information to you, Detective Cassidy," he said, ignoring the question. "Don't allow anyone to try to enter this building. All the doors and windows are armed with explosives. We have no regard for our own lives. We'd like to allow Frank to live, but we will kill him if our single demand is not met. We have planned for this day for over a decade, so we are prepared. We would like to achieve our goals without unnecessary loss of life."

Cassidy was silent.

Bret spoke again, his tone softer now. "Would you like to speak to Frank?"

"Yes."

A speakerphone button was pushed.

"Tom?" a distant voice said.

"Hello, Frank. How are you?"

"I'm a little down," Frank said.

"We're in a basement," Bret said. "I believe that's what he's trying to hint at."

"Is Irene there with you?" Frank asked.

"She'll be along a little later," Cassidy said.

"He's lying to you," Bret said. "She's in the building."

"What?" Frank shouted.

"I'm sorry, Frank," Bret said. "She's in the building. Samuel doesn't know. I've told her about the doors."

"But Samuel could be out looking for her right now!" Frank said.

"I'm afraid we'll have to be going now, Detective Cassidy. I'm turning the ringer off, by the way. I'll call you a little later."

He hung up.

"What's the chopper say?" Cassidy said.

"Two people moving around in opposite ends of the building."

"Stay hidden, Irene," Cassidy said.

"Mrs. Harriman needs to talk to you," Hank said, listening on the radio. "Says it's urgent."

"Mrs. Harriman?" Cassidy said, still thinking of Irene.

"Bea Harriman."

"I can't leave this situation to go down there and—"

"She has some people from Bakersfield with her, sir. She said to tell you she has what Hocus wants."

Cassidy stood stock still. "Go down there and tell Mrs. Harriman— Never mind. Listen, Hank, make sure the captain is spreading word to SWAT about those entrances. Tell them about the cameras, too. I'll take the portable phone with me."

He walked slowly toward the group of people standing with Bea Harriman. He'd calmed himself by the time he reached them. Cecilia Parker. Nathan Cook. Gus Matthews. Bear Bradshaw.

"Y'all have a nice trip from Bakersfield?"

"You know why we're here," Cecilia began.

"Oh, yes, Ms. Parker, I know. And I'm surprised four law enforcement officers—retired or not—could be such damned fools. You come here with some noble intentions, I suppose, but the truth is, Frank is alive because Hocus doesn't have what it wants. And you know we are not going to send anyone here into that building. We'd be signing your death warrant, and probably Frank's and Irene's at the same time. We are not in the business of vigilante justice here. You give me time, and we'll get Frank and Irene out of that building alive. Hocus will just have to accept that things are not going to happen exactly the way they wanted them to happen. It's my job to get them to that point—peacefully."

"But we know why they are doing this," Cecilia began. "And we—"

"And you are going to be arrested if you try to interfere in any way. I won't hesitate. Do you understand?"

He waited.

"We understand," Bradshaw said. "I told you what would happen. Let's go."

He got angry looks from all of them. Cook and Matthews stomped off. Cecilia moved slowly, helping Bradshaw, both of them clearly as angry as the others. He didn't care. They were a distraction he didn't need. Only Bea Harriman stayed behind with Pete, Rachel, and Jack.

Cassidy walked back to the negotiator's post.

"Any word?" he asked.

"No," Freeman said. "But the drawings arrived."

Cassidy looked back at the group. Pete Baird was walking away now.

"SWAT have copies of these, too?"

"Yes, sir."

Cassidy unrolled the building plans, then turned to

stare at Pete Baird's retreating back. "Hank," he said, "I want someone to watch those people. Baird included."

"Someone is watching them, sir. We have guards—"

"No. I want our people to keep an eye on them, even if they've left the area. Especially if they've left the area."

38

THEY PULLED INTO THE UNDERGROUND parking garage and waited.

"Excellent, Cecilia," Nathan Cook said after a moment.

She didn't smile until Gus said, "You're a hell of a driver. I don't think I could have shaken them that fast myself."

"We might not be in the clear yet," Bear said.

"You old hen," Gus said. "Of course we are."

"Having second thoughts?" Nat asked her.

"Shut up, Cookie," Gus growled. "Don't try to work that shit on anybody."

"I wasn't trying to talk her out of it, Gus," Nat said. "I'm as determined as any of you are."

"I doubt that," Bear said. "Now hurry up. Who knows what they're doing to the boy while you shoot your fancy yap off."

"He's not a boy," Nat said.

Cecilia popped open the trunk, stepped out of the car. "Let's get this over with," she said.

The others got out. Gus walked around a little. "All clear," he said.

Nat started to unbutton his shirt, paused when he saw she was staring at him. "Would you please look the other way?"

"No," she said. "I won't. I don't have an injured leg, and I don't feel as sorry for you as Gus does."

"I don't feel sorry for the bastard," Gus said to her.

Nat shrugged, continued to undress. "Whatever. If you feel you must guard me, fine. But I haven't fought any of you on any of this. And I don't know what I've ever done to harm you, Cecilia."

"You let me believe you were someone you weren't. Hurry up and strip."

39

I TOOK THE FLASHLIGHT and key and crawled up the ladder. Hoping to God it wasn't what Bret had called an "armed" door, I unlocked the access door. Gingerly I pushed it open. Nothing happened.

I listened for a moment before continuing to climb through the access. I heard the sound of the helicopter passing overhead. Nothing else. I moved through the opening and looked around.

I was in a space between the roof of the building and the "house" and stage below, an area called the catwalk: part of a large grid of suspended, narrow metal walkways—also called catwalks and used for access to lights and other equipment above the house and stage. The term came back to me from a great distance—I had briefly dated a stage manager in my freshman year of college. We split up when he discovered I wasn't ready to go directly from the overture to the third act with him. An interesting man, but even with a bonus prize of free matinee tickets, he wasn't worth it.

The stage manager had believed in ghosts and was convinced that all old theaters were haunted. Looking along the Starlight's catwalk with nothing more than a flashlight in my hand, I was convinced he was right about that. Although almost everything up here seemed fairly new, one misstep on the newest of catwalks would lead to a long fall. I crept along, passing lighting fixtures and electrical cords. I heard a gear turn and froze.

Eventually working up enough courage to shine the flashlight in the direction the sound came from, I saw that it was a videocamera. I couldn't see the lens end, which extended into the wall and was surrounded by rubber.

Moving cautiously, shining the flashlight along the walls of the building, I saw that there were four cameras up here, one in each corner of the catwalk. There might be others in the part of the theater nearest the alley, which wasn't accessible from the catwalk. I sat still for a time, considering my options. The cameras were undoubtedly being used by Hocus to monitor what went on outside the building, the movements of the police. Although there might be other cameras elsewhere in the building, if I disabled these, I might give Cassidy a much needed advantage. On the other hand, if Hocus saw their monitors start to blink out, their first reaction would probably be to come up here and find out what was going on. If Bret came looking for me, I might be all right, even if he was angry about the cameras. But Samuel?

I thought of Faye Taft and gave a shudder.

Still, it might be a chance worth taking. I might be able to elude him. Any theater was full of hiding places.

They were probably in such a hiding place themselves. They had left the stage, but I hadn't heard them moving through the house or up to the projection booth. I had seen no lights on in the area below the catwalk. They were probably somewhere behind or beneath the stage, then.

If I ran along the catwalk—dangerous even in full light—from one end of the building to the other, I might make it. I couldn't just turn off the cameras. I'd have to make sure they couldn't be repaired quickly, or it wouldn't be worth the risk.

I studied the camera nearest me. I pushed at the thick rubber lining that surrounded the lens end of the camera. It gave way easily, and bright daylight came in through the small opening in the wall. I let my eyes adjust to it and looked out around the little space left by the camera. I couldn't see anything outside the building, but I could hear the helicopter more clearly. The opening was larger than the camera itself, made to allow the camera to move for various angles.

To my relief, the camera was fastened to an arm by a simple camera screw, similar to one on a tripod. The arm itself had separate controls. If I unscrewed the mount and yanked the power supply loose, I could shove the camera through the opening in the wall.

I thought out the pattern I would need to follow. There were four ways to exit a catwalk. Up through the roof, but the roof access was probably booby-trapped. Down a set of stairs onto the stage or down the ladder into the projection booth—the two safest options. The final exit would be just that—a fall from one of the walks.

For several reasons I decided to disable the cameras nearest the projection booth first. That would prevent Bret and Samuel from monitoring any police activity at the front of the building, where Cassidy and his friends would have more room to move than the blind alley at the back.

The covering over the projection booth ceiling was a solid floor, not the narrow catwalk ramps that I'd have to take to reach the cameras at the stage end. It would be easier to take out the booth-end cameras first. I also knew the only other exit from the projection booth was a single stairway, while the stage would offer more chances for evasion if need be. Hocus might come up the stage entrance to the catwalk to see what was happening to the cameras, but that was a chance I'd have to take.

I walked to the stage entrance, opened the unlocked door, and listened. Silence and darkness. The flashlight revealed little beyond the stairway itself. Near the door, a set of large cardboard boxes stood on a platform. A closer look showed this platform to be the top of the mechanical lift I had seen on the stage below. There were no controls on the platform, or I might have had another way down. Reading the box labels, I saw they were speakers. A new sound system for the old theater, in the process of being installed. I used one of the smaller boxes to prop open the stairway door.

Mapping my escape along the way, I went to each camera, pushed off the rubber guards, loosened the mounting screws. Back near the projection booth I took several deep breaths, thought of orange blossoms, and yanked the first camera's power cord, then shoved it out onto the street.

I skipped the pleasure of watching it crash and ran to the other corner at the front of the building and did the same to that camera. Now the long run down the catwalk to the camera at stage left. I tried to move as quickly and quietly as possible. I dropped the third camera and was moving to the fourth when the booth access door flew open, a shaft of light coming through it. I turned off my flashlight, prayed faster than I ran.

I forced myself to continue toward the camera, even as I saw a man crawling through the space. He was already pulling a gun from his waistband, though, so I detoured toward the stage stairway. He yelled, "Stop!" But he wasn't looking directly at me, and I realized that his eyes had not adjusted to the dark. He had no flashlight, only the gun in his hand. I reached the stairway door, moved the box, then turned and toppled the other speaker boxes. I heard a shot as I closed the door behind me.

I grabbed the stair rail, turned on the flashlight for a brief second, then moved like hell down the stairwell. I reached a landing, turned the light on again just long enough to read a sign on a door that said FLY GALLERY.

I knew the fly gallery would be another narrow walkway, an area alongside the rigging for the mechanisms that operated curtains and backdrops. Counterweighted ropes would raise and lower curtains, borders, and backdrops from this area over the stage called "the flies." There would be no exit from the other end, and I would be about sixty feet above the stage. Without entering the fly gallery, I opened and closed its door with a loud bang, then continued down the metal stairs.

I could hear my pursuer struggling with the boxes as I reached the part of the stairwell that opened onto the stage itself. One box fell to the seats with a loud crash.

I reached the stage and turned right. I used the flashlight again, this time to find the rigging. I went to the area where the flyman—the person who raises and lowers the scenery and curtains—would work during a production. There were dozens of line sets. I turned off the flashlight, tucked it into my jeans, and began moving along the line sets, releasing all of them, lowering curtains and backdrops like crazy.

This made noise in the fly gallery, and I could hear my pursuer opening the door I had passed. I reached the end of the line sets and bumped into a console: the on-stage controls lights. I hesitated, then worked my way around it. I risked the flashlight once more as I heard the fly gallery door slam shut again. I chose a relatively unobstructed path between a curtain and backdrop, then turned off the flashlight. I began tip-toeing along the path, trying to get to the other side of the stage without revealing my presence. I heard my pursuer reach the stage.

"Who are you?" I heard him call.

It was Samuel. I didn't answer.

"You can't get out of here, you know." He tripped over something as he said this and swore as he fell. I listened but could not hear his footsteps. I moved a little farther, stumbled over one of Bret's magician's props. I grabbed the curtain to keep from falling. It made a soft noise as it swayed, but it didn't rip or drop.

I waited, regained my balance, and moved on. I could hear Samuel again now. He was moving closer to the light console. I hurried forward, stumbled again.

The house lights came on. I was not far from the other side of the stage. I lurched to my feet, ran into the wings.

Suddenly there was a familiar whistling sound—the sound of the alarm I had heard in the delivery bay. I kept running, moving backstage.

I passed a red handle and pulled it. A fire alarm. Loud bells overpowered the whistling sound. The fire curtain plummeted, slowing slightly when it was about eight feet above the stage floor, blocking the house lights. I saw Samuel cross beneath it just as the stage, cut off from the house now, was enveloped in darkness once again.

I turned on the flashlight and ran.

40

C AMERAS, SIR."
Cassidy took his eyes from the binoculars and looked at Hank Freeman.

"SWAT said she's disabling the cameras," Hank clarified. "That's what was dropping off the building. The rubber pieces were some sort of weatherproofing. The cameras have followed. She's dropped all but one."

"I'll be damned," Cassidy said, listening to the endless ringing of the phone line connected to his headset. Under his breath he said, "Pick up the phone, Bret."

Freeman was frowning now, listening over his own headset. "One of them is chasing her."

They heard the pop of gunfire.

Cassidy picked up a hand radio. "Hold on."

Hank Freeman heard Bredloe ordering everyone to hold their fire. Bredloe's voice was less calm, he thought. He never knew how Cassidy managed this part of it. The worse it got for everybody else, the calmer Cassidy would be. The helicopter pilot was talking now, and Freeman listened over the headset.

"She's still moving," Hank said. "They're farther apart."

Into the radio Cassidy said, "You copy that, Captain?"

Bredloe said he did.

"Pick up the phone," Cassidy said into the headset again.

As if Bret had heard Cassidy willing him to do so, the answer came.

"Detective Cassidy?"

"Yes, Bret," Cassidy answered, smiling. "I'm here."

"Was that your gunfire?"

"No, Bret, that was yours."

"Samuel?"

"I think so. He apparently took a shot at Irene."

There was a long silence.

"What's he shooting with?" Cassidy asked.

"I don't know. I don't know. Did he . . . ?"

Cassidy waited.

"Is she all right?" Bret asked.

"I can't tell you, Bret."

"Why not?" he asked. "That part of the building isn't shielded."

"What part of the building?"

"All of it. All of it except the room I'm in can be seen on your thermal sensors. Where is she?"

Cassidy didn't answer.

"I don't want to hurt her!"

"I know you don't," Cassidy said easily. "You and Samuel are different in that way, I suppose."

"Yes. We are. He'll kill her! Where is she?"

But before Cassidy could reply, he heard the sound of breaking glass. Bret shouted, "No, don't! Don't! Oh, God! Oh, God!"

There was a high whistling sound in the background.

"Ignore that alarm," Bret said to Cassidy in a weak voice, and hung up.

"Hank, tell the tactical folks to ignore all—"

They heard the loud ringing of a fire alarm.

Cassidy picked up a hand radio. "Ignore it. False alarm."

He heard Bredloe repeating the order.

They listened as the bells rang.

41

S AMUEL RAN ACROSS the loading dock to the basement door. He used a key to shut off the fire alarm. His ears were still ringing from the damned thing. Fucking asshole intruder. How did he sneak in? That was worrisome. He would take care of the intruder later. If he was lucky, the jerk would blow himself to kingdom come.

He entered another code, and the whistling sound ceased. Jesus, what next? Things weren't going right. He unlocked another panel and turned on a screen that allowed him to view the basement room.

Bret was lying on the floor. Frank Harriman was bending over him.

Samuel frantically punched the intercom button. "Get the fuck away from him!" he screamed into the mike. "Get the fuck away from him *now* if you want to live, you son of a bitch!"

Frank lifted his manacled hands in the air, backed

awkwardly away from Bret. He couldn't see the camera, so he turned toward the voice. "He fainted," Frank said. "He's okay, he just fainted."

Samuel's breath was coming hard, painfully. "Stay away from him," he repeated, nearly in tears, but now he could see that Frank's hand was bleeding. The blood. That's what must have made Bret faint.

"What did you do to your hand?" Samuel asked.

Frank didn't answer, just looked around for the camera.

"I asked a question. *Answer me!*"

"I pulled the IV out," Frank said.

Bret moaned.

"Let me help him," Frank said.

"You go near him, I'll kill you. Go into the bathroom," Samuel ordered. "Go in there and close the door. If he sees the blood, he'll faint again."

Reluctantly, looking down at Bret as he passed him, Frank moved into the bathroom and closed the door.

With shaking fingers Samuel entered the code, then hurried down to Bret. He rearmed the alarm, noting that the keypad had blood on it. He'd have to wipe that off later.

Bret's eyes fluttered open.

"Samuel?" He tried to sit up.

"I'm here. You're still pale. Let me help you." When he had situated Bret on the stairs so that he could sit more comfortably, Samuel said, "Are you hurt anywhere? Did you hit your head when you fainted?"

"No, I think Frank caught me." He looked around. "Where is he?"

"In the bathroom. It's okay. Just relax. Don't look

over there—I'll clean up that mess. You just put your head down."

"Embarrassing," Bret said, putting his head between his knees.

"No, it's not. Don't worry about that. And forget about him. The fan runs when the light is on, so he can't hear us."

"Maybe you should see if he's all right. He was bleeding."

"Not that badly," Samuel said. "He'll be okay. He can rinse it off in the sink, wrap it in a towel. He's smart enough to do that."

"He broke the morphine bottle. Pulled his IV catheter out. Tried to enter the alarm code."

"I should have waited, made sure he went under."

"He pinched the tubing shut. I don't think he got any of it."

"Son of a bitch," Samuel growled, looking toward the bathroom.

"I don't blame him," Bret said.

"What?"

"I don't blame him. And every time I hear those manacles—"

"Relax, relax," Samuel soothed.

"I would go crazy, Samuel. If someone did that to me, I'd go crazy. I couldn't take it."

"Shh. It's all right. No one has hurt him, Bret. Not really."

"We have. The morphine—it's just like the chains. It's a chemical chain, that's all. He knows it. It makes him feel helpless. And when he thought you had shot his wife, it must have been just like—"

"When he thought I had *what?*"

"Shot his wife. Did you shoot her?"

"What are you talking about?"

"Irene Kelly. That's who's in the building."

Samuel stared at him in silence. "You *lied* to me," he said, incredulous.

"Yes. I'm sorry if that hurts you."

"If it hurts me? Of course it does!"

"Just sit with me here for a minute, Samuel. Just sit with me. Like we used to, when we were silent."

Samuel almost rebelled, but something in Bret's voice worried him. So he didn't say anything.

Within a few minutes he was calm. The silences always did this for him. In school, when they were younger, if someone made him angry, Bret could calm him in this way. And he was reminded that Bret would not have asked for one of these shared silences unless, ironically, there was something important to be "said."

After a long time Samuel spoke. "It was because of Faye."

"Yes."

"Do you hate me for that?"

"No, of course not. But it's getting easier for you to hurt people, and I didn't want you to hurt Frank's wife. That's why I didn't tell you she was here, Samuel."

Another long silence stretched between them as Samuel thought about what Bret had said.

"You're so sure he's innocent?" he asked.

"Yes," Bret said without hesitation. "Aren't you?"

"I don't know."

"Are you willing to trust my judgment?"

After a long pause Samuel said, "Yes. But there's something you should know."

Bret waited.

"I haven't had a chance to tell you yet. When I went out, I went to a pay phone and called the paper to ask if my 'granddaughter,' Irene Kelly, had placed an ad like I asked her to. The one about John Oakhurst."

"And?"

"His wife knows who the policeman is."

42

H E HAD STOPPED COMING AFTER ME. After hiding in a wardrobe room for God knew how long, I decided he had given up on me, at least for the moment. Maybe he had bigger problems. Or maybe he decided I was going to die if I tried to leave the building and figured I wasn't worth the effort of pursuit.

I decided to do some cautious exploring.

I went through a large dressing room, scaring the bejesus out of myself when I caught my reflection in one of the many mirrors—at first, in the darkness, seeing the reflection only as another person moving in the room.

I almost went to the wall and turned on a light switch, but I decided not to become too cocky. Whatever had caused Samuel to give up his pursuit might be only a temporary delay.

I moved slowly through the back of the theater,

conserving the flashlight batteries as much as possible. Eventually I wandered into an office. A light was flashing on the desk. A ringing telephone.

I answered it, crawling under the desk to hide before I spoke.

"Hello?"

"Irene?" a surprised voice asked.

"Yes," I said, recognizing the drawling version of my name. "Glad Hank got in touch with you, Cassidy."

"I would have preferred to find you waiting for me on the *outside* of the building, but I reckon that was too much to ask. Where are you?"

"Alone in some kind of office. Do you know where Frank is?"

"Yes, but I'm not sure I should tell you. You've already been busier than a one-legged man in an ass-kickin' contest."

"I didn't exactly plan to be locked in here with them. Anything I can do for you while I'm here?"

"Hide. Stay clear of them. They get a hold of you, we've got twice the problem we had before. You understand that, don't you?"

The lights came on in the office.

Oh, shit, I thought.

"Irene?"

"She understands, Detective Cassidy," a voice said from another extension. "Say good-bye to him, Ms. Kelly."

"Bret?" Cassidy said.

Samuel walked around the desk. He was pointing a gun at me. He motioned me to come out.

"See you later, Cassidy," I said. I hung up the phone

and let Samuel lead me away. I noticed the light on the phone didn't go out. I tried to be heartened by that, by the fact that Cassidy was still talking to Bret. You'll see Frank, I told myself.

I was scared anyway.

He took me to a basement. As I came down the stairs, Frank looked up and saw me. He was still in chains, and his hand had a bigger bandage on it. He stood up. I ran to him.

He lifted his manacled hands over my head, held on to me as tightly as I held on to him. He was warm and alive and we were together. Maybe something will feel better to me someday, I thought, but I couldn't imagine what it would be.

Bret came closer, and Frank stood very still for a moment. Frank extended his arms. Bret unlocked the chains on Frank's wrists, pulled off the leather cuffs.

"Thank you," Frank said. He pulled me closer, in an embrace so fierce, I couldn't breathe. I didn't need to breathe.

"We'll give you some time alone," Bret said, and to our surprise, they left.

"Are you okay?" we asked each other in unison, and spent the next few moments crying in each other's arms. I leaned back and wiped the tears from his face. "Cassidy will get us out of here," I said.

He nodded, told me he loved me, and we both started crying again.

"I know you think I'm an ass, coming in here, getting caught—" I started to say, but he put his fingers over my lips and shook his head.

"No more of that," he said. "No matter what happens, we're not going to waste time on regrets."

I looked up at him, smiled a little, and said, "Do you think they've got cameras in here?"

He laughed. "Sure of it, I'm sorry to say. Microphones, too."

"Damn," I said.

"Damn," he said, and held me tight.

"In spy movies, they use this kind of time to talk about strategy," I said.

"Thank God we aren't spies," he said, and kissed me.

There was a ridiculously polite little knock on the basement door, and Bret came in, seeming embarrassed.

"Sorry to interrupt," he said, "but we need to talk to Detective Cassidy."

He put on a headset, spoke into it. "Any change?"

He listened, then said, "All right. I'm calling now. Stand by."

"Where's Samuel?" Frank asked.

"Keeping an eye on things. There seems to be some SWAT movement." He turned to me. "Ms. Kelly, are you willing to tell us the name of the man we're looking for?"

Frank looked at me in surprise. "You know?"

I didn't answer. Before Frank could say more, Bret said, "We'll talk about it later."

He lifted the phone and waited.

"Hello, Detective Cassidy. I'm putting the speakerphone on." He pressed a button, looked at us. "Would you please say something?"

We each said hello.

"Are you all right?" Cassidy asked.

"Yes," I answered. "We haven't been harmed."

"Are you giving up?" Bret asked him.

"Now, what makes you say a thing like that?" Cassidy asked.

"We've seen some SWAT movement," Bret answered.

"There hasn't been any SWAT movement," Cassidy said.

"Detective Cassidy," Bret said, "please don't lie."

"I'm not," Cassidy said. "Hold on, let me confirm what I just told you."

There was a moment's silence. "Bret?"

"Yes?"

"I apologize. You're right. It was completely unauthorized, and those men have been pulled back. You want to confirm that with Samuel?"

"Just a moment," Bret said. He spoke into the headset. "Samuel?" He listened, then said, "All right, Detective Cassidy. But now we're concerned that you may not have your part of the situation under control."

"Really?"

Bret seemed distracted. "Oh, no, I guess not. Samuel is telling me that those officers have been taken to the commander's post. Well, now, shall we talk?"

"Sure."

"Let's make everything plain, all right?"

"Plain?"

"Unmistakable. I thought I should tell you that we have a generator and plenty of supplies, should you decide to cut off power or water."

"No one is talking about doing anything like that, Bret."

"We also have gas masks and protective clothing.

Samuel and I do, I mean. If you try a chemical approach to this problem, Frank and Irene will suffer, not us. And we are, of course, the only ones who can arm and disarm the explosives."

"Bret, nobody wants—"

"No, of course not. But the situation should be made plain. Now, we want one thing. Just one thing. Not money, not notoriety, not innocent lives. We don't want a plane to fly us to Havana or any other nonsense like that. We simply want justice. That's all."

"Justice."

"Yes, Detective Cassidy, justice. It's all we live for. Literally. A life for four lives."

Cassidy let the silence stretch. Frank was watching me. I took his uninjured hand, squeezed it lightly. He held on.

"Ms. Kelly knows the man's name," Bret said.

"She tell you that?"

"Not directly, no. But—just a moment—"

I could hear Cassidy shouting, though. "Stop that man! Stop him!"

"No, Detective Cassidy!" Bret said. "Tell your men to stay back! I don't want the others to be hurt."

"Hold on," Cassidy said. We could hear Bredloe's voice over a bullhorn, saying, "Officer, halt where you are. That's an order! You are compromising negotiations and placing others' lives in danger. Halt!"

"Are you sure it's him?" Bret asked Samuel over the headset, turning on a television monitor. A street-level view of the area in front of the theater came on the screen. A man in a SWAT uniform was crossing the street with his hands up. Bret said, "I wish we could hear him talk."

Just then the man shouted, "Bret! Samuel! I'm the one you want."

"Who is that?" Frank said.

Over the headset Bret said, "Yes, just that one door." He moved to the phone, then said, "Detective Cassidy! Use your bullhorn. Tell that man to enter by the center door only. No other door. And no other officers."

"I can't allow that, Bret. We don't know that this man is the one you want. People often confess to crimes they didn't commit, out of some mistaken sense of—"

"He'll blow every one of us to hell and gone, sir, if you don't do exactly as we say. Some of your men will die, too. Samuel and I don't care about ourselves, but the Harrimans deserve better. Hurry, Detective Cassidy, he's getting closer."

But it was Bredloe's voice that made the announcement, even as I heard Cassidy say, "Captain, don't—"

"We'll call back soon," Bret said, hanging up. "Excuse me," he said to us, and hurried up the stairs. He paused at the door and tossed down a key. "Just in case," he said with a smile.

"Bret!" I called after him, but he paid no attention.

"Who is it?" Frank asked again.

"Nathan Cook," I said, picking up the key. I took a guess and tried them on the manacles on Frank's ankles. The locks opened.

"Cookie?" he said in disbelief, staring at the monitor, rubbing his ankles.

"Yes. Frank, I know he was your father's friend, but I don't trust him. I don't know what he's up to now, but it's bound to be some trick."

"You're sure he's the one?"

"Yes."

Frank looked at the monitor, then back at me. "Let's go," he said, and shouted, "Bret, wait!" as he began to run up the stairs.

Bret entered the lobby just ahead of us, ignoring our repeated shouts.

When we burst through the doors Samuel was smiling, holding a gun on Nathan Cook, whose hands were held high.

Cook was also smiling, until he saw Frank. "Ah, Frank," he said. "I don't suppose you'll ever forgive me—but I see you probably don't even know what this is about."

"I know," Frank said quietly.

Until that moment, perhaps he hadn't really believed that Nathan Cook was the man Hocus sought. But there was unmistakable fury in him now.

Cook raised a brow. "Yes, I guess you do."

"It's him all right," Samuel said. "His name is Nathan Cook."

"Are the doors rearmed?" Bret asked nervously.

Samuel nodded.

Bret moved to a phone near the box office. He picked it up. "Detective Cassidy? Nathan Cook has turned himself over to us. We've rearmed the doors. We'll release Detective Harriman and Ms. Kelly to you just as soon as we have Mr. Cook safely in custody."

"I can't tell you how I've waited for this to be resolved," Cook said.

"We waited first, remember?" Samuel said. "Powell got tired of waiting for you."

"Yes, I'm sorry," Cook said, which caused Samuel to laugh. He ignored the laughter and went on. "I didn't mean to take so long. It was daylight when I found the turnout, and I had to wait for darkness, and then for traffic to die down. I never expected Powell to become so violent."

Samuel laughed again.

"Drug dealing, Cookie?" Frank said. "My father would have strangled you with his bare hands."

"It wasn't serious dealing, Frank. I just wanted to make a point. The morons in Vice never should have demoted me. It was just a way to irritate them. I didn't even keep the money. I gave it away—small cash donations to good causes."

"Penance?" I asked. "Or avoiding the attention of Internal Affairs?"

"Please," Bret said quietly. "Nothing he has to say makes any difference." Cook glared at him, but Bret went on. "He can't excuse what he did. Even he knows that. That's why he came in here."

Cook dropped his gaze.

"Take off the helmet and Kevlar vest," Samuel ordered.

"Slowly," Frank said. Cook reached up for the helmet, dropped it to the floor. Began unfastening the vest.

"Cecilia and Gus and Bear thought I'd have to be forced to come down here and rescue you, Frank," Cook said. "They were wrong. This will end years of hell."

"You aren't rescuing anyone," Frank said angrily. "I can't believe you'd try to make yourself out to be a hero."

"Why not?" he said, swiftly pulling a gun out from beneath the vest. He aimed it directly at Samuel. "Drop it, son."

Samuel flinched at the word "son," but then he smiled.

"Don't even think about it," Cook said, glancing at Frank, who had moved slightly closer to him.

"Bret?" Samuel said.

"Yes?"

"Give Julian my love." He pulled the trigger.

The loud report of the shots came almost at the same time, Cook's a fraction of a second later, with Bret's scream. The lobby filled with the acrid stench of gunpowder.

Frank ran to Samuel, saying, "No—"

I glanced at Cook, looked away from what was left of his head as I took the gun out of his hand. I made myself feel for a pulse. I'll admit I didn't regret not finding one.

Bret was bent over Samuel, clinging to him, making sounds of misery and grief. I looked at Frank, who shook his head. He had taken Samuel's gun from him but simply set it aside, out of Bret's reach. I put Nathan Cook's gun next to it.

Frank sat next to Bret, holding on to him. His face reminded me of his face in the photo. I stood next to him, reached down, stroked my fingers through his hair. He reached up and took my hand, held on to it.

The phone was ringing. Frank glanced up at me. I didn't let go of him—I used my free hand to answer it.

"Cassidy?"

"Irene? We heard gunfire. Anyone need an ambulance?"

"No. Cook's dead. Samuel, too."

I heard him sigh. His voice was unsteady as he said, "The rest of you?"

"We're all okay. Tell them we're all okay. But—give us some time."

"I can hear Bret," he said.

"Yes. The doors are still armed, but I don't think Bret's going to hurt us. We just need to give him some time."

"He may not want to hurt you, but I can't tell you how dangerous he is right now—to himself especially, but maybe to you and Frank, too. Those two boys had what amounts to a suicide pact. Don't let him out of your sight. Where are the weapons?"

"Out of reach."

"Good. Make sure it stays that way, all right?"

"Yes."

"We've got to talk to him, get him to look at things differently."

"I don't think he's ready—"

"No, not right this second. Of course not. But I don't want any further harm to come to him, Irene."

"I know you don't, Cassidy."

I'm not sure how long we stayed there, huddled together on the floor. When it seemed to me that Frank was ready to hear it, I whispered some of Cassidy's concerns to him. Frank nodded, broke open the guns, took out the remaining bullets, and pocketed the weapons. Bret seemed oblivious of anyone other than Samuel.

When exhaustion finally began to slow Bret's grief, Frank gently pried his fingers from Samuel's shirt

Known for being afraid of blood, Bret was now bathed in it but seemed not to notice. We stood him between us and, putting our arms around him, walked back to the basement. He was in a state of total numbness by then, I think. We helped him wash up, but he just stared blankly into space. Frank found a stage outfit in one of the trunks and asked Bret if he wanted to change clothes.

Bret didn't answer but took the clothes and went into the bathroom.

"Maybe we shouldn't let him alone even to do that," I said.

"There's nothing he can harm himself with in there," Frank said. "I didn't even hand him a belt. But if he's not out in a few minutes, I'll check on him."

But Bret did come out, and his mood seemed to have changed. It made me want to call Cassidy. I exchanged a glance with Frank, who picked up the phone.

"I'm sorry," Bret said to him.

Frank put the phone back, waited.

"I wish I could give your own clothes back to you," Bret went on, "but they had blood on them and Samuel was afraid I would. . . ." He lowered his eyes. "I'm sorry. I don't think mine will fit you or I'd offer—"

"It's okay," Frank said. "Don't worry about it, all right?"

Bret hesitated, then nodded. Frank picked up the phone again. Bret made no objection, but seemed uneasy. Frank watched him carefully as he walked away, moved closer to me.

"What book are you reading, Ms. Kelly?" Bret asked politely.

"Call me Irene," I said. I reached into my back pocket—removed the forgotten paperback.

"Bret Harte," he said. "Read the title story sometime. About a group of misfits trapped in a snowstorm. The outcasts aren't saints—definitely sinners—but not really any worse than the people who kicked them out of town—better in some ways, I suppose. They're imperfect, in an imperfect world. But they do what they can in the face of adversity."

"It's the story with John Oakhurst in it?"

He smiled. "Yes. John Oakhurst. He pins the deuce of clubs to a tree—'at once the strongest and yet the weakest of the outcasts of Poker Flat.' "

I didn't understand the quote and was about to ask him what it meant, but Frank was calling him to the phone.

"They can leave at any time," Bret said to Cassidy. "I'll disarm the doors. But I'm staying here with Samuel."

"We aren't leaving without you," Frank said, beginning a standoff.

Cassidy talked to Bret for a long time, while Frank and I sat next to one another, waiting silently for the negotiator to coax Bret into leaving the dead—all of them—behind.

We heard Bret's side of the conversation change. Yes, he could always take his life later, so he didn't mind talking to Cassidy. And Cassidy, working his own magic, got Bret to talk about getting to know Frank and the Szals again and of dreams other than revenge. About how life might be different now and how there were some projects he'd like to see finished. The theater, for example.

"Do you think," Bret asked Frank at one point, "that we could really get to know one another?"

"Yes," Frank answered. "I enjoy talking to you, Bret."

"You aren't just saying that, are you?"

"No," Frank said. "I mean it."

He said, "I'm scared."

"I know," Frank said. "I was scared over the last few days, and you tried to help me. I'll try to help you, too. You won't have to go through anything alone."

"Okay," he said simply, and told Cassidy we would be coming out through the front doors in a few minutes.

He put on his white cape as we stood in the lobby, near the door. "How do I look?" he asked Frank.

"Great," he said. "Merlin would be proud."

"I'm scared," he said again, glancing over at Samuel's body.

"We're right here with you," Frank said, and put his arm around Bret's shoulders.

We pushed open the door. I stepped through first. Bright lights were shining. I put up a hand to shield my eyes, but Bret balked completely.

I could hear Cassidy telling them to cut some of the lights. We tried again.

It wasn't so bad the next time. I could see Cassidy waiting for us on the other side of the street. We walked out onto the sidewalk. We were free, I told myself. Frank was coming home. But with each step I was aware that guns were pointed at us, and I felt Bret's fear.

"What's wrong?" I heard Frank ask, and realized they had stopped walking. I waited, too.

"Chains," Bret said.

We saw what had halted his progress then: an officer holding a set of manacles.

"Get those goddamned chains the hell out of here," Frank yelled, obviously shocking everyone who knew him as quiet Frank Harriman.

Cassidy seemed equally impatient, and the chains were quickly removed from sight.

"Don't be afraid, you're safe now," Frank said.

Bret looked at Frank and smiled. "You said that the first time we met you. You really were our hero, you know," he said, and reached into his cape.

"Hold your fire!" Frank shouted, but the shot rang out before he finished the sentence. Bret's knees buckled. Frank clutched clumsily at him as he slumped, then gathered him into his arms. "Bret? Bret?"

People began to move toward us, but Frank fell to his knees and I moved with him, watching helplessly as he threw back his head and made a keening sound of anguish.

Cassidy was beside us, telling the others to leave us alone. I heard him ask softly, "What was he reaching for?"

Frank gently lifted Bret's hand, which still gripped the deuce of clubs.

"John Oakhurst," he said, "committed suicide."

EPILOGUE

I WATCHED FROM THE LANAI of our room at the Halekulani as my husband swam the length of the orchid pool underwater. His movements were strong and graceful as he crossed over the exquisite blue mosaic. When he broke the surface for a new breath, I found even these few yards between us a distance nearly too great. Perhaps sensing my gaze, he turned toward me, smiled, and beckoned. Too great a distance for him, as well.

Halekulani means "a house worthy of paradise," and it is. We had come to Waikiki because we had never been to it before, because we did not want to be anywhere we had ever been before. We decided to try to see things differently by seeing different things. We were cosseted here, fed delectable dishes, and in every other way taken care of in perfect style. We had saved for a rainy day, and when it had started pouring, Hawaii became our umbrella.

We needed it. We needed a time to be able to sleep in after nightmares, a place to sort through remembrances without spectators eyeing our reactions.

Several hours ahead of us, Las Piernas finished its day. My editor, elated a week ago by the most difficult story I've ever written in my life, would by now be angry that I wasn't around to take on a new assignment. My sister, out of town during our week of hell, would begrudge my leaving town for this brief taste of heaven.

Others would be dealing with the aftermath of that week in their own way. Cecilia, Gus, and Greg were back in Bakersfield, relieved that no one was pressing charges against them. Detailed investigations had revealed that Lang and Colson—who had little hope of avoiding prison—had each lost family members to addiction. Lieutenant Carlson, facing charges by Internal Affairs that he had leaked the story on Hocus, might not be a lieutenant by the time we returned. Bredloe, facing the chief's displeasure over allowing Nathan Cook to enter that theater, might not be a captain. Pete, given a day or two to realize that Frank really was safe, had taken a leave of absence to go fishing with Rachel. They'd invited Jack to go along, and he'd decided to take the dogs—who had been following Frank so mercilessly, we feared we might see them surfing into Waikiki Beach. Bea, who had a long talk with Frank about his older sister, was staying at our place, keeping Cody company. She'd bought a little frame for Frank's photo of Diana.

Cassidy was on Maui. That would be week two of our vacation.

Frank talked about leaving the department, about

trying some other line of work. I told him that I'd stay married to him even if he became a beach bum. He hadn't shaved the beard yet but otherwise had made no firm commitments.

"Probably not a smart time to make the decision," he had said yesterday.

Probably not.

But that world was hours ahead of us, more hours than simple longitude could measure. We were blissfully behind, moving at Hawaii's pace. The Hawaiians were good enough to teach us how to slow down.

At the edge of the pool Frank swam to meet me, reaching up as I stepped in.

For all the healing that we knew lay ahead of us, we had seen what Bret and Samuel sadly could not see, that damage need not destroy us, that what remains is often so much more than what was taken. And if, after all the pain of those days had passed, some part of our lives was still left in ruins, we would build on it our own Halekulani, our house worthy of paradise.

Or, I thought, sliding into the water and his arms, something damn close.

Visit
❖ Pocket Books ❖
online at

---

www.SimonSays.com

Keep up on the latest new releases from your favorite authors, as well as author appearances, news, chats, special offers and more.

SIMON & SCHUSTER
A VIACOM COMPANY
www.SimonSays.com

Pocket
Books